Her heart jumped when he spoke her name

"Sharon! Hey, dreamer." Calum's voice penetrated her thoughts. "Where's your fight gone?"

Where had it gone? "I'm pretending you're not here," Sharon managed to say.

He took her hand, and it was as if he had walked right into her fantasy. Her blood raced like a flooding river. A spurt of mischief bubbled inside her. "Have you ever held hands with a rattlesnake before?" she asked.

He looked at her in puzzlement, then flung back his head in laughter. "Maybe this little rattlesnake's fangs are at rest." His hands moved to massage her neck. "If I do this, will I activate them?"

Anticipating Calum's kiss turned her panic into fear. It wasn't that she didn't want to be in his arms—but that she wanted it too much!

LILIAN PEAKE
is also the author of these

Harlequin Presents

and these

Harlequin Romances

Many of these titles are available at your local bookseller.

For a free catalog listing all available Harlequin Romances
and Harlequin Presents, send your name and address to:

HARLEQUIN READER SERVICE
1440 South Priest Drive, Tempe, AZ 85281
Canadian address: Stratford, Ontario N5A 6W2

LILIAN PEAKE

passionate intruder

Harlequin Books

TORONTO • NEW YORK • LOS ANGELES • LONDON
AMSTERDAM • PARIS • SYDNEY • HAMBURG
STOCKHOLM • ATHENS • TOKYO • MILAN

Harlequin Presents first edition July 1983
ISBN 0-373-10612-2

Original hardcover edition published in 1982
by Mills & Boon Limited

CHAPTER ONE

As Sharon entered the living-room of her parents' home, a tall, middle-aged man stood up to greet her. He was a friend and client of her father, who was head of an accountancy firm.

Sharon shook the man's outstretched hand, then sat beside her mother as she put aside her knitting. Her father placed his beer glass on a coaster beside that of his friend.

'The island's a great place, Sharon,' Jack Wilson said, resuming his seat. 'It's small, it's green and it can turn even a breeze into a young gale. It'll fill your lungs with good fresh air. But I warn you, it's lonesome at times. I'm a born loner, always have been. That's why I bought the place, as a hideaway and somewhere I can paint my business cares out of my system.'

'I'm certain it's just what I want, Mr Wilson,' Sharon assured him.

'A tiny little island off the west coast of Scotland?' Mrs Mason shook her head, asking with some anxiety. 'There's shelter of some sort, isn't there, Jack?'

'A hut, fairly roomy, made of wood. It's really a large room with a bed in the corner, cooking stove, oil heater. A few bits of furniture.'

'Any drinking water?' her father asked.

'It'll be taken across by the ferry in large quantities. There are buckets to catch the rainwater for washing and so on. The necessary's round the back. A bit primitive, but,' Jack smiled broadly, 'it's only a kind of vacation, isn't it?'

'It certainly is,' Sharon's mother pronounced. 'We

couldn't ever visit her there if she never came back.'

The others laughed.

'I'm not quite sure,' her father commented, 'why she wants to condemn herself to that kind of solitary confinement, even for a short time.'

Jack replied at once, 'It won't be that solitary. Did I forget to tell you, Sharon? There's a film unit going over there the same time as you. I'm helping to finance the making of the film. I usually travel to the island by helicopter, but I've asked them to take you across in the ferry boat they've hired for the duration of their stay.'

'That's good of you, Mr Wilson,' Sharon commented, smiling.

'It was no trouble, either to them or to me. You'll be doing the crossing with the props, provisions, actors, cameras, the lot. I've rented the island to them for as long as they want it. Needed a rugged island background, they said. Heard I owned Cuilla and I played along with their wishes.'

'That really means I won't be alone, doesn't it?' Sharon remarked thoughtfully.

'Sorry, Sharon. Want to change your mind?'

'I think it might be interesting,' her mother commented, retrieving her knitting. 'And I'm glad you'll have company, dear. I won't be so worried about you.'

'If the men turn out to be womanisers,' her husband laughed, 'you'll be sorry you said that!'

'Oh dear!' The knitting hit Mrs Mason's lap. 'I never thought of that.'

'It's okay, Mum. I can look after myself.' Sharon bent to kiss her mother's cheek.

'Oh, and Sharon,' Jack eased himself to the front of the chair again, 'this letter.' He pulled an envelope from his pocket. 'Would you give it to a friend of mine who'll be on the island, too? You'll find him somewhere about.'

Sharon looked for an address. 'Caldar. Is that all?'

'It's all you'll need to find him.'

'You mean he's a member of the film company?'

'You could say that,' Jack Wilson answered. 'He won't be on your ferry. Wait till you get to Cuilla, then ask. All right, my dear?'

Sharon nodded and smiled. 'Will deliver.'

That evening, Sharon paused in her packing and stared at the boxes containing the wedding gifts which were piled neatly along one wall of her bedroom. Her mother had placed them there, carrying each with regretful but loving care.

Not one of the givers of the presents would take back a single item.

'Such a tragedy,' they'd said. 'Let her keep them as a memento.' Of what? Sharon had wondered with bitterness. Of a pre-marital desertion which had shattered her dreams and devastated her future?

The press had besieged Daryl's father, but he had passed them on to her. 'Give them his love story,' he had pleaded. 'That's what they want. Fill in the boyhood angle—make something up if you don't know the facts. I can't cope, Sharon. I'm too full of grieving for Daryl, and so is my wife. And she's not in full health. You were his fiancée. I know you lived together before—well, before the wedding that never was.'

'Mr Irwin,' Sharon had protested, 'that's just not true!'

'Oh, don't be coy, dear,' he'd coaxed. 'Daryl told us you did. It'll make good reading, Sharon. That's what the papers want these days, not the truth.'

'I—I couldn't tell lies like that, Mr Irwin.'

'Look, dear,' he had pleaded, 'my heart's not too good. I can't take the strain.'

So Sharon had told the reporters the bare facts, un-embellished, no punches pulled. Then she had told them to make what they liked of it, and they had taken her at her word. When the newspaper eventually ran the story, it had become a series in three parts. It had been embroidered with lies and exaggerations.

She had been made to look a worshipper of every woman's dream man, and a lifeless shadow of the true hero of the tale—the handsome, heart-wrecking, world-renowned Olympic yachtsman, Daryl Irwin, whose final battle was fought not against other men, but against the roaring elements themselves. He had died, with many others, in a yacht race over which a relentless storm had raged. Had he survived and the storm never happened, they said, he would again have won.

'I'm still in love with him,' the reporter had claimed to quote the bereaved fiancée. 'I'll never forget Daryl Irwin. I shall love him as long as I live.'

On reading the final episode—which was what the report had really been: pure fiction, not even faction—she had thrown the newspaper across the room. The fee they had paid her was large. She had given it to charity. And that, she recalled, still staring at the presents, was a fact that had gone completely unreported.

It had all happened three months ago, but it would take a very long time for the memories to die. Her heart had not died. It beat on strongly, defying any man who dared to tamper with it. Never again, she had sworn, would she be fooled by near-idolatry or dreams.

In any future relationship with a man, illusion would not be allowed to cloud her vision of him as a real human being, no matter how famous, nor how celebrated he might be. As she fastened the straps of the back-pack and slid the zips of the hand luggage, she knew that her chances of meeting such an exalted creature for the second time in her twenty-four years were non-existent.

The crossing was unbelievably calm, but the skipper

advised his passengers not to be deceived. It could be rough at times, he informed them, sometimes so rough they couldn't operate the ferry, whether or not it was privately hired.

Sharon was mistaken for a member of the film company. It amused her to be drawn into the conversation of actors and electricians and sound engineers. When their talk became so technical that she could not understand them, she felt it was time she told them she was only along for the ride.

A fair-haired man stood beside her for much of the time. He was tall and blue-eyed and Sharon wondered where he fitted in to the group.

'What's your job?' she asked. 'Something arty, like design?'

'Do I look arty?' he asked. She nodded and he laughed. The sound, to Sharon's ear's, sounded oddly inhibited for so attractive a man. 'Guess my job,' he challenged her.

'I give up. You tell me.'

'Would you be surprised if I told you I was an actor?'

'Don't pull my leg,' she laughed. 'You'll be telling me next you're the leading man.'

'Right first time,' he answered.

Sharon stared across the water at the distant hills. He had to be fooling. His manner was so hesitant, so self-effacing he was surely one of the technicians. If she told him of her doubts, he would be hurt, so she exclaimed, simulating astonishment and pleasure.

'Are you really? What's your name?'

'Lee Banks.' He looked at her expecting a reaction.

Sharon had never heard of him, but she turned actress herself commendably well. Her blue-green eyes shimmered like a tropical sea.

'You're not, are you? How wonderful to meet you, Mr Banks.' She offered her hand and he took it and held it.

His obvious gratification at her delight astounded her. Where was the self-assurance of his fellow-professionals? How could such a diffident person project on to the screen all the roles required of him? She gave up the puzzle and gazed at the family photographs he had produced from his wallet.

His wife was beautiful, his young son and daughter showing promise of equally good looks in the future. Putting them away, he said with a sudden gravity, 'My wife's divorced me.'

'Oh, dear!' He had caught her off balance and Sharon could only mouth platitudes. 'I'm so sorry.'

He shrugged, and she wondered again at his lack of fight. As a diversion, she looked around. 'Where's your leading lady?'

'She's a bitch.'

Sharon almost choked. 'I'm sorry, I didn't understand——?'

'I said, she's a bitch.' He smiled. 'In the film, I mean. It's Maida Halliday.'

It was a name so well-known, Sharon recognised it instantly. There was no need to pretend surprise in her case. How could this man's ability to act rise to that woman's standards? The search for solitude on a Scottish island, although that solitude had been invaded, might, as her mother had said, be interesting after all.

The boat docked at the jetty. Once, the skipper explained, it had been a busy place, this island, with crofters and sheep and weaving. Now it had all gone, but the jetty still stood to bring the sheep farmers over to inspect their flocks.

Sharon left the group with a wave and followed the skipper's directions to Jack Wilson's hut. The man was, it seemed, a well-known figure to the local people.

As she climbed the steep slope to a plateau, the hut came into view. Sharon felt in her bag for the key Jack Wilson had given her. Beside the hut, a tent was firmly planted. Mr Wilson had not told her about this. Its colour was orange, presumably so that it would be noticed in an emergency.

With some anxiety, Sharon stared at it. In her mind, it presented that emergency. She had come here for solitude, but that, it seemed, would be the last thing she would get.

If the occupant was a member of the filming team, having come across in advance of the crowd, then she would speak to whoever was in charge. The tent was mobile, whereas the hut was not, so it was the tent that would have to go.

Putting down her hand luggage and easing off the back-pack, Sharon used the key. It scraped noisily in an apparently rusty lock. Something made her turn and she found herself staring into two grey eyes set into a face which seemed chiselled, grooves and frown included, out of rock. Topping it all were layers of thick brown hair.

Which proved, if proof was needed, Sharon thought, that the tent's occupant was most definitely male. His very attitude told of his machismo, of a forceful masculinity. Fists on hips, legs straddled, he eyed her jet black hair, blue-green eyes, tapering chin and wide mouth.

Sharon had never before been examined so analytically, with male assessment interwoven like an intricate pattern into a fabric. Resentment welled at the scrutiny bordering on insolence to which he was subjecting her.

Who had the greater right to be there—she with Jack Wilson's permission to live in the hut, or this stranger with his tent arrogantly hammered into place by its guy ropes and tent pegs so as to trespass like an intruder on to the plateau of peace and quiet which she had come here to find?

A craggy brow arched. 'Lost your way?' the man asked. The timbre of his voice was deep, the tone faintly caustic.

With eyes which she hoped matched his in coolness, she returned his very personal examination of her in full. Broad shoulders pushed at his half-buttoned navy-blue shirt, breadth of hips balanced shoulder-width, while sinewy thighs were imprisoned by the tight jeans he wore.

Her eyes lifted and the mockery in his knocked her senses reeling. Colour sprang to her cheeks as his amusement at her investigating gaze showed through. 'Would you like me to bare my heart as well as my chest?'

'You have a heart as well as macho, Mr——?' Her smiling question elicited no similar response. After a pause, in which she turned the handle of the hut door, she went on, 'I think it's you who've lost your way. I guess you're one of the film crew.' She glanced at the garishly coloured tent. 'I'd be glad if you'd move that down the hill to where they're pitching camp.'

Sharon pushed open the door and looked around. On the low pine bed across the hut were a couple of rolled sleeping bags. There were folding garden chairs, a wooden table, cooking facilities along the opposite wall. The two windows were hung with country-print curtains.

As she stopped to pick up her belongings, the stranger commented, 'Before you go in, I'd like to warn you you're trespassing. The hut, like the island, belongs to Jack Wilson——'

'Who's a friend of my father's. He gave me the key.' She smiled sweetly. 'Plus permission to borrow the hut for as long as I want.' Then she remembered, raking in her pocket. 'This letter, I've got to deliver it. Do you happen to know someone called Caldar? Friend of Mr Wilson's. Could be man or woman.'

'Man, without doubt.' His hand came out for it.

'You? *Your* name's Caldar?'

'Mr Caldar.' His eyes glinted. 'But drop the Mr. Your name is——?'

'Mason—Miss Mason. But drop the "Miss".' It was a return shot. Had it gone home?

His laughter followed her irritable entry into the hut. So her sarcasm had misfired. He carried in the zipped bag she had left outside, intending to return for it. Thanking him briefly, she waited for him to leave. Instead, he lounged against the cooking stove.

'Sharon Mason. I've been expecting you.'

He knew her name! Which at once gave him the advantage over her. 'Well, I wasn't expecting you, Mr— Mr Caldar. Unfortunately for me, I can't go one up on you by calling you by your first name.'

He gazed back at her lazily, omitting to supply it.

'And, as I said just now, I'd be happy if you'd join your colleagues down the hill.'

'Who said they were my colleagues?'

'If they aren't, then what are you doing here?'

'I pass.'

Sharon brought a sigh from her depths. 'Look, Mr Caldar,' her eyes glittered like sunlight sparkling off the sea, 'I came here to be alone. *To be alone*, do you hear? I've had just about as much as I can take from life for a while. I've come a long, long way. I came to convalesce—not physically, but kind of mentally, spiritually, not in the religious but in the aesthetic sense. In other words, to find myself again.'

His stance did not alter. Fingers slipped into waistband, legs crossed at the ankles, he waited.

'Now do you understand why I want solitude? And

why I want your tent, plus you, moved from beside Mr Wilson's hut?'

He leaned forward and picked up the letter from the table where he had put it. He flipped open the flap and read the letter, and the grooves on his face deepened with his smile. It did not hold humour. 'You'll just have to want, Miss Mason. I stay right here. I have Jack Wilson's permission.'

'I don't believe you! Mr Wilson told me it might be lonely here, except for the film crew——' Realisation hit her. 'Which means you *are* one of the team down there. So why can't you move?'

'How you do jump to conclusions. Here.' He offered her the letter.

'Dear Cal,' the note ran, 'I'm sending you some company—distinctly female. Warning: Do not handle the goods. Fragile. Treat with care. Sharon's a lady—yes, there are still some around, whatever you say. Use whatever you want from the hut, but ask first. Okay, friend? Best wishes, Jack.'

Sharon folded the letter and returned it. 'If you aren't connected with the film people, then who are you?'

'Maybe I'm just a guy who, like you, wants to retreat for a while from the hurly-burly and who craves for a bit of peace.'

Her eyes scanned him again. It was as though they were drawn by a magnet inside him, drawing her. Even standing a foot or two away, she could feel his power pulling, tugging. Not only was he strong in physique, his mind had an uncanny strength, too.

In some ways it frightened her. She had had enough of men to last her for a very long time. After Daryl, she had vowed to be no man's puppet. Her destiny was her own, not someone else's to jerk around, then leave her lifeless.

'If you'll forgive my saying so, Mr—Caldar, you look

tough enough to withstand a volcanic eruption, even if you were standing right on top of it.'

He smiled, again without mirth. 'Maybe I am. Nothing can part me from myself. I'm my own man.'

'To quote the poet John Donne, No man is an island, entire of itself.' Her smile was genuine. She was enjoying the verbal fencing match.

'This man is, Miss Mason, entire of himself. Not a single woman, not even if she were the most beautiful in the world, will ever be allowed to touch my secret self. Not even you.' His eyes were hooded now. 'And another thing—a woman's love is something I don't need, either.'

Noises drifted in, the cries of seabirds, a shout or two from the film-makers, laughter on the breeze.

A strange disappointment had entered Sharon's body, striking her like a live match and firing her deepest feelings into a brief, searing flame.

Her laugh was hollow, not uncaring as she had intended. 'That's something you won't get from me. Nor do I regard myself as good-looking, let alone beautiful. I'm not after admiration, love or sex. That's a "keep off" warning, Mr Caldar.'

His raking gaze dismissed her from top to toe. 'That I do not need,' he tossed back at her, anger hissing in his gaze like a firework hitting water. 'Look on yourself as far as I'm concerned as being on the banned list.' His mouth tightened unpleasantly. 'Strictly not wanted.'

Anger rumbled and mushroomed. 'Will you get out of here?' Sharon demanded tensely. 'I've had a long journey. If there's nothing you want from the hut, then go, will you?' After a pause to steady her hard-beating heart, she went on, 'If I sound impolite, I just don't care. You seem to have made rudeness into a fine art yourself.'

'There's one thing I want,' he answered, lifting himself upright, unmoved by her explosion of words. 'The typewriter over there.'

'Typewriter? Why, do you write letters to yourself?'

He confronted her, arms folded, legs stiff. He was near enough for her to feel his breath on her face. 'Yes, Miss Mason. Letters to my inner man, to that secret me I told you about.'

His nearness unnerved her. 'Would you be serious?' His smile at her plea was fleeting and, in the way it put a shine in his eyes, magical. 'Are you—are you the film-makers' scriptwriter?'

He shook his head very slowly. 'Cold. Try again, lady.'

'Not a—not a writer?'

'Warm, very warm. In fact, you're burning your fingers.'

'Books?' He nodded. Sharon frowned. 'Caldar? I can't say I've heard of you.'

'Good. That's the way I like it. Now, that typewriter.' It was already in its carrying case. He turned at the entrance. 'I'll leave the table for you.'

'Thanks. I'll need it for all the friends I invite to my candlelit dinners.'

His gaze held a transient gleam. 'Top marks for sour-ness, Miss Mason. It almost equals mine. We should get along really well, you in your love nest, me in mine.'

When the wooden door struck home, Sharon felt as though someone had switched off the sun. It was even-ing now and she had eaten a cold meal from cans. Summer daylight lingered in these northern parts. The air outside smelled good, the semi-distant sound of the sea was sweet. A breeze blew, fluffing her dark hair.

The tent side bulged momentarily as its occupant moved around. As she turned her back on its bright colour—which, against the sunset-painted sky, did not for once look out of place—she wondered how so tall a man as her neighbour could stand the cramped size.

Forcibly, she took her mind from him. She would banish him from her thoughts as he, no doubt, had banished her.

A weariness overcame her. It closed down her senses and her mind curled up for the night. It could take no more new impressions, demanding to be rested like her limbs and nervous system.

Someone had collected water in a bucket and placed it near to the plastic washbowl. It must, she decided, have been standing there since Mr Wilson had last visited the place. Before washing, she ventured into a darkness which was still not entirely without light. White stretches of high cloud reflected the rays of a long-set sun.

It was not difficult finding 'the necessary', as Jack Wilson had called it. As she emerged, her heart thumped. The outline of a man stood a polite distance away.

'S-sorry to keep you,' she stammered, embarrassment and shock making her stammer. 'Do——' she cleared her throat, 'do you use this, too?'

'I do. Does it upset your sensibilities?' The voice was deep with amusement.

'I—no, I don't really mind at all.'

'Just as well.' The outline solidified into the three-dimensional figure of a man. 'It could be very, very awkward if you did.'

Sharon laughed, feeling for a passing moment a sweeping sense of happiness. Here was security, should the need ever arise, another human being to turn to . . . Except that he had told her she was strictly not wanted.

'Goodnight,' she said, walking back. If she had waited for an answer, she would still be there, for none came.

Waking after a night's deep sleep to the wild island sounds was a wonderful experience. Washing and dress-

ing were things to be accomplished quickly, so as to
waste not a moment of time.

There were cereal packets in a wooden cupboard, and
powdered milk. Crispbread stood beside jams and mar-
malade to spread on it. With her appetite appeased,
Sharon wandered outside. A glance at the splash of
orange a few steps away told her that the stranger had
not taken up his tent and walked during the night.

The thought was pleasing to her, but that very
pleasure worried her. The presence of the man should
mean nothing, except maybe as an irritant. Yes, she
appeased her reasoning mind, that was it. It gave her a
purpose in life—to rid herself of him and his tent. Only
then could she enjoy the solitude which Mr Wilson had
promised.

As if she had willed him out, he pushed head first
through the tent flaps. Sharon's frigid 'good morning'
elicited a curt nod. He was bare to the waistband of his
jeans, and the tightened belt buckle revealed no spare
waistline flesh.

The rest of him was muscular and tough—tough as
his character, Sharon thought. Yes, he and his body
went well together. As far as he was concerned, he could
keep them both.

With a lift of the heart, she scanned the panorama of
grey-blue sea and cloud-dappled sky. Distant mountains
on other islands rose, daring the clouds to cover them,
then fell away in slopes and hollows. Her gaze came
homing to Cuilla, down the hill she had climbed.

Overnight, temporary cabins had been erected. People
reduced in stature by the distance moved like busy
matchstick people in a Lowry painting. Maybe that's
what they are, Sharon mused, inventions of my brain so
that I wouldn't be too lonely ...

With the fingers of her mind, she grabbed back the
thought and stuffed it away. Loneliness was something

she did not fear. In fact—her disparaging eyes sought out her neighbour and antagonist—she had come here specifically for that purpose, hadn't she?

He seemed to have been watching her, and her heart jolted with shock. In trying to shut him out, she thought he would have vanished, as though she had invented him, too. Invent that hunk of sarcastic, egotistical male? She smiled. She would have needed to be desperate to do that!

A thick eyebrow lifted. 'There's something about me that makes you laugh? That's a bonus. No other woman has found me funny before. "Irresistible, charming, sexy, lecherous"—I'm quoting—but never a subject for laughter. That really is something.' He bent down to enter the tent. 'And it would have to be you.'

Laughter bubbled out of her, she could not stop it. She had never felt so happy, not even when she had been Daryl Irwin's fiancée. Certainly not then. Looking back now, she realised what a miserable time she had really had. Yet once, her whole existence had centred on him, her reason for living just to become his wife.

'Good God, the woman's human!' The voice came growling from the interior of the tent.

Smiling, Sharon made her way down the stony path which had been made by time and the plod of feet, away from the hut where once, Jack Wilson had told her, a crofter's cottage had stood.

It was a different world on the flat land at the base of the hill. To the right was a concreted area bearing the letter 'H'. There, she assumed, was the helipad on which Mr Wilson's helicopter landed whenever he visited the island.

Back at the film village which had grown up overnight, mud had been churned up. There were the marks of a Land Rover's tyres, the imprint of the booted feet of men in charge of props, or constructing the temporary buildings.

'You one of the make-up girls?' a passing man wanted to know.

'Just looking.' She used the phrase spoken so often by her in London's department stores when a hopeful assistant had approached. London was a long, long way from here, she thought thankfully.

'Keep out of the way, then, will you?' The man spoke bluntly but kindly. He turned as he walked away. 'Looking for who?' he asked as if it had just occurred to him he might be able to help.

Sharon had to think fast. 'Er—Lee Banks? Is he around?'

'Lee?' The man's eyes were not quite so kindly. 'He's around somewhere. If you keep looking, you'll trip over him somewhere. Hero-worship? Or close relationship?'

Sharon coloured. 'Neither. Guess again.'

The man's respect crept warily back, but cynicism still held it at bay. He went on his way. Stealthily she climbed three wooden steps and pushed open a door. There was a table made of planks of wood on trestles. Around it sat a group of people. Carefully Sharon withdrew, walking backwards down the steps to stand on a large, hard foot.

Arms came round her waist, just a little too intimately. Struggling to remove them, she said, 'Sorry, I didn't see you. Let me go, will you?' The arms did not move, and looking up and over her shoulder, she saw a face which turned her heart over. Then she struggled some more. 'I said let me go!'

The man from the tent swung her round and lowered her, turning her to face him. With his boots, his dusty jeans and open-necked shirt, his brown hair springing thickly and spilling to skim his brows, he looked every inch the casual wanderer he pretended to be.

His hands rested on her shoulders. 'What are you

expecting me to do—rape you down there in the mud with an audience of technicians and extras?'

'I just don't like being manhandled,' she hit back, smoothing her hair.

'No?' His eyes were slits. 'Sharon Mason, you could have fooled me.'

'What do you know about me?' she asked, less certain now and wondering, wondering if he knew . . .

He did not answer the question. Instead, he jerked his thumb at the cabin he had ventured into. 'Can't you read? The notice on the door says, Story Conference in progress. No unauthorised admittance.' He took a step upwards. 'So why are you going in there?' Sharon asked. A curl of his lips was his only response, but she was determined to get an answer out of him. 'You told me you had nothing to do with the film team.'

Another slow smile appeared, then he disappeared through the forbidden door.

From inside the cabin, she heard raised voices say, 'Hi, Cal,' and 'Late again, Cal.'

Cal? She thought. Was his name really Caldar? And if so, Caldar what?

There was a clattering noise from inside another building. Since the word on one door said 'Entrance', while another farther along bore the words 'No Admittance', Sharon took a chance and entered. It was a self-service canteen and seemed established enough to have been there longer than the other cabins.

Jack Wilson had told her the film company's ferry she would catch was not the first to go to the island. It seemed that the production team had their priorities right, Sharon reflected. Food equalled warmth and energy, and the latter was an eessential which the prevailing conditions certainly required.

Even lifting your feet high and finding a non-muddy area in which to place them needed an energy output that surprised her. Commuterland was never like this, with its flat streets and underground trains and motor traffic to minimise a person's need to use his feet at all.

The smell of coffee was an invitation she could not resist. Luckily, in her parka pocket there were a few coins left over from her train journey. The counter assistants were friendly, their accents Scottish. Like everyone else, they assumed she was one of the film-makers.

Emerging later and descending the steps, her ears and eyes were caught by an eruption from the conference cabin. The door swung open, swung shut, and the man called Cal made grinding boot-prints in the mud as he stomped past the girl who was staring at him.

'Cal?' she called.

His head shot round. His face was a cold mask of anger, making her flinch as if it was she who had caused his wrath. Impetuously, she ran to walk at his side. 'What happened?' she asked, offering sympathy.

His icy eyes turned on her. 'Get out of my way,' he rasped. 'Of all things, I don't want your company.'

The rebuff hurt as he must have known it would. She rallied at once and called after him, 'And the last thing I want is yours!'

He had spoilt her morning, taken away her laughter. With slow, wide strides, she climbed the hill in his tracks. Looking up, she saw the tent flaps swing, swallowing him up.

For a while, Sharon stood outside the hut and listened. Out of angry thuds and fulsome swearing came the sound of a pounding typewriter. Entering her hut, she took down from a shelf a book she had brought, but she could not concentrate.

Throwing it aside, she pulled on her jacket and emerged into the daylight. The pounding of the type-writer keys went on with scarcely a pause. The fresh air was calling with its swooping, squawking, ever-present gulls. She strode away from the plateau, upwards towards the hilltop in whose shelter the hut had been erected.

Here was the solitude she had come to find. Here spread the wide sky, while below, the Atlantic licked the island's shores. Scattered near and far were other islands, some smaller, others larger, bearing rocky hillsides and sun-bathed, rounded summits.

Everywhere she looked, there were sheep. Even on Cuilla, they dotted the hillside and plains. Farmers from the mainland owned them, Mr Wilson had explained, having let out tracts of the island as pasture for grazing. At intervals, the farmers came over and, when necessary, tended them. Here and there were sheep pens and windbreaks behind which the sheep could shelter from the winter's biting winds.

Sharon sat down on a stone slab, staring across the water. What had his comment meant? *Sharon Mason, you could have fooled me.* Had he read the three-part series she was alleged to have written about Daryl Irwin's love life?

Even now, the story line had made her flinch. That was what it had been—not the truth but invented by the journalist who had interviewed her. It had been sensationalised out of all recognition, probably by the newspaper's editor. It had been printed with her own name written large just beneath the screaming headline.

Her father had urged her to sue the newspaper, but she had recoiled from the idea. Not only would it have brought even more unwanted publicity, she had no case. Hadn't she told the journalist to make what he liked of her story?

At the time, she had been too hounded and exhausted to care. For two years, the report had declared, Sharon Mason had lived with the star of the yachting world.

She had sailed with him, crewed for him, standing at his side in storm and in calm. If only the readers had known how scared of sailing she had been!

Not once had she shared Daryl's bed. He had made love to her, spoken endearments, bought her gifts, but had never pressed her for any greater intimacy. All this she had interpreted as a sign that he had loved her too much to expect more of her, that he was prepared to wait until they were married.

How naïve she had been in her adoration of him. Only later had she discovered that he had another woman in his life, hidden away out of sight. So why had she agreed to marry him?

He was her dream, her idol whom she had adored. She had mistaken that adoration for love. For two years she had worn his ring, waiting for him as he raced each race, coming home the victor almost every time. When she tentatively suggested that they might marry, at first he had rejected the idea. Then, to her astonishment, as he practised for the major yacht race of the year, he had agreed.

The night before the wedding he had taken her to dine at an expensive hotel on the south coast, overlooking the area from which the yacht race would start. They had dined and danced, then he had told her he wanted to go down to the yacht club and make sure all was well with his yacht.

'Can I come with you?' she had asked, but he had persuaded her with kisses to remain.

'Wait for me here,' he'd told her. 'I won't be long.'

From the steps of the hotel, she had watched him walk away into the darkness.

CHAPTER TWO

IT was not until evening that Sharon's neighbour emerged from his tent. She was reading outside, using the two steps up to the hut entrance as a seat.

He nodded at her and she smiled. Remote, enigmatic, he looked around as if seeking refreshment from the sea and distant hills. There was a driving necessity inside her to make verbal contact. Maybe she had been wrong about her ability to tolerate unbroken solitude. Or maybe it was just that this mysterious man, with his soul-probing eyes, disturbed her too much for her peace of mind.

'You acknowledged my existence,' she nudged, her hair swinging as she looked up at him. 'That's a cause for celebration it itself!'

He smiled, not at her but at two seagulls, one in swooping pursuit of the other.

There was a silence which he seemed in no hurry to break. 'You——' she needed courage to scale his barriers, 'you've worked hard today. Nothing but tap, tap from your orange-coloured hideaway.'

A mere lifting of his brows was the only answer he offered.

'That's a contradiction in terms, isn't it?' she persisted. 'A bright colour for a secret hiding place.'

Slowly, he swivelled from the waist, hands on hips. He gave her a lingering look, then turned fully. 'So you're in a talkative mood, eh? You want my attention like a domestic pet offering its paw.' He was near her now, looking down at the top of her head. His correct analysis had embarrassed her.

25

His fingers curled round her forearm, but although she flinched, he did not remove his hold. Instead he urged her sideways.

'Move up,' he ordered. 'There's just about room for two.'

Jerkily, Sharon obeyed. When their hips made contact, she felt a flash of feeling. As his thighs pressed against hers, a curious excitement combed through the nerves of her skin. Their eyes clashed, hers holding surprise, his sardonic amusement.

'What——' she moistened her lips, 'what does Caldar stand for?'

'You really want to know?'

She nodded and rubbed her thumbs over the glossy finish of the book's flimsy cover. Why was he hesitating? Did he need to take so long?

'You couldn't just call me Cal?' he asked at length.

She shook her head.

His shoulders lifted and fell, causing a tingle of friction between them. 'It's a kind of code Jack Wilson and I worked out. To hide my identity.'

'Why, are you a criminal?'

He threw back his head in laughter and she saw, with a stir of unfamiliar feeling the tensing of the muscles in his neck. At last he answered, 'Some might call me that.' He took a deep breath, let it out. 'If I didn't tell you now, you'd hear sooner or later from that bunch down there.' He frowned, rubbing at a dusty patch on his jeans. 'I'm Calum Darwin.'

She stared at him. 'You are?' Then she frowned. 'Oh dear!'

'Something wrong?' he drawled sarcastically.

'Don't they call you the Millionaire Man? Made a fortune out of your books?'

'Right.'

'Scorns the rich life, wanders the world, plenty of

women but strictly no ties?'

'You've been reading the blurb put out by my agents, not to mention my publishers.'

'On the back of the book. Plus a photograph.' She grinned up at him. 'Your devoted readers should see you now!'

'Disappointed,' he sneered, 'that I don't live up to my smart-suited, slicked-back-hair image which that photographer's studio portrait presents?'

'No.' She shook her head decisively. 'I've read two of your books. To be honest, I couldn't understand them.'

He smiled thoughtfully as he flexed his fingers, as though the concentrated typing session had made them ache. During the long pause that followed, Sharon flicked and reflicked the pages of her paperback. So he was a famous writer. The knowledge made her just a little sad.

'There's something missing,' he commented, startling her.

Her eyebrows lifted questioningly.

'The instant admiration, the gasps of delight. The praise, the adulation. The expressions of longing to possess the ability to earn a fortune that I seem to have.' He turned his head and fixed his gaze on hers. 'The adoration, the dreamy look in women's eyes as they stare at me.' He was smiling now, but she tore her eyes from his.

'I've had my fill of adoring the unreachable, of dreaming dreams that turn into nightmares. I'll never hero-worship any male ever again. I'll promise you something, Mr Darwin.' He looked down at her quizzically. 'I'll never adore you,' she continued. 'I shall never see you as a "dream man". To me, you'll always be an ordinary person who has the ability to write unintelligible but highly marketable books.'

The fire that had roared inside her had burned her

cheeks red. She flung her book to the ground and clasped her hands until they hurt.

'Wow,' he said softly, assuming an exaggerated drawl, 'is something eating you, as those guys down there would say.'

Despite herself, she laughed. He had made the tension in her twang, then he had joked and it had slackened, leaving her relaxed again.

'So you'll never adore me. I shall never be your dream man.'

'Nope.'

His arm went round her shoulders and he turned her, tilting her face so that he could look into it. His grey eyes searched hers, then his mouth descended, zooming in on her startled lips. His kisses touched down from one corner of her mouth to the other.

When he lifted his head, her wide eyes stared at him. 'Why?' she whispered.

'Why not?' was his answer. Then his kiss hardened, pressing her mouth until she allowed him access. He did not plunder, but seemed set only on satisfying his taste buds. Then it was over, but he did not remove his arm.

The fact that she had liked his kissing meant that she had to fight him with every weapon. 'Proving your masculinity, Mr Darwin?' she provoked.

'No. Just doing what my friend Jack Wilson gave me permission to do—using whatever I want from the hut.'

Sharon twisted from his hold and stood in front of him. 'You were *using* me?'

He leaned slightly forward, elbows on his knees, hands lightly clasped. 'In my tent, most of my needs are catered for. There's just one that isn't.' His eyes skimmed her figure, narrowly assessing.

'I'm not here to be "used" in that way,' she retorted furiously. 'The sooner you understand that, Mr Darwin, the better it will be for both of us!' She was all the more annoyed because the woman in her was doing battle with her reasoning mind. It was good to be held by him, it was saying. 'Anyway,' Sharon finished, 'Mr Wilson said "ask first".'

'But I did, Miss Mason, I did.' His smile mocked her. 'My first two or three kisses were just a testing of your reaction. You didn't emit a "no" signal. You just sat there waiting for more.'

'You think you have the answer to everything, don't you?' she returned, conscious that she was losing out in their oddly disturbing skirmish. 'Well, Mr Wilson also said, don't handle the goods, fragile, Sharon's a lady.'

He laughed shortly. 'So you don't mind being referred to as "goods".' He watched her lips draw in and he smiled. 'Point two, no woman's a lady where men and her sexuality are concerned.'

'You think you know it all where women are concerned, don't you?'

'Not all. Enough—enough to know you can't trust a single one of them any more than you can trust a rattlesnake.'

'I've got news for you, Mr Darwin. You're talking right now to the exception to your rule.'

He stood up slowly, sliding his hands into his jeans pockets. '*You*? I wouldn't trust you any farther than I could see you.'

It was spoken with such venom that she reeled. 'Me? What have I ever done to make you say that?'

He strolled away to stare across the water. He was as remote again as the darkening, distant hills, his essence as uncatchable as those swooping gulls. Like an unwanted character in his books, he had dismissed her from his mind.

When she said 'goodnight', he did not answer. It was as though, for him, she had ceased to exist.

Down the hill, the angular structure and unnatural white of the hastily-constructed buildings contrasted starkly with the greens and browns and rocky greys of which the island was formed.

The small scurrying figures attracted Sharon constantly. Although she had come for solitude, she had already started to question the correctness of her idea. Being with others, even if they were strangers, took her mind away from the past more effectively than the complete loneliness she had originally sought. Again, next morning, she did not even try to restrain her footsteps when they took her downwards.

It seemed she was accepted now, since most of the people she met smiled at her. One of them, ascending the steps of the cabin where yesterday she had so nearly gatecrashed the story conference, called out, 'Cal in a better mood this morning?'

'I don't know,' she answered, 'I haven't seen him.'

'Sharon?' She turned, recognising the hesitant voice. 'They told me you were looking for me yesterday.'

'Oh, it didn't matter, Lee. There were so many strangers. I was looking for a familiar face.'

He pretended to be hurt. 'Is that all you wanted? You've damaged my ego.' He had typewritten pages under his arm. 'I've been getting to know the place. We spent yesterday tramping the island for the right spot to set part of the film.'

'What kind of story, Lee? Historical, romantic or what?'

He pushed back his fair hair. His slacks were the worse for wear, his sweater crewnecked. He frowned. 'Don't you know? It's a spy story. Part of the action takes place in——' he consulted the script, 'an island hideout.'

'Are you a goodie or a baddie?' she asked, smiling.

'Hero. They're always good, aren't they?'

'Not always. They can be what's called, I think, anti-heroes, not at all good. Is it based on a book? Or are they making it up as they go along?'

'Don't you really know who wrote the story?'

She shook her head, checked it then stared. 'You don't mean——' She pointed up the hill. 'Calum Darwin?' Lee nodded. 'But he said he had no connection with you down here.'

'His little joke. Read any of his stuff? The book's called *Come Night, Come Day*. It had rave reviews when it came out.'

Sharon shook her head again. 'I think I'll get a cup of coffee. Don't let me hold you up.'

'There's not much to do evenings, Sharon. Can I visit you up there tonight?'

Sharon frowned and tried to sound casual. 'To do what, Lee?'

'Talk, walk. Whatever you want.'

She considered, but could find no possible reason why she should refuse. It would be pleasant to have company, since her neighbour seemed to take pleasure in denying her his.

'Why not?' she replied.

He seemed pleased and waved, continuing on his way. Hands in her pockets, she stared around—and caught the eye of the tall, lean man who seemed to have been watching her. She turned on her heel and made for the café, collecting her coffee and finding a table.

There were a few people scattered around. One or two nodded as though they accepted her, no questions asked. As she emptied a sachet of sugar into her cup, Calum Darwin came through the door. The others looked up, one or two called, 'Hi, Cal.'

He nodded in reply but did not look at anyone in particular. I might as well be invisible, Sharon thought, staring at her swirling coffee. There were footsteps. He's going past, she thought.

'Mind if I join you?'

She did not look at him. 'If you can bear to.'

A chair scraped, his spoon clattered and she watched his coffee go round and round.

'Why didn't you tell me you wrote the book they're filming?'

His eyes held hers. 'I thought it was common knowledge. Why else would I be here?'

'You told me you had nothing to do with these people.'

'I'm just keeping a watching brief, as they say. I attended that story conference yesterday to keep up to date with the twists and turns of the director's mind.'

'You came out of there furious. Did you spend the rest of the day putting right what they thought was wrong?'

'Did I hell! I started another book.'

Sharon was bewildered. 'But Calum——' it was the first time she had used his name and it felt good on her lips, 'it's your story they're filming.'

'Once, only once have I taken an active part in helping to put one of my books on to the big screen. I hardly recognised the end result. Since then, I vowed never again.'

Sharon shook her head, still not understanding.

'If you feel as strongly as that, why don't you go and tell them?'

His broad shoulders lifted under his shirt. 'I tried, yesterday, but it was like shouting at a volcano to stop it erupting.' He pushed back his chair, nodded to Sharon and walked away.

Disappointment lowered her emotional temperature. He was like one of those seabirds the ornithologists go wild about, she thought despondently—rare, elusive and maddeningly untouchable to the ordinary person. And am I an 'ordinary person'! she reflected in self-mockery.

She watched the muscles move in his thighs, remembering their feel against her. Through her lashes, she saw the leanness just above his waistband and wondered how it would feel to hold him there. Shaking the thoughts away, she heard him speak, his voice still rasping a little with the remnants of his anger, as he lingered for a moment beside one of the occupied tables.

When the door slammed on him, she sighed. It would have been so good, she thought, if he had invited her to go with them. If only he were just an average man, down on her level. Then she could talk to him of everyday things, feel easy with him, and be on laughing terms. That was something else, she thought. He rarely laughed, except in mockery.

One of the women behind the counter called out to her, 'Going up the hill to watch the filming? Lee's there.'

Sharon nodded and thanked her. Emerging into the sharp sunlight, she guessed that her quest yesterday for Lee Banks had gone around via the grapevine.

Making enquiries, she was told the direction to take to find the action. It was difficult terrain to negotiate, Sharon discovered. No sooner had she made it to the top of a rocky incline than she was descending on to stone, only to climb again.

The sound of raised voices told her she was almost there. The sea made a sun-dappled backdrop to the sudden rise in the level of the land. It was on this particular rocky promontory that she saw two figures. One was that of Lee Banks, in a loose, short leather jacket and jeans, his hands lifted above his head. An imitation gun bulged from his pocket.

The other was that of a redhead whose body was encased in a brown velvet one-piece suit. In her hand

was a gun and it was levelled at Lee. The girl stood with
her back to the rocks below. Slowly, hands still raised,
Lee was approaching her. She was trapped, but still her
confidence was supreme.

Sharon felt her heart pounding. It was as if it were
really happening. Like a child wanting to share her en-
joyment, she looked at the nearest person. About to
return her attention to the scene, she saw who that
person was.

Calum Darwin was smiling at her cynically. He was
completely unmoved by the action on the rocks. If I
were the writer of the story, she thought, I'd be delighted
to see my characters coming to life. Eagerly, she looked
back at the actors.

As she watched, she saw the Lee Banks she had come
to know taken over by the character he was playing.
There was menace in his every move, yet cleverly muted
by an attitude of pleading as he approached the threatening woman, all the time silently daring her to 'shoot'.

When he sprang at her, knocking her gun away,
Sharon stifled a scream. The woman clawed the air as if
about to fall backwards down the rock face. Lee's arm
caught her waist just in time to prevent her death-
plunge. With the woman at his mercy, the menace in
him surfaced and something inside Sharon cringed at
his acting.

Was he acting? she asked herself, or was this the real
Lee Banks? Had she been fooled by the hesitant manner
he used when he talked to her—or was that hesitancy
an act? The scene was cut and the tension in the onlookers slackened.

'So you've had your fill of adoring the out-of-reach
dream man?' a voice gritted beside her. 'You'll never
hero-worship any male ever again? I'm quoting your
words, lady.'

'Me—adoring Lee? What do you mean?' Sharon

challenged, wishing she could remove the jeering expression from Calum's eyes.

'The way you were gazing at him just now, it looked as though you wanted nothing more from life than to become his dream girl.'

'I was watching the action,' she flared. 'It was so exciting——'

'You mean *he* was so exciting.'

'No, I don't. Oh, I wish you'd leave me alone!' She turned and scrambled down between the film crew, retracing her steps. Calum was not far behind, keeping pace, then overtaking her, but waiting at the foot until she caught up with him.

He seemed about to walk with her up the hill to the hut. She turned on him. 'You told me I wasn't wanted. I'm telling you now that you're not wanted.'

He smiled down at her. 'Over the years, Sharon, I've grown a skin as thick as an elephant's hide. A few velvet-tipped barbs from you won't penetrate it.'

Why did her heart have to jerk when he spoke her name? She mustn't let herself down and fall for him. Yet why else did she wish that he would take her hand as they walked and entwine it with his? Why did she keep getting this 'good to be alive' feeling whenever he was near?

'Hey, dreamer,' his voice came softly, 'I'm still with you. Where's your fight gone?'

He was right—where had it gone? She had to extract herself from the sentimental quicksands into which she seemed unwittingly to have stepped. Repeat to yourself, she told herself fiercely, I do not feel a single thing for this man—except dislike.

All the same, it was difficult urging her mind to deliver up a smart retort. 'I'm pretending you're not here,' she managed, only to hear his jeering laughter.

At that moment, he did take her hand, and it was as

if he had walked right into her fantasy. His action was like flicking a switch to start her heart thumping instead of merely pumping. The blood in her veins raced like a rising river in flood conditions.

What of her vow that she would never fall again for a man famous enough to be considered public property? Glancing covertly at his careless style of dress, the mud-clogged boots into which he had pushed his well-fitting but creased jeans, she could imagine no more unlikely a person as a cult figure than this one.

Trying to judge his mood, she glanced up at his ruggedly handsome profile. He seemed to be deep in thought, but a spurt of mischief she never even knew she had founted inside her. She would get his attention if it killed her! 'Have you ever held hands with a rattle-snake before?'

He looked at her in puzzlement for a passing second, then flung back his head in laughter. They were at the hut now and he released her hand. He looked at the palm that had rubbed against hers. 'No swelling from an injection of venom. Maybe this little rattler's fangs are at rest.' His hand rested on her shoulder, then moved slowly to hold the side of her neck. 'If I do this, will I activate them?'

A shiver caught her off guard. He must have felt it, since his eyes gleamed. Panicking, she clasped her fingers round his wrist in an effort to eradicate the source of disturbance to her body's equilibrium. His hand was immovable and it was impelling her towards him. The kiss that was coming turned her panic into a deep fear.

It wasn't that she did not want to be in his arms—just that she wanted it too much. Self-defence in the form of abuse came to her aid. 'Are you so deprived of an outlet for your male desire you'd even stoop to making love to a female on your "hate list"?'

He let her go at once. Relief mixed itself with mortifi-

cation and an absurd sense of rejection. Hadn't she in-
itiated his disgusted dismissal of her? An apology
hovered in her head, but her compressed lips imprisoned
it. Sadly, she saw him turn on his heel and disappear
into his hideaway.

During the afternoon, the air freshened. Sharon
pulled on a thick sweater and went to the door to stare
around her. Clouds were gathering and she wondered
how long it would be before they shed their contents. A
side-glance told her that the tent's occupant was not
visible. He was, however, audible.

The typewriter tapped incessantly, with an occasional
pause. It was almost as if he were pouring out his anger
on it, but anger against what—or whom?

Towards evening, she returned to the door to watch
for Lee. She had begun to regret her acceptance of his
suggestion that he might visit her. Part of her hoped he
had forgotten. When his figure did appear at the foot of
the hill, she felt little pleasure.

As she sat on the steps waiting, Calum came out of
his tent. He stood for a moment looking round, his life-
sculpted head lifting to survey the heavy clouds. He
turned as she watched him, and the colour which
invaded her cheeks dismayed her. Why did she have to
give away all her inner secrets to this man?

His gaze moved downhill and his expression turned
cynical at the sight of the man who was by now nearing
his goal.

'Why didn't you run to greet him,' was the grating,
goading question, 'like in the romantic movies of old?
You seem to have an old-fashioned crush, as they used
to call it, on the famous star. Don't mind me, go ahead
and run into his arms. His wife has only just run out of
them.' He watched the other man's approach. 'He's
come to visit you for old-fashioned reasons. Primitive,
in fact. No doubt you're willing to oblige.'

'Will you be quiet!' she snapped. 'It's a friendly visit, nothing more.'

His cynical laughter hit the air as Lee stood puffing a little from his climb. Calum nodded at the newcomer and turned, still full of amusement, to enter his tent.

'Don't you get on with Calum Darwin?' Lee asked as he followed Sharon into the hut.

Sharon laughed. 'That's about as possible as getting friendly with a herd of wild elephants. Take a seat, Lee. There's a garden chair against the wall. Just unfold it and put it where you want.'

'Next to yours,' Lee said promptly, and did so.

The faintest shadow of a doubt passed across Sharon's mind at the implication behind Lee's words. All the same, she said brightly, 'Sorry I can't offer you a drink.'

'It doesn't matter,' Lee answered. 'If that was all I'd wanted, I could have had one in the bar down there.'

Sharon sat beside him, pulling at the neck of her sweater. 'What do you want, Lee?' she asked quietly.

He hesitated, studied his own hands, looked at her askance, then answered, 'A chat, maybe coffee if you make some. I was feeling lonely.'

The suspicions that Calum's sarcastic remark had aroused about Lee's reasons for coming began to trouble her. Earlier, she had seen Lee act. Although the familiar diffidence was there now, did another personality lurk beneath the surface? Was Lee acting yet another role in his repertoire?

Irritably, she told herself not to be so stupid as to believe anything Calum Darwin said about another human being. He seemed warped in his approach to his fellow creatures, whatever their sex. Managing to relax, she asked Lee about his career.

He seemed to shrug off the subject. 'Usual thing. Trained to be a mechanical engineer, but got the acting bug at college. Went to drama school. Small parts. Eventually I was spotted as someone with potential, and here I am.'

'At the top.' He seemed uninterested in the praise in the statement, but again she wondered if it was an act.

'Much good it did me. My wife walked out on me, taking the kids.' He looked fully at her. 'I'm single again.'

Sharon's smile was strained, apprehension growing as to his intentions—or hopes. At least Calum wasn't far away. Hearing the crunch of footsteps, she went to the window. 'Coffee?' she asked over her shoulder. Calum was descending the hill. In a few moments he would be quite out of earshot. She hoped Lee had not heard.

Busying herself at the stove, she praised the scene she had watched that morning. 'I think Maida Halliday is beautiful. Does she act well?'

It was babbling, Sharon knew, but it filled the heavy silence.

He took his coffee from her, refusing the sugar. 'When she's in a role she likes. Opposite a male lead she likes.'

'Does she like you?' Sharon asked, smiling.

He paused before he replied, 'She might, if she hadn't got her eyes on a bigger fish.'

Sharon's heart seemed to contract. She knew the answer before she asked it. 'Who might that be?' Had she sounded casual enough?

It seemed so, since he answered, stirring his coffee, 'Calum Darwin. He hasn't shown himself to be unwilling.'

'He's just gone out.' Then Sharon cursed herself for giving the fact away.

'That'll be to Maida's cabin. Or to go for a drink at the makeshift bar they've got. Or both. Darwin can knock it back when he likes.' He stopped again, then added, 'He's a tough customer.'

'He surely doesn't live here all the time, Lee?'

He shook his fair head. 'Just likes to live rough now and then. It's good publicity.'

'Calum doesn't strike me as the sort to seek publicity.'

Sharon studied Lee's face covertly. He was certainly handsome, enough to turn any woman's head except her own. She'd had enough of good-looking hero-types. They were usually more in love with themselves, she reflected acidly, than anyone else in their world.

It was about an hour later that Lee got up to go. 'I've really enjoyed being with you, Sharon.'

The door stood half-open and Sharon wished he would go through it.

'There's a kind of mock-up movie house down there,' he told her. 'Courtesy of Jack Wilson. They watch the day's takes in it. Would you come with me some time to see a film?'

'Maybe.' Some time sounded pleasantly vague. 'How did they get all this stuff over, Lee? By ferry?'

He nodded. 'Specially laid on by Mr Wilson for the film unit's benefit. He's got a financial stake in the film, but I expect you knew that?'

'He told me. I said I wanted a week or two of solitude and he offered me the use of this hut. He said there'd be a film crew coming over with me, but I didn't expect a kind of miniature Oxford Circus on a tiny Scottish island!'

Lee laughed, then pulled her to him, placing a presumptuous and unbelievably ineffectual kiss on her astonished mouth. She tried pushing at him, but he held the position as if waiting for a director to shout 'Cut!'

When the crunching footsteps, which Sharon in her confusion had not heard, came to a stop outside Lee let her go. He was smiling and he lifted a hand to run it over her hair. Only she could see that it was shaking.

'Have I come at the right or the wrong time?' the familiar voice enquired smoothly. 'Was the lady enjoying it or hating it? From this angle, it looked as if she was revelling in every second.'

'Go away!' Sharon snapped. Of all the people to come at that moment, she thought furiously, it would have to be Calum. She knew exactly what kind of construction he would put on the scene.

'See you again soon, Sharon,' Lee promised, his subtle actor's tone plainly reinforcing Calum's conjecture. Throwing a smile at Calum, Lee ran down the hill like a lover whose expectations had been fulfilled.

'Go on,' Sharon lifted her head high and stood on the step, hands on hips, 'call me a hypocrite, tell me how I'm going back on my statement that I'd never get involved with a hero-figure!'

A wind had sprung up, blowing strongly, tossing her black hair in all directions. He took a measured stride towards her. 'You've said it for me,' he commented, as if his mind was not entirely on the subject. His hands lifted to move the strands of hair away from her face, resting on her temples the better to study her features.

'Strange,' he remarked, 'you don't look used.'

Sharon jerked away. 'I hope you enjoyed *using* Maida's cabin this evening,' she attacked again.

'So that's where you think I've been. Who told you? Ah, Golden Boy Banks.' He smiled unpleasantly. 'I didn't just use Maida's cabin . . .' The words were left dangling to taunt.

Colour sprang to her cheeks. 'You said the other day you wouldn't trust a woman. Hasn't anyone told you men can't be trusted, either?'

He studied her speculatively. 'Trusted to what? With what? Or,' as an answer suggested itself, 'should it be with whom?' His smile was wide. 'You wouldn't be jealous?'

'*Jealous?*' Sharon had meant it to sound full of amusement, but it came out as almost a shriek. The wind took it away and played with it, returning it augmented. 'You're flattering yourself,' she finished with commendable scorn.

With a strained, 'Excuse me', she walked past him and turned towards the sheltering hill above them.

'Where are you going?'

Sharon didn't answer. He repeated his question and she turned her head at last. 'For a walk. And it's none of your business. I'm just a rattlesnake to you. Why should you worry about me?'

'You're here through Jack Wilson's generosity. So am I. I feel a certain responsibility for your welfare. If you go for a walk, your welfare's going to suffer.'

'You're joking! Walking is good for you.'

'Not when it's getting dark and the wind's rising and those great clouds out beyond,' he indicated the hills across the near-black sea, 'are going to loose their contents on us in a very short time.'

Sharon hesitated. If she returned at his bidding, it would mean he had won his point. Then he would gloat, if not aloud, then with a maddening look. Her feet made the decision, taking her upwards.

There was a pounding of booted feet and an arm curved round her neck from the rear. 'Stop it!' she cried, almost choking, but he did not let her go. Her head was back against his shoulder and the feel of his body against her created a havoc inside her which no storm, however strong, could equal.

Against her will, her head stopped forcing itself forward. Instead, it lay against him. His arm loosened and after a few moments he turned her, holding her from him.

Her hair blew everywhere, while the wind made furrows through the thickness of his, parting it in all the wrong places. His eyes were a deep blue now, coloured by the sky's darkening canopy. She saw the hollows of his cheeks beneath the high cheekbones, tapering to a ridged jawline.

His brows were pleated into a frown. The marks which time and a life lived hard had put there would never go, she hazarded. Calum's lips were a thin, hard line, but even as she watched, they seemed to soften. He had been watching her, she realised, as studiedly as she had been looking at him. A tenderness was creeping into his features and it had her heartbeats all over the place.

Over their heads was a piece of sunlit sky, as if it was making a last valiant effort to fend off the approaching storm. There was a glow all around as she felt herself pulled against him. Once more, she knew the pleasure of being close to the solid rock of his chest, his hips and legs.

His arms enveloped her and the wind battered at them, trying its best to topple them or rend them apart. Nothing, she thought, parting her lips for the taste of his kiss, could tear me away from him at this moment. His mouth explored and demanded a return. She melted into him, feeling the sinews of his neck muscles ripple beneath her curving fingers.

Around her, his arms were like lashed ropes, pressing against her so that she struggled to breathe. He kissed and kissed again, until her thoughts reeled mindlessly. His hands slipped beneath her parka, moving upwards and seeking for her warm, thrusting shape.

Even through the thickness of her sweater his moulding hands aroused her into clutching at him. Slowly he was bending her backwards and unresistingly she went. Drugged by his kisses, she offered him no barriers to surmount.

Yet he chose not to take advantage of her lowered defences. Gently he lifted her upright, took away his lips and looked deeply into her eyes, as dark now as the restless sea below. She could find nothing to say. His expression remained serious and unreadable. Trying a smile, and discovering that at that moment it was useless as a means of communication, she pulled her jacket into place.

'Goodnight, Calum,' she whispered. He did not reply.

Finding her way with care in the near-darkness, she descended the short distance to the hut. Before going in, she walked a few yards and stood contemplating the wild sky-scene. Clouds massed enormously in every direction. The sea, wave upon wave of it, hit at the base of the cliffs. It was a sight that filled her with an incredible pleasure. This was Nature obeying no laws but its own.

As she made her way to the hut, she heard sounds from Calum's tent. He too, during that time of kissing, seemed to have felt that irresistible pull which existed between them. Standing for a moment on the wooden steps, she felt it again. Was he willing her to join him? Or was it her imagination playing a tantalising game?

With a sigh, she closed the door and sank on to the bed. Well, she told herself, she had her solitude. The frightening thing was that she didn't want it any more.

CHAPTER THREE

AT first, Sharon could not sleep. The sound of an angry sea hitting at the great rocks which were the island of Cuilla made her wonder, in her tired state, if the roaring Atlantic was seeking to sink the place.

Daryl's yacht had sunk in such a storm. She moved restlessly. Was the rest of her life to be haunted by storms? When he had walked out of the hotel the night before their wedding, he had gone straight down to his yacht.

On the boat was a woman. He had known she would be there. She was his secret lover. It was she who had crewed for him on the many occasions that a woman had been seen on board by pressmen and photographers. Since the engagement had lasted a long two years, the journalists had reasonably assumed that it had been his fiancée who was helping him.

By midnight, Sharon remembered, she had become so worried about Daryl's failure to return, she had contacted the police. At once they had agreed to help. They had gone down to the yacht's mooring place where they had found Daryl. He had resisted their persuasion to rejoin his fiancée at the hotel.

He had a companion, they'd told her, reporting back, a woman he'd called Roxana. His message to his fiancée had been that he was sorry but there would be no wedding . . .

Sharon stared into the darkness, remembering her parents' dismay when she had called them, giving them the news. Her father had left his bed and driven from London to collect her from the south coast hotel. Her mother had frantically contacted guests informing them of the change of plan.

Afterwards, Sharon learned that her mother had been so humiliated by the cancellation, she had made up a plausible story. Daryl, she'd invented, had known of the risks involved and had told Sharon he would not marry her until the race was behind him.   ·

The story had been swallowed whole by every invited guest. Their sympathy and understanding had been immediate. They were never to know that Daryl had already changed his mind about the marriage and that, even had the circumstances been different, it would never have taken place.

It was as though the skies were descending. The pounding on the roof awakened her and over it all was the howling of the gale rising now and then to a high-pitched scream.

Everything rattled—the windows which were firmly closed, the door which had seemed tight in its frame. Draughts had turned into young gales themselves. In the cocooned warmth of her sleeping bag, Sharon wondered how long the hut would withstand the elements' battering. The thought of the roof being lifted completely away filled her with dread.

As she lay there listening, she grew worried for Calum's safety. If the hut felt as if it were rocking on its foundations, how was he faring in his flimsy tent? Just how flimsy it was she learnt a few minutes later.

There was a hammering on the door and a shout of 'Let me in, will you?'

She scrambled out of bed. Covered as she was only by lightweight pyjamas, the low temperature hit her. With shaking hands, she put a match to the gas lamp. Without waiting to find extra covering, she dived for the door, unbolted it, released the catch and pulled it open, helped against her will by the power of the wind.

Calum stepped in, oilskins billowing, his booted feet leaving their soaking imprint on the floor-covering of the hut. He held a half-filled backpack, which he dropped quickly. Sharon struggled to close the door, holding it in place with her shoulder while she locked it. Then she turned and stood with her back against it, surveying the intruder.

His outer covering was running with water, dripping to make pools around him. He half-turned to see where she was, and only when his eyes lingered did she realise how much of her he could see. Her loose pink semi-transparent top and knee-length pyjama trousers hid little, while her outline thrust and curved uninhibitedly under the clinging, man-made cloth.

His only comment was. 'Don't just stand there, help me out of these things.' His face was wet, too, and droplets of water rested on his eyebrows and long lashes.

'Sorry,' she responded, 'I'm still half asleep.' Her bare feet tiptoed to him.

His glance skimmed her again, this time including her ruffled hair. 'You look fit to eat. Luckily for you, my appetite's been blunted. The tent descended around me.' He was removing his oilskin leggings. He saw her cover her smiling mouth. 'You can laugh, woman. If you'd been there with me——' His gaze flicked her again as he unfastened his jacket. 'We won't go into that. Come on, get me out of this.'

Sharon went round the back of him and tugged the jacket free of his shoulders and arms. The oilskin came off with a jerk and flung itself against her, wrapping itself lovingly around her upper half.

She squealed at the dampness and he laughed. 'It must have taken on the personality of its owner,' Sharon quipped. 'It can't leave a girl alone!'

'It's your animal magnetism,' he rejoined, looking at her askance.

'*My* animal magnetism?' She shook her head. 'You've got that, not——'

Realising what she had said, her voice trailed into silence. Anxiously she looked at him. What was he thinking now?

To hide her embarrassment, she held the oilskin jacket away from her to let it drip. He was looking at her and she followed his eyes. The wet pyjama top was clinging boldly to her every curve. No wonder his eyes were gleaming, despite his state.

'A towel,' she muttered, and turned away.

'For me?'

'For myself. I'm wet through.'

'And beautiful. Leave it.'

'But I——'

'You're wet, I'm soaked. Give me the towel, will you?' His tone was imperious and sharp. She did not move. 'Please,' came from him softly.

'You'll have to share mine,' she warned.

'Who cares?' He put the towel to his face and inhaled. 'Mm—the sweetness of you,' he murmured with sarcasm. He rubbed around his neck, then handed back the towel. 'I'll finish off with my own.' He crouched down. 'I've got a clean one in here. Lucky I never completely unpacked.'

His wet sweater came off first and Sharon took it from him, draping it over a chair back. His shirt followed which she spread on the seat. He rubbed his damp skin vigorously, throwing the towel down. When he started unfastening the buckle of his belt, Sharon's fingers pressed into her cheek.

'Calum, I——' His raised eyebrows formed a question. 'I'd rather you didn't——'

'Didn't what?' He inspected his clothes to see what he

was doing wrong. His head came up disbelievingly. 'You're not asking me not to remove my jeans?'

She nodded faintly, her heart sinking as she saw the derision in his eyes.

'You, Sharon Mason, are asking me not to strip? You, with your past history?'

A slim shoulder lifted and drooped. She went for a towel to dry herself, turning her back on him. For a few moments, there was only the sound of the storm. Strangely, since he had arrived, its intensity seemed to have lessened, but that, she guessed, would not last.

The towel was being taken and he was turning her, just as he had earlier in the twilight out there. 'I told you not to,' he said. He was urging her towards him, but she stiffened.

'Not again, Calum. If you need a woman, go back to Maida Halliday.'

Had she said too much? She hadn't meant to provoke him, but it seemed she had succeeded, judging by the thinning of his lips.

'A woman's something I'll never *need*. Take, maybe, even use, but not *need*. I told you my opinion of the breed, and that included you. And why the hell should I go trekking down to Maida's place when you're here, saying "Take me, I'm yours for the asking"?'

He jerked her off balance, so that she fell against him, but she made herself go as rigid as a piece of sculptured rock. His roving hands had already found their way beneath her loose pyjama top. The touch of him on her sensitised skin, on her waist and stomach, brought her nerves to fever pitch.

He whispered against her ear, 'Loosen up, baby. Come on, give.'

'Give what?' she snapped through clenched teeth. His hands were skimming the full shape of her and she was battling with her own arousing needs as well as with the man arousing them. 'I haven't got a history, nor have I got a past. You've got the wrong girl. I'm the one who came for peace and solitude, remember?'

His laugh was grating, grazing her mind. 'Stop talking and let me take what I want. You're a cheap little——'

She lifted her hands to pull at his hair, but he caught her wrists and forced her arms to her sides. She compressed her lips to prevent the tears from forming, but the thickness in her voice gave her away.

'I let you come in here out of pity. You needed help and I was sorry for you. What do you do but take advantage of my kindness of heart and treat me as if I was a—a woman of the streets? So now who's behaving like a snake?'

He let her go without another word. He grabbed back his towel and rubbed at his damp hair, throwing the towel down again. Then he looked around.

'Got a spare sleeping bag?'

She went straight to it in the corner, untying the string that secured it in a roll. She hoped he wouldn't notice her trembling hands.

'Okay, thanks,' he said shortly, 'I'll do it. You get back to bed.'

Doing as he directed, Sharon climbed on to the wooden-structured bed and slipped down into the warmth the bag still held. He glanced at her, unfastened his jeans and removed them. One eyebrow lifted as he asked sardonically,

'You don't object to a man in underpants?' She shook her head. 'Thank God for that,' he said with mock-relief, and unzipped the sleeping bag. 'I'd be wearing less than this at a swimming pool.'

He went to extinguish the lamp and over the rustling sound he made in settling down, Sharon heard the increasing whine of the gale. He moved about for a while, then a torch came on. He got out of the sleeping bag and went across to his back-pack.

'Looking for something?' she asked politely.

'What does it look like?' he snapped.

'I was only trying to be helpful.' If he noticed the waver in her voice he gave no sign.

In the glow from the torch, his lean body looked white. There seemed to be immense strength in the moving shoulders and arms, a strength which beckoned her unbearably. She felt a surge of longing to be wrapped around by them in the haven of security they would offer, shelter from the storm around them, from the storms of life.

Of life? She caught at her thoughts, scolding them. She wouldn't know him for that length of time. Once they left this island, whatever there was between them— and there was little enough—would disappear as if it had never been.

As he pulled a sweater from the bag, she asked, 'Are you cold?'

'Why, are you going to offer to warm me up?' He straightened and the columns of his thighs drew her gaze. There was an inherent strength all over this man, not only in his powerful body but in his mind, too. Instinctively she knew that it would take a mighty storm indeed to destroy him.

Her reply hid her secret feelings. 'I'd sooner warm up an—an iceberg than you!'

Calum bent over her. 'Don't tempt me, baby. One pull at that zip around you and I'd be beside you before you'd know I'd moved. And you couldn't do a damned thing about it, could you? Admit it.'

She stirred restlessly. 'I admit it, but I told you, I'm going to have nothing more to do with men for a long, long time.'

To her relief, he moved away, saying, 'All I wanted

was a pillow.' He folded the sweater, got back into the bag and zipped it around him. The torch clicked off.

The whine of the wind grew stronger again, the crashing waves so loud it seemed they must be climbing the hill to get at them. Had Calum gone to sleep? A movement gave her the answer.

'Your tent—will it blow away, Calum?' she asked, her voice small against the storm's roar.

'I secured the fabric with bits of rock, so it should be safe. Anyway, it's my worry, not yours.'

She turned her head sharply towards the wooden wall beside her. Why was he being so unpleasant? If only she could get back to sleep ... Even if she did, she told herself despondently, he would invade her dreams. There seemed to be no way of escaping him.

'Why didn't you try to help your fiancé when he was drowning?' Her head swivelled back but in the darkness, he could not see her astonishment. 'Why,' he persisted, 'did you shout, "Save me, not him—save me, not Daryl"?'

He knew about her connection with the famous young yachtsman? He knew about her engagement to Daryl Irwin? All this time he had known, yet had never said a word!

So many questions, so many answers clamoured to be spoken but all she could manage was, 'Where—where did you read that?'

'In the newspapers. Where else?'

'You mean that story about Daryl the paper published as a serial?'

'I said newspapers, plural. It was a report, a factual report.' He seemed to be waiting for an answer. None came his way, so he went on, 'It wasn't, of course, mentioned in the series you're talking about.'

'Why "of course"?'

'You wrote it, your name was splashed all over it.

Naturally, you wouldn't tell a tale that could be held against you.' She heard his head turn. 'I suppose you're now going to deny you cried out to be saved, at the expense of your loved one?'

'If I did, would you believe me?' Her voice was weary now.

'No, because all the national dailies carried it.'

'Do you believe everything you read in the papers?' she asked dully, knowing it was useless to try reasoning with him.

'No, but witnesses agreed they'd heard you screaming to be saved first. Even the rescuers were shocked.'

It was true, Sharon knew, that the woman they had seen floundering in the mountainous seas had shrieked those words. But by then she also knew that the pleas had been pointless, because the rescue parties had told her later that Daryl had already gone under. The woman who had cried out had been saved, handed over to friends and had not been seen since.

Daryl's parents had pleaded with Sharon to keep the presence of the mystery woman on their son's yacht a secret. Nothing must spoil his memory in the eyes of the public, his father had said. Out of compassion for them, Sharon had agreed, but she had paid a terrible price.

'You haven't answered my question.' Calum's harsh voice came at her through the darkness. The storm was loud around them, but Sharon could only hear the storm which raged in her heart. She raised herself on to her elbows.

'Why?' she hit back, her voice high-pitched. 'Because I'm a no-good selfish sleep-around bitch who cares for no one but myself? That's the answer you wanted, isn't it?'

There was no sound from him.

'Now I know,' she added bitterly, 'that you've acted both judge and jury and convicted me without even allowing me the scant justice of saying a word in defence of myself.' She lowered her head to the pillow again.

There was a long silence. She said into it, without knowing whether Calum had gone to sleep or was as wakeful as she was. 'I know, too, why you've called me names, even—even equating me with a snake. I understand now why there's been a constant undercurrent of nastiness in your attitude towards me. I can't think,' she cursed the stifled sob, 'how you could bring yourself to k-kiss me.'

There was a rustle as he seemed to lift himself. 'Do you want me to get out of here?' The gale howled, rattling everything as if it were demented.

Words shrilled in her mind, badgering to get out. *Come and love me like I love you.* 'Yes, no—oh, I don't know,' she moaned, turning her sobs to the pillow.

There was a movement and he came to stand beside her, a tall, mysterious figure in the darkness. He shifted her bodily in the sleeping bag, then lay at her side, sliding down the zip to her waist.

He put his cheek to hers, dampening his skin with her tears. He turned his face to kiss the wet saltiness into his own mouth. A hand smoothed back her hair, then lingered lightly on her throat, stilling the sobs. His other hand slid beneath her, rolling her towards him.

Her throat was freed and a strange coldness touched her where his warmth had been. His hand was moving down, arousing a warmth of its own, finding what he was seeking—the hardening shapes of her breasts.

Her arm curved around his neck and she was taking his intimate, thrusting kisses with a passionate eagerness which she could not, nor wanted to, control.

'Sharon, baby,' he murmured, 'let me take you . . .'

If he had not said those words, she acknowledged afterwards, she would, only moments later, have belonged irrevocably to him. It was not her inhibitions that stopped her, nor shyness, but his demand for her to *give* herself while he *took* her . . .

'That's all a man ever wants,' she cried out in protest, fighting off his hands, 'take, take from a woman, who gives and gives. Leave me alone, just let me be!'

Calum freed her immediately. After a few moments he swung his legs to the floor.

'I didn't mean you to go out,' she told him hastily. 'I'm—I'm not turning you outside in this.'

'Thank you kindly, ma'am,' his sarcastic answer flicked back and he returned to his sleeping bag, lying completely still.

Sharon re-fastened the zip and moved on to her side. The tumult inside her was dying down, but her thoughts were in chaos. Why had life turned so sour on her? Three months ago she had been an engaged woman, poised to marry and be happy ever after . . .

Three months ago she had been naïve and years younger. Looking back, she wondered how she could not have seen that, by agreeing to marry Daryl Irwin, she had committed herself to being sacrificed on the altar of a man's conceit. The loss of his life, much though she regretted it, had in reality given her back her own. For that, at least, she guessed she should be thankful.

When she woke up, she felt refreshed, and wondered why. Her subconscious mind had momentarily blanked out the events of the dark hours. There was an odd silence which told her the storm had receded and the wind was no longer doing its best to demolish the wooden hut in which she had slept.

Slept—but not alone. It all came back and she turned to discover that she was indeed alone again. Calum had gone but had cleared away so neatly it was as if he had never been there.

As she peered into the jug which she kept filled with rainwater for washing, it seemed that he had washed in her bowl before leaving. Having herself washed all over and dressed, she opened the door carefully, expecting to have it wrenched by the wind out of her hand.

There were noises outside as if someone was working, and she looked out to see Calum repairing the damage the gale had wrought. The tent was almost fully secured by its guy ropes and pegs. He paused in his hammering to look at her, but it seemed that his interest was of short duration. The hammer lifted and descended as if there had been no interruption.

His voice came across to her over the noise he was making, saying expressionlessly, 'Thanks for letting me use your place.'

Sharon nodded, then realised he would not have seen the action. 'Would you like some coffee?' she asked.

'Thanks, but no.'

It was a rebuff in itself. Feeling hurt, then telling herself how stupid it was, she went back for a jacket. It was too late for breakfast. The canteen below would have something she could eat. As she made her way down the path, the hammering stopped.

If he was wondering where she was going, then he could just wonder, she thought rebelliously. After his condemning attitude in the early hours, even if it was followed by those inexplicable moments of tenderness, there could be no more doubt in her mind as to where she stood with him. The hammering started again, which meant that he had been watching her.

Bracing her shoulders, she told herself that it was all over now, not that there had ever really been anything. She was free of men, all of them. Maybe, she considered, if I think it often enough, I'll be able to convince myself it's true!

They were busy at the foot of the hill. The gale had

lifted flimsy roofs clean away from even flimsier walls, doors had been blown in or torn off, props tossed about. The canteen, however, was functioning normally, or so it seemed by the clatter of crockery coming from its interior.

One of the cameramen stopped her. 'Any damage up there where you are?'

Sharon shook her head. 'The hut's unscathed, although I kept thinking the roof would go any minute.'

'Jack Wilson had that place built too well for any storm to harm it,' the man answered. 'It would take a typhoon to make any impression, and I think even that would skirt round it out of respect for its owner!'

Sharon laughed, her eyes lighting up at the thought, and the cameraman's eyes considered her reflectively. 'You should be in this film,' he remarked. 'You've got something.' He glanced up the hill. 'I'll bet our friend Calum hasn't missed it, either. How's his tent?'

'It was flattened, but he——' The light went out of her eyes. She had so nearly started a rumour and that was something she could do without. 'He managed,' she finished, and lifted her hand.

Lee was lining up at the counter. He did not smile as she joined him. Embarrassed, she looked around, quietly awaiting her turn. The canteen was half full and most of its patrons seemed to be staring at her.

Sharon pulled at Lee's jacket. 'What's wrong with me? Is there a smut on my nose or something? Everyone's staring.'

Lee half turned, then moved his tray along. 'Nothing's wrong—with your face.'

'What's the matter with you—and everyone?' She pushed her tray after his, taking a buttered fruit bun and asking for coffee. Lee waited while she paid.

Carrying her tray, she followed him to an empty table. The eyes followed, too, but she shut them out. He stood by a chair but waited for her to take a seat. This politeness from a man like Lee surprised her just a little.

'Lee, what's the matter with everybody?' She filled her mouth with bun.

Lee drank some coffee, then lifted his shoulders. 'Could be they're wondering. About you and Calum.'

Frowning, Sharon went on eating her bun. Swallowing a mouthful, she said, 'There's nothing to wonder about.'

'Isn't there?' His voice was full of meaning and as she chewed, Sharon watched him. Which Lee was this—the real one, or the actor? 'I was on my way up to you early this morning to see if you were all right.'

'Thanks a lot,' Sharon remarked, to fill the silence, 'but I was okay.'

'So it seemed. I saw Calum Darwin coming out of your hut. He looked as though he'd just got out of bed.' He looked at her expectantly.

'He had. I gave him shelter for the night. Didn't you see his flattened tent?'

He nodded, then took a sip of coffee. 'He could have wrecked that deliberately.'

Sharon put her cup down with a clatter. 'You mean to get into the hut with me? You can't mean it!'

'Or you could have suggested it,' he continued doggedly, 'to make it look as if it was flattened. Or you two could have connived, to hide the truth.'

'What truth? What are you getting at, Lee?'

'That you've started an affair.'

'Oh, for heaven's sake! Didn't you hear the storm? Would you have turned somebody away? Could you have put up a tent strongly enough to withstand the force of that little squall?'

'Don't try and deny anything, Sharon,' Lee answered, assuming a sudden weariness. She could recognise this one, she thought with a secret smile, this was the great star acting the rejected lover role.

Rejected lover? Had she hit on the truth? Was he on the way to believing she was his property? 'I don't have to report to you who I allow or don't allow in my hut!' she said angrily.

'Thanks for confirming my suspicions.'

She pushed back her chair. 'You've no right to talk to me like that, Lee! Just because we've been friendly——'

'If you're talking about us as if our friendship was in the past, that's confirmation of my suspicions twice over.'

'Oh, for goodness' sake!' She looked around. 'Is that why they've been looking at me—because of Calum sleeping in my hut?' His shrug was expressive. 'Who told them? You?'

Lee shook his head. 'When he came out of your hut, he followed me down, but he didn't say anything. He went straight to the canteen for some food. People asked him if he was all right and he said he was fine. He'd spent the night with a lady—in her hut.'

Sharon stood up. 'So that's how they know.' She gazed around, seeing the curiosity in the watching eyes. 'I'll—I'll——' Her face drained of colour. Oh no, she thought, not again! Just like it was before with Daryl, the half-accusing looks, the meaningful glances ... How long would it be before the abuse followed?

Lee went round to her. 'Take it easy, Sharon. These people are used to it. They won't talk, not outside this island.'

'I know, they'll just make nasty remarks among themselves. It'll be something to entertain them. Don't they know he's got Maida? That I'm not his sort?'

'Is that true, Sharon?' Lee asked, hope rekindling in his eyes.

'Of course it's true.' She pulled on her jacket. ' 'Bye, Lee.'

Calum had hammered in the final peg when she reached him. She put her hands on her hips and stared down at him, waiting for her breathing to ease. He must have known she was there, but he did not lift his head.

'You know what you are?' she attacked.

He looked up briefly. 'No. Tell me.'

'You're nothing but a rotten, low-down traitor!' He straightened so that she had to look up to him. His eyebrows were arched, his expression cool. 'You,' she pointed an accusing finger, 'went down there first thing this morning and lied to them about us.'

'Hardly a lie, was it, when it was true.'

'It was true that you slept in my hut, but you didn't spend the night with me, which is what you let them think down there!'

'Is there another description for sleeping on your floor? If so, I'd like to know. As a writer, it might help my powers of description.'

'Stop being so supercilious,' she choked. 'You know you implied we slept *together*. What's more, you did it intentionally.'

Calum shrugged. 'Whether I did or not, people being what they are, it's the first thing they think of. And the more you deny it, the more they believe it's true.'

'You don't know—you don't realise what damage you've done,' she declared, her voice rising.

'Damage? By implying we slept together? Come on into the twentieth century, honey.'

'I hate your cynicism,' Sharon cried, near to tears. 'You don't know what it's like to be on the receiving end of the public's self-righteous condemnation!'

Turning, she ran into the hut, closing the door but finding a foot in the way. 'You're not coming in,' she declared, but found the door swinging back against her.

He pushed his way in, shutting the door with his foot.

'Well, what is it like?' he asked, planting his feet firmly apart and folding his arms.

'You want to know? I'll tell you. Day after day, abusive letters poured through the letterbox of my parents' house. Why? Because I lived there—I who had, or so they supposed, broken all the moral and spiritual laws they could think of, by deserting my fiancé in his last moments. Like you, they'd seen it in the papers, so it must be true, they argued.'

His face was stony. She had not penetrated his mental barriers, nor altered his conviction that, despite her protestations, she had been at fault.

'There were phone calls, obscene and threatening. They disturbed my parents' sleep as well as mine. All day and most of the nights, that telephone rang, nearly driving us mad. So now you know why I wanted to find some peace. Now you know why I promised myself I'd never get tangled up again with a famous man. In fact, I never even believed it could happen to me twice. Now you see what you've done to me—started off the rumours, the gossip, the trail of watching eyes that wouldn't leave me alone.'

For a long time he looked at her, saw her shaking hands pull out a chair, dwelt on her flushed cheeks as she gazed up at him.

'When you've calmed down,' he stated, with maddening calm, 'I'll make a proposition.'

'I'm calm,' she claimed, 'I'm calm. Tell me your proposition.'

'That we return to the mainland and marry.'

'Marriage?' she stormed. 'Is that what you're offering, like soothing ointment on a wound? Like a sweetie to a child after you've just trodden on its hand?'

'Will you stop being hysterical?' He watched as she leant her elbows on the table and covered her eyes. After a moment, he continued. 'Our marriage would mean nothing. I would make no demands.'

Sharon shook her head, still concealing her face. 'I'd be in the news again, wouldn't I? I can see it all. The public would start slinging mud again, the papers would tear my character and integrity apart once more ... How *could* I have been so callous, they would say, as to forget so quickly the man I loved that in the space of three months or so I'd married someone else?'

She heard him approaching and stiffened in anticipation of his touch. He caught hold of her wrists to move them from her face, but found her arms had stiffened.

He pulled her round and to her feet. 'Relax, baby.' His voice was low and sensual. As he pulled her closer, she lifted her head so as to watch the movement of his mobile lips. 'We would set a time limit for the marriage, then we'd start divorce proceedings. When it's over, I'd be off your back and you off mine.'

Her heart was hammering against her ribs as she fought off the disappointment his words created. 'That would be another blot on my character, wouldn't it? Everyone would blame me for the divorce because of my so-called past. If you were just an ordinary man, no one would notice, but you're well-known, honoured, celebrated wherever you go. You'd get the sympathy, I'd get the condemnation.'

He traced the line of her finely tapered eyebrows, used his thumb to pull down her chin, thus parting her lips. He put his mouth on hers, invading it slowly, arousingly until she closed her eyes and could hardly breathe.

When she opened them again, he was smiling down at her, looking into her wondering eyes and seeing their vulnerability.

'If that's what you think would happen, then we would do things gradually,' she heard him say through the mists that were rising to cloud her mind. 'We'd separate for a while, then quietly divorce each other. There are ways around everything if you look for them.'

How could he be making potent, deliberate love to her, yet in the same breath be talking of separation?

'Why do you look so worried, Sharon? I told you, it would be a simple civil ceremony and an exchange of rings. You'd have my name and my protection—for just as long as you felt you needed it. No need to worry about telling me you're ready to announce the separation. Rest assured that I'm self-contained, I have no need of a woman in my life, a permanent woman.'

Sharon stared back at him. If only he had spoken in anger or bitterness about his lack of the need of a woman to share his future, then she might have been able to salvage a crumb of hope.

He had spoken so rationally, with such reasonableness she despaired. 'I told you once,' she responded, looking at the dark stubble around his chin and longing to run her fingertips over it, 'in fact I made a promise, that I'd never adore you.'

'I hadn't forgotten.' He shrugged, releasing her. 'So I'll never be your dream man. I also told you that you were on my strictly-not-wanted list. Our marriage would make no difference to either statement.'

A shiver ran the length of her, but she did not let him see it. 'Do you really expect me to accept your offer of marriage when you put the vital question so *charmingly?*' She ignored his lifting eyebrow. 'You're an accomplished wooer, Calum,' she jeered. 'Your passionate declaration makes me hunger for you.'

'You want me to woo you? You'd like me to be passionate?'

Her sarcasm had aroused his anger at last, but now she was afraid of having awoken his dormant desires. Afraid, because if he did take her into his arms, he would learn from the responses of her body secrets which her lips would never tell him.

His hand had come out, but she backed away, evading it. 'Thank you, but no to both questions.'

'Do I take it you're turning down my offer of marriage?' he enquired coldly. 'You're prepared to harden yourself to the innuendoes about our relationship, the knowing looks?'

'I've seen them already,' she declared, 'and——'

'And they made you come running back up here to me to tear me to bits for telling them the truth. If I hadn't told them the truth, they would have made it up—how we spent our night together, what we did.'

Defeated by his logic, she sank down. 'Oh, for heaven's sake let me think. Just let me think.'

He went so quietly she did not realise she was alone until she lifted her head from her hands.

Her uncertainties had not been resolved even when she emerged into the sunlight after her midday meal. She hadn't eaten much. Her appetite had left her.

Her thoughts had rattled round her head like jigsaw pieces in a box. She had not been able to fit together a single part of the picture. The cool breeze made a jacket necessary. As she turned to retrace her steps and find one, there was the sound of feminine laughter from Calum's tent. Sharon froze, cold with shock. He had asked her to marry him, yet he had Maida Halliday in there to—to what?

Wasn't she now reacting in exactly the same way as all the others had reacted on hearing about Calum's spending the night in her hut? But hadn't she far more reason to be suspicious, after being told by Calum himself, the day he had visited Maida, that he hadn't just used her cabin . . .

This was what it would be like, she thought, if I ever agreed to marry him—watching the women in his life come and go, while I would have to remain at a distance. You can't do it, her other self whispered, you can't love a man, be married to him, yet have him treat you like a stranger.

As she emerged again, pulling on her jacket, Maida came, head and shoulders first, from Calum's tent. He followed her, straightening from easing through the flaps. Maida's look was hostile, Calum's unreadable. He was pulling on a sweater. Why had he taken it off? Sharon wondered, torturing herself.

Maida's slacks were a slinky black velvet, her blue-knitted cardigan buttoned to the neck. Her red-gold hair hung long and shining, her brown eyes flashed a 'hate' message in Sharon's direction.

The woman turned, smiling, to Calum. 'How do you manage it, Calum?' her husky voice enquired. 'A night with Miss Mason and an energetic afternoon with me.' Her arms wrapped around one of his, which hung loose. 'Hey, Mr Superman, can we do it again some time?'

Calum removed his arm from Maida's possession. His head moved sideways, indicating that Maida should go. Lifting a hand, she went, singing, down the hill.

'A jerk of the head and the woman you've just made use of goes without question,' Sharon commented bitterly. 'Do you honestly think I could marry a man who treats women like dirt as you do?'

'You've made two inaccurate, and if I may say so, damned cheeky assumptions. But I'm darned if I'm going to say a word in my own defence. If it gives you a feeling of revenge to condemn me without trial—I'm quoting your words—then carry on.' He strolled towards her, his hands in his pockets pushing the edges of his sweater out of place. 'Is that your answer to my offer? You're saying "no" to marrying me?'

'I'm saying "no" to marrying you.'

His eyes narrowed. 'You're an ungrateful bitch. But

it's what I should have expected, after reading your story in the papers.'

He passed her, his elbow hitting her arm as he swung down the hill path. He made no apology, leaving her rubbing at the sharp pain. If he had glanced back, he would have seen the rising tears. It wasn't the physical pain which had caused them. It was the hurt he had inflicted by his contempt for what he, and thousands of others, had mistakenly believed she had done.

CHAPTER FOUR

SHARON descended the hill but branched away from the film unit's camp site. Passing others and seeing one or two familiar faces, she smiled and they nodded back.

A group of young men followed her progress. The male look in their eyes made her embarrassed. Then one of them broke away, approaching her. 'Hey, is it true your name's Sharon?' She nodded, her heart taking a dive. Had she assumed right as to what was coming? 'Sharon Mason,' the young man persisted, 'fiancée of the late Daryl Irwin?'

'How did you guess?' It was meant to be sarcastic, but the man took it as a question.

'It's all around the camp.'

'How interesting.' Had he got the brush-off note yet?

He looked embarrassed. 'Just thought you'd like to know. That's why everyone was so surprised to hear you'd taken up with Cal Darwin. A bit quick, wasn't it? I mean, after the way Daryl Irwin died and you shouting to be—it was in the papers,' he finished defensively.

Her eyes flared and he backed away. Sharon continued her walk, leaving the group he had rejoined staring after her. Her fists clenched in her jacket pockets, her teeth pressed together, her eyes closed hard for a few seconds.

Would the accusations never go away? Would they follow her for the rest of her life?

The harbour stretched right and left, formed by a natural bay. The old pier had come back to life with the arrival of the film team. Here and there an anchored rowing boat bobbed on the waves. On the dirt road away from the pier, one or two cars were parked, having apparently come over on the ferry.

Just across the bay, cliffs towered, descending in a near-straight line to the water's edge. In the distance were round-topped hills, light grey when the sun caught them but seeming a dappled brown when the clouds took over the sky. All the time, gulls cried to each other, spreading their great wings, swooping or flapping in flight.

Turning, she started climbing, which seemed inevitable on that island. There was little flat land indeed. She had no idea where she was going, finding after a few moments that the terrain was rough to the feet. Once or twice she slipped on loose rock and bent down to hold a tuft of grass to steady herself.

A voice came up to her. 'Where are you going?' Having recognised its owner, she did not stop. The question was repeated and the anger in it this time had the effect its owner plainly wanted.

'Don't go walking unprepared,' Calum shouted, his hands cupped to amplify the words. 'Not safe. Dangerous. Come down!' Stolidly she stared back at him as he stood, made small by the gradient and the distance, but stiffly commanding nonetheless. 'Or I'll come and get you!'

Fragments of laughter floated up, taunting her and making her stand her ground. He started up the slope. How far did he intend to climb? Far enough to frighten her? When he came relentlessly on, Sharon turned and climbed, too, but tension influenced her muscles. Against her will, her pace slowed.

Panicking, she used her hands to help her up the steepening incline, but it was not enough. He was gaining on her. At the moment that she stopped to gasp for breath, he was catching hold of her hips, tugging her back towards him.

Exhausted by fear as she was, her legs could not take the strain of her backward momentum. She fell against him, crying out in fright as she thought they would both go tumbling.

It seemed he had prepared himself for the extra weight, bracing his leg muscles and his body. After a few seconds of teetering balance, his footholds held and his arms were round her like steel hawsers. He swung her slowly round until she was below him, his arms crossing against her breasts. It was an intimate hold and Sharon heard shouts of encouragement and ribald laughter from below.

'Leave go of me, will you?' she said hoarsely. 'What are they going to think now?'

'That I intend sleeping with you tonight as well as last night.'

'Well, you're not, not ever. Let me go, or I'll struggle until we both roll down the hill.'

'You'd get the most bruises on those rocks—you're softer than I am.' His hands held her breasts beneath her jacket. 'Much softer.'

In defiance, she twisted and jerked to free herself, but his hold grew tighter. He was hurting her now, his thumb and forefinger pressing cruelly where no man had ever hurt her before, not even Daryl. Her breasts started to throb and tears of defeat as well as pain filled her eyes.

The laughter from below was louder, growing raucous. 'Listen to them,' she choked, 'what are they going to say about us down there after this?'

'They're going to say,' he twisted her round as if she were a spinning top and she saw the rigidity of his jaw, 'in their slightly crude way, that I've got myself a handful in more ways than one. They'll envy me and wish me luck. The men will. The women will envy *you*.'

Sharon shook her head fiercely. 'They'll condemn me

for my low morals, for not shouting and screaming for help against you.'

'Be your age. No woman in this situation in this day and age would do that.'

'No?' She pulled free and he let her go. 'You don't know, you just don't know. I've had it up to here,' she pointed at her neck, 'with criticism and reproach and other human beings sitting in judgment on me.'

'Can you blame people for being nasty to you after what you shouted in that storm that killed your fiancé?'

Sharon started to protest her innocence, but stopped herself from even trying to persuade him that everything he'd read about her was false. A sense of utter defeat made her shoulders droop.

Her eyes lifted to the distant hills. 'Where's the peace and quiet I came for?' She turned on him. 'If it hadn't been for you, I would have found it.'

His hand started coming towards her, but she flinched. His eyes hardened. 'Don't try and blame me, Sharon. It's your past, not your present, that has denied you that peace. I did my best to help you over this bad patch by my offer of marriage, but you turned it down. You'll have to take the consequences—alone.' He went past her and preceded her down the hill.

If only you loved me, she wanted to cry out after him. But he just went on walking away.

When she reached the camp site, the audience had dispersed. Lee Banks emerged from a cabin marked 'office'.

'Hi, Sharon.' He smiled, his blond hair blown by the breeze, his shoulders slouching a little. His eyes were a shade wary and she asked aggressively,

'I suppose you were among the crowd staring at the day's rushes? Pity the director missed it. He might have decided to make room for it in the film.'

'Why worry?' Lee dismissed. 'It gave them a bit of much-needed entertainment. Life can be a bit dull here after a while.'

'That's what I came here for,' she declared, 'except I called it solitude.' She looked around. 'Where did Calum go?'

'To find Maida.' He watched Sharon's face and seemed to take some pleasure in the way it lost colour. 'You can't win against her, Sharon. She's got him—here. Back in London, she'll be added to his list of cast-offs and he'll get himself another woman to take her place. I bet he's tried it on with you.'

There was a pain in her mind provoking the desire to cry. 'He's always trying it on with me. Last night——'

'It's obvious what happened last night,' Lee broke in, 'after the way he treated you this morning. And you didn't even fight him, did you?'

Strange how Lee sounded so bitter. Why should he envy Calum his ability to attract women? He probably had thousands of female fans all over the world. Yet, she reminded herself, his wife had left him. Had that hurt so much he couldn't forget it?

'There's a movie on in the cinema. Come and see it with me?' He looked at his watch. 'It's just about to start.' He named the film, which she had not seen.

'It would make a change,' she agreed. When he put his arm round her waist, she did not object. I might just as well add to their list of accusations against me, she thought, with an uncaring shrug of her shoulders.

On the way, one or two men acknowledged Lee. 'Hi there,' he answered. Was there the faintest sound of self-congratulation in his voice? 'Come on,' he invited, pushing open the door. 'By the way, I'm in the movie. Does that put you off?'

She laughed. 'Are you good or bad in this one?'

'I'm the bad guy, but I get the girl.'

'That's a new twist,' Sharon commented as she followed Lee into the semi-darkness.

Yet again, Sharon marvelled at the change which came over Lee when he was acting. It did not seem possible that the man portrayed as having such aggression on the screen was sitting so quietly beside her now, passively watching his own image as if it were another person.

As they emerged into the daylight, Calum, with Maida at his side, left the canteen. In his hand was a beer can and he ripped off the tab. Tipping back his head, he drank, watching with slitted eyes as Sharon walked away from the cinema with Lee beside her.

Maida wore a cream silk blouse, Sharon noted, certain that the actress had deliberately chosen a size too small. From her waistband, black pants curved themselves around the rest of her.

So what, Sharon thought, if my hair isn't red, my parka looks secondhand, my jeans have mud around the hems? I'm real, not a photofit dream woman, who's a sex symbol on the big screen with whom the world's men fall in love. She can have almost any man she wants, but she can't keep a single one of them. How many divorces and relationships had this woman had? she asked herself with not a little touch of self-satisfaction.

She caught Calum's reflective gaze over his tipped-up beer can and coloured. Had he guessed her thoughts about Maida? All right, she wanted to shout, what else can I be but jealous when the woman I've silently been castigating has you at her beck and call?

Calum wiped his mouth with his wrist, looked round for a waste bin and, with an upward sweep of his arm, aimed and hurled. The can went straight in. His grin was broad as he turned back to Sharon, but it was Maida who clapped her hands.

'Enjoy the film, Sharon?' Calum asked, adding mockingly, 'and did it make it all the more titillating having the hero of the story sitting by your side?'

Sharon's cheeks turned pink, which annoyed her. 'I object to your choice of words!'

He reached out an arm and caught her by the back of the neck, pulling her towards him. He forced her head down to his shoulder. 'Turning prude, honey? Last night——'

'Stop talking about last night!' she cried, trying to lift her head.

'Why? Is it too precious to you to let the world know all the things that happened between us?'

'You bastard, Calum Darwin!' The words were torn out of her, desperation acting like claws on the skin of her self-restraint. His other hand went round her waist, strengthening his hold on her. 'You know darned well we slept—just slept——'

'Afterwards, honey, deeply.'

His distortion of the truth aroused in her a frenzy of anger. She managed to prise his hand from her waist and turned and twisted madly, succeeding in freeing her neck and enduring the pain her struggles had brought about.

'How could you say such things, how *could* you?' she asked, her blue-green eyes darker now like the sea being crossed by a sun shadow. 'After all I've told you, too!'

'I know who you are,' Maida sneered. 'You're the girl who——'

'Shut up, Maida.' Calum's curt tones had an immediate effect, but Maida's eyes widened with astonishment. His hand clasped her shoulder, his fingers moulding the flesh under the silkiness of her blouse. 'We sat at the bar talking too long. We'll take a walk, go down to the harbour.'

Maida's surprise apparently robbed her of objections.

Sharon gave her full marks for taking every chance of greater intimacy with her man of the moment. Maida clung with both arms to his, putting her head on the shoulder which Sharon's own head had so recently occupied. I hope her hair picks up some of mine, she thought acidly.

'I'm going back to the hut,' she told Lee, who stood frowning beside her.

'What did Maida mean, Sharon, when she said she knew who you were?'

He didn't know? Thank heaven for that, she reflected. That's one person less to look at me with that damning disapproval.

'Probably meant I'm the girl who knows Jack Wilson, the financial backer of the film they're making here.'

This seemed to satisfy the male star of that film. He might be a good actor, and his good looks make his fans' hearts beat faster, Sharon reasoned with just a shade of malice, but it could hardly be said that he had a five-star brain.

'Busy this evening?' Lee asked, his fair hair lifting in the breeze. Some women, Sharon thought, would be trembling at the thought of being in this man's arms. Strange how he leaves me cold.

She shook her head, pushing her own hair from her eyes.

'I'll come and see you. Okay?'

Sharon's slim shoulders rose and fell. 'Why not?'

As she reached the hut door, she paused to listen to the tapping from Calum's tent. His walk with Maida could not have been a long one. Maybe they didn't make it to the harbour. Personally, she couldn't see Maida Halliday taking a step more than she needed anywhere, certainly not if there was a prospect of churned-up mud at the end of it.

Inserting the key, she heard the movement of the flaps

leading out of Calum's tent. Hands in pockets, he regarded her. 'Going walkies?' he asked, making her smile.

She shook her head. 'Why?'

'For a suburbanite like you, it's not walking country.'

'You, of course, can go striding up and down those hills like a native.'

'So sarcastic, and yet she's got such a pretty face.'

With an angry movement she turned the key, pushing open the door.

'The answer to your question is yes,' he said. 'I know the landscape and it's not for the novice. I've stayed here many times—alone.'

'Lee said you have a liking for living rough. He said you did it for publicity.'

The sensual lips hardened. 'And you believe his every word. Have you fallen for *his* pretty face? Is that why you refuse to marry me?'

'Me, fallen for Lee Banks? I'd as soon fall for a bundle of straw!'

'You don't like blond-haired men? Daryl Irwin was blond, was he not?'

'Stop cross-questioning me!' She came down the wooden steps to face him. 'I'll tell you why I refused that offer of marriage. It was because you made it. You, Calum Darwin, who couldn't care a damn for anyone except yourself!'

He watched her mount the steps, his expression unreadable. 'If you ever decide——' his words detained her. Was he renewing his offer? If so, she would have to refuse again, but it would hurt like having a tooth wrenched out without anaesthetic.

'Yes?' she asked quietly.

'To go walking,' he continued, and her pulses slowed to sluggish with disappointment, 'remember that dangers lurk up there,' he indicated the hills, the rocks, the

bushes and the brown patches of last year's heather preparing secretly to bloom, 'hidden and misleading, like
sudden dips in the ground and bogs.'

Her eyes holding his wavered. These things she hadn't
known. 'Thanks for telling me,' she remarked, and went
into the hut.

When, later, the knock came, she jumped, having forgotten that Lee had invited himself to visit her. She
closed the book she had found on the shelf above the
bed. It was one of Calum's and bore his signature,
addressed to 'my good friend, Jack'.

Putting the book aside, she opened the door to find
Lee's head nodding at someone behind him. As she
closed the door, Sharon asked, 'I assume that was
Calum?'

'Who else? Does he scrutinise all your visitors, or only
the male ones?'

'I don't have visitors—except you, of course.' She
found smiling at him a strain, but at least he was company and formed a barrier between her thoughts and
her next-door neighbour. 'He said when I arrived up
here that because I knew Jack Wilson, who'd loaned me
the use of this hut, he, Calum, felt some kind of
responsibility for me.'

'Did he use that as an excuse to sleep with you last
night?'

The shock she felt made her catch her breath. His tone,
his expression was out of character. Her instinct was to
recoil from him, run to the door and order him out.

Her reaction must have shown, because he seemed
contrite at once, returning to normal. He found a seat.
'Sorry—but losing your wife and child to another man
makes you bitter about every female. Ask Calum.'

'What do you mean—he's been married?' Had he
noticed her dismay? It seemed he was too wrapped up in
his own thoughts.

'Nearly, not quite. It was a few years ago, I was told. He was twenty-seven, she was twenty. He's thirty-three now.'

'Which makes it six years ago. He's nine years older than I am,' Sharon mused.

'Apparently, just before the wedding, the whole thing was called off. The girl had run off with a man twenty-five years older than herself.'

'Was the story in the papers?'

Lee shook his head. 'He was a journalist at the time, not the kind of cult figure he is now. Then he started writing and two years later his first book became a bestseller. Since then he's never looked back.'

Sharon walked around restlessly, switching on the cassette recorder she had brought with her. Her own kind of music filled the hut and she adjusted the volume to background level. It would help to gloss over any silences, she reasoned.

While she made coffee, Lee glanced through the books on the shelf. 'Yours?' he asked. She explained that they belonged mostly to Jack Wilson.

'He seems to be a fan of Calum's,' Lee commented, taking one down and flicking through it.

'Ever read any of his?' Sharon asked, finding the carton of milk she had bought from the canteen.

'I'm not a great reader,' Lee dismissed. 'Even if I were, I doubt if I'd climb to his intellectual heights.'

Sharon offered Lee a cup from a tray she had found. 'I've read one or two, but they were about international intrigue. Plenty of drama, action and, apparently, fact. How he got to know it all, I don't know.'

She sat on the other sprung garden chair, stirring her coffee although it had no sugar. She felt she had to have something to do.

'Travelled the world, wore disguises, or so the publicity said.' He drank his coffee.

'Of course,' Sharon considered thoughtfully, 'he was once a journalist.'

'Investigative. Anyone who wanted any kind of fact would go to him.'

'Publicity again?'

'Book jacket.' Lee smiled at her and put down his cup.

Something about his expression alerted her. She placed her cup on the floor. When he said, 'I didn't come to talk, Sharon,' she stood up, gripping the chair back.

Her smile was fixed as she asked, 'What did you come for, Lee?'

'What does a man usually visit a woman for? What you gave Calum Darwin last night. Besides, I know who you are now—Maida told me. You're the girl who let Daryl Irwin drown. You're worse than my wife. At least she let me live.'

Sharon wanted to leap at him, but restrained herself because intuition told her it was in her own interest. 'It's not true, Lee, what you said,' she answered mildly, hoping to calm him.

Alarmed, she saw his knuckles whiten as he too gripped the chair. Jekyll and Hyde, she thought, frightened, docile man and aggressive actor. Hadn't she seen him on the screen that afternoon? His frantic strength had even then amazed her. Now, the thought of it terrified her.

'Of course it's true. It was in the papers—I remember reading all about it. And your own story. Like all women you're worthless, so,' he moved nearer, 'I'm going to have my own back on my wife—through you.'

He was nearer the door than she was and he knew it. 'Don't be silly, Lee,' she said, in as normal a voice as she could manage.

'What about? I haven't done a thing.'

It's in your mind, she thought—then he moved, quickly, slyly, as he had in the film. She tried to dodge, but he had caught her arms, pulling her with them. The feel of him revolted her.

'R-rape's against the law,' she humoured him, trying to smile.

'Who's to know? Calum's gone down the hill. He can't help you.'

Was it true? she wondered, starting to shake. Slowly he was easing her down towards the floor. She would not let her knees bend. Oh God, she thought, what shall I do?

Lee's eyes were wild. 'Calum took what he wanted, so why shouldn't I?'

He pushed her backwards and she lost her balance. The floor's impact winded her. 'No, Lee, no, please, please!' He seemed deaf to her entreaties. The background music played on. Feverishly, he was pulling at her sweater, searching for her waistband. Sharon twisted her legs, slithering round and breaking away.

Before he could extricate his thoughts from their near-hypnotised state, she had wrenched open the door and screamed 'Calum!' It was hopeless, she knew, since he wasn't there, but it might just have served to halt Lee's pursuit.

Her estimation of his reaction had been wrong. As she put a foot outside, he leapt at her, dragging her round, trying to find her constantly shifting mouth. He managed to find a corner, but she screamed again. His hands were round her neck now, and it was then that fear made her scream inside.

In his state, she knew, he might not even have been aware of what he was doing—until it was too late. She was fighting for her life. The fingers were tightening, her breath was growing more rasping. 'No,' she whispered hoarsely, 'no!'

'I'm going to drown you, like you should have drowned the day your fiancé died.'

'Lee,' she heard her voice rasp, 'don't, please don't . . .'

There was a groan as someone crumpled to the floor. She discovered that she had been freed. It was not herself down there, but Lee. He was writhing in agony.

'Sharon, get out of here.'

'Calum,' she croaked, holding her aching neck, 'oh, Calum! Thank you, thank you . . .'

Then she crumpled, too, in a heap at Calum's feet.

Regaining consciousness, seemingly hours later, she opened her eyes to a lighted lantern suspended from the wooden rafters. Outside, it was almost dark. There was no music, no raised voices, only a breathing silence.

Breathing? Whose? Lee's or her own? Then she recalled what had happened and looked across the hut at the figure in the chair. Calum was there, calmly reading.

'Calum?' He put his book aside and came to stand beside her. 'What happened to Lee?'

'You mean, did I decide to finish him off? I was tempted. He hasn't got quite such a pretty face at the moment.'

She stretched out her hand. He looked at it, but did not take it in his. She hid her disappointment and slowly moved it back. 'If you hadn't come, Calum——' She felt her neck.

'I can see the bruises.'

'He didn't know what he was doing, he——'

'Are you trying to defend him?'

'For trying to kill me?'

'I doubt if he would have gone that far.'

'He was possessed, Calum. He was playing a part.'

'He'll need layers of make-up to hide what I've done to him,' grated Calum. 'Otherwise, he won't be playing any part for a while.'

His attitude puzzled her. He seemed to hold himself aloof, yet he had apparently given Lee, her attacker, a rough time on her behalf. Also, he must have had sufficient feeling for her to carry her here to the bed.

'How did Lee get back to base?' she asked, more to make Calum talk than out of any real interest.

'He staggered down. Why, do you think I carried him?'

Refusing to allow his sarcasm to rile her, she enquired, 'And how long was I unconscious?'

'I soon got you round from your faint, then I put you here and you went to sleep on me.'

'So you decided to baby-sit?' Had her effort to lighten the atmosphere succeeded?

His mind, it seemed, was on more intimate things, judging by the raking look he gave her recumbent body. ' "Baby" is right,' he drawled.

Then she remembered—he had called her 'baby' when he had kissed her and touched her, in a very different context from the one in which she had used the word.

Colouring deeply, she turned her head away. 'Sorry.' A feeling of desolation swept her. 'I'm sorry about the whole thing. He and I talked, I made coffee, then he lunged at me.'

'What did you expect him to do—sit and twiddle his thumbs while a beautiful, provocative female body flitted back and forward in front of him?'

Her head came round sharply at his scathing tone. 'He said he would come and see me, that's all. I thought he might be company, so I agreed. He invited himself.'

'But you didn't discourage him, did you? Stop trying to blind me with your innocence. You must have known what was in his mind—exactly what he thought was in your mind. And who knows, he might have been right, despite the screams and the fainting fit.'

Sharon swung her legs to the floor, started to stand, but her legs refused to take her weight. 'Are you implying I wasn't really frightened? That I faked the faint?'

He shrugged, leaning against the cooker and pocketing his hands. 'Maybe he was a little rougher than you'd expected.'

'That's right—refuse to believe me like you always do and like everyone else. I've been attacked physically this evening. You might as well finish the job by attacking me verbally.' She rallied her fading spirits. 'It was your fault,' she accused, 'for putting round that lie about us. Lee said he wanted what I'd given you last night. *That's* when it sank in just why he'd come, and by then it was too late to stop him.'

She tried her legs again and they carried her. She went across the room to stare out at the last great brush-strokes of lingering light from the long-set sun. 'Because of you, I nearly died tonight.' Shock was having its way at last, thickening her voice, giving warning of the tears to come. She felt her neck and winced even at her own touch.

Hands came from behind, removing her fingers. A shiver shook her, but his touch, curiously, did not hurt. It soothed, it comforted—and it began to arouse. Her muscles tensed. It was her senses he was assaulting, not her body.

'These bruises don't mean he was going to kill you.' His voice had softened now. 'This is some men's way of making love.' Slowly, he turned her, seeking and holding her eyes. 'It's not my way, Sharon.'

His investigating fingers were caressing now. Her breathing was shallow, not through fear, this time but through pleasure. 'When I screamed for you,' she whispered, 'he told me you'd gone down the hill and weren't there to help me.'

'An old trick, honey.' He eased her head back against his shoulder, running his palms over her throat, breasts and hips. Strange, she thought, how potently she could feel the friction of his hands against her when she was fully dressed. Only then did she realise she was wearing night clothes.

He had sensed a change in her and loosened his hold. She faced him. 'Who undressed me? You?'

He looked about him mockingly. 'Did you bring a nursemaid with you? Come on, my sweet. Who else but me? All women are the same physiologically and as you must have guessed by now, I'd hardly qualify as an un-initiated male.' His tone was warm, his hands on her seductive. His kiss on her quivering, waiting mouth was teasing and tormenting, making her pout it in a silent request for the real thing.

Still refusing to satisfy her demand, he lifted his head. 'Do you mind my having seen your body?'

Her lips were curved into a tremulous smile, her eyes glowing like the last of the light in the sky as she shook her head. 'I'm glad,' she murmured, 'I'm glad.'

Under her pyjama top, his hands slid upwards and behind her to her shoulders, moving round and down and following her curving waist to hips and thighs. Then, upwards again to find her swelling shape to linger and stroke with his thumbs where earlier in the day he had inflicted pain.

In her delight Sharon murmured his name until his mouth imprisoned hers. She swayed into his arms and he cradled her, and she felt the warmth of his intensifying desire. The moment he released her mouth and held her away to look deep into her eyes, she murmured.

'I'm drowning in you, Calum.' A tiny frown puckered her brow. 'Lee said he would drown me like I should have drowned with Daryl, but he was wrong. Everyone was wrong. Do you believe me, Calum? You must believe me.'

His grey eyes darkened like the rock on the hills under a cloud shadow. His body grew cold, his hold hardening painfully before he pushed her away. She felt as if she had been grazed and cut by that rock, as he had warned her earlier when she had threatened to struggle until they both rolled down the hill.

They were rolling down it now, bumping and bouncing until she wanted to shriek with pain. Their friendship, relationship, whatever others called it—it was falling out of sight, condemned finally to split apart and shatter into tiny pieces.

He answered coldly, 'I don't believe you.'

'You've got a closed mind,' she accused, hugging her waist to try and stop the shivering. 'How can you function as a writer if your mind is closed to the truth? I thought all writers—good ones, and everyone says that's what you are—respected truth and sought after it relentlessly until they found it. You're blind to it, Calum, you're a useless writer.' Her eyes were almost blinded by tears. 'Why don't you just give up and live on your millions? They've perverted your insight. They must have, because you can't see the truth when it's staring you in the face.'

He picked up his jacket, shrugged into it and without a glance back, left her.

CHAPTER FIVE

SHARON had slept after Calum had left her. Far from feeling refreshed, however, an underlying sense of depression lurked. Or was it, she wondered, apprehension of what might lie in store which made her eyes heavy and her limbs feel weighted?

Outside, her gaze was drawn to the tent which nestled beside the hut. If, instead of quarrelling, she had nestled against the occupant and thanked him for all he had done to help her, would their parting, if there had been one, have taken a very different form?

Voices, raised and argumentative, carried from Calum's tent. The conversation, judging by the lull, appeared to have ended. The flaps moved across the opening and a man emerged. He was short, rotund and flushed. That he was still annoyed was evident by the bluntness of his question as he saw Sharon.

'Who the hell are you?' he asked, his second chin quivering. 'One of the extras?'

His name, Sharon recalled, was Galton Hardaker. His position in the hierarchy of the film unit was that of director. This fact, she reasoned, still did not give him the right to be so rude.

'You could say that,' was her snappy reply. 'Maybe impartial observer would be a better description.' She tossed the key to the hut in her palm, a fact he was not slow to notice. Behind the man, Calum had taken up a position of amused, expectant waiting.

'That key,' Galton Hardaker barked, 'where did you get it? Only J.W. can use that dump——' he indicated the hut, 'which he misguidedly calls his sanctuary but which I'd call something far less complimentary!'

Sharon felt she could see how this man had gained the high position he held in the film world. He was opinionated and uncaring about other people's feelings.

'Mr Wilson is a friend of my family. He loaned the hut to me. I came for a peaceful holiday, but I found you and your friends in occupation.'

He stared at her. 'You've got a lot to say for yourself. Are you trying to get yourself a part in the film?'

Sharon laughed, but stopped when she discovered Calum was grinning malevolently. 'Don't be silly.' Galton Hardaker looked taken aback by her outspokenness. 'How could I be? I'm not beautiful, am I?'

'That,' remarked Mr Hardaker, his experienced eyes busy over her, 'is a matter of opinion. Isn't it, Calum?'

There was intent to annoy in Calum's answer. 'Is it? I haven't looked at the girl for long enough to assess her charms.'

'Why, you——' Sharon caught her breath and compressed her lips.

Galton laughed, his head thrown back as far as his short neck would allow. The laughter came to an abrupt end. 'You wouldn't be the girl——' He turned to Calum. 'She's not the cause of the punch-up?'

'When one of your hand-picked stars tried to throttle and rape my next-door neighbour, I go to her aid, don't I, like the knight in shining armour my fans think I am.'

Mr Hardaker stared at Sharon unpleasantly. 'So you're the reason the filming's come to a stop.'

'I'm sorry about that, Mr Hardaker, but if it hadn't been for Calum, my heartbeats would have come to a stop.' A spurt of mischief urged her on in her battle of wits against this man. 'Would you like to see my bruises?'

'No, thanks. Voyeurism, even secondhand, is hardly my line—good grief,' as he saw Sharon's neck, 'who did that?' His thumb pointed backwards. 'Him?'

'Wrong, Galton. Throttling's not *my* line. Why else did I beat up Lee Banks?'

Galton Hardaker paled. 'But why did he do it?'

'Use your tiny mind, Galton.'

Mr Hardaker looked round at Sharon. 'Because he wanted, and you——'

She nodded. 'Wouldn't give.'

'For crying out loud,' the director said, 'I'll have to import some of his fans to pander to his——'

'Ego,' Calum interpolated smoothly.

The director grinned, his double chin tripling. He glanced at Sharon. 'I told you you were beautiful, darling, didn't I?' Cheerfully, which was surprising in the circumstances, he descended the hill.

There was a strained silence as they watched him go. Sharon knew she would have to be the one to make the first move conversationally. 'I'm—I'm sorry for what I said about you last night, Calum. About your writing, I mean.'

'It's of no consequence.' His reply was so harshly spoken she knew that he was not speaking honestly. But there was no way now in which she could reach him. His barriers were well and truly up, built high and unscalable.

'What's happening?' she asked at last.

'Filming's suspended until male lead recovers.'

'Was Mr Hardaker angry?'

'He was. We had one colossal row.'

Another short silence, then, 'Are they leaving?' Sharon enquired.

Calum nodded. 'But returning at a later date, season and weather permitting, of course.'

'Are—are you leaving, too?'

'Yes. Why?'

'You told me at first that you weren't connected with

the film people down there, that's why. Now you're leaving when they are.'

'So what? I'm going, all the same. What about you?'

Her long sigh came unpremeditatedly. 'Maybe I'll get my peace and quiet at last.'

Was this the end of their acquaintance? She forced herself to face the fact that it was. The day he went away he would leave her behind but take her heart with him, and he wouldn't even know.

There was a helicopter's unmistakable sound. It came into view against the cloudy sky, stalled to a hover and slowly lowered on to the island's helipad. Her heart throbbed faster as the helicopter's noise slowed down.

'Who's that for?' she asked.

'Me. I own it. Can I offer you a lift?'

'To London? No, thanks.'

Sharon looked at him, to discover that he was looking at her. His brown Fair Isle sweater was rollnecked, his casual slacks a well-fitting darker brown. His 'going places' appearance should have warned her, as should his shaven cheeks which, so often since she had known him, had remained rough and dark with bristle all day. Still he looked and she pushed back her windblown hair agitatedly.

'How long will the helicopter wait?' she asked, colouring with embarrassment.

'As long as I want.' His hand stretched out. 'Sharon?'

She had two choices—either she could ignore it as he had hers last night, or she could walk the distance between then. Without hesitation, she walked across and put her hand in his. He pulled her close, the full length of his body. Her low-burning fires leapt to new life at the feel of him.

He ran his fingers into her hair and put his mouth on hers in a long, drugging kiss. When he raised his head, he said, 'Last night, when I got you round, know what I called you?' She mouthed 'no'. 'My midnight girl—your black, black hair.' He caught a lock of it, twisted and held it tightly. He was hurting her, but she would not tell him. 'Skin so smooth, a kiss like an intoxicating drink.' She wanted the moment to go on and on.

'Cal-um!' A voice shouted from the foot of the hill, but he ignored it.

'My offer still holds good. Marry me and I'll protect your name.'

Only with the immense exercise of her self-control did she check the tears from invading her eyes. She shook her head and he dropped his arms.

'Thanks,' she answered, her voice as steady as she could make it, 'but I'm sure I can take anything that comes my way.'

Marry me and protect your name—did he know so little about a woman's needs that he thought that this was all she wanted from the man she loved—for she knew now without a single doubt that she loved him. He had proposed, but she could not accept. He didn't love her!

He was aloof again, withdrawn into himself. 'Goodbye, Sharon.'

Her smile was tremulous so she spoke lightly to hide it. 'See you around—on your book jackets!'

He smiled faintly, then ducked to disappear into his tent. When she emerged from the hut some time later, it was to watch the helicopter rising and flying off into the far distance.

Sharon walked down to the harbour, strolling to the end of the pier where a ferry boat was moored.

The skipper leaned on his elbows on the pier rail, smoking a cigarette. He was bearded, grey-haired and, like his vessel, looked weathered by the sea. He nodded to Sharon, tapped his cigarette ash into the water and asked,

'Are you coming on board, lassie?'

'Not this time, thanks.'

'We won't be making many more trips for a wee while after this. Better make up your mind soon.'

'I've an arrangement with Mr Wilson. Do you know him?'

'Aye, we all know Jack Wilson. You, too?'

Sharon nodded. 'My father's friend. He's sending his helicopter for me in about three weeks' time.'

'You'll find it lonely on your own. Although maybe they'll be leaving one or two people behind to watch over the stuff. I've been told to bring supplies now and then, so they must be.'

Sharon nodded, a little relieved, although reluctant to admit it even to herself. A shiver struck her and the captain asked, 'Are you cold, then?' She nodded, turning up her collar, although she could not sort out whether it was the temperature or the departure of the man she had grown to love that had caused it.

'It's the wind,' the man explained. 'It's blowing almost all the time here.'

'Is there much snow in winter?' Sharon asked, glancing up at the hills.

'Not only winter, but spring, too. The snow rarely settles in any quantity for more than a short while, though. The air's too moist and salty for it to linger long. There's the Gulf Stream, you see—it influences the climate.'

Sharon nodded. 'Well, I'll be on my way.'

The skipper lifted a hand. 'Mind how you go,' he warned. 'The rocks get very slippery at times.'

As she approached the hut, she saw tucked under the wooden steps the typewriter Calum had borrowed. It must have been there, she realised, as she had emerged, but had been so busy watching the helicopter's departure she had missed it.

Pulling the typewriter out, she saw there was a note attached to the handle. 'Thought you might be sleeping off your bruises, so I didn't knock. Thanks for the memories. Caldar.'

It was the name she had first known him by when, in her innocence, she had arrived at the island for the solitude and rest cure she was so sure it would give her. If she had known how her coming would tear to shreds not only her mind's peace but her heart, too, would she still have come? She answered her own question with a silent yet resounding 'yes'.

Most of the afternoon she spent reading, interspersed with lying on the bed, with the sound of taped music as a background to the turmoil of her thoughts. When she found she could think of no one but Calum, no matter how she tried to wrench her mind to dwell on other subjects, she paced the hut and wondered with some dismay how to cope with the strange and ironic turn her life had taken.

It was evening when the restlessness within her grew too strong to ignore. The rocky landscape beckoned, its wild aspect equalling the state of her emotions. She was in a mental wilderness, and only the transference of herself to a similar environment would help her adjust to Calum's absence. He had grown to be so much a part of her, she felt, now that he had gone, as if the life-force within her had been drained away.

After a bite to eat—he seemed to have taken her appetite with him too, she thought, smiling ruefully—she pulled on boots and an extra layer under her parka and made her way upwards.

The walking, as she had been told, was not easy, but it was a challenge which took her mind from her problems. Each step had to be taken carefully and, since there were bogs, assessed before each was taken. Higher now, Sharon turned to find that her progress had not been as great as she had imagined.

The camping area of the film unit was still in sight. The figures moving around looked minute. They were making their way to and from the pier where the ferry still waited. One figure caught her attention. It was clothed in a brilliant emerald colour. This in itself helped it to stand out noticeably from the browns and greys of the background.

There was no doubting that the figure was female. Only one woman on this island, Sharon decided, would wear such an outfit, which meant that Maida had not left the island with Calum. This was some relief, although it offered little consolation. He had probably given Maida his address, Sharon thought bitterly, even if he had omitted to inform his 'next-door neighbour' of his place of residence.

Walking on, she came across a wall beyond which was a line of ancient and long-abandoned stone crofts. They were mostly in ruins, with only the walls remaining. It seemed that sheep used them now as a shelter, since here and there pieces of sheep's wool clung to the rough stonework.

The view from the hilltop was magnificent. There were few directions, Sharon discovered, in which she could look without seeing mountains or islands on the horizon. The sun gave a hint of homing to the beckoning horizon, on its way filling the sky with muted colours which were caught by the sea, smooth in its evening calm, turning the pastel shades to brilliance, like a copyist outdoing the original painting.

For a long time Sharon sat on the hill, gazing at the beauty, wishing Calum were there to share it with her. She had come for the loneliness and here it was, all around her. The beauty was overwhelming, the sound of bleating sheep evoking memories of childhood days in the countryside.

From time to time, a curlew called, the song it sang lifting on the wind. Now she was utterly alone, and it was a strange and eerie feeling. Memories floated feather-like into her mind. The day Daryl had asked her to marry him she had asked,

'Why bother to propose marriage when you're married to the sea?'

His answer had been unselfconscious and childishly honest. 'Having a wife will add a human touch to my public image. Every time I win,' he had continued, unabashed, 'you'll be there to greet me, drink the champagne with me.'

Even then she had not seen through his words to the conceit beneath.

He had gazed out of the car window. 'A beautiful, admiring woman at the moment of victory,' he had mused, 'will make all the other women who are watching identify madly with her—you.' He had turned to her, taking her hand.

Sharon recalled how she had smiled into Daryl's eyes, and not a single doubt about her acceptance of him as her husband-to-be had entered her mind. Only later, a seeming lifetime later, had she come to realise how blind her faith in him had been.

As she stared at the changing sky-colours, the spectacular display dying away now and leaving a clear but darkening turquoise sky, the shape of a head seemed to etch itself against the scene, looking so real she nearly stretched out to touch it. It was not an image of Daryl, of whom she had been thinking; it was the face and features of Calum Darwin.

A double hoot from a ship's siren came climbing up the hill, brought by the wind. The ferry was departing at last. How long, Sharon wondered, before it returned?

As she prepared to descend, walking with greater care in the half-light in case she stepped into an unseen ditch or blundered into the awful menace of a bog, she had come to a decision. When the ferry came again, she would go back to the mainland and make her way home.

The following two days she spent tidying up generally, cleaning the hut with the mops and bucket which Jack Wilson had pushed into a corner. Then she had taken sea water from the harbour in a pail and carried it up the hill to wash a few items, drying them in the sun and wind, before packing them.

After that it was only a matter of waiting—simple enough, Sharon had thought, until she had to endure the creeping minutes which reluctantly formed themselves into plodding hours.

Following the familiar path one morning to the dwindling camp site, she discovered that six or seven people were still in residence. Two women served in the canteen, whereas there had been four of them. Sharon was delighted to discover it was still open.

As she stirred her coffee, her eyes, in their constant search for the absent ferry, automatically swung to gaze through the nearest window. There was a burst of feminine laughter outside and the canteen door opened to admit Maida Halliday.

The woman's stare did not hold the surprise which Sharon had expected. Maida plainly knew that she had not left the island. No friendliness was offered in the actress's demeanour, and Sharon gladly reciprocated her coolness. A member of the film crew she had seen before asked Sharon if he could join her.

He stirred his tea, saying, 'Don't know how much longer we've got to wait until the leading man's face is in a fit enough condition to go in front of the cameras.' He looked at Sharon with a touch of annoyance. 'Rumour's going round that you were the cause of the fight.'

'Is it?' Sharon's voice was flat. 'You never know with rumours—whether they're true or not, I mean.'

'So it's true, then? If not, you'd have denied it.'

'Ah, but would you have believed me?' Sharon threw back.

'Not a matter of whether I'd believe it. It's that one you've got to reckon with if it is.' His head bent towards the leading lady. 'She was mad when she saw Lee's face.'

'Was it bad?'

The man seemed surprised at Sharon's genuine interest. 'Two blue-black eyes, swollen lips, a cut on his cheekbone.'

'Oh-oh dear!' The words came out on a long, faintly dismayed note. 'No wonder Mr Hardaker was angry. Where is he, by the way?'

'Went with Cal. Why?'

Sharon smiled, pushing away her empty cup and rising. 'He asked me if I wanted a part in the film. I'm so bored with waiting for the ferry, if he asked me now, I might even say yes.'

'Another week before that comes back,' the man said.

Sharon kept her disappointment to herself. 'I guess I can wait that long.'

'Before you see Cal again?' the man asked cheekily.

'Maybe it's before I see Lee again,' she answered, leaving the man frowning in surprise.

The week of waiting seemed all set to turn itself into two when the sound of the siren for which Sharon had been waiting had her swinging out of bed. In a fever of haste she washed and dressed, then raced down to the harbour as the skipper stepped ashore.

'Don't go without me,' Sharon gasped. 'I've decided to leave the island and go home.'

The skipper nodded in his wise way. His name, she

had been told, was MacAlister. 'Thought a Sassenach like you, and a female on top of it, wouldn't stay the course.'

'It's not that,' she started to explain, a little angry, 'it's because I——'

I'm only half here and want to find the other part of me before it slips out of my grasp ... How could she say such a thing to such a life-toughened man?

'We'll be leaving this afternoon, lassie. You can come on board this morning if you like.'

'I like,' Sharon echoed, and hurried back to the hut.

On the long train journey back to her parent's house in the suburbs of London, Sharon recalled her meeting with Maida Halliday. The member of the film crew who had said it was 'that one' she would have to reckon with had been right.

Maida had approached as she had leaned on the ferry boat's rail. Hearing the quick footsteps, Sharon had guessed at once that danger loomed, not ahead, but from behind. She turned quickly in a purely defensive action.

It was plain from the actress's expression that her claws had been especially sharpened. 'Heard from Lee?' Sharon asked brightly, intending to pre-empt Maida's attack. It seemed, from Maida's reaction, that she was on the wrong track.

'To hell with Lee,' Maida snapped. 'Why are you returning to the mainland? I thought you were in search of a rest cure from the baying hounds of the press?'

'Oh?' Sharon's eyebrows rose in what she hoped was a supercilious manner. 'Who told you that?'

'It's common knowledge on the island. People have eyes to recognise you with from press photographs and to read everything that was printed about you.'

'Lies, all lies,' Sharon returned smoothly, wondering

how long she would be able to maintain the pose of a bored celebrity.

'Lies?' Maida spat. 'It's not a lie that you're chasing after Calum, is it?' The woman smiled at Sharon's heightening colour. 'I hit the jackpot there, didn't I?'

'Unfortunately for you—or maybe fortunately?—I won't be seeing Calum again. We said goodbye before he left for home.'

'A short and sweet affair? Mm, it sounds like Calum.'

'Short, sweet non-affair, Miss Halliday.' Sharon turned back to gaze at the hills of the mainland rising out of the mist. 'If you're so crazy about him, go and get him. He's yours.' Her smile was sugar-sweet. 'I give him to you with my love.'

Maida had stared, apparently nonplussed, turned on her heel and stumped away across the deck. Sharon's smile was bitter this time. It was a victory of sorts, but it tasted sour.

Hours later, she emerged from the taxi she had found at the London train terminus. She had managed to persuade the cab driver to take her home to the outlying area of Greater London in which her parents lived. It was daylight now, and after he had helped her with her bags, she gave him the fare plus a tip which made him smile.

Although she had slept in the train, it had been sporadic and shallow. Fatigue weighed heavily on her eyelids and thought-processes. Even so, as she looked at the house she realised there was something wrong. It was night-time, yet all the curtains were opened, even those in her parents' bedroom.

Entering the house, she called to them, but her voice boomeranged at her from the walls. On a notepad near the entrance, she saw the words, scribbled by her mother, 'Remember tell milkman no milk until further notice.' So they had gone away. Sharon was vaguely troubled, yet did not know why.

After making herself some hot chocolate, she went to bed and slept until the sounds connected with everyday living woke her with a start. It was midday and outside the sun shone, coaxing her to leave her bed.

A snack meal was all she wanted, after which she dialled Jack Wilson's business number. It took a few minutes for her call to be passed through to his office, and she felt a surge of reassurance as she heard his familiar voice.

'Sharon, my dear, you weren't due back—via my very own helicopter—for ten or so days. Did you get weary for company, after all?'

'I loved it on your island, Mr Wilson, and I'll be going back there some time soon, if you'll let me.'

'It's yours whenever you want it,' Jack Wilson answered. 'Now about your parents——'

'They're not here, Mr Wilson. Where have they gone?'

Jack laughed. 'You sound like a lost lamb! They're taking a holiday. It was like this. Even after you'd left, the calls kept coming—you know, *those* calls.'

'And they made Mum ill?'

'Just fed up to the back teeth, Sharon,' Jack answered with a laugh. 'Your dad, too. So they took themselves off on a three-week cruise to the Med. They went a couple of days ago—packed in a hurry. Hoped you'd understand if you came back and they weren't here.'

'Of course I understand. I'm only sorry they were driven away.'

'Your mother wasn't—said she'd been trying for years to get your father on a cruise. He agreed at once, deciding it was the only way they could take themselves out of reach of a telephone. Although I do believe there's a telephone link with the ship at most ports of call.'

'I'm glad, really,' Sharon replied. 'They needed a break, especially Dad.'

'True. By the way,' Sharon smiled as Jack's voice changed gear to 'gossipy', 'how did you and Caldar get on, eh?'

'Did you set that up, Mr Wilson—me in the hut and nestling beside me in a tent rough-hewn, rough-living, tough-minded genius Calum Darwin?'

Jack Wilson sounded as though he was rocking with laughter. 'You sound as if you've swallowed a couple of mouthfuls of the blurb on one of his books! I plead a little bit guilty, but when I told him about you, he didn't seem to mind,' he added dryly.

'You might have told me, Mr Wilson.'

'Wouldn't you have gone, dear?'

'I—well, I——'

'That's right, tell an old man not to pry into your private thoughts. You've had more than enough of that to last a lifetime, I imagine. Well, if you want to get back to Cuilla at any time, just let me know.'

One day, she promised herself, she really would return—when all the intruders had gone and there was only herself and the gulls and the sheep. Turning on her father's stereo equipment and tuning to the music she liked, she lay back on the carpet's good quality pile and thought.

It would be necessary to sort out her life, to eliminate Calum Darwin's image from her mind; to rip away the past and discard the ruined material like dress fabric which had gone wrong in the cutting.

Rising, she switched off the radio and dropped into a chair. There was something different, she sensed, from the last time she had been home. It was the silence! No telephone to ring and ring, never stopping, jangling the nerve chords in her brain. There was no abuse in her ear, nor threats which sent arrows of fear twanging through the wires until she felt punctured in every part of her.

Vowing she would not put on the radio again, thus introducing noise, she picked up a book, sat back and listened to the peace, as she had sat on that island hilltop and gloried in the silence.

Next day she went shopping, using her mother's little car. It was wonderful to wander through the crowds of shoppers with not a single doubtful glance cast in her direction. The passing of time had given her back her anonymity, something she had come to regard as her most precious possession.

As she opened the door, the telephone rang. For a sickening moment she stared at it, then told herself to stop being foolish. Who would know she was back at home?

All the same, her hand shook as she lifted the receiver.

'Jack here. You okay, Sharon? Just checking—you know, in your parents' absence.'

'That's good of you, Mr Wilson.' Her breath came more slowly now, relief flooding her cheeks with colour. 'I'm fine, thanks. You know what I'm doing? Enjoying the silence, the way no one stares at me. Do you know what I mean?'

'Only too well, my dear. After what your parents told me, it's a wonder you stayed sane, the three of you. Look after yourself, Sharon, and if there's anything I can do, just call me.'

'I will, Mr Wilson. And thanks.'

The day passed as quietly as the previous day. As she wandered round the well-kept garden, however, Sharon felt a familiar restlessness creep up on her like a friend tiptoeing from behind and clamping their hands over her eyes and saying, 'Guess who?'

There was no need to guess. He was in her thoughts constantly. He would not go away. Part of her wished she had accepted his offer of marriage, while the other part regretted that he had ever made it. He had been offering her his protection, when she had wanted his love.

How would she have felt now if she had accepted his offer? Like a joyously happy bride, or a discarded, still inviolate nuisance of a wife? She had to face facts. Since she was a living, breathing woman and not an actress in a romantic film, the latter would apply.

It was mid-afternoon. Sharon was making herself a pot of tea when the telephone rang. This time she approached it with more confidence. It was Mr Wilson again, asking if she was managing alone. She was wrong, since a woman's voice responded.

'Is that Miss Sharon Mason?' the woman wanted to know. The question was asked briskly and with confidence.

Since Sharon could see no reason for denying her true identity, she agreed that she was indeed Miss Sharon Mason.

'This is Elizabeth Derry of the *Morning Journal*. I have it on good authority, Miss Mason, that on a film location on a remote Scottish island, there occurred a— shall we say—a physical dispute between two well-known men——' Sharon started to protest, but the reporter went on, 'one of whom was Calum Darwin, the writer and novelist, and the other Lee Banks, the film actor. Would you like to confirm that this is true, Miss Mason?'

'I would not *like to confirm* anything, Miss Derry,' Sharon answered politely but with a tinge of sarcasm. 'Thank you for calling.'

'Miss Mason,' the reporter seemed anxious that they were not cut off, 'I was given this information by a very reliable source——'

'And of course, being a good journalist, you wouldn't care to reveal your source,' Sharon replied cuttingly.

It was obvious, she decided, that her cutting edge must have needed sharpening, since the young woman came back cheerfully, 'That's true, Miss Mason. You seem to know all about the ethics of journalists.'

'Do they have any?' was Sharon's still polite response.

Plainly put out, the reporter pressed on, 'I was also informed that you are now a very good friend of Mr Darwin——'

'You can tell your precious "source" to go jump in the river!'

'Only three months,' the reporter continued, 'after the tragic loss of your late fiancé, Daryl Irwin. Would you care to confirm or deny those rumours, Miss Mason?'

Sharon crashed the receiver down and put a shaking hand to her head. Who? Who could have done this to her? Who knew enough to inform the press so confidently of what had happened on the island of Cuilla?

Lee, perhaps? No, he would be hiding himself until his wounds had healed. Maida, maybe? She would hardly tell the world that the man she regarded as her own had ignored her and started an affair with another woman.

Which left only one person, Sharon concluded angrily—Calum himself. 'Wanders the world,' the blurb on his book covers had said, 'strictly no ties.' No ties—that was the reason he had told the press.

He might have offered marriage, but he had made it clear that it hadn't meant a thing, other than a piece of paper giving her the right to use his surname. On returning to the everyday world, he had realised how near he had come to putting the noose round his own neck.

What better way of avoiding that kind of trouble than by making it public property, thus forcing her into denying it? And how had he known of her return? From who else but Maida? As she walked away from the telephone, its ring summoned her back. If it was Calum, calling her to gloat over his small but significant triumph over her . . .

'*Evening Record* here. Is that Miss Sharon——?'

She dropped the receiver back as if it were burning her hand. Almost at once it rang again. For a few moments she let it ring, then picked it up to tell them to go away. 'Miss Mason,' the man said, 'there's a story circulating about you and Mr Calum Darwin. It seems that the actor Lee Banks is also involved——'

'Then go and talk to them,' she said through clenched teeth, and hung up.

Removing the receiver and listening to the dialling tone, she sighed thankfully, knowing it would not disturb her again. She switched on the music and let her mind meander through the immediate past.

'No man is an island,' she had quoted at Calum. 'This man is,' he'd answered at once. Why hadn't she heeded the warning in his words and shielded her bruised emotions, instead of allowing them to be subjected to the batterings of yet another man's charms, a man even more beyond her reach than the first?

Having dressed next morning, she went down the stairs and saw that she had not replaced the receiver before going to bed. Something compelled her now to reach out and pick it up. She dropped it into place as quickly as if it might bite her, then smiled at herself.

The morning's paper was pushed into the letterbox. She pulled it out, taking the newspaper with her. She was eating the toast she had made when the telephone rang. As she hurried to answer it, she knew why she had felt the need to replace the receiver. In case Calum had somehow discovered her address and number and was calling . . .

Tripping over the words, she said the number, then she listened. The colour drained from her face, and she clutched the windowsill for support. Cutting off the string of abusive phrases, she covered her eyes. The obscene calls had started again.

Those journalists—what had they printed? She ran back to the kitchen and opened out the tabloid newspaper. Nothing on the front page, but on page two her own picture, taken earlier in the year when Daryl had been at her side, gazed, smiling, back at her.

The headline screamed, ' "Save me first" yacht girl causes punch-up.' 'Daryl's sweetheart lets his memory drown: Takes two more famous men on board.' The report went on, 'Sharon shares out her love between celebrated novelist Calum Darwin and handsome star Lee Banks. "I deny I'm having affairs with both of them," Miss Mason declared yesterday. Which,' the reporter went joyfully on, 'only leaves one of them. Which one is the lucky guy?'

Sharon threw the paper across the room, then the telephone rang. Was it Jack Wilson, concerned about her welfare? It was another spate of abuse which, once again, she cut off.

Dialling Jack's number, she drummed her fingers. 'Mr Wilson, please.' She gave her name and was put through immediately. His secretary answered.

'So sorry, Miss Mason. Mr Wilson did try to call you, but I kept getting the engaged signal. It was early, because he was in a rush to catch a plane.'

'I—I took . . .' What was the use of explaining the situation to Mr Wilson's secretary? 'I see. Will Mr Wilson be away long?'

'A few days, maybe ten,' was the vague answer. Sharon thanked the woman and rang off.

The urge to telephone the newspaper which had been delivered to the house was strong, but reason stopped her from taking such an action. Since it was two other papers that had telephoned, it was unpleasantly obvious that the story had been passed from one reporter to another, all along the line.

To get away from the house and the agitated state that was beginning to creep up on her, Sharon drove into the town. Friends of her parents passed her in the high street. They nodded and smiled, but they did not stop to speak.

Other people she knew pretended they had not seen her, or stared unsmilingly. It was all so familiar. She knew it would get worse before it got better—if it ever did get better. How could she issue denials? Who would print them, except as a platform from which to launch yet another series of libellous reports about her private life? Nor could she go up to people in the street and say, 'The papers have got it all wrong. I'm innocent of their allegations . . .' They would think she had taken leave of her senses.

As she turned the key and let herself in, the telephone rang. She steeled herself to ignore it—until the sound made her head feel as if it was spinning. With the receiver in her hand, she listened for a moment to confirm it was yet another abusive call, then she clicked the buttons down with a shaking finger. For the second time she put the receiver on the table.

The shaking spread to the rest of her. It did not stop until she had rested in a chair and reasoned herself into a calmer state. This was worse than the last time. Then, she had had her parents' support. They had formed a barrier between herself and the outside world.

The letterbox clattered and Sharon dragged herself from the chair to pick up the mail. One glance at the oddly-written envelopes told her they were poison pen letters. Just to make sure she was right, she opened one, then tore all three into tiny shreds.

Later that day she reconnected the telephone. Half an hour later it rang. She was in the middle of cooking her evening meal. Steeling herself to an unnatural calmness, she picked up the telephone. The voice was disguised, high-pitched and female. 'Who——' Sharon began, but the caller hung up.

Sinking to the floor, she held her head. Her palms were moist, her fingers trembling. She took a few deep breaths to steady herself—then the ringing started again.

Springing to her feet, she screamed into the phone, before the caller could speak, 'Leave me alone, do you hear? Stop abusing me, stop pestering me, stop driving me nearly mad! I can't stand any more of it, I can't take it,' she was sobbing now, 'I shall, I shall . . .'

Again, her legs collapsed beneath her and she had folded down to the floor. The receiver dangled, unheeded. A voice said, 'Sharon? Sharon? Are you there? Will you listen to me? Will you answer me?'

For a moment, the trembling stopped. Her head came up, her eyes wide with disbelief. She scrambled to her feet, seized the receiver. 'Calum?' she asked wonderingly. There was only a blurring sound in reply. He had gone

CHAPTER SIX

SOMEONE was dragging her by the armpits. They were wanting her to stand up. She was on a slope and there was grass underneath her. Or was it? Her finger-pads felt and it was carpet tile. She was lying on the stairs, stiff from her sprawled position.

'What happened?' she asked no one in particular. 'Did I fall down the stairs or something?'

Her body was being half-lifted downwards. A hard male body supported her. Then she was on a level surface and her head fell forward to rest on a broad, solid shoulder.

'For heavens sake, don't go to sleep on me again. I fight a man for her virtue and she goes to sleep on me! I almost get caught for speeding coming to stand by her in her adversity and she passes out on me. Baby, aren't you *ever* awake?'

'I'm not your baby.' The denial came automatically. Then the realisation dawned as to who this man might be, and her head jerked upright. 'Get out of here!'

'Not on your sweet life, Sharon mine. I'm not leaving you now.'

The phone rang. He must have replaced the receiver. 'You,' she accused, pointing towards the shrill, commanding sound, 'you're the cause of that thing ringing and ringing!'

'Can't your father afford to get himself one of the quieter variety that trills or buzzes? What do you do to stop that darned thing?'

'Of course he can afford it. He's just old-fashioned. And you stop the noise by lifting the mouthpiece.' She hoped Calum heard the sarcasm. He just smiled.

'You don't say,' he commented dryly, and did just that. For a few moments he listened, then cut off, a deep frown creasing his forehead. 'Is that what you've been hearing every time you answered that shrieking monster's call?' Sharon nodded. 'No wonder you've nearly been driven out of your mind!'

'Thanks a lot for your sympathy. It's a bit hypocritical on your part, though, isn't it? You were the one who started the rumours, whispered hints to the press about us so that I would have to deny the rumour. What you probably didn't take into account was the fact that they would rake up my—my past, add it on to your nasty innuendoes—and come up with the wrong but oh-so-sensational answer.'

Sharon led the way into the main living-room. Calum followed slowly, looking around, taking in the ex-pensive-looking furnishings, noting the silver trophies displayed on sideboard and mantelpiece.

'Your father's obviously a keen something.' His lifted eyebrows invited an answer.

'Golfer. Which is how he met Jack Wilson. My father's Mr Wilson's accountant.'

'Ah.' He moved towards her. 'That explains the per-vading feeling of affluence, the indulged good taste.' He lifted her chin with one finger. 'That certain air of quality his offspring possesses.'

Sharon shook her head free, hoping also to shake off the excitement the touch of him aroused after endless days without him. It was a vain hope, since he had only to be there in front of her to make her blood flow faster.

'How did you get in, anyway?' she asked.

He tossed and caught a bunch of keys. 'Courtesy of our mutual friend Jack Wilson. In his absence, he asked me to keep a fraternal eye on you.' He laughed at the mixture of emotions passing across her face. 'It's okay, my friend,' he bent to brush her startled lips, 'I told him once again that was the last thing I felt towards you.'

The telephone rang again. 'There, you see what you've done to me!' Sharon cried, half-covering her ears. 'Your lies——'

'I'm a liar now?' His eyes had turned as dark as the Scottish mountains as night descended. 'According to you,' the ringing went on, 'I'm a gossip columnist's dream. I feed those "birds of prey" with seeds of doubt about acquaintances and friends alike. I——' He gripped her shoulders. The ringing did not stop.

He strode to the door and turned, saying grimly, 'You'd better not listen to what I'm going to say to the louse on the end of the line this time. A well-brought-up girl like you won't appreciate my flow of invective.'

Sharon dropped on to the couch and seized a cushion, burying her face and covering her ears. A few minutes later Calum returned. She emerged, blinking in the light he had switched on.

'What happened?' she asked. 'Did the caller take fright at your terrible language?'

He shook his head, coming to stand in front of her. 'No abuse this time. It was the press asking impudent questions. So I took advantage of their interest in us. I've just announced our engagement, plus the date of our wedding.'

Sharon stared up at him. 'You can't have done! I haven't agreed to marry you.'

'A couple of days from now,' he responded implacably, 'you will become my wife.'

She stood up, facing him. 'Who says so?'

'The press will say so. Tomorrow you'll see it in your morning paper.'

'Why, you miserable——' Her hand gripped the sleeve of his sweater, bunching it, but he grasped her wrist so tightly, she was forced to let go. 'Why couldn't you have told them to leave me alone? Why didn't you insist they stopped printing lies about me, and told the truth instead?'

A muscle in his jaw moved. 'Did you really expect me, a one-time journalist, to try to persuade them to suppress the facts? Remember the thing called freedom of the press?'

'Freedom to tell lies?' she stormed. 'I tell you, it's not the truth they're printing about me.'

'It's the truth to them, Sharon.' His arm went round her waist and he pulled her nearer. 'Tell me something, honey. Are you able to produce any evidence to prove your contention that everything that has been printed about you is untrue?'

Give them his love story, Daryl's father had pleaded. I'm too full of grieving. You were his fiancée. I know you lived together ... When she had started to refuse, she remembered, he had reminded her of his heart trouble and that he couldn't take all the strain. How would she feel now if she suddenly talked to the press, telling them the truth?

Her head drooped, but Calum lifted it, gazing keenly into her eyes. They had clouded with pain. 'I can't produce a shred of evidence, Calum.' She moved away and he let her go.

The letterbox rattled, and Sharon sank to the couch. 'Poison pen,' she muttered. 'Don't bother to go.'

He did go, opened the envelope, read the contents, crumpled all the paper into a tight ball and hurled it at the waste paper bin. Then the telephone rang. Sharon clapped her hands over her ears. 'I can't stand it!' she cried.

Calum went out, lifted off the receiver, clicked the buttons to silence the string of words and the telephone in one act.

He came back, raked a hand through the thick layers of his hair and slid his hands into his slacks pockets. Her eyes were drawn to the hard-boned hips, his leanness, his strength which she longed to feel against and around her, protecting her from the abyss which seemed all set to swallow her up.

'When I made my offer of marriage,' he said quietly, 'on Cuilla, and you turned it down, you said "thanks, but I'm sure I can take anything that comes my way." '

'All right,' her throat was tight with threatening tears, 'so I was wrong. Thank you for offering to marry me, to protect me.' She took a breath. 'I accept your offer of your name and your protection.'

There was a pause, but she could not see his expression. If their eyes were to meet, he would read in them her love for him, which he didn't want. And she could not bear to witness his total lack of feeling for her.

'My name and my protection it is,' he responded briskly. 'I shall give you that, no more, no less.'

'I shall expect no more,' she answered, cursing the touch of bitterness that had crept in. 'As you said, it will be a marriage with a time limit, after which divorce proceedings will be started.'

'I also said,' he reminded her, 'you could have my protection for as long as you needed it.'

I'll need it for ever, she thought. Aloud, she replied, her voice as empty as an echo, 'For as long as I need it.'

It was just as she closed the catches of the bulging second suitcase that doubts about living under Calum's roof, about marrying him at all, began to creep in.

Tugging it so that the handle was uppermost, she leant on it, still kneeling, her cheeks in her hands. It was a drastic step she was taking, for all that Calum had promised only protection, with an 'opting out' clause in their strange agreement.

If only her mother had been home! They would have sat on the bed and discussed the problem, looking at it from all angles. What would her mother's advice be about this loveless marriage she would, in a few days, have contracted herself into? Marry him, she could almost hear her mother's voice saying, if you love him, Sharon, marry him—provided you are strong enough to accept the consequences. Yes, she knew what those 'consequences' would be. After a year, maybe two, the parting would come. Only one of them would suffer—herself. She meant nothing to Calum. He wouldn't feel the terrible wrenching sensation she would experience. Nor would there be any offspring, simply because there would be no lovemaking.

A heavy sigh escaped her and she stared unseeingly at the carpet. 'Having second thoughts?' Calum's voice mocked her from the doorway.

Sharon shrugged without changing her position. 'It's quiet now,' she offered. 'Maybe it's all dying down. You know how events are done to death by the media, then they sense the public's tiring of it and they leave it alone?' She looked up at him. 'Perhaps they'll leave me alone now.'

Calum turned and went. Sharon heard the telephone receiver being replaced. Before Calum could reach the top of the stairs, the ringing splintered the silence. He leant against the door frame. 'How much more proof do you want?'

Sharon clapped her hands over her ears. 'Stop that noise, please stop it!'

'Is there an extension phone anywhere up here?'

'Across there, in my parents' bedroom. On a bedside table.'

Calum's voice drifted across. He was answering the caller: 'Yes,' he was saying, 'I am Calum Darwin. I confirm my engagement to Miss Mason. Wedding date to be fixed. Sorry, nothing more to add to my statement.'

Sharon heard the click, indicating that he had cut off the discussion.

'That, Miss Mason,' he stated, coming out of the main bedroom, 'was an international news agency. Evidence enough of the world's interest, let alone the home media?'

'You're famous,' she half-muttered, 'and I swore I'd never become involved again with an internationally-known personality. I never even thought it was possible.' She pressed her fingers against her temples. 'I'm sorry, Calum, I can't go through with it.' She went to unfasten the suitcase catches, but he was there, seizing them and carrying them down the stairs.

'Bring them back!' she shrieked. 'I told you—no deal.'

'I've often wondered,' he shouted back at her from the entrance hall, 'if you really were the coward they made you out to be. Now I know you are.' He dropped the cases and made for the door.

'Calum, don't go,' she pleaded. 'I'll—I'll marry you.'

'What makes you think,' he returned unpleasantly, 'that I'll have you now?'

The knowledge of her own innocence of any guilt caused a fury to lash her, making her sway like a tree in a hurricane. 'So what do you want me to do,' she flung at him, 'get down on my knees and beg you to marry me—you, the great and wonderful writer, who has such insight and compassion for his self-created characters, but none at all for real-life human beings?'

Taking his time, he climbed the stairs. Slowly Sharon backed away into her bedroom and he followed. Spreading his hands over his hips, he looked down at her. She had changed from slacks and blouse after he had told her he would take her out to a meal before they went on to his place.

His eyes appreciated the short-sleeved yellow dress, with its stand-up collar and buttons reaching to her narrow waist. His glance caressed the deep blackness of her silky hair, the colour-stained cheeks; travelled down to her legs and neat ankles.

A faint smile deepened the grooves around his mouth, his eyes became flecked with the rays from the setting sun. His hand came out. Wonderingly, she placed hers in it.

'I have compassion,' he said softly, 'for this human being. Aren't I taking her under my protection, holding her close, keeping the baying newshounds at a distance?'

Swallowing deeply, she nodded, but her emotions would keep clogging her throat so that she couldn't speak. She studied the heavy brows, the deep furrows between them that would never go away.

Would she ever be allowed to be near enough to the man to smooth those frown marks with her finger, making those serious and cool grey eyes glow with warmth, the ridged jaw relax, those resolute lips soften into a smile from which all trace of life's ironic twists and turns had been banished?

Her feet were moving, she was being eased towards him. Before her reason could start off the buzzer with its pre-set alarm, she was wrapped in his arms and yielding to his demanding mouth. It was a kiss of the body, too, as his leg pushed between hers and she felt herself bending under the pressure he exerted.

The hardness of his muscles made inroads into the softness of her flesh. She knew of his growing desire, creating an answering warmth inside her. Her fingers gripped his shirt sleeves lest she lose her balance. Then she recalled the day on the island when he had taken the full force of her on that slope, holding them both steady against all odds. He would not let her fall.

As he lifted her upright, her pulses drummed, her blood ran through her veins like burning lava. 'Calum, oh, Calum,' she whispered, and felt her mouth waywardly seeking for his like a half-drunken person reaching out once again for yet another, and then another drink. He gave her that 'drink' with a willingness that had her limbs weakening with delight.

It took a full minute for her to realise his lips were hardening and withdrawing. He let her go so suddenly she had to bend double to ward off a faint. When she recovered, she sat on the bed, to find that he was across the room, gazing at the wedding gifts.

'These boxes. What are they?' His voice was cold. All passion and warmth had been driven out by the sight of them.

Sharon explained. 'My mother tried to give them back, but no one would take them. They said I'd suffered enough by losing Daryl.'

He swung round, his grey eyes like steel clashing and throwing off sparks. '*You* suffered? You lived with him for two years, as your heartrending story said. You were as good as married to him, yet at the moment of his drowning you screamed out to be saved first. And they called that *suffering*?'

She had started to shake her head, but stopped, knowing he would walk all over any denial she might make. 'You don't understand,' was all she could say, but even that brought another deluge of fury on to her head.

'You're so right! I damned well don't understand how any woman could be so callous about the man she loved. Presumably,' he indicated the gifts, 'you still love him—or rather, his memory. Otherwise, why are they still there? Why haven't you given them to charity?'

Her eyes lifted at last. It would be useless to tell him how the press had pestered almost from the moment of

Daryl's drowning, how the phone calls and written abuse started immediately after the publication of her so-called 'love story'. 'It's a family matter,' she told him coolly. 'Their fate will be decided when my parents return.'

'When we marry, I want them to be disposed of as soon as can be arranged.'

'They're mine,' she rallied. 'You'll have no say in what happens to them.'

'When we marry,' he repeated, 'they will become ours, just as my home and its contents will become yours. They,' he nodded to the stacked boxes, 'will be distributed at the earliest opportunity. Otherwise, my love,' he spoke through his teeth, 'I shall myself get rid of them. Do you understand?'

'Only too well, thank you.' She faced him. 'I also understand I'm getting myself involved—too involved—with a selfish brute who would stop at nothing to get his own way. I refuse to m——' Marry you, she had been intending to say, but the telephone rang again. Her hands lifted to shut out the noise, but she checked them.

'I'm answering this one,' she stated, running to the door, 'and if it's one of your journalist friends, I'm going to deny . . .' she had reached her parents' bedroom and he was not far behind, 'everything you told them,' she lifted the receiver, 'about our engagement.'

His hand came out as she got the earpiece to her ear. She wrestled with him for possession of the instrument, but he would not let go. She lowered her head and nipped his skin, at which he released the phone, uttering a furious expletive.

Her eyes flashed in triumph, as she said to the caller, 'If that's the press, I'm announcing the breaking off of——' She listened.

'Oh dear, darling,' her mother's voice soothed, 'have

you broken something valuable?'

'M-Mum?' Sharon stammered. 'Oh, Mum, you don't know how glad—yes, I'm—I'm fine.' She wished Calum would go away. 'You and Dad? You're where? Calling by radio telephone link from the ship? You're nearing Naples? That's wonderful!'

'We didn't expect you'd be home, Sharon. Did you start wanting company again? Was it too lonely?'

'I wasn't lonely at all,' Sharon explained, 'but it's too complicated to tell you about it now. You haven't got long? I know, but I must tell you and Dad something.' She glanced over her shoulder. Calum was leaning against the doorway, arms folded, smiling sarcastically. 'Will you go away?' she hissed, covering the mouthpiece, but he did not move. 'I'm—I'm getting married, Mum. Three days from now. No, you don't know him. Well,' she gave another 'get lost' glance at the indolent figure behind her, 'maybe you do. You might have—have heard of him. It's——'

'Yes, darling?' Her mother could hardly wait.

'It's Calum Darwin. Yes, the writer. How did I meet him? On Mr Wilson's little island. Yes,' she was glad her mother could not see her strained smile, 'it was a—a strange kind of place to——' she swallowed hard, 'to meet one's future h-husband.' The word almost stuck in her throat.

'Sharon dear,' her mother sounded choked, too, but with pleasure, 'you must be so happy.' There was a subdued whisper. 'I've just told your dad, and he's as pleased as I am.'

'Do you love him, Sharon?' her father's voice boomed, and she heard a movement behind her. Arms coiled round her, crossing over at her breasts. Her heart beat faster, her blood sang in her ears.

'Yes, yes, Dad, of course I—I love him.'

'Good. That's all I wanted to hear. Good luck, dear. I 'll hand over.'

'A kind of whirlwind romance, wasn't it?' her mother commented, and Sharon could almost see her mother's flushed cheeks and eyes bright with the anticipated happiness of her daughter. 'And such a famous man.' Her voice lowered. 'He wouldn't be anywhere around, would he, dear? I'd really love a word——'

Hard male lips were imprinting their silent possessiveness around the back of her neck, spreading an electrifying tingle like a necklace of live wire over her skin.

'Stop it!' she mouthed over her shoulder, but her protest elicited only a soft laugh.

'Yes, he's right here, Mum.' She covered the mouthpiece, holding it out. 'My mother—she'd love to talk to you.'

With seeming reluctance, his arms let her go and he took the receiver, his smile wide with mockery.

'Mrs Mason?' he said. 'I'm delighted to speak to you. Yes, I'm sure we shall be extremely happy.' His eyes reached round to taunt in unison with his words. 'She's the girl I've been waiting for, Mrs Mason, no doubt about it. And she's just said,' his smile flashed, showing white teeth, 'I'm the man she's been looking for all her life. Yes, I know about that episode.' His voice had gained a faint edge. 'It's behind her now. Together, we'll erase the past——'

Sharon slipped from the room, unable to listen to the inventions of a supposedly wildly infatuated husband-to-be.

Her suitcases were down in the hall. She stared at them, standing there deserted. Her instinct was to go down and bring them back, unpack their contents—and that would be the end of this nightmare. She held her head, admitting to herself that she had now become too involved to back out.

The press had been informed. A denial now would

only worsen matters where the publicity angle was concerned. Her parents had been told and were delighted by the news.

There was a whisper from nowhere which told her that with herself, at least, she could be truthful. More than anything in the world, she wanted to marry Calum Darwin. But on the terms agreed between them? Even on those terms, she silently acknowledged.

As she turned, she saw Calum watching her. 'Your parents quite understood,' he informed her, 'that we chose not to wait for them to return. Your mother was just a little upset—until I told her we loved each other so much we wanted the ceremony behind us, so that we could start our blissfully happy marriage as soon as possible.'

Sharon returned to her bedroom to pick up her jacket and handbag. 'You lie very easily, don't you?' she remarked with deliberate casualness.

He was not riled as she had anticipated. 'Being a writer helps,' was his sarcastic comment. She turned away, only to feel his hand on her shoulder pulling her round to face him.

'Show me some of that love you told your father you have for me.'

'You know I——' She did, she did love him! So how could she deny it? 'I had to say that, didn't I? If I had told my father "no", they'd have come flying back to discover why I was marrying you. And to try to stop me.'

His eyes flickered and he repeated his demand. 'Show me some of that love.'

A breath dragged at her lungs. She shook her head. 'I——' There was no moving him, she could see that. Hesitantly, her hands held his shoulders. Two steps forward, then she went on tiptoe. Her lips reached out to his mouth. He turned his head away.

Annoyed with him, with herself for even beginning to obey his order, she pulled away. 'It's ridiculous,' she said. 'How can I even start?'

Incredulously he looked at her. 'Don't you know how to make love to a man? What did your late fiancé teach you when you lived together? Nothing?'

'You don't have to be "taught" when you love a man,' she flicked back. 'You just seem to know . . .' The words tailed off. She couldn't go on, simply because she just 'didn't know'. It was that simple. 'Anyway,' she rallied, 'we didn't live together—I told you.'

He gave her a throwaway glance. 'You lie easily, too. Come on, we'll go and eat.'

Even as they were making their way down the stairs, the telephone rang.

'Leave it,' Calum snapped.

'I'm going to answer,' Sharon insisted. 'It might be my parents again.' He blocked her way down, so she turned and raced up to the extension. Listening, she heard enough to make her grip the receiver before flinging it down.

'I did warn you,' Calum commented unsympathetically.

They sat at a candlelit table in a restaurant bearing a Tudor façade. The meal was good, the presence of the vitally-alive man seated opposite her making Sharon's taste buds function at peak form. Even dry bread, she reasoned, would have tasted wonderful in the circumstances.

Part of her wanted to feel euphoric because in only a few hours' time she would become this man's wife. The more rational part of her held her emotions tethered, telling her that to Calum her intrusion into his life held purely nuisance value. This she knew she would have to accept and live with all the time she bore his name.

During the meal, he had seemed preoccupied. This had left her thoughts free to roam. They did not go far, only stretching across the table to touch, in her imagination, those grooved cheeks, that hard jaw. His jacket was of fawn cord, casually yet well styled. He had found a tie in his car, and this in itself had lifted him into a different category of person from the wide-open-spaces individual she had come to know so well on the island.

When at last he surfaced to reality, the meal was over. He smiled, searching for his credit card. 'You'll make me a good wife, Miss Mason. You know when to leave me to my thoughts.'

She smiled back. 'I wouldn't have dared to intrude on them,' she replied, thinking, As you have intruded on my innermost being, stealing all my self-reliance and causing me to be only half alive when you're not here. 'That thing you call your secret self—you said it was something no woman would be allowed to know, and most certainly not me.'

'And then you gave me the "keep off" sign.'

Her smile was banished. 'That's something you'll always get from me.'

His face echoed her seriousness as he rose, helping her with her jacket.

Calum's home was on the edge of the countryside, some miles north of the London suburb where Sharon had lived with her parents. It was almost dark by the time they approached the house, but Sharon could see in the headlights' glare the way the drive opened out into a circular sweep of gravel.

The engine noise faded, leaving the silence of a deepening darkness. Calum turned, resting his arm along the back of Sharon's seat. 'Shall I carry you over the threshold as all good bridegrooms should?' he asked, voice and eyes mocking.

'I'm not your bride,' Sharon replied tartly.

'In two days' time you will be.'

'Two days? That's simply not possible. The notice would be too short.'

'Notice of our marriage has already been given. The evening you arrived back on the mainland, you phoned Jack Wilson. Correct?'

Sharon nodded.

'He called me right after that. Next morning I went out and bought a licence. Here it is.' He pulled it from an inner pocket.

Sharon stared. 'But by then I'd decided I wouldn't need anyone's protection, not even my parents'. The press and the public had stopped pestering me. They'd forgotten the whole episode. Then,' her gaze widened, 'it all began again. A reporter phoned me . . .' She grasped his arm, shaking it. 'You *must* have told them! You must have called your press contacts and told them I was back in circulation.'

His hand came across and gripped her wrist, throwing it from him.

'I know why you did it,' she accused. 'Publicity is what you were after, wasn't it?' She stared fiercely at his profile sculpted against the darkness. 'I understand all about that subject. I asked Daryl once why he'd asked me to marry him when he was really married to the sea.' She spoke bitterly and gazed through the windscreen.

Pausing, she glanced at him again. Calum had not moved and she wondered if he was listening. Determinedly, she continued.

'Know what he told me? Having a fiancée added the human touch to his public image. He said,' her voice wavered and she felt the cool glance of her companion upon her, 'that a beautiful woman by his side at the moment of victory made all the women watching the television and seeing the pictures in the papers identify madly with me and worship him as I worshipped him.' She added in a whisper, 'He said nothing about loving me.'

The only move Calum made was to push the marriage licence back into his pocket.

'So now perhaps you understand,' she finished, 'why I'd made up my mind never to get entangled with another famous man. Also, why I didn't want to marry you. Now, because of *your* search for publicity, all the nastiness has started again.'

Calum opened his door, climbed out and walked unhurriedly to the passenger's side. He motioned to Sharon to get out. 'I could answer your accusations,' he said coldly, 'but I'm damned if I'm going to bother.'

Sharon felt she could not let the subject drop. They faced each other, a mere pace apart. She could feel his body-warmth coming at her, magnet-like drawing her towards him. 'Why did you do it, Calum?' she asked with a break in her voice.

A hand came out and outlined her waist and hip. 'You think of a reason, honey.' The endearment sounded hollow. 'You tell me why I did it.'

'You thought—you thought it was time you killed your playboy image?'

'Is that what you think? How would that tie in with the accusation you made on the island that I lived rough for the sake of publicity?'

For a moment she was disconcerted, then she offered the only answer she could think of. 'Some people on your social level will do anything for publicity.'

'Listen, Sharon. I don't give a damn for social levels. I earn and live by the exercise of my intellect, not the people I might occasionally have to mix with. The only publicity a good writer needs is the quality of the writing he turns out, plus his ability to satisfy the readers of the category he's chosen to write for. Stop equating me with your late lover Daryl Irwin. He needed publicity to boost his confidence sufficiently to win yacht race after yacht race. I'm not in the game of winning races.'

'Or even hearts,' she retorted, immediately regretting the words.

His arm went round her shoulders and he propelled her towards the house. 'I'm not out to win your heart, honey. Mine's not on offer, either. Do I make myself clear?'

Sharon came to a halt. She could not still her trembling lip. 'You're an ice-cold brute. The thought of even taking your name fills me with horror.'

'Will you stop being melodramatic?' He turned her, his hands on her waist. The moon sailed out from behind a cloud, but its light showed her nothing in his face to give her hope.

He went on, 'You still haven't come to terms with your immediate future, have you? In two days' time, you and I will go through a ceremony which will make me your husband and at the same time deliver you to me, legally and indisputably, as my wife.'

She tried to wriggle free, but he held her firmly.

'After that,' he pursued the subject relentlessly, 'I can take you to bed with me and keep you there for as long as I decide.' His fingers turned her rebellious face towards him. 'Afterwards, I can push you out and,' his mouth lowered, surprising hers, then lifted, 'tell you to get the hell out of my room.'

Tearing free, Sharon ran back down the drive. His footsteps were gaining on her. She was caught by her jacket collar, jerked round and marched unceremoniously towards the house.

Calum used his key and urged her inside, closing the door, and switching on the light. Only then did he release her. Her eyes flashed as she faced him. 'Next time

I'll run faster,' she asserted. 'You can't make me marry you.'

His look was long and penetrating. He opened the door. 'Right. You can go.'

For a moment, she felt like a climber who had lost her balance, then she rallied. 'When I'm ready to go, I'll go, I promise you.' She made a commendable effort to sound offhanded.

A smile passed over his lips. 'I'll get your cases,' he said, going outside. Returning with them, he put them down. 'I'll carry them upstairs later.' He gestured to a door.

As she went towards it, Sharon's eyes followed the bold sweep of the staircase. The floor area of the entrance hall, she estimated, was large enough in itself to be used as a lounge.

'It's a beautiful house, Calum,' she commented, adding with an impish smile, 'and it definitely puts you into the higher-than-high income bracket!'

He smiled faintly and stood back, allowing her to precede him into the living-room. Its spaciousness struck her first, its aura of good living and even better taste. To one side there were floor-to-ceiling bookshelves. Another wall bore a rectangularly hung group of paintings, modern and varied in subject.

The velvet-covered three-piece suite stood on a beige carpet. There was, along yet another wall, a spread of stereo equipment, complete with floor-standing speakers. 'Just looking at it relaxes you,' Sharon said, with an appreciative sigh.

'No doubts now about marrying me?' She caught the irony in his glance and grew angry.

'I could live in a tent with the man I loved.'

A quizzical eyebrow rose. 'We must try it some time.'

He had put her on the defensive. 'I didn't say you were the man I loved.'

'Then why did you lie to your parents?' He appeared to enjoy the confusion his words had caused, and gave a good imitation of a sigh. 'I really thought you meant it.'

'What good would it have been if I had meant it?' she blurted out. 'You wouldn't be any use to a loving wife. You're self-contained. You told me. Plus you quoted John Donne. You're "an island", you said, "entire of yourself".'

'Under our verbal agreement,' he returned coldly, 'I have no intention of being of use to my wife, loving or otherwise. So why the accusation?'

Her only defence now was to retort, 'I'm sorry. How stupid of me to forget.' Her sarcasm elicited no comeback from him. She turned away, listening to his footsteps receding. Remorse, plus her love for him, made her call, 'Calum?' The footsteps stopped. 'I really am sorry.'

His broad back, which was towards her, slackened like anger leaving him. He faced her, waiting.

Under his cold regard, she said, 'You're doing me a favour, Calum. I'll never be able to—to repay you.' The hard line of his mouth gave her no encouragement to continue. All the same, she did. 'Not—not even when we're married. Because of that verbal agreement. So I want you to know how grateful I am for all you're doing to help me.'

His lazy stride brought him to face her. His eyes held a strange light and his hand cupped her face. 'We could tear that agreement up. I could make love to you—passionate love—if that's what you want.'

Her blue-green eyes, with their sea-depths, shone into the winter grey of his, and the light in them grew brighter. For a moment Calum regarded her tremulous smile, then blotted it out with his rough kiss. As if it was not enough, his arms gathered her to him, and she felt the reined passion within him straining to break free.

Her arms wrapped about his neck and she made no attempt to hide how much her desire was rising to make an ardent response to his. Then it was as if they were back on the island and harsh words drifted into her mind like the rough sea hammering at the cliffs.

You? he'd said. I wouldn't trust you any farther than I could see you. You're on the banned list, he'd informed her, strictly not wanted. Rattler, he'd called her, a snake ... And he had said, *You*, with your past history?

His lips were on her throat now, his hand cupping the thrusting shape of her. He was crumpling that verbal agreement with his lips and his caressing hands and she could not—would not—let him.

Her growing fury gave her strength and she managed to convey, by her twisting, struggling body, that she had had enough. Slowly his head lifted and he saw the storm in her eyes.

Sharon tugged her dress into place, retreating a few steps. ' "If that's what you want", you said,' she quoted his words. 'What I want! How kind of you to give your lovemaking away! Well, you can keep it. I don't want your love offered to me as if I were a charity, as if you were doing me a kindness.'

'Doing you a kindness? Honey, I was doing myself a favour. A man has his needs. After two years with your late fiancé, you should know that.'

She was shaking her head when the telephone rang. She put her bunched fist to her mouth, her eyes lifting to his in fear. 'It isn't the press, surely? They wouldn't know I was here.'

He was on his way to answer, entering another room, half-closing the door. 'Who?' he asked. 'Maida, honey! Yes, I've been out. Where have I been? Dining out, if you must know. Alone? Why should I tell you? Yes, you can come round, I've a spare hour or so. Fifteen minutes? I'll be right here on the doorstep to welcome you.' The receiver crashed down.

Sharon turned to go back to the living-room, but she was too slow.

'Enjoy what you heard?' Calum queried. 'That agreement remains intact. So I'm free as a bird to have whatever damned woman to this house that I want. Understand?'

She moistened her lips. 'I understand.'

'Good. I'll take your cases up to your room. Follow me.'

Sharon trod each stair as if it burned her feet. Her instinct was to run again, but she had already faced the fact that she could not run for ever. Even if she did, the shadow of this man would follow her wherever she went.

It was large for a guestroom and, no doubt about it, furnished with feminine occupation in mind. Calum lifted her cases to a stand. 'Unpack at your leisure. The bathroom is through that door. You'll be here for quite a time, so make yourself at home. Oh, and——' he paused at the door, 'in your own interests, while Maida's here I would advise you to stay in your room. If she sees you, she'll tell the world, and you wouldn't want that all over again, would you?'

His cruel provocation incensed her. 'Do you know something, Mr Darwin?' she spat, eyes flaring. 'I'm beginning to hate you!'

His wide shoulders lifted. 'So you're starting to hate me. Before many weeks have passed, my love, you'll probably wish you'd never met me.'

CHAPTER SEVEN

IF he can invite Maida here, then I could invite any man I liked. The thought buoyed up her wilting spirits, causing her to push back her shoulders in defiance as she gazed through the bedroom window into the darkness.

In the lights coming from the house, she could just see the outline of Maida's small car. The door bell had chimed at the moment that Calum had reached the foot of the stairs.

In her desire to remain unseen, Sharon had not gone to the top of the stairs to see where he had taken his visitor, but the thought of that long and comfortable couch teased her mind unbearably.

Turning from the window, she wandered round the bedroom, liking the delicate shade of green in which it had been furnished. There was hidden lighting, a table was pushed up to a full-length mirror, with a stool on which to sit to apply make-up or arrange her hair.

That night she slept deeply. Here, she sensed, was security, with Calum's house offering her the same unwavering stability and barrier to life's poisoned barbs which had so often made her their target in the past few months.

Dressing after a quick shower, she hoped Calum would not object to her simple style of dress. Spending the day in jeans and casual top on the island was one thing. Wearing similar clothes while living in a rich man's house was another, even though that 'rich man' had not so long ago lived beside her in a tent.

Sharon's thoughts rebelled at the thought of discovering Maida making Calum's breakfast. No smell of cooking greeted her as she found her way to the kitchen. There were two unwashed cups on the breakfast bar and a used coffee pot. The most modern array of kitchen equipment she had seen gleamed in the bright daylight.

It was then that the silence struck her. Was Calum out? Or had he gone to spend the night with Maida? The thought fired her footsteps into action. They took her to the slightly opened door she had passed on her way to the kitchen.

Easing the door open, she stepped inside. With a shock, she saw that Calum was stretched full-length, shirt open, shoes removed, on what appeared to be a divan bed, minus headboard, running along one wall. Here again were floor-to-ceiling bookshelves, built-in this time, the books at all angles as if often consulted and carelessly replaced.

Filling the bay window was a cushion-covered window-seat overlooking a flower-filled garden, which appeared to stretch endlessly, except that it went down a slope and out of sight.

Pine cabinets, side-by-side, bulged open with sheets of manuscript and proof copies. Chaos reigned happily, and it seemed to Sharon to be an area into which the housekeeper had been forbidden to stray.

'I don't recall giving you permission to enter my den.' The icy voice had her spinning round to gaze at the hard grey eyes of the speaker.

The idea that he would exclude her, who tomorrow would be his wife, from his place of work incensed her. 'It's obvious you've let someone enter part of your *secret self*, isn't it?' She pointed to two used coffee mugs standing on an extension desk. 'Plus two more in the kitchen. It was Maida, wasn't it?' she accused, ignoring her own better judgment which urged her to silence. She indicated the bed on which he lay. 'Is this where you and she spent the night, then you turned her out before I came down?'

He was on his feet before she could blink. 'Are you standing in judgment on me? You dare to do that, with your polluted past?' His face was white with anger, and Sharon trembled inwardly. She had delved too deeply with her verbal sword-thrusts and discovered a sleeping tiger.

He was gripping her shoulders now and shaking her, but it seemed it was not enough for him to see her pale face moving backwards and forwards, her eyes glazed with fear. He propelled her backwards until she fell on the bed. He lifted her legs and threw them down, so that she was lying flat.

His hands tore open her buttoned top, jerking it off her arms. His face had changed and she stared into the eyes of a terrifying stranger. 'Please, Calum, don't, *don't* . . .'

He was not listening. Now he was beside her, unfastening her bra and hurling it away. His mouth covered the rising peaks of her breasts, bringing to them, without gentleness or compassion, a thrusting hardness which had her body arching to please him, to do with her whatever he wanted.

Until she felt the roughness of his flesh against the length of her she did not realise that his hands had been busy removing all barriers to his access to every part of her.

This was something she had never known, this abandonment of all restraint, this desire to please, to give of herself in her entirety. She whispered his name and gripped his bare shoulders, moving her curling fingers to rake through his hair.

Then she remembered that, only hours earlier, he had been making love to Maida, probably in this room and on this bed. She managed to free her mouth from his. 'You—you called *me* the polluted one,' she accused, 'when it's really you who's polluted.' She pushed at his shoulders but made no impression. 'It isn't long since Maida was here, where I am now, and you and she . . .' Her voice faltered at the thought.

'Say what you like,' he said harshly, 'I'm making you mine. Tomorrow, we shall marry——'

Her head turned from side to side to evade his searching mouth. 'We made an agreement . . . you said you wouldn't touch me, wouldn't have any use for me as a wife.' She knew she was talking in vain.

'You've forgotten one thing.' His head lifted and his hard grey eyes held hers in bondage. 'The agreement doesn't yet apply. We aren't yet married.'

He gave her no chance to reply. His mouth clamped over hers, forcing back her head until it sank into the cushion beneath it. She felt the sharpness of his teeth pressing into the sensitive interior of her lips, but even that sensation was overriden by the feel of his feathering palm moving downwards over the fullness and the curving shape of her, bringing every part he touched to throbbing life.

In the pit of her stomach there was an ache, and she knew now that this could only be appeased by allowing him to take everything that he demanded of her. Her mind was too dazed now to force her body to offer any resistance.

When she felt his possessive hand finding and stroking intimate parts of her, she cried out in her need for him. His hard body moved to cover hers and the woman in her welcomed the forcefulness of his unbounded desire.

There was one plea she had to make and she whispered, 'Please, oh, please be careful. I've never . . .'

He had not heeded her words and she could not contain within her throat the cry that was torn from her. Through the mists, she heard the catch of his breath, then she was lost in him.

The ecstasy of belonging to him was singing within her. She had not yet descended from the heights to which his possession had lifted her, when she heard him say huskily,

'Sharon mine, you should have told me.'

'I tried, I tried,' she whispered back, her fingers pressing into his hard-muscled back, then moving convulsively across the breadth of his shoulders.

He was placing light kisses along her mouth, down her throat to nuzzle the softness of her breasts, making them tingle yet again. It was as though he had not heard her. 'Baby, why didn't you say I was the first?' His passion lingered, lighting the moments that followed like those island sunsets.

He was no longer possessed by an insistent demand, but tender and caressing. He had been satiated and in that state, forgiving. She wondered if he knew it was she, Sharon, to whom he was talking and not Maida who, only hours before, had been with him.

His hands held her face and his mouth twisted to cross hers, forcing open her lips so that he could explore once more her mouth's sweetness.

His eyes held a look of intense pleasure, something beyond her understanding. Her knowledge of men was small, but she knew by his face that she must have pleased him. Together, they had reached a summit, and the joy of attaining it still throbbed within her.

Tenderly, she cradled his head on her breast, until he moved to place his head beside hers. He slept, his arms around her, holding her possessively where his cheek had just rested.

Carefully Sharon reached down to the floor for the quilt which had been over him, pulling it to cover them both. Then she lay watching, through the still-pulled curtains, the sun on its path across the windows. At first, she mused, he had invaded her life. Then he had stormed into her mind. Now he had intruded upon her heart and finally, most treasured fact of all, upon her body.

Whether or not he wanted her love, he had it, and for ever. He was her first and only lover. Although tomorrow she would become his wife, she had to accept that she would never be able to tell him of the love she felt for him.

Her eyelids fluttered and closed. Side by side, they slept.

The shrilling of the telephone awoke them. Reluctantly, Sharon surfaced from her dream, to find that the dream was indeed reality and that she was locked in Calum's arms.

When Calum moved, she clung to him. Something told her that if she let him go, he would never return. His fingers started to prise her hands from around his waist, and at once she moved her arms, experiencing a pinprick of anguish that, having made such passionate love to her, he should now be so anxious to release himself from her hold.

Seeing his body fully for the first time, just before he pulled on some clothes, gave her a shock. The sinewy toughness of his thighs, his leanness, the absence of any surplus flesh, put admiration into her gaze and shyness into her eyes.

His raised brows told her he had witnessed her inspection of him and that he was amused. The memory of the feel of him against her speeded up her pulse rate and she experienced another shock—at the way the very feminine responses inside herself were reactivated at the thought and the sight of him.

He went out, silencing the phone at last. He seemed to be speaking from the entrance hall, despite the fact that there was an extension telephone on his desk. It had, it seemed, been switched off, since the ringing sound had not come from that.

Sharon tried her best not to listen, but he had left the door ajar and his voice filtered in. 'Maida? Yes, I was expecting you to call me.'

Rising from the bed, Sharon bent slowly to pick up her scattered clothes, putting them on. Her heart had been floating on a cloud; now it was in fragments at her feet. Like a used and discarded woman, Calum had left her to speak to the one who really meant something to him.

Tomorrow he would become her husband in the eyes of the law. Today he spoke to his mistress with welcome in his voice, within the hearing of the woman he was so soon to marry.

Sinking to the bed, she waited, hands clasped. At least she knew he had another woman. Daryl had kept his a secret to the very end.

Calum appeared at the door. 'I'm lunching with Maida.'

Sharon did not raise her head. 'So I gathered from your conversation.'

'I don't know what you're thinking, but it's business. We're discussing her interpretation of her part in the film.' Sharon was silent. He picked up his shirt. 'I'm going to have a shower.' Sharon nodded. 'You, too?'

Sharon shrugged. 'Later.'

'Something wrong?'

She did not answer.

'Get yourself an outfit for the wedding.' Again she nodded. 'Need some money?'

'No, thank you. My bank account balances. My cheques don't bounce.'

'Okay, okay, I just asked.' He came to stand in front of her. At last she looked at him, hoping to find the lover, but instead, the 'island man' stood there, self-contained, his 'secret self' intact. 'I never asked you before—do you have a job?'

'I work for my father. I'm a secretary to one of the partners in his accounting firm.' Her jaw jutted defiantly. 'He pays me well, my father. He's not mean, just because I'm a member of the family.'

If he could go back to his rough-hewn self, then so could she.

'Dad gave me time off to recover from—from past events.' Her hard smile hid her misery at the sight of his thinning lips. Had they, only a few hours ago, coaxed her into giving over her body into his keeping? 'I went to Cuilla to get away from it all, but I had to meet you. Ironic, wasn't it?'

He did not answer. When he had reached the door, she called him and he stopped. 'Doesn't it prove anything, Calum?'

'Doesn't what prove what?'

She stood and faced him across the room. 'Are you being deliberately obtuse?' She felt like crying. Her tensing muscles held the feeling in place. 'Our—our lovemaking . . . you being the first.' Still he did not speak. She could not contain her anger. 'Doesn't it tell you that Daryl and I weren't lovers, and that I didn't live with him for two years?'

'It tells me that, yes.'

'So can't you, with your writer's mind, deduce from that that other reports about me might have been wrong?'

There was a pause. His eyes did a swift digest of her assets, ending with her flushed face and tousled black hair. 'While admitting that the report about your living with your late fiancé was untrue, I can't use the fact as a basis for conceding that the other stories the press printed about your relationship with him were incorrect.

One simple thing stops me—your assertion that you're unable to produce a shred of evidence to the contrary.'

Steadily she held his gaze. He waited, seemingly giving her yet another chance to clear herself, then with a shrug he turned and went up the stairs.

Sharon ran into the hall. 'Can I come with you when you meet Maida for lunch?' She expected a negative in reply, and she was not disappointed.

'The answer's "no".'

'So I can call anyone I like—any *man* I like—and ask him to take me out to a meal.'

Calum seemed about to nod, but checked the action. 'Which man?' He was leaning on one arm on the banister rail.

Her shoulders lifted. 'Any man I fancy. Lee Banks, maybe.'

He started down the stairs, flinging away his shirt. Sharon forced herself not to back away. He stopped at the foot. His fingers gripped her shoulders, pulling her against the length of him. Her hands found his bare ribs, pushing at them in an effort to hold him off, but the feel of his leanness, the muscular toughness just above his waistband threatened to fan the fires of her desire.

'If I catch you dating that swine Lee Banks, I'll flay you to within an inch of your life.' He shook her. 'Do you hear?'

'You wouldn't dare!' Her words were brave, but inwardly she trembled.

'You dared me earlier. Are you repeating your folly?' His hands moved to rest on his hips. 'Maybe you want a repeat performance. I can oblige. I'm on peak form.' She shook her head miserably, still remembering the joy and after that, the tenderness. A 'performance'—was that how he regarded those precious moments of passion?

He went on, 'As for *daring* to flay you, if you provoked me enough I'd dare, my girl, even though you might bear the scars for the rest of your life.'

She turned her back on him and walked towards the kitchen, hearing him mount the stairs. There was food in the fridge. There were pans and crockery too, but her appetite had left her. She'd make herself some coffee after her shower. The daily papers had dropped to the porch floor.

Taking them through to the kitchen, she placed them on the breakfast bar top. One was a quality paper, the other in a tabloid format. For a few minutes she searched in the first paper for a mention of Calum's announcement, finding it tucked away discreetly in a corner.

When she looked at the second newspaper, there was no need for her to search for anything. It came right out and hit her eyes—a photograph of herself, smiling brilliantly, and taken at the celebration of one of Daryl's triumphs. His picture had been carefully cut away. There was another, of Calum this time, apparently escorting a woman friend. Her identity was not revealed, since her picture had suffered the same fate as Daryl's.

It was not so much the photographs as the words that aroused her anger. Whereas the wording of the larger paper had been discretion itself, the other devoted half of its front page to the subject.

' "Save Me First" girl Sharon to wed millionaire writer Calum Darwin,' the headlines shrieked. 'Mr Darwin, one-time investigative journalist, announced his engagement in a telephone conversation with our reporter. Did Mr Darwin not consider the change of heart on his bride-to-be's part to be rather sudden, not to say a little insensitive in the circumstances?

'Mr Darwin carefully dodged the question. 'It was a whirlwind romance,' Calum Darwin claimed. 'We met,

I saw, she conquered.' See next page,' the instruction directed.

The reporter than launched into a replay of the last moments of Daryl Irwin, Olympic yachtsman, and the part 'his fiancée' had alledgedly played in saving herself before the great man. There it was again, the 'facts' that weren't facts, the 'truth' that was a bunch of lies from start to finish.

Rolling the paper into the shape of a stick, Sharon hammered the breakfast stool seat with it, then hurled it across the room. She had not aimed at the doorway, but it went flying through it, to be caught and met with a curse and a question, 'What the hell's going on here?'

Calum was dressed for going out. In his dark suit and sober tie, he looked like the man whose photograph she had first seen on his book covers—self-assured, handsome and utterly beyond reach. Yet all this was not for her, but for Maida Halliday, the real woman in his life.

The thought took her words in answer up a note or two. 'Read it,' she cried, 'it's all there, all over again. Your announcement tore open the garbage bag of untruths that most newspapers store about well-known individuals in the cellars or the "morgues" in the filing cabinets of their offices.'

He read the offending passages. It did not take him long. Sharon flopped on to the stool. 'Why can't they leave me alone now? Why can't I sue them for defamation of character or something?'

Calum folded the paper and tossed it on to a work top. 'It wouldn't be worth your father's money.'

'My father's?' she asked uncertainly. 'Tomorrow I shall be your wife.'

'Precisely.' He strolled towards her, hands in pockets. 'After a few days, it will all die down again. They'll lose interest in you. Resorting to litigation would only fan the flames and keep the fire burning for months.'

Sharon's leg swung as she stared at the tiled floor. Calum's fingers lifted her chin, but if she had expected tenderness, her hopes were immediately dashed. His smile was cynical as he commented,

'In any case, if I'm going to spend money going to law on someone's behalf, I make darned sure first that I shall win my case. Since you've admitted to me more than once that you can produce no evidence to prove your innocence of the things the media are accusing you of—sorry, lady,' his lips brushed hers, 'no sale.'

She gave a heavy sigh, then looked him over. 'You smell nice. You've shaved,' she remarked. 'You're smoother now than when we—when we——' with her thumb she indicated the room where he worked.

His arms went round her and with his cheek he pushed her head aside to nuzzle her neck. 'You look nice, too,' he muttered, between kisses. 'You smell nice as well.'

Cold shivers made her skin prickly at the touch of him and she threw back her head. 'I haven't washed,' she pointed out, 'so how——?'

'You have a "woman" scent, and it's all your own, deliciously feminine. I'm hooked on it, baby, and I can't keep away from you.'

He lifted his head and smiled into her eyes. Her heart was hammering. Was he remembering the delights of their lovemaking? Something made her probe. 'You're lying about Maida, Calum. She stayed on and slept with you there before I did. Those coffee mugs——'

He withdrew from all contact, moving away. His eyes had cooled to zero.

'Were all mine,' he interposed. 'I worked, drank coffee, worked again. I slept for a time on the couch—which is why it's been made up as a bed—then I made more coffee and worked again. Right through the night, until you came into my dream.'

'Don't try and soft-soap me, Calum, with pretty

phrases.' She was deadly serious now. 'I'll have my own back and ask you to produce evidence that Maida didn't stay the night—or part of it.'

'I'm damned if I'm going to lower myself to the level of a henpecked husband by defending any real or mythical night with another woman.' His features had angled into hardness. 'We're not even married yet. And even when we are, you know the score.'

'Freedom on both sides.'

'On both sides,' he agreed.

'I'll remember that,' she hit back, 'when I'm inviting a man to join me for the evening!'

His only reaction was to stare coldly at her defiant face, then to rake her body with a frozen glance. 'Go and find something better to wear. Someone might call, and what a story it would make if the future Mrs Calum Darwin opened the door looking like a teenager after an all-night party.'

She was off the stool and leaping at him. 'Why, you——'

The telephone rang. He bowed mockingly and went to answer it.

'Your housekeeper hasn't come,' she called after him.

'I gave her an indefinite vacation. I said I'd call her when I wanted her back.'

So the caller was not his housekeeper. Was it Maida again? It seemed it was not. Calum shouted her name, then handed her the receiver.

'Not the press?' she whispered, her eyes widening.

He shook his head. 'Our first congratulatory message, delivered verbally.'

Sharon frowned. 'Yes?' she queried uncertainly. 'Who is that?'

'You may not remember me, young woman.' The voice was deep and full, as if the man was wide-bodied with a wide-ranging imagination to match. 'Am I speaking to that little make-up girl I saw with Calum on the island that day? Or was it an extra I called you?'

'Mr Hardaker!'

'Galton Hardaker, no less, director of your fiancé's film, *Come Night, Come Day*.'

'It's not my film,' Calum muttered in the background.

'I felt I should offer my congratulations,' Galton Hardaker went on. 'I'm delighted that my old friend Calum has been caught at last. And by such a notorious young woman, too!'

'Mr Hardaker, please . . .' Sharon's voice faltered. 'Don't believe everything you read in the papers about me.'

'My dear, I'm too old a hand to believe a word the newspapers say.'

'My—my fiancé does, Mr Hardaker.'

'Ah, that's because he's my junior by twenty-odd years. Too young to disbelieve anything he reads. Remember he was a journalist once, writing those lies about other people.'

Calum grunted behind her, muttering a curse or two. Galton Hardaker heard him and his growling laugh came over the wire.

'Also,' Galton went on, 'he has a personal interest in those stories cooked up by his one-time colleagues. Tell him that, investigation being his speciality, he should do a little of it where his future wife's past is concerned. He owes that to her, at least.'

Eyes bright with hope, Sharon turned to Calum. 'Did you hear that?'

'I did. So what does he want me to do—go through the archives of all the tabloid newspapers on the market?'

'You don't *want* to prove me right, do you?' she accused, and heard laughter from the earpiece. 'Sorry, Mr Hardaker.'

'Am I eavesdropping on the first family quarrel? Never let it be said you two had a fight with each other on your wedding eve! Is Calum there?'

Sharon handed over. 'Two o'clock tomorrow, Galton. A small reception afterwards at a nearby hotel.' Calum named the place. 'You'll act as a witness? Good. Yes, I've got a second person—Maida.'

CHAPTER EIGHT

THE wedding ring felt strange on Sharon's finger. There was no engagement ring to accompany it. Calum had asked her if she would like one, but she had refused. If he had produced one and pushed it unasked on to her finger, she would have been delighted. Even if it had meant nothing to him, she could have held on to the tiny thread of hope that he had had sufficient feeling for her to go into a shop and choose one.

Now she felt the gold band and turned it round and round. Her thoughts followed a similar path. She was dazed and dazzled and bewildered. The ceremony and the reception were over. With Calum beside her, they were walking away from the hotel with the sounds of voices wishing them happiness and joy in the future.

Sharon asked herself, What joy, what future? She brushed confetti from the shoulders of her cream-coloured two-piece suit and from around the neck of her shell-pink blouse. In spite of the agreement they had made about going their separate ways, the radiance of a bride illuminated her blue-green eyes and put a curve around her well-shaped lips.

Turning to look at Calum—who gazed straight ahead—she saw confetti on his jacket. Reaching up, she brushed it from his shoulder—and a camera flashed.

'No!' The shriek came involuntarily from her, revealing that her fear of the news media lay just beneath her skin.

At once Calum's arm went round her waist and he drew her close to his side. He halted, holding her still, and the camera flashed again. He was looking at the photographer and the other young man beside him.

'Want something?' Calum drawled.

The photographer laughed uncomfortably. 'Thought you'd welcome the publicity, Mr Darwin.'

'The readability of my writing is all the publicity I need, thanks.'

'What about your wife? Can we have a word with her, then?'

Sharon raised her head and looked beseechingly at Calum's hard-hewn profile. 'Calum?' she asked.

When he answered, 'Why don't you ask her?' Sharon pressed agitated fingers into his arm.

'You can't let me down now,' she whispered.

'Stand on your own two feet, honey,' was his callous reply.

'But you offered me the protection of your name——'

'Which you now have. I didn't undertake to be your mouthpiece. Fight your own battles with the media.'

Sick at heart at his shattering change of attitude now she was his wife, Sharon turned to the two men. 'What do you want to know?'

'How does it feel, Mrs Darwin, to be the wife of a famous, not to say rich man, only three months after losing the other famous man you were to marry?'

Sharon made a play of consulting her watch. 'Two hours since we married.' Her smile was convincingly bright. 'Ask me in two years.'

'Which is how long you were engaged to Daryl Irwin.'

'My,' she hit back, 'you've been doing your homework!'

The young man looked disgruntled. 'How do the late Mr Irwin's parents feel about your marrying so soon after the loss of their son?'

It was a barbed question, probably out of revenge for

her sarcastic attitude. 'Try asking them.' She felt Calum like a rock beside her, but they were not touching.

'Any regrets, Mrs Darwin, about crying out for help while your late fiancé was drowning beside you?'

'He had already gone down. It would have been useless . . .' She realised then that she had played right into the reporter's hands. Her face was flushed again, not with radiance this time, but sheer fury. 'I wasn't there, was I? *I was not there!*'

'No, you weren't, Mrs Darwin. By then you were safely in the arms of the rescuer. You'd saved your own skin.'

'If you know so much,' she flung back, 'why bother to question me? Go and make up the story out of your own head.'

'Isn't that what you said last time, Mrs Darwin?'

Her body started trembling and she hardly noticed Calum's hand grip hers. 'Are you from that—that particular newspaper?'

'I am. Which is how I "did my homework", Mrs Darwin.'

'Then you know all there is to know.' The man was closing his notebook. 'Except one thing,' Sharon continued. He opened it again. 'Which is this.' Her head came up, the small cream-coloured hat she wore perching on top of it. She lifted her hand which was in the firm clasp of the man beside her. 'I love my husband more than I ever thought it possible to love any man. And that is the truth, which I hope you will print like a shining light among all the rest of your lies.'

'We could sue you for slander, Mrs Darwin,' the reporter threatened, only half serious.

'Go right ahead and sue,' she called from over her shoulder as she walked away with Calum at her side. 'I could tell you a story that would make the ink in your journalistic veins turn cold at the thought of all the libel actions *I* could bring against *you*!'

There was no response from the reporter who, with his colleague, walked in the opposite direction.

Calum's car was parked at the rear of the hotel. Sharon sat staring through the windscreen at a brick wall. Her husband sat beside her studying the wall as if he had never seen one like it.

'You handled them well. You sounded like an old hand at the question-parrying game. Why did you appeal to me to come to your aid?'

'Maybe because I was afraid I'd—well, say too much.'

He turned his frown on her. 'Too much? About what?'

The truth was tearing at her throat in its effort to get out, but she swallowed it down. They hadn't forgotten, those newsmen, had they? If she told Calum, he was still journalist enough to make every effort to set the record straight, for his journalistic principles' sake, if not his wife's.

Then the Irwins would be involved, plus Daryl's secret liaison with an unknown woman which, Daryl's father had said, would besmirch his son's still sacred reputation and his wonderful record of victories. It was these thoughts that kept her silent.

'About what?' Calum repeated, but Sharon only shook her head. Had she done enough to allay Calum's suspicions?

'About our—our agreement,' she invented. Calum's expression hardened visibly and he fired the engine.

The house still lacked the feel of a home. There was no warmth of welcome, nothing to make you run into it as if it had arms to wrap around you and tell you that this was where you belonged.

Sharon knew the reason the moment she stepped over the threshold. There was no joking about carrying her over, no melting of body into body, no smile even from the man with whom, earlier that afternoon, she had exchanged the solemn vows of the marriage ceremony.

They went into the living-room. The empty couches and armchairs were a hollow welcome, but the only one she knew she would receive. Their quality reminded her that she had married a rich man. Handsome as Calum looked in his good-quality suit, white shirt and silk tie, there was plenty about him, too, to remind her of his wealth.

His ease of manner came from a knowledge of his proven intellectual ability, his acknowledged status in the world of creative writing. He invited her to sit down. She did so, feeling more like his guest than his bride. He went with an inbuilt self-possession to the drinks cupboard, pouring what he now knew to be his wife's favourite choice.

He held it out to her and lifted his own. 'To us,' he said simply, and she drank with him.

His gaze lingered on her. 'I can just see, through the layer of cosmetics, the girl I first saw on Cuilla.' He sat on the arm of a chair.

Sharon stared at her drink. 'Did—did you like that girl?'

There was a pause, then, 'She intrigued me. Her sharp tongue and her refusal to knuckle under to mankind— and I mean "man"—were a challenge I couldn't resist.'

She smiled. 'Sometimes, you were very rude to me.'

'And you, of course, were politeness itself to me.' She heard the irony and looked up to see his smile.

'You—you acted the adoring husband very well this afternoon, especially at the reception.' He didn't answer, so she supplied her own answer. 'I suppose that was because your literary agent was there, plus a photographer, and Galton Hardaker.'

'I notice you've left out Maida.'

Her head came up swiftly. '*You* should have left out Maida. It made me ill the way you told Galton you'd asked her to be the second witness without telling me first, without even consulting me.'

'You made no objection when I came off the phone.'

'What would have been the use? It was a *fait accompli*, wasn't it? I couldn't see you telling your——' she stopped herself quickly, not wishing to provoke his anger at such a time, 'anybody, having asked them, that you didn't want them at your wedding after all.' She paused. 'All the same,' her smile underlined the lingering brightness in her eyes, 'thank you for pretending you— you loved me.'

He lifted his drink and looked through it as if admiring its colour. 'It wasn't difficult,' he answered at length. His eyes did a swift survey of her clothes and the shape beneath it. 'You're beautiful,' he spoke softly, 'eminently desirable and——' with a meaningful glance, 'very nice to know.'

She wanted to run over to him, put her arms around his neck and pull him down to kiss her. She closed her eyes, picturing the scene, feeling his arms come round her, delighting in his kiss. She opened them to find him staring broodingly at her.

He turned, put down his empty glass and went out. His quick footsteps took the stairs with ease. Sharon heard him moving about overhead and wondered which room she was supposed to occupy. This was their wedding night. Would Calum expect her to share his bed just this once, sleep with him . . . And would they make love?

The thought, without the action, made her throb with longing for the touch of him. Was it only yesterday morning they had lain entangled, sleeping deeply and with complete content after coming together with such a sunburst of passion?

It was some time before she followed him upstairs. Would he take her somewhere special for their evening meal? Surely that didn't contravene the terms of their agreement?

He came out of his room, and she could hardly breathe at the sight of him. His fine clothes had gone. In their place were jeans, a rollnecked sweater and a brown quilted zipped jacket. On his shoulder hung a rucksack. His feet were booted. He had turned back into the island man!

'Where are you going?' she asked in a hoarse whisper.

'Back to Cuilla. Any objections?' His eyes were as remote as the distant mountains seen from the island's hills.

Yes, she wanted to scream, yes, oh yes! How could you leave me like this, without warning, without even a kiss?

She braced her shoulders. 'None at all,' she answered.

'What will you do?'

'You don't really care a jot what I do. However, I shall probably go back to work. The man I work for, my father's partner, probably needs my help by now.'

'There's no need for you to continue working. I've more than enough money for the two of us.'

'That's nice to know.' If he had noticed the sarcasm, he didn't show it. 'But I'd prefer to remain independent of you financially. After all, I'm only a temporary addition to your life, aren't I? When you finally ditch me, I certainly won't lower myself to claw alimony from you. And if you offered it, I'd throw it right back.'

He worked his rucksack round to his back. 'I'll certainly sleep all the better for hearing that piece of news, honey,' he answered caustically, then started down the stairs.

'How——' she had to clear her throat to speak with

sufficient clarity, 'how are you travelling to the island? By car?'

'At this time of day? No, my love,' he spoke mockingly from the foot of the stairs, 'by my own helicopter, which I keep tucked away in the three acres of land which go with this place. I hire a pilot to take me there, then he'll bring it back here.' He raised his hand. 'We must meet again some time. But give me good notice, won't you? My social diary is full until well into the future.' His smile was cynical as he looked up at her.

Sharon did not answer. Had she done so, he would have heard the tears which were gathering in her throat.

'Take care, *Mrs Darwin*,' he called, letting himself out of the house.

After two restless weeks alone in Calum's house, Sharon packed her bags, dressed in jeans, shirt and parka and made for the nearest railway station.

She left the house only three days before her parents were expected back from their cruise. Much as she loved them, she did not feel able to cope with their questions and their probing as to why, on their wedding day, Calum had walked out on her.

Travelling north by train, she arrived at the west coast of Scotland many hours later. Since it was almost dark, she decided to stay the night at the small hotel overlooking the sea. Even when she had started her journey, she knew she would be taking a chance on there being a ferry chartered to take people and props to Cuilla for the film unit. By morning, she hoped, one might arrive.

It was early August and even though it was not yet autumn, there was, next morning, a faint chill in the air. Nearby, there was a shop selling handmade sweaters in the intricate patterns for which some of the Scottish islands were famous.

There were women's kilts for sale, too, in attractive

colours, thick-knit jackets and scarves. Sharon bought some of the woollen and machine-woven garments, nodding in complete agreement when the woman behind the counter told her that not all the manmade cloth in the world could keep a person as warm as wool.

Back in her hotel room, she pushed away the light-weight jacket she had been wearing and pulled a sweater over her blouse. Over it all she wore her new jacket and revelled in its warmth.

Wandering down the quay—this was not an official landing place at which regular ferry services docked—she asked a fisherman who tended his net whether Captain MacAlister's ferry was due to sail that day.

'Ay, lassie,' the man said, giving a weatherbeaten smile. 'You're lucky. He'll be along soon. Is it Cuilla you'll be going to? Well, I did hear they're starting film-ing again over there, so he's things to take out for the director, Mr Hardaker.' He looked up at her. 'You wouldn't be one of the actors, would you?'

Sharon laughed, shaking her head. 'That's another to add to my list. I've been called an extra, a make-up girl and now an actress. No, I'm just a—well, an onlooker, I suppose. I was really in search of peace and quiet.' And my husband, she thought but did not say.

The man laughed. 'You'll no' get much peace while the film crew's in occupation, lassie. Best stay here for that.'

Sharon shook her head and thanked the man, wandering away. It was while she was drinking down her cup of coffee and gazing through the hotel window that she saw Captain MacAlister's ferry sail slowly into view. Paying for the coffee, she pulled on her back-pack, seized her zipped bags and hurried outside.

The ferry crew were readying the boat for mooring. As Sharon waited, she saw the captain on the bridge. He looked, if anything, a little more weather-worn than before, although only a relatively short time had passed since she had last seen him.

He cupped his hands and called, 'You've got an hour or so to wait, young lady, before we sail, but you're welcome on board.'

Sharon nodded, decided to buy a few sandwiches for her lunch and returned to the hotel for them. Arriving back at the quay, she was helped aboard by one of the crew. Seeing some wooden stairs, she climbed down them, finding herself in an area with fixed wooden tables and benches. It was called the saloon.

Dropping her luggage, she found a paperback book and sat back to read it and await the ferry's departure. After a while, other people came down to join her. They nodded but made no attempt to talk to her. Their conversation was exclusively of the film, and she guessed they were some of the people she had seen milling around the film unit's camping site the last time she was there.

Absorbed in her book, only hunger pangs reminded her of her uneaten sandwiches. These she ate, still reading, not caring to look up in case Lee Banks, whom she half feared to meet again, had arrived on board. Listening to the chattering voices, she could not hear any that resembled his. Since she sat apart, he would have come across to her, which could only mean he was not there.

The ferry docked at the jetty. By this time, Sharon had joined the others on deck. With misgivings, yet with a growing excitement, she looked up at the hills of Cuilla, seeking out the hut and the orange-coloured tent. The hut was there—a tiny speck from that distance—but the tent was missing. Did that mean that Calum had decided to live down at the camp site, in more comfortable surroundings than he had occupied before?

Waving to the captain, she laughed as he called out that he was glad that she'd had the good sense, usually lacking in a Sassenach, to come back so soon to one of Scotland's beautiful islands.

The hill path leading to the hut seemed steeper than she remembered, but she gritted her teeth and carried her three bags up to her destination. The key was in her purse. She turned the lock, but it would not move. Puzzled, she drew out the key, looked at it and put it back. Still the lock would not turn—except one way, and that was in the 'lock' position.

At once she unlocked it, reclaiming the key and putting it away. A thought had struck her that had made her breath catch in her throat. Someone was in occupation, and she did not need three guesses as to that person's identity.

Her first thought was to run back, down that hill, straight on to the ferry. The door was creaking open. Calum stood there, hair falling over his forehead, face unshaven, rollnecked sweater up to his shadowed chin. The chance to run had gone.

'Yes?' His voice was cold, his grooved face expressionless.

Wasn't he going to let her in? she wondered, trying to smile. 'You—you don't look surprised to see me.'

'I watched you walk off the ferry and climb the hill.'

'Oh.' This was ridiculous, she thought. This man was her husband. Did he have to be so distant? And did she have to feel so shy? 'Can I——' she peered past him, 'can I come in?'

'If you must.' He stood back and she carried in two of her three bags. He did not carry in the remaining piece of luggage.

Sharon looked around. 'I see you've been working hard. Is it a new book you've started?' Do I have to sound so sickeningly hearty? she wondered.

He did not answer the question. 'Why are you here?' Dropping her bags, she looked at him with surprise.

'I'd have thought that was obvious. I've come back to Cuilla.'

'Rain is wet. Now tell me why you're here.'

'Why are you behaving so—so obnoxiously? I've travelled a long way——'

'Overnight? No? You stayed at the hotel?' She nodded. 'Which means you left yesterday. Why?'

She turned the question round. 'Why did you come back?'

'They're filming here again.'

'From which you've dissociated yourself—you told me that last time, so that's no reason for returning. All right, why did I come back?' She pretended to think. 'Ah, I know. I've still got some vacation left. In fact, with my father as my employer, it could be a vacation without end, if I wanted.'

He folded his arms, his eyes taking in her woollen outfit, which had obviously been newly, and locally, bought. 'Now tell me the real reason.'

'What do you want me to say?' she retorted, unzipping her jacket and looking round in vain for a clear space on which to put it. 'That I couldn't live without you?' Which was true, she admitted silently. 'That I've spent sleepless nights missing your arms around me?' True again, she thought. 'Sorry to disappoint you, but they would all be untruths.'

'Have the press been getting at you again? Is that why you're here?'

'They haven't printed a word about me—us. There hasn't been a phone call. They didn't even use that photograph they took of us on our wedding day.'

He nodded without surprise. 'When they told their editor what you said, he probably wouldn't touch the story.'

'I didn't really mean those threats,' she protested, looking as bewildered as she felt.

'They weren't to know that. One little whisper of a libel action goes a long way in the newspaper world.'

'So I almost got the better of them,' said Sharon, with a reminiscent smile.

'Almost,' he agreed, regarding her thoughtfully. 'Besides, they may have scented another story buried deep among your words.' His eyebrows lifted in a question.

I won't answer it, she thought. I only wish I could, but for the sake of Daryl's parents, I must keep silent about that side—*my* side—of it.

With a lift of the shoulders, she turned away. 'There isn't another story.' There was a long silence. 'Anyway,' she said finally, 'the persecution seems to have stopped at last—from all sides.'

'So the object of our marriage has been achieved.'

'Yes. Thank you.' The formality of their behaviour towards each other, when all she really wanted was to turn and throw herself into his arms, made her want to laugh and cry together. 'How did you get into the hut?'

'Jack Wilson called to see me on his way to the airport. I asked him for his spare key.'

'You told him you wanted it for us to spend our honeymoon here?' she asked over her shoulder.

'He jumped to that conclusion without help from me.'

She nodded, then looked round. 'The—the bed,' she indicated the mound of pillows, sleeping bags, plus discarded clothing, 'can I sleep on that now I'm back?'

'And I camp out in the tent again?'

Sharon pretended to consider. Had she really hoped he would say, You can sleep beside me if you like? 'You could——' she faced him, tugging down her new sweater, 'you could sleep on the floor like you did during that storm, if you like.'

He bowed over his folded arms. 'I appreciate your thoughtfulness, madam. However, having thought it over,' his narrowed glance ran the length of her, 'I've decided to do the gentlemanly thing and put up the tent—for you.'

She was about to thank him, when his meaning hit her. With an agitated hand she pushed back her hair. 'You don't mean I should be the one to sleep in the tent?'

'First come,' he looked round, 'first to occupy. I was first.'

'You were first before, yet you slept in the tent.'

'That was different.' His smile told her he held all the cards—and the hut.

'Yes, it was different,' she agreed. 'We weren't married then. Now we are.'

'To give you my protection, nothing else.'

'Not—not even consideration?' Why did her voice have to waver so?

'On what grounds—that you're a female member of the species? Not on your life. According to women, they're liberated, equal to men. I slept out there. Now it's your turn.'

'But, Calum——' to her intense annoyance, her eyes filled, not with selfpity but with sorrow at his unyielding attitude towards her, 'I'm your wife! Even—even if we don't share the bed, I could at least sleep on the floor here like you did. Couldn't I?' She moistened her lips and felt a tear or two course down her cheeks.

A few strides took him to her. With the back of his hand he wiped at the moistness, bent to kiss the tremulous mouth. 'No.'

She took a deep breath which sucked away her sadness and put anger in its place. 'Why, you——'

His hand covered her mouth, then he took her shoulder and propelled her outside. In a few moments, her jacket and baggage followed.

'You can't do this to me. I'm your wife!' She thrust out her hand and showed him her wedding ring. 'Besides, I——' she looked at him doubtfully, 'I've never put up a tent in my life.'

'No, I didn't think you had, which is why I said I'd do it. The tent's round the back, next to the "necessary".' His brief grin brought back memories of the first day she had met him.

All the time he hammered, she fought a verbal battle, but it was slightly one-sided owing to his curt replies.

'I haven't got a sleeping bag, for a start,' she informed him.

'There's a spare one in the hut.'

'There's nowhere I can put my clothes. They'll get damp. Where can I keep food?'

'I'll make a concession,' his mocking smile flashed up at her briefly, 'I'll share my tins and packets with you.'

'But I've never——'

'Roughed it. Then it's time you learnt.' He rammed the final peg home and straightened. 'You can move in now. The groundsheet's clean and effective. You may get a few flying insects in. Use a repellent, just in case. There's a tube in the hut.'

'I won't sleep, Calum, I know I won't.' Her voice held a deep appeal, echoed in her eyes.

Calum tilted her chin, gazed into her depths, and with a finger, followed the line of her lips. 'Did I remember to tell you you're beautiful, that night you slept with me?' He stood away from her wondering, hopeful eyes. 'Some day some man who can bring himself to trust you will love your body, baby, as much as I do.'

He was playing with her emotions like a ball swinging on a long piece of elastic.

'Trust me?' she cried, on the edge of tears. 'You can

trust me, I swear you can trust me. Can't you read between the lines?'

His head was shaking slowly. 'I can't see any lines, so how do you expect me to read between them?' She could find no answer. 'There isn't another story, you said.' He seemed to be waiting again. At last he murmured, 'Please excuse me. I have work to do.'

Moments later, the hut door closed and the sound of a tapping typewriter reached her ears. Lifting the tent flaps, she hoisted in her bags, then retreated backwards, into the fresh, salt-laden air.

Gulls were still flying and crying, the sheep were still contentedly eating. The sea was like a human face, reflecting the moods of the clouds, sometimes blue-gold with glints of sunbeams, sometimes grey as massed clouds drifted by.

The hills beyond climbed and fell away. Promontories of land tapered to points, forming natural bays. The ferryboat moved gently at its mooring. The captain, as usual, was in no hurry to leave. Rocky hillocks were grey and rounded, except where they reflected the sun's gold. Last year's heather, brown now, awaited this year's sighting of purple and green.

Below, the camp site seemed busy, as if preparations were well under way for a new start to the filming. Sharon wondered if Lee Banks had returned. Was Maida down there, too? The thought squeezed at her heart and she turned quickly to retreat into the tent.

Flopping on to the ground sheet, she drew up her knees. She felt for her jacket, then remembered she had left it in the hut. The sleeping bag was in there, too. Soon she would have to disturb Calum and ask for them.

Her chin rested on her hand, her elbow on a knee. It wasn't fair, she told herself. All right, so Calum had arrived first, but he could at least have let her share the hut. Trying to think of an uncluttered open space where she could have put her belongings, let alone slept, she shook her head.

Just as Daryl had been married to the sea, so Calum was married to his writing. I have a genius, she told herself wryly, for forming relationships with men who put me second. With Daryl, she'd come third. This she had learned the hard way, the tragic way. At least, she thought again, I knew about Calum's other woman before I agreed to marry him.

A deep weariness came over her and she lay back, putting her arm across her eyes. The tears, she reminded herself, would make her new sweater wet, but that didn't stop them coming. Here she lay, she thought, with the ring still feeling new on her finger, with her husband a few strides away. She had been rejected by him as thoroughly as the media-led public had rejected her.

He had married her to give her his protection! It was her husband now from whom she needed protection, she thought. Murmurs of words came into her mind from the recent past. A woman's love is something I don't need, he'd said. I wouldn't trust you any farther than I could see you . . . I'll promise you something, Mr Darwin, I'll never adore you, I'll never regard you as a 'dream man' . . .

Sharon rolled over on to her front, trying to gulp back the tears. *He* was her dream man, she did adore him. He had her love and her heart. It was his for the rest of her life. But he didn't need it—he'd told her so.

Our marriage, he'd said, would mean nothing. I'll make no demands. On those terms, she had accepted him, and it was on those terms he was determined that their marriage would continue. We'll set a time limit, he had promised. How long was his 'time limit'?

Turning over and standing up, she ran fingers through

her hair, found a handkerchief and dried her eyes. Maybe, she tried consoling herself, that time limit was a blessing in disguise. Once the divorce was through, she would be able to get on with her life, even if she had to live the length of it without her heart.

CHAPTER NINE

BEING compelled to knock on the door of the hut made her fret. Access to my own husband, she argued silently, while waiting for the door to open, should be free and without barriers.

Looking about her, she noticed that a helicopter occupied the helipad. She knew it was not Calum's by the letters G.H. which were painted in red on the side—Galton Hardaker's, she interpreted, which meant that he had arrived.

Calum pulled irritably at the door and stood regarding her. At first he seemed to be only half aware, the other half, Sharon hazarded, still being with the book he was writing.

His eyes were busy all over her, all the same. 'Your hair needs combing,' he remarked, opening the door wider so that she could enter. He closed it again. 'You've been crying.'

'Sorry to inflict my unattractive face on you,' she responded tartly. 'You're so right—I've been crying. There's no mirror in the tent, so I couldn't check on how terrible I looked.'

He took a rectangular mirror from a shelf and handed it to her.

'Why crying?' he asked, leaning on his shoulder against the wall.

'For my sins of the past, maybe?' she answered with asperity.

'For the untimely loss of a very special man?' he hazarded.

She shrugged, knowing he meant Daryl. 'If it pleases

you to think so.' She thought, He's right—he's the very special man I've lost.

'Can't you forget that Olympic sailor? Does he haunt you even now?'

Her smile was hard, otherwise her lips would have trembled. 'Yes, it plagues me the way I screamed to be rescued before he was.'

He frowned, unbelieving. 'You can joke about something you did that was so cowardly, so craven?'

She flinched at his harsh words, but answered unwaveringly, 'I can joke about something that didn't happen.'

'Proof?' His face was mask-like, his eyes piercing.

Her shoulders sagged. 'No proof to offer, Calum.'

'What do you want?'

She forced herself to meet his icy gaze. 'My jacket, the sleeping-bag. Please.'

He handed them to her, one by one, including the mirror. Hugging the bundle to her, she found it difficult to dispose of the jacket. Calum took it from her and draped it across her back. For a few moments, his hands rested on her shoulders. She wanted to turn her head and rest her cheek against his knuckles, but she did not move.

His grip seemed to tighten, then his hands fell away. At the door, she threw a 'thank you' over her shoulder and made her way carefully down the wooden steps. The door closed behind her.

By the time she had sorted through her bags, selecting the items she would need most, she was ready for an evening meal. Sitting back on her heels, she refused to entertain the idea of knocking yet again on Calum's door and asking for a tin, a saucepan and some means of heating the food.

Looking down at the camp site, she thought she saw someone entering the building which last time was the canteen. Pulling on her jacket, she made her way down the hill to the place which seemed still to be the central eating place. Hands were lifted in recognition and cheerful salutes, while friendly, unquestioning smiles came her way.

The women behind the self-service counter recognised her, too. They chatted for a few moments, expressing their pleasure at the reappearance of all the old faces. Sharon held her tray, looking round for a table.

Her eyes encountered the animated face of Maida Halliday. As usual, she was surrounded by men. Unexpectedly, the woman looked up, seeing Sharon. For a few seconds her expression held total distaste, then the actress in her took over.

Her smile was sparkling and entirely false, reminding Sharon of her wedding day. She had still not really forgiven Calum for asking Maida to act as one of the witnesses. Maida had sparkled then, too, especially when Calum was near.

Sharon carried her tray to an empty table. It was a simple salad meal she had selected, with coffee to follow. While the sound of voices ebbed and flowed around her, she pretended to be absorbed in eating.

'So you married him.' The tone of voice was subdued, but the edge was serrated. Sharon looked up quickly. Lee Banks was smiling with his mouth while his eyes stayed empty. As usual, there appeared to be two personalities warring inside him.

'What did you say?' It took her a few moments to adjust. 'Oh, oh yes.' She looked at her ring. 'How did you hear?'

'Maida told me. May I sit down?' He pulled out a chair. 'I saw the announcement of your engagement in the papers. My guess that day he was seen coming out of your hut that you were having an affair with him must have been right, but why did you have to marry him, Sharon?'

She forked over her salad, her appetite gone. 'Couldn't it have been that I fell in love?'

'Calum Darwin wouldn't marry a girl because she was in love with him. He'd run the other way.'

You can say that again, Sharon thought grimly. 'Well, there's the proof.' She extended her hand, indicating the wedding ring.

'Is that all? No sapphire and diamonds to go with it?'

Sharon hid her wedding ring under the table. 'Your face——' she gave it an exaggerated inspection, 'it's—it's just as handsome as it ever was.'

'No thanks to the man you married.'

'No, well, he—he was only acting like a man in love, I suppose.'

'Darwin—in *love*? Look, Sharon, there must be some reason why he married you, but don't fool yourself it was because he found he couldn't live without you.' A thought struck him. 'You're not expecting——?'

Slowly she shook her head. Swallowing some more food, she put down the fork. 'Did you see the tent go up this morning, beside the hut?'

Lee nodded. 'That's my residence. He—he won't allow me into the hut.'

Lee released a sigh, as if he had solved a problem. 'So that's how it is.' He glanced at his watch. 'I'll have to go. There's a conference about restarting filming. Look, Sharon, can I see you tonight? We could talk——'

She was already shaking her head. The threat Calum had made about what he would do to her if she ever dated Lee Banks would never be forgotten. He had, she was sure, meant every word.

'Sorry, Lee.' She pushed at a piece of lettuce on her plate. 'I'm a married lady now.' She attempted a smile. 'Can't entertain male visitors. Sorry.'

'Just a chat, Sharon. Anyway, he can't keep you on a leash. He's no angel himself.'

That last statement hurt, but she kept her wince to herself. ' 'Bye, Lee. See you around—down here—sometime.'

Lee left, leaving a draught from the slammed door. Sharon was draining her cup when the chair opposite her was occupied again. The presence of the man hit her before she lifted her eyes.

'Calum darling,' she said, her raised voice a reasonable imitation of Maida's, 'fancy seeing you.' She felt the waves of Maida's fury without looking at her.

An unwilling smile touched Calum's lips. When he spoke, it was like a stinging slap. 'Arranged a secret rendezvous with Banks?'

She willed her heart to a slower beat. 'Yes,' was her sarcastic rejoinder, 'he's taking me to the steamiest night spot in town.' Her smile was tight. 'It'll teach me all the things a wife-in-name should know about how to entice a reluctant husband into her tent.'

His eyelids flickered, but it seemed he was too intent on cross-examining her to smile. 'Now give me a straight answer. Are you meeting Banks somewhere?'

'No.' Her voice was flat.

'Good. Keep it that way.' Her rebellious green-blue eyes lifted to his, but his words thrust straight back at her. 'Another thing—I'd be obliged if you'd refrain from discussing our private affairs with other people.' Sharon frowned, not understanding. 'I heard you drawing his attention to the tent and your residence there.'

'Private?' she challenged. 'You call that "private"? The whole world can see it. Anyone can look up the hill and see me going in and out of the tent.'

'Is that what's eating you—the fact that it embarrasses you not only that your husband refuses to sleep with you, but that everyone can see it with their own eyes?'

'No, it's not——' What was she about to do? Tell

him it hurt her physically to be rejected by him as a lover? 'Yes,' she finished hurriedly, 'that's right. On the other hand,' she added with a flash of malice, 'it gives me greater freedom.'

His jaw stiffened, drawing her attention to his unshaven appearance. His dark silk shirt was partly unbuttoned, revealing a glimpse of chest hairs. His jacket was open, its collar uplifted, giving him a rakish, exciting air.

'Knowing about your past, I also know you wouldn't have the courage to invite Banks into your tent, not after my threat.'

Her eyes blazed. 'First, you know nothing about my past, except what the media have told you. Second, don't question my courage, Calum. I could tell you a story that would make your opinion of me turn upside down.'

He leaned on his elbows and his face came nearer, the face she had grown to love. She could see the faintest trace of lines around his eyes that she had not noticed before, and a deepening of the time-created grooves in his cheeks.

'Tell me that story, baby,' he invited, his voice low and coaxing, his eyes caressing her features.

She turned her coffee spoon from end to end. 'Sorry, the book's out of print. If you get my meaning.'

His touch was rough as his fingers pinched her cheeks, forcing her to look at him. It flashed into her mind that he looked just a little older. 'I get your meaning, sweetheart. The book was never written, except in the papers.' He released her. 'I bet you made a packet from that series of three "life stories".'

'I gave the fee to charity,' she answered dully. 'My father's got the receipt and the letter of thanks to prove it.'

He scraped back his chair and left the canteen, not even bothering to acknowledge Maida's cry of 'Hey, Cal, wait for me!'

That first night in the tent was the most difficult she had ever had to endure. Washing facilities were primitive, there was nowhere to put her cosmetics, nor her comb, towel or, when she had pulled on her pyjamas, her clothes.

The night air had a chill she had not expected. The lamp Calum had given her shed a less-than-adequate glow. Yet when *he* had used the tent, he had managed to cope with ease, even using a typewriter to tap out page after page of typescript.

He, of course, was hardened to rough living. Hadn't Lee told her? Curling up in the sleeping-bag, she told herself that, given time, she might even come to enjoy dwelling in the great outdoors. How much time, she did not care to estimate.

Sleep would not come. With her torch, Sharon counted the quarter hours on her wrist-watch. At a quarter past one she had had enough. Pulling on her zipped jacket, socks and boots, she staggered outside and hammered on Calum's door.

Even if there had not still been a light inside, she would have aroused him. He loomed large and irritated inside the hut. He wore a high-necked Fair Isle sweater. His hair was untidy, as if long fingers had raked it for ideas. His jeans were faded and hugged his thighs and hips.

'What the hell do you want? Can't you see I'm busy?'

'Can't *you* see I'm c-cold and tired out with tiredness? I just can't relax, I can't get to sleep. I'm—I'm lonely, Calum.'

He put out an impatient hand and tugged her in. 'So what do you want?' He extended his arms, looking at them. 'These to come round you and warm you? You wouldn't relax in these, either, once I got them wound around that shape of yours.'

She shook her head. 'There were noises, Calum, as if

someone was wandering about. I was afraid.'

His mouth widened in a grin. 'Didn't it occur to you they might be sheep?' She shook her head again. 'They often come around at night. Didn't they bleat?'

'If they had, I'd have bleated back. At least they'd have been someone to talk to.'

His head was thrown back, his frame rumbled with laughter. Sharon glanced around, seeing nothing but chaos. Typewritten sheets were strewn on every flat space, even the floor.

'Calum,' her tone was soft, 'please can I sleep in here?' She looked at the bed. 'In that, while you're not using it. An hour or two's sleep, and I'll be fine. That's all I'd need, Calum.'

'Sorry, no deal.' Her face fell, but her despondency did not move him an inch. 'You can make some coffee, if you like.'

Everything was concealed under paper. Finding the mugs on a shelf half hidden by bulging folders, she searched for the instant coffee. It was on its side and she caught it before it rolled on to the floor.

'I don't know how you can *think* in this chaos,' she remarked to his back as he sorted through papers. She put water on to boil. 'What you need is a wife who——'

He dropped his pencil and faced her. 'Who what?'

At once she knew what was in his mind. 'Who looks after you,' she finished, avoiding his eyes. 'Cancel that. I should have said a woman, not a wife. You've got the first and can't wait to get rid of the second.'

Her head lifted proudly as they stared at each other, his expression uncompromising, hers challenging.

'Kettle's boiling,' he pointed out, breaking the brittle silence.

They drank the coffee, he standing, she on the bed. She felt the tug of him, the sheer, masculine pull of the man. She wanted to run to him, hold him and plead with him to hold her, too.

With her knuckles she rubbed her eyes, massaged her temples, pushed back her hair. Her whole body cried out for rest and a release from this intolerable tension. The rest might be within her reach, but the tension would be with her for the unforeseeable future. Only one man held the key to it, and he would be in no mood, ever, to release her from it.

Fatigue won, and she put down her empty cup. Drawing up her legs, she rolled over on to the bed, burrowing under the scattered clothing, and slept.

In full daylight, she was awoken by a noise. A key turned in the lock. There was no sign in the hut of Calum, nor of where he had slept. It had not been at her side, that was clear. The clothes had been removed and she was covered by an opened sleeping bag.

Calum entered, closing the door and leaning back against it, arms folded. 'You achieved your objective,' he said, eyes in shadow, the stubble round his chin blacker than ever. 'You slept in the bed.'

Sharon sat up, pushing aside the cover and swinging her legs to the floor. Her boots stood empty, waiting for her feet to fill them. 'Thanks,' she smiled at him, 'for taking them off.' She looked down at herself. Nothing else had been removed. She should have been pleased, but she was not. He still hadn't wanted to touch her.

'Where did you sleep?' she asked cheerfully.

He walked slowly across to her, rubbing his fist against her chin. 'In the tent, you cheeky kitten.'

'That's better than being a rattlesnake,' she remarked, laughing into his eyes and taking up his lighter mood. 'At least you can stroke a kitten.' She could have bitten her tongue out.

'Is that an invitation?' he rapped out, forcing her chin up.

Her eyelashes drooped. 'No.' Freeing herself from his hold, she pulled on her boots. 'Thanks for the night's rest.' She looked up at him. 'You badly need a shave.'

'Oh, do I?' Like lightning striking, he sat on the bed, pulling her beside him. Then he impelled her cheek until it was against his face, moving his head so that the stubble rubbed against her.

Pain like a thousand needles against the smoothness of her skin made her shriek out for him to stop. When he did, her cheek burned and throbbed. Pulling away, she accused, 'Why are you always trying to hurt me?' Tears filled her eyes and her voice grew thick. 'Why can't you be nice to me for once, just once?'

For a long moment Calum regarded her, then his hand cupped her chin, his mouth covered hers. He moved so that his arms were around her. Against her own wishes, she responded, she couldn't help herself. Why do I love him so much? she thought in self-reproach. Why can't I hate him for the things he does to me?

His hands were under her sweater now, pulling open the buttons of her pyjama top and running his hands over the shape of her like a parched man satiating his thirst. His mouth claimed hers entirely, taking it over and exploring it in its entirety.

His caressing hands were creating havoc with her senses, her resistance, already low where he was concerned, had almost disappeared. Her head went back and his mouth followed, electrifying every part it touched.

Then it was over. He moved away to stand at the window, hands in pockets, his breathing uneven. Sharon held her face, hiding it. Her breathing was ragged, as if she had been running to the top of a mountain, only to discover that its summit had been blown away and there was only a gaping hole to swallow her up. He could do this to her, then walk away!

Well, she had her pride. She could walk away, too. On weakened legs, she made it to the door, opened it and went out. In the tent, she threw herself full-length on the sleeping bag, gathering it to her because he had used it.

Once again she was conscious of the soreness of her cheek where his had rubbed. Now she nursed it tenderly. The feel of him was all she had left.

For all of the following morning she slept. Despite the hardness of the ground beneath her, in spite of the fact that her dreams were haunted by Calum's unyielding face, sleep had come to her.

Using the collected rainwater, she managed to wash and dress. Deciding she could not face going down to the canteen in case Calum was there, she opened a tin or two and ate on paper plates. In spite of her long rest, she felt enervated and uncaring.

Pulling a paperback from her bag, she settled down to read the day away. This she managed, until her body clock told her it was time for an evening meal. Only the canteen could provide that. She did not want to make herself ill by starving herself. How much longer, she wondered, was it worth staying on Cuilla?

In her heart, she had to admit that the only reason for returning had been to find Calum again. He plainly did not want her. He would probably be happier if she left.

Hunger conquered in the end. The canteen was busy, but Sharon found an empty table. It was a simple, tasty and hot meal she had chosen for a change. As she transferred the cutlery from tray to table-top, the entrance door swung to the sound of a familiarly deep voice.

Her head turned quickly, almost defensively, and she met her husband's eyes. Galton Hardaker was with him. 'Over there,' Galton indicated Sharon, 'we'll join your wife.' Cupping his hands, he bellowed uninhibitedly, as only a person in complete command could do, 'Keep two places, Sharon!'

Nodding, she felt relief that Galton Hardaker would at least help the conversation along. Galton's face was brimming with good-humour. Calum's glance was detached and cool. They approached, carrying their trays.

Pulling out a chair, Galton patted his already protruding stomach. 'I need this food to re-energise my brain. An argument with your husband, Sharon, takes it out of me, even me, the great director of international fame.' His wink took the boast out of the words.

Sharon, eating hungrily, did not look at Calum, who was seated opposite her. 'I'm surprised, Mr——' A hand came out and the word 'Galton' was interjected. Sharon smiled. 'I'm surprised, Galton, that someone with your power to say "Do it my way" should bother to argue with a member of the film unit.'

'I'm not a member of the bloody film unit,' Calum growled.

Galton nudged Calum with his elbow. 'Listen to him, yet the film's based on his book.'

'You had me fooled,' Calum's voice was scratchy. 'I thought the story-line was an invention from out of your head.'

'He once told me, Galton,' Sharon confided, flashing a provocative smile at her husband, 'that he was an island and needed no one to share his solitude. Which can only mean he's not a team man.'

'That's got nothing to do with it,' Calum responded irritably. Galton glanced from one to the other. Calum went on, 'When they stop messing about with the script

I produced for them, maybe I'll take an interest.'

Galton leaned on his elbow, his head turned to study the angry profile of the man beside him.

Calum drained his cup and clattered it on to the saucer. 'They read the book, decide to film it—remember I'm a "big name" author—then their scriptwriters get going on it. The accountants are shouting, Cut the costs. The actors have their say, even sometimes altering the dialogue, which is an essential part and woven into the tapestry of the story. They aren't writers, they don't know this.'

'Calum,' Sharon cautioned with some embarrassment, 'the director's sitting beside you.'

Galton shook his head. 'I can take it right there, Sharon.' He indicated his chin. Sharon was amazed at the man's good humour in view of Calum's attack.

'The director,' Calum went on, unabashed, 'has got his mind on the box office, so he puts his own ideas into it, taking out some of mine. In the end, it's not mine any more.'

'Which, maybe,' Sharon interposed, hoping to placate her husband, 'is why people often come out of the cinema saying, It wasn't like that in the book.'

Calum nodded. 'Nothing can alter the relationship between the reader and the written word. Films will never entirely take over, simply because they aren't able to present the twists and nuances put there by the writer.'

Galton laughed. 'Finished using me as a punchball?' Calum's smile was fleeting. 'Okay, so now I want to change the subject and ask you something.'

Calum's raised eyebrows turned towards the director. He followed Galton's eyes and focussed on his wife's pale, unhappy face. 'Why, Calum,' Galton queried, 'if you're so keen on my presenting on screen a truly truthful version of your book, don't you pursue the truth

where your charming and intelligent wife is concerned?'
Galton had hit back at Calum's accusation, but in his own
way.

Anger gave a hard angle to Calum's jawline. 'You
put him up to this,' he accused Sharon.

She was shaking her head miserably when Galton commented, 'I know the state of undeclared war between you. I
saw her picture in the papers four or so months ago. I read
her so-called story. Having met her, I don't believe a word
of it, nor the allegations. You don't have to be as old as I
am to notice the unanswered questions.'

'There's the subject of our discussion,' Calum
answered savagely. 'Ask her for the answers. I hope you
have better luck than I've had.'

Sharon played madly with the glass salt container,
then she put it down. The movement of her hand took
even herself by surprise. It closed over Calum's which
rested on the table. Her smile was tremulous and sweet.
'Calum?' she whispered.

Calum's eyes grazed her features much as his face
had earlier scraped her cheek. She did not shrink from
his hard stare. Instead, she noticed again how he seemed
to have aged, and her heart went out to him, wanting to
cradle him against her breasts, as she had when they
had made love on their wedding eve.

He jerked his hand free and stood up, tall and commanding. 'Coming, Galton?'

The director gave a sigh and shook his head. Then he
patted Sharon's shoulder. The action was louder than a
thousand comforting words.

As Calum passed Maida's table, she caught at his
sleeve and tugged him back. Inviting him to bend lower,
she whispered in his ear, but he shook his head. Then
she whispered again and he raised a shoulder, but she
mouthed the word, 'Tomorrow?' He nodded unsmilingly, then continued on his way.

Her eyes dancing, Maida turned to look in triumph at Sharon. Galton opened the door, saying nothing, but the way he stamped outside spoke volumes. After a while Sharon wandered out, hands in the pockets of her woollen jacket. Pulling at the zip, she shivered. It was August, but here the evening air grew chilly before autumn showed its face. Or was the shiver caused by the promise in Maida's eyes as she had stared after Calum's retreating back?

Sharon's footsteps dragged as she climbed the hill. Reaching the top, she gazed about her. A noise brought her eyes round swiftly. There was the roaring sound of a helicopter engine starting up. A man was at the controls while another climbed awkwardly in. Others hung around, at a distance, watching it rise.

Galton had gone! But he had been the passenger, no doubt about that. Who was at the controls? As the evening passed and there was no sign of Calum, the question was answered for her. So Calum held a pilot's licence, after all. Was he doing Galton a favour by flying him back to the mainland?

If so, why had he not told her? How could he fly away into the evening sky without a single word, not even telling her when he would be back? Her heart seemed to have weights tied to it as she tried to sleep that evening. All the time she listened for Calum's footsteps, even in the early hours when she was wakeful and fretting at being so alone, feeling so bereft.

Maybe he had gone to Maida's place? But that possibility was even more difficult to accept than his desertion of her. She drifted into a light sleep, only to be awoken by a heavy breathing sound outside. Terror gripped her—then she heard a pathetic bleat. A sheep—it was a sheep! In her relief, she almost laughed. Now I've got company, she told herself, turning on to her side. At last she slept.

The day passed with no sign of Calum's return. As the hours went by, Sharon felt less and less able to face the others down the hill. Instead she went for short walks and read her book.

Watching the sun lower itself behind the darkness of the distant hills, she tried to convince herself that she was not watching for the helicopter's return. Even if it did come back, Galton could have found himself another pilot, leaving Calum on the mainland.

Fatigue hit her early, caused, she decided, by the interrupted nature of her sleep the night before. Be honest, she scolded herself as she prepared for bed, it's the weariness of waiting for Calum that's got at you.

It was half an hour to midnight when the sound of the returning helicopter aroused her. Hurriedly she pulled on a sweater, slid halfway back into the sleeping bag and waited for the climbing strides which would tell her that Calum was back.

Twenty minutes later, those footsteps came, but with them were lighter footsteps, too. A whisper of voices told Sharon that her husband was not alone. A trilling of feminine laughter told her, also, the identity of his companion. Pulling off her sweater, Sharon burrowed down into the bag.

The actress was playing a part, no doubt about it—that of seductress and lover. Sharon wanted to burst in there, using her key, tearing the woman apart. Maida was where she, as Calum's wife, should be—welcoming him back after hours of unexplained absence.

Pushing away the thrust of primitive jealousy, she tried to sleep, but the laughter rang in her ears, although she covered them. It was locked into her mind just as surely as Maida was locked in Calum's arms.

Listening against her will, Sharon heard a rustling sound. It did not trouble her this time, since she knew now for certain that Calum had been right about the straying sheep.

Her hearing seemed to have grown more acute. This time she discerned a difference. As the noise came nearer, Sharon's fists clenched. It was certainly no sheep that pulled open the tent flaps. No sheep had fair hair gleaming in the light of a camping lantern, nor could it speak.

'Sharon?' Lee Banks straightened from bending to enter.

'I'm in bed,' she whispered hoarsely. 'Will you go away?'

'I only wanted to talk. I haven't seen you all day. Calum's back. I didn't know he'd gone, otherwise I'd have come sooner.'

'I'm glad you didn't know,' she said fiercely. 'I wouldn't have wanted you up here. I was happier on my own.'

He sat cross-legged beside the sleeping bag. 'I know all about your "happiness"—and your unhappiness, Sharon. I've been watching you, and I've seen how your marriage to Calum is tearing you apart.' He rested a hand on her hip, but her arm flailed, pushing it away. 'He's a solitary, darling, you must have known that when you agreed to marry him.'

'Don't call me darling!'

'He doesn't want a wife trailing round behind him. He roams the world. I did tell you.'

'Will you please go?' She was growing frightened now. What part was Lee Banks, the actor, playing tonight, for heaven's sake?

'Maida's with him. Did you hear her? I followed them up the hill, but I made sure they didn't see me. He'll divorce you, Sharon, just like my wife divorced me. We're two of a kind, Sharon, so I thought I'd come to offer you my shoulder to cry on.'

A door opened, a bubbling feminine voice said, ' 'Night, darling. Pleasant dreams.' There was a tantalising pause. Was Calum kissing her? 'You're quite a guy, aren't you?' Maida went on softly. 'Not only a famous writer, you hold a pilot's licence, too.' Another pause. 'You really do things to me, Calum darling.'

Sharon waited for his reply, but none came that she could hear. Footsteps half-ran down the hill. Lee stared at the groundsheet, waiting for the door to close. After a few long moments—was Calum listening?—there was the creak of rusty hinges and the door key turning.

Lee moved nearer so that he was touching against the sleeping bag. Sharon tensed, feeling helpless. 'I want comfort from you, too, Sharon. You're the only one who can give it to me. No one else cares.' His voice lowered. 'Let me love you, darling, let me hold you.'

The spurned lover, Sharon thought, that was his role at that moment, seeking reassurance in another woman's arms. Well, she resolved, they weren't going to be her arms. But how to get him out, and without Calum hearing anything? It was essential that Calum heard nothing. She had never forgotten his warning. And anyway, she wanted to go running into his arms to tell him how much she had missed him.

Taking a breath, she took the only path she could think of. 'Calum's threatened me, Lee, that if he—he finds you here, or anywhere near me, he'll thrash me, so please go now—quickly!'

He stretched out beside her, putting a protective arm across her waist. 'If he so much as touches you——'

She had got her timing disastrously wrong. The situation she had painted had had an electrifying effect on his actor's imagination.

A hand touched her hip and she was racked by a growing fear. Looking down, she discovered that the zip fastener was opened down to her feet. He must have moved it, inch by inch, as he talked to her.

'No, Lee, please, Lee. I told you what Calum would do . . .'

'Stay quiet, then,' his mouth was seeking hers as she strained away from him, 'and he won't hear a thing.' His arms were round her now, and in the subdued lighting, she saw a strange and frightening look in his eyes. His role had switched to that of predator, man after woman.

It was no longer within her power to control events. He spread himself across her, finding her elusive mouth, pressing down on it, clutching at her hair.

Thrashing about, Sharon hit out with her fists, freeing her lips and screaming for Calum. Lee put a hand over her mouth, but she bit its flesh. Swearing with pain, he stopped as a door opened. He scrambled up, snatched his lantern and went to the entrance.

Sharon had gone silent, covering her ears and closing her eyes. Not again, she thought, not another fight.

'You louse!' Calum's snarling voice penetrated her guard. 'Get away from my wife and get down that hill fast—unless you want me to mess up that pretty face of yours for a second time. And after this bout, it'll never be the same again!'

Feet pounded into the distance. There was silence. Slowly, in the grip of a primeval fear, Sharon lifted her fingers from her eyes. Holding a torch and playing its light all over her to linger on her frightened face, Calum stood at the entrance.

CHAPTER TEN

'GET up.' His expression was black and menacing in the shadow. Frozen with terror, Sharon could not move. Two strides brought him beside her. He ran the light over the dishevelment of her flimsy pyjama suit, then with his free hand he bent down, reached out and gripped her wrist, dragging her to her feet in one action.

Turning, he pulled her behind him to the open air. 'No shoes, Calum,' she gasped, 'I'm wearing no shoes!'

He did not slacken his pace. With the torch, he found his way, pushing her up the steps and into the hut. He slammed the door and locked it.

'Right,' he unbuttoned his shirt, removing it, 'you've asked for it.'

His gaze held hers as she stood, shivering a little, her hands clenched and moist at her side. In one movement he came to stand in front of her, his eyes burning with a rumbling fury. When the eruption came, Sharon knew she would go under, floundering, crying with pain. Her eyes grew heavy as tears gathered behind them. It was so unfair!

Some of her jacket buttons had come open in her struggle with Lee. Her hair was all over the place, like the beating of her heart.

'How did you like that swine's lovemaking, my faithful wife?' he grated. He pushed up her chin, jerking back her head. The line of his mouth was so tight his teeth showed, his breathing so deep his chest expanded and contracted, revealing his leanness and the muscle power in his arms. It seemed he had had a shave, but it must have been a few hours back, for the stubble was appearing again.

In the low lighting he looked devilish, uncaring, capable of anything. Moving quickly, his hand ripped open the rest of her jacket. He tugged it off, bunching it and throwing it across the room. Then his arms had her trapped, holding her so close she could hardly breathe. His mouth savaged hers, brutalising inside as well as outside.

Tasting blood, Sharon was swept by a feeling of weakness. Her arms needed something to cling to. They curled about his neck. When he had finished with her mouth, it throbbed. Pushing her away, the better to look her over, he ran his hands over her shoulders, her arms, her waist, leaving until the last the poignantly sensitive swell of her breasts.

His mouth replaced his hands, which pushed her backwards, the better to kiss and fondle. Scarcely able to think, or to control the rising longing inside her to be one again with this man she loved, she whispered, 'Please, Calum . . .'

'Please Calum what?' he rasped. ' "Leave me alone because I'm exhausted from my lover's lovemaking"?'

'Lee's not my lover, Calum. It may have looked that way to you, but——'

'It would even have looked that way to Galton, who looks on you as the essence of purity and loyalty,' he growled. He released her, his hands going to his belt. 'I said I'd thrash you if Banks so much as went near you again.'

Sharon paled but lifted up her head, crossing her hands over her breasts. 'Thrash if you want, Calum. I know I'm in the right—*in every way*.' She held his gaze boldly. 'That should help to ease the pain you'd be inflicting, plus the pain of my knowing that even a man as highly principled as you would stoop to such a thing.'

His thumbs hooked round his belt and he gazed at

her steadily, unreadably.

'And I love you, Calum. I'll take anything you hand out. My—my love for you won't change. You see, I'd forgive you . . .' Her voice wavered. 'Although I'd never, ever, be able to forget what you did to me.'

He moved slowly towards her. 'You have courage, sweetheart, but it's all for nothing. I've never hit a woman in my life, and I certainly don't intend to start now. But this I will do—make you mine in a way you'll never forget.'

'I can't stop you doing anything, Calum. I don't have your physical strength.' She spoke hoarsely, but would not show her fear.

He moved without warning, swinging her into his arms. By the time he dropped her on to the bed, he had removed all her barriers. When he threw himself beside her, he too wore nothing. He pulled her to him, handling her harshly, his stroking hands hard on the smoothness of her skin.

His mouth possessed first, burning a rough trail from throat to shoulders to breasts. His hands made their searing mark on her most secret places. When she was crying out his name and clutching the flesh of his shoulders as if he might be swept away by the tide of his own passion, he possessed her utterly and she abandoned herself to him. It was as if they had merged into one entity and could never again be parted.

'Sharon, baby, my own, my wife.' The wild sea of his desire had died down, leaving him tender and passionate in the afterglow.

'Calum?' He was still holding her, stroking her hair. 'Will you believe me if I tell you Lee Banks tried to force himself on me but that you came just in time?'

'I'll believe you. From now on, I'll believe every single word you say.'

Sharon's eyes widened with delight and amazement. 'Calum? Do you know what you're saying?' She rolled on to her side and shook his shoulder. 'Tell me you aren't still on a cloud, that you're aware of what you've said?'

'I'm aware, oh yes,' his palm slid around the fullness of her breast, 'I'm aware, my love.'

Sharon found a rug on the floor and tugged it over them. She needed time to think. 'Tell me,' she shook his arm, 'tell me why you've changed your mind about me.'

He clamped her to him. 'If you'll stop trying to shake me to pieces——'

'I promise. Now, please, what's happened to make you trust me?'

'It all began, let me see,' he ran a nail up and down his stubbled cheek, 'the day a young woman with haunted eyes brought me a letter.' He kissed her lightly. 'I'd seen her before, of course, in the papers. I'd heard things, so many things about her. It grew and grew, that feeling that I had to discover the truth.'

Sharon rested her cheek against the rough one. 'And each time you tried to get me to speak out, I refused.'

'You refused. I came to a dead end. Yesterday evening, I couldn't stand it any longer. After that meal Galton and I had with you, hearing Galton's conviction that you were hiding something—he told me that later—I asked if I could borrow his helicopter and go to London.'

'He went with you. I was watching and saw him climb in.'

Calum moved on to his back, cushioning his head. 'I asked him along as a witness. He was delighted to oblige.'

Sharon waited, lying beside him, staring into the semi-darkness of the hut.

'I was going crazy,' Calum went on, 'being married to

you, yet not having you as my wife. Know what I mean?'

. So he wanted her as his wife, not because he loved her? 'I think I know what you mean.' Sharon withdrew from all contact with him. 'That you felt the normal desires yet that agreement was in the way?' His head turned towards her. 'But—but you had Maida, Calum.'

'To hell with the agreement, and to hell with Maida.' He raised himself on to his elbow. 'If you think she was my mistress, then forget it. She wanted to be. Even when she saw the competition—and sensed my feelings for you—she still thought she could win. She kept inviting herself here on the pretext of going over the script. I wanted to work on my book. I almost had to push her out.' He subsided on to the pillow. 'Satisfied?'

'Yes, Calum. But——'

'But—I had to know for sure about you. I had the feeling you might be shielding someone.' She nodded vigorously. 'Hence my journey to the mainland, where I turned back the clock and became an investigative journalist again.' He looked at her again. 'I know it all, Sharon.'

She was silent, holding still.

'I couldn't rest until I knew the truth. If *you* couldn't produce any proof that the press stories were untrue, I had to produce it instead. First, Galton and I called on your parents' house. They'd only been home a day from their cruise.'

'How are they?' Sharon asked eagerly. 'Did they enjoy it?'

'They're fine, they loved every minute and they send you their love.' He smiled, turning her face so that he could kiss her lightly. He grew serious again. 'Your father told me he knew the whole of your story, but without your permission, he couldn't reveal it. He put me on to Irwin's parents.'

Her eyes widened. 'You called there?'

'We did. My investigative reporter's "nose" was finally scenting out the trail to the truth. Mr Irwin told me everything, including the promise you'd made to shield his wife and himself from the publicity and its consequences. He was shocked to hear about all you'd been through. I had already told him I was your husband but that all the unresolved doubts and uncertainties were in danger of wrecking our marriage.'

Sharon sighed deeply. 'So now you know it all.'

'Now I know that, far from deserving the abuse you received, you should really be given a medal for being a heroine.'

'Thank you, kind sir,' she said, her eyes bright with mischief, but with happiness also at being freed at last from the burden of his castigation.

'I called on my press contacts and told them about my discoveries.' He must have sensed her sudden tension and rolled her round, holding her. 'Going on my past experience as a journalist, I'll tell you what the papers will do. The more sensation-seeking ones will tuck the item away in a corner, giving it a couple of inches of space.' He smiled. 'They never like to admit they were wrong, nor to spoil the story they first thought of.'

'The better quality ones?' Sharon prompted.

'They'll put the story probably on page two or three,' he hazarded, 'underneath a photograph of the two of us. Their report will exonerate you completely. Since they gave the allegations so little coverage in the first place, they've got nothing to lose by telling the truth now.'

'A complete reversal, in fact, of how the press treated the original story.'

'You've guessed right. Now, come here, baby. I'm cold without you.' Sharon slid into his arms.

Something compelled her to whisper, 'You were

engaged once, Calum, but the girl ran away just before the wedding. Lee told me . . .' Should she have mentioned his name?

Calum was frowning, but not at the person she had anticipated. 'All that seems years ago—it was years ago. She was an error I would have spent years regretting if the marriage had taken place.'

'Like me,' Sharon ventured, 'with Daryl. If I'd discovered after the wedding about this other woman he had . . .'

He held her even more closely. 'And now there's just us.'

Her finger traced his dark brows. 'When did it begin with you?'

'The moment I saw you trudging up the hill loaded with baggage. Your first words to me were impudent, to say the least. Jack Wilson had warned me before I left home that "the rest of my life would be arriving soon". He said you'd bring a letter. By the time you'd given me that letter, I was the rest of your life, too.'

'Darling,' she whispered, parting her lips for his kiss. It did not come.

'Except,' he added, 'for those doubts about you that nearly drove me mad.'

'Yet you offered me your protection by marrying me.'

'Protection be damned!' He pulled her the length of him. 'I wanted to get my ring on your finger. I wanted you, woman. Do you understand? I *wanted* you.' A flare of passion lit his face as he studied her. 'Eyes as warm and inviting as a tropical sea. I could drown in them.' His hands held the sides of her head. 'Hair so black I once called you "my midnight girl". Now you're my "midnight woman".' His mouth lowered to her waiting lips. He promised softly,

'From now to eternity, I shall share my "island", and

my secret self, with you and only you—the woman I love more than life.'

'I never guessed, darling. I've loved you all this time without any hope that you'd ever love me in return.' She ran a finger over his dark brows.

Calum held her away. 'Just a few words I'm going to make you eat, my love. That "promise" you made——'

'That I'd never adore you? I retract it, darling, every single word. You're my dream man and always will be. I do adore you—madly. I need you, but most of all I love you with every tiny part of me. Now are you satisfied?'

'No, my midnight woman,' he said, pulling her still closer, 'nor will I ever be, where you're concerned, to the end of our lives.'

Harlequin® Plus
A WORD ABOUT THE AUTHOR

Lilian Peake grew up in North Essex, a region about sixty miles northeast of London, England. She became secretary to a local mystery author, gaining valuable insight into how an author functions.

Before she wrote her first Harlequin, Lilian also worked as a journalist, a career that included a stint with a London fashion magazine. This experience was to help with background for her fourth novel, *The Real Thing* (Harlequin Romance #1650). Unlike her mystery-author employer, who dictated his work, Lilian found she had to type her manuscripts herself. "I have to see my thoughts in front of my eyes," she explains.

Though two of her book titles are *Master of the House* and *Man in Charge*, Lilian maintains that women should play a much bigger role in running the world than they do at present. To this end, she believes, education is the key.

Lilian Peake's first Harlequin, *This Moment in Time* (Romance #1572), was published in 1972.

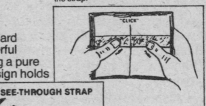

Enter a uniquely exciting world of romance with the new

Harlequin American Romances.^{T.M.}

Harlequin American Romances are the first romances to explore today's new love relationships. These compelling romance novels reach into the hearts and minds of women across North America...probing the most intimate moments of romance, love and desire.

You'll follow romantic heroines and irresistible men as they boldly face confusing choices. Career first, love later? Love without marriage? Long-distance relationships? All the experiences that make love real are captured in the tender, loving pages of the new **Harlequin American Romances.**

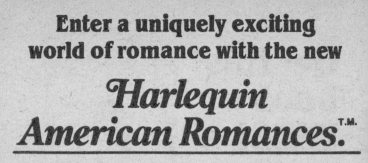

What makes North American women so different when it comes to love? Find out in the new **Harlequin American Romances!**

Send for your introductory FREE book now!

AR-SUB-2

Get this book FREE!

Beyond Imagination

One of the greatest broken-field runners of the 1970s, O.J. Simpson seems to be the embodiment of success. The complete Hollywood package, he is a professional athlete, network-sports commentator, television and film actor, and a corporate pitch man. For twenty years he has been afloat on a sea of money and privilege pumped his way by networks and studios.

Then in one horrible week his entire life was transformed before the eyes of 100 million television viewers. From that Monday morning when we turned on our sets to see O.J. in handcuffs at his Brentwood home to the Friday evening when we were riveted to our sets as O.J.'s slow-motion car chase played out across both the California freeway system and the national psyche, we watched in complete shock and disbelief.

Way Beyond the Headlines

What was the real story behind the events that turned O.J. Simpson's life into a a vortex of tragedy? For the first time anywhere, this exciting *Globe* Book details the *real* story behind O.J. Simpson. Beyond the headlines, beyond the sound bites, *Juice: The O.J. Simpson Tragedy* gives the first in-depth and up-to-the-minute portrait of Orenthal James Simpson as he faces a gripping trial for his life.

GLOBE BOOKS

JUICE
The O.J. Simpson Tragedy

Larry Browne
Paul Francis
Senior Editors

Robert Taylor
Project Director

Princeton Publishing West

JUICE: THE TRAGEDY OF O.J. SIMPSON

© 1994   Globe Communications Corporation and
          Princeton Publishing West, Inc.

ISBN: 1-885840-00-4

Cover photograph by Enrico Ferorelli
Complete list of photo credits follows page 210.

Production: BLAZE I.P.I.

Printed in the United States of America
by Offset Paperback Mfrs., Inc.

First Printing, June 1994

10   9   8   7   6   5   4   3   2

Acknowledgements

Dozens of *Globe* staffers and stringers contributed to this book. The authors would like to specially thank Managing Editor Robert Taylor and West Coast Bureau Chief Mary Ann Norbom for their sterling efforts in bringing it all together.

In addition, we'd like to thank the following: Lo Mae Lai, Chris Doherty, Bob Michals, Mike Kerrigan, Jack Carter, Kathy Tracy, Paul Bannister, Adrian Havill, John I. Jones, Ian Markham-Smith, Sharon McDonnell, Bonnie Robinson, Marie Terry, Rafe Klinger, Kim Humphreys, John Nelander. Also: Debbie Morse, Irene Internoscia, Diana Siegfried, Bernadette Roedel, Gary Camolli, Peter Brennan.

The editors at Princeton Publishing West would like to thank Tom Colbert of IR&D Inc. and Terry Raskyn of *Globe* for bringing this project together. In addition, we would like to thank Edward Sax, James Wohl, Dan Paulson, Dave Zable, Phil Bunton, Don Allen, Steve Schragis, Erwin Vertleib, Jeff Wald, Dr. James L. Mastrich, and PBC Stories, Inc.

Without all these people, this book would not have been possible.

*This book is dedicated
to those victims of domestic violence
who will read these pages
and recognize their monster
and fear for their own safety.
Please seek help.*

**1-800 572-SAFE
The Domestic Violence Help Line**

**(201) 625-6215
Self-Help Clearing House**

**(213) 989-7841
Families Anonymous**

**(215) 348-5664
Network of Victims Assistance (NOVA)**

Check the front pages of your phone book for the nearest
community shelter or counseling hot line.

Contents

Foreword

I've been a newsman in L.A. for over a quarter of a century and I would like to comment, from an objective but personal perspective, on the journalistic fever that runs rampant through L.A. in general and the Hollywood entertainment and celebrity community in particular. The Hollywood community is unique. Its relationship with the press and with journalists is as symbiotic as any relationship can be. The community needs the press to promote the industry, the stars, the movies, and the television specials. Careers rise or fall on the level and type of press coverage movies get, and the entertainment community exerts extreme pressure to make sure the coverage is good.

Hollywood celebrities are like mini-industries themselves with business, personal, and publicity managers. It's the publicity managers who work with the press, sometimes making clients available, sometimes begging for coverage, and sometimes actually setting the rules for what type of coverage the press can get. More often than not the press goes along because the media correspondents know that celebrity stories only increase circulation. Hollywood sells! That's the way it's been ever since the founding of the motion picture industry out here just after the turn of the century.

O.J.'s press has always been good. But now that he's behind bars and the nation's news correspondents have turned on themselves, the old criticisms of "pack journalism," "checkbook journalism," and "feeding frenzy" have again risen to the surface. Only this time, the Hollywood community itself is raising some of these charges. The news media has been accused of trying O.J. in the press and of disclosing leaks and information about the case so as to compromise O.J.'s constitutional rights, prejudging O.J. on the 10 P.M. news, and digging up stories based on rumor and innuendo.

So? What's wrong with that? Basically, that's what's known as a free press doing its job.

First, nobody in the press out-and-out accused O.J. of anything. When L.A. Prosecutor Marcia Clark goes before a bank of cameras and microphones and announces at a press conference that O.J. *is* the killer instead of O.J. is the *alleged* killer, what are we supposed to do: turn off the cameras? Marcia Clark said what she said. Our job is to report it—not judge it.

Second, why blame reporters for a feeding frenzy or for engaging in pack journalism? Hollywood thrives on pack journalism and feeding frenzies during the good times; they have no right to complain when one of their own falls from grace on a Friday afternoon.

Third, I never read in the American constitution that the press has the job of protecting the constitutional rights of the people accused of crimes, no matter how important those people are. The press's only job is to report the truth as they understand it. Once the press is turned loose, good reporters will sniff out stories and their editors will tell them what's ready for print or broadcast and what needs more digging.

This is exactly what's happening in the O.J. Simpson

case. We didn't step over the line. If anything, in Hollywood, the line stepped over us. The press is routinely manipulated and exploited by handlers and public information officers as they disclose facts to enhance their position or to hurt the other side, promising us exclusives in exchange for deals on the handling or spin of the stories. It's all a big cauldron of Who-Needs-What-From-Whom. Nobody seems to mind until the really big story breaks involving Hollywood royalty. That's when the accusations start flying about the press.

In the Simpson story, the press was simply doing its job. In a routine case the evidence, the police planning, and the prosecution strategy would all have been disclosed to us in some way or form. But in the Simpson case the rules have changed. The police and the prosecutors chose to withhold information. When the rules change, the press wants to know why. The press has to dig on its own. Dig we must—and dig we did. We found witnesses, we found sources, we found public documents. Only this time, we're being slammed for it.

Now, we're all at Parker Center waiting for the moment when O.J. is to arrive. But there is no O.J. Time passes. It's now the afternoon and Commander Gascon gets up to address the gathered media and announces that "O.J. Simpson is a fugitive from justice." He announces that the LAPD has no idea where O.J. is; the fugitive is "in the wind." You can hear an audible gasp from the audience; the assembled press corps is in shock. We've played by every rule, and now we learn that the cops have let their suspect escape. No surveillance in a double-murder special circumstances? They simply took his word and left it at that? At that moment, there was a shared—but unspoken—assumption on the part of the press that now all bets were off. If The Juice is on the loose, then the press has as much right to find him as the police have. Doesn't matter who it is.

The chase is on. Whatever happened after that—the helicopters, the camera work, the interviews with anybody we could dig up, the human-interest sidebars, the press of journalists covering every minute of the Friday-afternoon adventure—was not only entirely legitimate, it was *exactly* what the press is supposed to do.

So if somebody is mad about the way the press covered a case of a fugitive on the run, that's just too bad. O.J. Simpson was given such special treatment by the police and prosecutors that the moment the press played the hardball it was supposed to, suddenly we became prejudicial in the eyes of some of our critics. If anything, the press went in the opposite direction with someone who lived and thrived in the media every day since his entry into the pros. From now on the press will gather every piece of information it can.

We broadcast! We publish! If there is a battle of press leaks, don't blame the press, blame the leaker. We're not going to sugar-coat the news. You deserve better than that. You, the public, hold no special privilege nor preferential position. But you do deserve the truth.

Jeff Wald
Executive Director—News Programming
KCOP–TV, Los Angeles

A Trail
of Blood

The quiet darkness of the peaceful, affluent westside Los Angeles neighborhood of Brentwood was shattered by a single chilling scream. A solitary jogger noticed a river of blood flowing beneath the gate of a fashionable town house at 875 South Bundy Drive. She peeked inside and froze in horror. Two bodies, savagely mutilated, were right there on the ground. One, a female, was in a fetal position on her side, her feet drawn up to her chest. The other, a young man, was in a sitting position against the stone portion of the gate. He was slumped sickeningly over on his right side. Neither one was moving. Earlier, the jogger had found Nicole Simpson's frantic dog scurrying up the street.

It was 12:10 A.M., Monday, June 13, 1994. The most shocking Hollywood murder of the decade—and what was soon to become its biggest and most publicized of all time, had been discovered. Events began to move very quickly in the early morning hours.

Globe's West Coast bureau chief, Mary Ann Norbom, was at home asleep at 3 A.M., when her phone rang. A breathless freelance reporter screamed: "Two bodies have been found at O.J. Simpson's house. I just heard it on my police scanner."

Norbom raced to her home office. She called reporters Chris Doherty and Lo Mae Lai and dispatched them to O.J.'s mansion. She was about to call a photographer to join them when her phone rang again. It was the freelancer who had provided the original tip. "Wrong," he shouted. "Wrong! The bodies are at his ex-wife's house! Not O.J.'s!"

Norbom paged Lai and Doherty. While she waited for them to respond, she called two photographers and told them to get over to the South Bundy Drive address. Doherty called from a pay phone near O.J.'s house. Before she could speak, he said: "Everything's quiet here. Nothing's going on," sure that his night's sleep had been disturbed by yet another false lead.

But it would be more than 24 hours before Doherty saw his bed again. "Get to 875 South Bundy Drive," Norbom snapped. "What the hell's going on there?" Doherty shot back. "That's where the bodies are," Norbom said.

Norbom then threw on her clothes and headed for her car. Ironically, the murders took place only three blocks from *Globe's* office in Los Angeles, but she lived an hour and a half away in Santa Barbara. As she sped through the night, her cellular phone was buzzing.

Calls went out to anyone she could think of who knew O.J. or his ex-wife, Nicole. Staff reporters, freelance writers, photographers, Tinseltown socialites, sports figures, and people who may have known O.J. because they worked in broadcasting or advertising, the two areas he was currently involved in.

Norbom had made more than thirty calls before she hit the office at 5 A.M. But she still had one more set of calls to make. The incredible day that was just beginning to dawn was Monday, and that day was *Globe's* press day. The execs and senior editors at the main editorial office in Boca Raton, Florida, had to know as soon as possible: This was not going to be an ordinary closing.

The first call went to *Globe's* Editorial Director Phil Bunton. "Phil," she said. "You've got to hold some space. Something very big may be happening." Like a self-replicating organism, each call spawned another. Bunton was on the phone immediately to Managing Editor Robert Taylor, who in turn ordered two reporters to the Boca office to prepare an obit on O.J.—just in case he was one of the victims. He also alerted Photo Editor Ron Haines to round up every photo of O.J. and Nicole he could lay his hands on.

Bunton called Director of Production Gary Camolli, who dialed the four plants around America where *Globe* is printed and directed them to expect the paper to be late.

Meanwhile, the black night was softening into a pre-dawn haze on South Bundy Drive. Police had cordoned off Nicole Simpson's house with yellow "crime scene" tape. Word was spreading rapidly that a tragedy had occurred. Globe's Doherty and Lai were joined by other reporters and photographers, all jostling for the best vantage points with the TV crews that had also begun to assemble. Scores of news vans pulled up and satellite antennas began rising from their roofs on single shafts, their arms opening, concave faces rotating toward their uplinks, just like a meadow of flowers trying to catch the morning sun.

Two bodies were removed. As the Medical Examiner's vans roared off, Doherty pushed past two burly police officers and peeked up the walkway. It was a sea of blood, punctuated by the paw prints of Nicole's Akita dog, which had been pacing and fussing near the curled-up body of his slain mistress.

Meanwhile, in Boca Raton, the office was a frenzied hive of activity, deadline was only hours away, and all they were getting were rumors . . . and speculation . . . and still more rumors feeding on the ones than had surfaced before. Call after call, and nothing definitive. The questions mounted: Who had been killed? Why had they been killed? Where were Nicole's two children?

And where was O.J. Simpson?

Finally, the answers started to come. The dead were identified as Nicole Brown Simpson, 35, and a 25-year-old mystery man named Ronald Lyle Goldman. The children were asleep in the house when the brutal murders were committed. O.J. was in Chicago for a business meeting.

Then the bombshell dropped. Word leaked from the Los Angeles Police Department that O.J., who had been summoned back from Chicago for questioning, was the only suspect in the savage murder of his beautiful ex-wife.

It was the start of a saga that would hold America spellbound—images that will live forever in our minds as a man changed right before our eyes: the great sports legend O.J. in handcuffs; murder suspect O.J. Simpson standing by his ex-wife's grave holding their children by the hand; the incredible, bizarre, slow-speed pursuit of Simpson the fugitive along the river of freeways intersecting Los Angeles County and the narrow serpentine streets of Brentwood; the standoff in the driveway of his home as he handed over his gun and was arrested and booked for murder with special circumstances as Prisoner Number 4013970; a shattered Orenthal James Simpson, hardly recognizable as the O.J. we've all come to know and love, in court facing the heinous charges, steadied by the hand of his lawyer.

And *Globe* was there from the very beginning.

The Steep Streets of San Francisco

The streets of San Francisco's Potrero Hill section stretch steeply up towards the sky—and then suddenly plunge down, down, down to the depths of despair. The Hill is a poor black ghetto in California's most sparkling city, and spread over both sides of the hill like a plague is a government housing development known simply as The Project.

Most of The Project residents wake up with—and go to bed with—grinding poverty and little hope that things will ever get any better. Some are welfare recipients, some eke out a poverty level wage, and still others peddle drugs small-time on the street. Some are gang members who know that prestige comes with a knife or a gun, that money comes hard and goes easy, and that fame and death are often related.

All of them know Orenthal James Simpson. He is one of the few lucky ones who got out, escaped to the glitter of Hollywood, to white-linen table-cloths in restaurants and multi million-dollar mansions in Brentwood with sparkling pools, bright green tennis courts, and heavy wrought-iron gates that slam shut behind him with a meaningful rich man's clang at night.

Yet for all his wealth and success, O.J. never forgot his roots and his people have never forgotten him. He is their hope, their symbol of freedom, and when they think of him, they can't help but wonder if maybe a few more—maybe those who can run fast enough, hit hard enough, or slam-dunk with enough conviction—maybe they, like O.J., can still escape The Hill.

Like a religious icon, O.J.'s image looms in sun-faded paint on the facade of the well-worn Potrero recreation center. It is a portrait of O.J. in his football uniform, wearing the Number 32 he made famous as a high-stepping broken-field running back for the Buffalo Bills.

A plaque memorializes his high school years in the school's display case outside the main office. A bronze bust of O.J. greets passengers at the international airport. His name adorns his high school stadium, and the letters "OJ" are chiseled into the concrete outside 906 Connecticut, the apartment where he grew up.

"Whenever I get home to San Francisco," he once said, "I like to go up on Potrero Hill. Sometimes I like to go up and walk in the park when nobody's up there but me. I kind of feel I'm getting strength from the earth where I grew up. It's a thrill."

But tourists don't ever visit Potrero Hill. It's gang turf, just as it was when O.J. was growing up in the '60s. It is still a place where strangers are eyed warily and with hostility. It is a place where National Guardsmen were called out to quell rioting after a black kid was shot by white cop.

It was O.J.'s 'hood.

In Larry Fox's book, *Born to Run*, Eunice Simpson describes the lusty infant boy she held in her arms for the very first time at Stanford University Hospital on a hot July day in 1947 this way: "The fattest of my four—a heavy baby."

And in *O.J.: The Story of Football's Fabulous O.J. Simpson*, author Bill Libby says that Eunice's sister, who loved outlandish names, was the person who suggested the names for the baby: Orenthal, "after some French actor or something" and James, for O.J.'s father, a custodian at the Federal Reserve Bank. The aunt tagged her own children with names like Stuart, Stanley and Pamela, but left O.J. with his unusual handle and dubbed another nephew Gursell.

"Orenthal!" O.J. understandably sighed. "She must have been sick once and it just came up," he quips in author A. S. Young's book *Black Champions of the Gridiron*.

At birth, the superstar-to-be was solidly built, but he suffered from the nutritional disease, rickets. By the time he was two his father had deserted the family—although he returned years later—and O.J. was virtually crippled.

"He had trouble trying to walk and we noticed his legs were weak," said Eunice. "The doctor said it was a calcium deficiency."

As a single mother eking out an existence on her meager pay as an orderly in a psychiatric ward, Eunice was unable to afford proper medical care for her baby boy and was also unwilling to follow the doctors' suggestion that they operate to straighten his bones. Instead, she asked nurses at her workplace, San Francisco General Hospital, for advice, and then she fashioned a pair of braces for her baby's legs.

For months she religiously put them on and took them off, massaging O.J.'s tiny legs with baby oil to prevent sores—tending to him and caring for her family in the few hours she wasn't slaving away at her grueling job. It seemed almost a miracle, but the makeshift braces worked perfectly.

And although O.J.'s legs are still bowed even today, thanks to his mother's loving attention, his legs grew stronger and stronger, eventually carrying him far away from her—and over The Hill to fame and fortune.

The family, which by now included Shirley, O.J., Carmelita, and Leon, moved often. And each time, things got worse. Years later, O.J. recalled: "It seemed that every time my mama got a pay raise, we'd lose some government money and we'd be worse off. I still can't work out why we kept getting worse and worse government housing when we were supposed to be getting a little better off."

It was a heavy load for the woman who was determined her children would escape the grimness of Potrero Hill, but she struggled along. Her youngest son struggled too—with his fists—in the streets of The Hill. By the time O.J. was 12, his friends and the older boys he looked up to were thieves and muggers: juvenile offenders, most of whom were headed for lives behind bars.

And the adolescent O.J. was hardly any different. He pried off car hubcaps and ripped out radios; he shoplifted beer and wine off store shelves, and became street-wise and self-sufficient.

"I was very cocky," he later admitted. "I started fights and gate-crashed dances. I was lucky. I did things, stole things, took cars for joyrides, but I wasn't caught much."

Twice, cops who caught him where he shouldn't have been drove him home and let him go with only a warning. Once, when he need a ride to a party, O.J. prowled a row of cars and found one with the keys left in it. It was a stick shift, something he'd never driven before. But he had seen it done and that's all he needed. O.J. and his pals climbed in.

That was the easy part.

O.J. stalled the car on a hill just as a police cruiser pulled alongside. Desperately, he tried again and again to start the motor. No dice. His buddies flung open the doors and ran for their lives. The cop climbed out of his cruiser just as O.J. managed to start his stolen vehicle. Then he peeled away with the police in pursuit.

The chase didn't last long. Once O.J. was out of sight around a corner, he swerved the car into the curb by a used-car lot, leaped out and slid under another car. He could see the policeman's shoes as he patrolled the aisles of cars, searching. O.J. crept away, then sprinted unseen into an alleyway, where he hid on a second-story balcony. Again, the cop followed. For several heart-pounding minutes, O.J. lay motionless, praying to escape. Eventually, he did—but he was soon in trouble again.

By now his group of Potrero kids had started a gang they called The Superiors. O.J. was the acknowledged leader, quick thinking and able to fast-talk his way out of serious trouble. Later, he belonged to a street gang named the Persian Warriors.

"He could grow a full beard, even when he was just 15," said an admiring Josiah 'Joe' Bell, a member of O.J.'s group. "He looked older than everyone and acted older and we all looked up to him.

None of us had fathers at home, so O.J. became like a father."

During this time, O.J.'s dad Jimmy Lee was living a few blocks away and wielded an important influence on him—especially when Eunice needed a strong hand to give him a spanking. And, according to the *New York Times*, he doled out punishment to his son with a belt.

"I resented his absence," O.J. said in an interview with *Parents* magazine, "especially when I became a teenager and was trying to find out who I was. I really needed a man around then for guidance."

In the weeks after his arrest, *Globe* unearthed a bombshell secret about O.J.'s wandering dad. According to The Juice's childhood pals, Jimmy Lee Simpson was a homosexual known as "Sweet Jimmy" who left his wife for another man—and died of AIDS-related cancer in 1986.

"Forty years ago, nobody really talked about it," confided Everett Ray Hawkins. "But it was common knowledge in the neighborhood. We all called him 'Sweet Jimmy' because he swished around real effeminate like. And he was seeing another man."

Hawkins told *Globe* that the superstar-to-be

was teased constantly about his father: "We'd act out like guys do, and by the age of 14 O.J. would laugh with us about him . . . but it was tough on him. He wanted to be close to his dad, but he also wanted to be macho. Being thought of as a tough guy in our neighborhood was everything. We all knew what we had to do to make it—be tougher than anyone. If there was even an inkling you were soft, people would make you out to be gay."

Another source close to young O.J. said "Sweet Jimmy" moved to San Francisco's Haight Ashbury hippie haven in the late Sixties and was later dubbed "Mama Simpson." In 1985, he became ill and checked into Kaiser Foundation Hospital. He died eight months later, at age 66.

"Sweet Jimmy's"death certificate cites the cause of death as cardiorespiratory failure following adenocarcinoma—stomach cancer. But Hawkins and others say flatly that O.J.'s dad died of AIDS.

"Back then it was called 'the gay cancer,' Hawkins recalled. "But we all knew better. We all heard about Sweet Jimmy being sick. He was in the hospital for eight months, but O.J. never came to see him.

"He only showed up for his dad's funeral."

And O.J. "listened to his mama," said Bell. "He

knew she was behind him all the way, but he'd best not cross her! We scuffled and ran around late, we played cards and dice, we strutted our stuff."

The Superiors threw rocks at buses, sneaked into ball games, and were generally rowdy. They'd sell programs at 49er games at old Kezar Stadium, then climb the fence to get the better seats. They collected seat cushions and returned them to concessionaires—at a nickel apiece—for extra cash. O.J. caught fish off Pier 90 and peddled them in The Project. He and his gang sold newspapers on street corners.

"And we got in fights," O.J. said.

After one gang rumble, he was arrested. "I gave my name as Burt Lancaster and the cop wrote it down in his notebook," he recalled. "I thought I was so smart. Then I spent a weekend in juvenile hall and I thought I was a man."

Eunice Simpson knew that her son's only hope of avoiding a future of crime or menial work lay in sport. She persuaded the baseball coach at St. Ignatius High School to give him a scholarship when he left Everett Junior High. The coach, mindful that O.J. had set the school record for the 60-yard dash and was a talented ballplayer, agreed.

But O.J., who was captain of his baseball team, threw his chance away. Against his coach's orders, he went to a dance and missed one baseball practice too many. The punishment was swift—the coach withdrew his offer.

It stung O.J. and could have cost him dearly. But Eunice Simpson was a tenacious woman with a will of tempered steel. She didn't give up. If he couldn't go to St. Ignatius, she'd get him into another school. All she knew was that she'd move heaven and earth before letting her son go to Mission High with the rest of The Superiors.

Somehow, trading on O.J.'s athletic abilities, she got him enrolled at a school across town. Galileo High, in San Francisco's North Beach area, was once a predominantly Italian school that had produced baseball legend Joe DiMaggio, basketball great Hank Luisetti, and champion golfer Lawson Little. When O.J. arrived, he found that most of the Italian-American students had been supplanted by Orientals; the school was utterly unlike Mission, where black and Latino gangs had ruled. He knew then and there that the cross-town bus ride meant he wouldn't be spending as much time with his old gang.

And the fact that his new schoolmates were mostly Asian meant that the tall, handsome black kid was one of the biggest tryouts for the football team. Coach Larry McInerney looked at his undersized Asian players and at the 165-pound O.J. and told him: "You play tackle." O.J. put on the helmet and pads and went to work.

McInerney knew enough about football, so that when he saw his newest recruit running, he swiftly changed his mind. "Backfield!" he told O.J. A star was emerging, even though McInerney and his fellow JV coach Jack McBride still didn't have the game plan down to a science.

Next they started O.J. as a defensive back. Then after that, they tried him as a receiver. Three mistakes in a row. Finally, O.J. began doing what he loved best—running with the ball. Running fast, running hard—running through, around, and past tacklers.

He never stopped running. The purple-and-orange-uniformed Number 28 ran his way through school in a sports uniform. It had been his supreme talent and now he was exercising it. He made carrying the football and weaving through defensive secondaries an art form that would take him all the way to the very top in the NFL.

But that was just about all the work he was doing when it came to school. "He was a very lazy student," recalled McBride. "And he never gave a thought to college or to anything much else, other than sports."

But in trouble or not, O.J. was never without his shadow, Al Cowlings. Al was always there for him. A playmate in the streets of Potrero Hill, a teammate on high school and professional football fields, and then later at O.J.'s side in Hollywood, Cowlings followed his hero everywhere.

The inseparable duo started football together at Galileo. They also finished it together at Galileo, and again finished it together with the San Francisco 49ers. Then, when O.J. led the Los Angeles Police Department on a bizarre, slow-motion chase that ended with his surrender in the driveway of his Brentwood mansion, Al went the distance and finished it with him again.

"He's still blocking for him," said Joe Angel, their high school quarterback. "He's still running interference, making sure the way's safe for O.J."

Theirs has been a lifelong liaison. When sides were picked on the playground, O.J. picked Al first. When fights were picked with their Superiors gang, Al stood by O.J. Al stuttered, so O.J. used his glib tongue to speak up for his friend. O.J. wasn't small, but Al stood a towering 6 feet, 3 inches and weighed 230 pounds by the time he was 16 years old.

"We ran together everywhere," Al said. "We partied, played cards, went everywhere together.

We have always been buddies. O.J. had a habit of promoting fights with guys from other neighborhoods. And then he'd disappear. I got my nose busted a number of times on account of him."

And then there were their antics with the ladies; for example, there was the time they went to watch a high school playoff game together. Said Cowlings: "There was a certain lady who was supposed to have eyes for me, and O.J. was telling her I had eyes for her, which was not exactly the case. Anyway, she told her boyfriend I was digging her. Right after the game, there's a tap on my shoulder and the boyfriend and two of his buddies let me have it. O.J.? He was nowhere to be seen."

But Al had the last laugh. The pair were riding a neighborhood bus when O.J. spotted a local beauty—and he gave her a friendly pinch as she passed. "She knocked him between two seats and jumped on him," said Al, hooting with laughter at the memory. "I was laughing like hell. O.J. was embarrassed—but there wasn't much he could do. She had four older brothers."

Another time O.J. and Al were thrown in a paddy wagon together and taken home with a warning. "We'd been out pretty late and the cops had stopped us," Al recalled. "They asked our names and O.J. said 'Orenthal James.' They thought he was trying to be smart with them. He told them he wasn't and just about had them convinced when they asked the third guy with us what his name was. He said 'General Blue.' They didn't wait a second—just threw us into the wagon. The funny thing was, his name really *was* General Blue!"

A lot less funny, but something that Al was able to forgive his best friend for, was the situation with Marguerite Whitley. Vivacious Marguerite was his high school sweetheart, but the sometimes-inarticulate teen was having trouble talking to her, and so he and asked O.J. to intercede on his behalf.

"It was like asking the fox to guard the chicken coop," said 'Joe' Bell. "Al, he's not that smart. O.J. was always smarter than a lot of guys." It didn't take long before Marguerite and O.J. were dating. They eventually married; she was 19, he just one year older.

At first Al reacted with fury to the loss of his sweetheart, but eventually he was able to shrug it off. This was strangely atypical behavior for an angry young man who was suspended five times at Galileo, usually for brawling, but it perhaps points out just how strong was the bond between the two men.

O.J. was often caught fighting, too, but the star athlete was able to talk his way out of suspensions, once even being given the remainder of the week off—"for a rest."

Al, Bell, and O.J. were always on the fringes of trouble. Bell eventually went to jail for selling marijuana to a high school teacher, so it was no surprise when the JV coach caught them playing dice in the school bathrooms. Coach McBride stared down his star players, whom he had just caught red-handed. It was the day of an important school game. What he did next stunned young O.J., who expected to be let off with a slap on the wrist.

"He turned us in to the dean," said O.J. "It meant we wouldn't be able to play." But O.J.'s quick thinking saved him. The coach escorted the trio to the dean's office and said he'd caught them playing craps. He gave the principal the dice he'd confiscated and left. O.J., who had followed Bell and Al, promptly turned to leave, too.

"Where are you going, Simpson?" asked the dean. O.J. looked innocent. "I wasn't shooting craps," he declared. "Coach just asked me to help bring these guys down here." Back in the locker room, McBride asked O.J. if he'd been suspended, to which he was truthfully able to reply: "No."

"Fortunately, the dean left their punishments up to me," said McBride. "They were the three best players on my JV football team. I knew when I turned them in they might not be able to play in our game that day, but that was my job." And so McBride opted to bench his three errant stars.

"We all felt rotten," said O.J. "McBride gave us a tongue-lashing that made us feel even worse, saying we weren't just wrecking ourselves but we were letting down the whole team. He said we'd stay on the bench that day.

"When the game started, there we were—like three stooges on the bench, watching our team getting pushed all the way down the field. I recall how irresponsible I felt. When Poly (Polytechnic High) got inside our 5-yard line, the agony became so unbearable none of us could watch."

Then McBride sent the trio in with a brusque: "Get in there and stop them before this gets out of hand." It was O.J.'s first great day on a football field. He poured out his frustrations with not one, but six touchdown runs, for 87, 75, 60, 20, 15 and 12 yards as Galileo then went on to an easy win. He later said that McBride's handling of the incident had made an indelible impression on him.

"He told me: 'If you want respect, you're going to have to act in a respectable way,' " the budding star said. "I heard him, and I began to straighten myself out."

Bell didn't get the message right away. But a

bit later when he was in jail, he saw a football photograph of O.J. in a newspaper. Shocked, Bell vowed: "If *he* can make it, so can I." It's an insight into how O.J. was viewed in school and it's also a clue to Joe Bell's character that he went on to play college football and today has a successful antique business.

It was about this time that O.J.'s growing feeling t⌄. ⌄e should straighten himself out truly surfaced. He'd been arrested for taking part in a gang fight and had spent the weekend in juvenile hall. He came home to receive a telephone call from the great Willie Mays, a baseball legend and one of O.J.'s personal heroes.

He never did find out how Mays learned about his arrest, but he suspects that one of his football coaches—or perhaps even his mother Eunice—might have dropped the dime. The result was dramatic. O.J. was invited to Mays' home, a mansion that overawed the unruly kid from The Project.

"There were no speeches, no stay-away-from-drugs talk," O.J. said. "It was just time with Willie. To have my hero pay attention to me made me feel I must be special, too."

The gist of Willie's talk to the impressionable teen was that O.J. had a special gift for football and that should use it against the best. If that meant testing himself, so be it—there wasn't any point thinking you were the best if you didn't test yourself against those who were. But Willie had another message, too.

"You might become famous, but you'll have an obligation," he told O.J. "You must set a decent example for other young people. Live right, remember your friends and family, and only pick those you trust to be your friends."

O.J. looked at the sumptuous surroundings that sports had enabled this great man to acquire, and he resolved to get away from petty crime and concentrate on becoming the champion football player he felt he could truly be. Back home, he told Eunice of his new resolve. Not surprisingly, she reinforced it.

"You'd best get away from what you're doing before you find yourself behind bars," she warned her headstrong son.

Later, in the speech he gave at his induction into the Football Hall of Fame, O.J. said: "She kept me on track all those years. She was the most important person in my life. You just don't know what it is to be eight years old and all your friends think you have the best mother in the neighborhood."

Eunice responded: "My job as a psychiatric technician may have helped me as a mother. A lot of times when O.J. would get in trouble or the other kids would get in trouble, I'd tell them: 'You kids act just like my patients.'

"And sometimes I found myself being very firm with them, treating them like I'd treat my patients. I didn't really think O.J. would turn out the way he did, but he always said: 'One of these days, you're going to read about me.'

"And my oldest daughter would always say: 'In the police report.' "

The Dude on a
White Horse

From the moment he saw team mascot Tommy
Trojan, the young, wide-eyed high school football
star O.J. Simpson knew he just had to go to the
University of Southern California. "In 1962 or '63,
I was watching the Rose Bowl," he recalled. "USC

was playing and this dude in a big cape on a white horse came galloping out on the field. I couldn't believe it and I decided right then that that was the college I was going to."

And USC, located a little more than a Hail Mary pass from his current cramped cell at L.A. Men's Central Jail, would in fact become the place where the street-smart ghetto kid first become a national hero. Getting there, however, wouldn't be as easy as a broken field run. Not at all.

The widely respected PAC–8 school had high standards, and a mere C-minus average from high school just wasn't good enough to get O.J. into Southern Cal. Instead, his grades were just high enough to get him into two years of junior college at the City College of San Francisco (CCSF).

Ironically, an education wasn't the only benefit he reaped at CCSF. Had he continued to hang out on Potrero Hill, he would surely have been drafted into the Army just like his brother and so many other young men his age—and O.J. could easily have begun his career dodging bullets in Viet Nam instead of eluding tacklers on the gridiron.

But more importantly, it was while he was faking defenders out of their shoes on his junior college team that his long-time love affair with USC became mutual—and the Trojans discovered that they wanted O.J. just as badly as he wanted them.

At the end of his first year O.J. scored three touchdowns to lead 20–point underdog CCSF to a shocking 40–20 upset over powerful Long Beach City College in the Prune Bowl. Southern Cal assistant coaches Marv Goux and Jim Strangeland had attended the game to scout two highly touted Long Beach stars, Mike Battle and Earl McCullough, but they left with their mouths watering for a taste of The Juice.

"You'll be seeing us again soon," Goux promised him.

As the giddy Trojan scouts left the locker room, O.J.'s overjoyed coach Dutch Elston grabbed him. "Southern Cal! That's where you want to go. That's big-time football," Dutch yelled. O.J.'s dream of playing where the "dude on the white horse came galloping out on the field" before all the games and after each and every Southern Cal score was suddenly inching closer to reality.

Still, the prestigious university was not waiting for him with open arms. In the first place, the "basket weaving" classes he took at CCSF didn't impress the Trojans; nor were they offering any under-the-table money like a lot of the other "football factory" schools which were wooing O.J. with cash and cars.

At some colleges, the coaches were in the habit of pointing out their star athletes as they took a tour of the campus with prospective recruits. Football players were very easy to find. They were the ones driving spanking-new Cadillac convertibles and wearing alligator-hide cowboy boots.

But at Southern Cal, players wore jeans and walked to class. Coaches didn't have to wave cash and shiny cars under O.J.'s nose because they had something far more valuable to offer—respect. The Trojans played regularly on national TV, and exposure like that could help a star player land a big-bucks career in the NFL. Besides, a degree from USC was really worth something.

Still, a poor ghetto kid had to listen to the lucrative offers made by other schools. Arizona State made a particularly good one: they had arranged for O.J., his mom, and his best girl, Marguerite Whitley, to fly to Phoenix for a recruiting trip. The three made it only as far as the airport. There, the Arizona State coach who was with them excused himself and walked into the rest room.

Big mistake. A Utah coach, who had been following the prize player, swooped down on the confused entourage when their Arizona State escort disappeared. The open-field tackle of the star runner was not at all appreciated by the ASU coach.

"They started arguing. They were fighting over me," O.J. would later boast.

And he liked what the Utah coach had to say best. He never left the airport that day. A few weeks later, O.J. signed a non-binding letter of intent to attend the University of Utah. As he started to pack, he was interrupted by a well-timed phone call. It was Marv Goux, the Trojan coach O.J. had wowed in the Prune Bowl.

"Tell the truth, O.J., he said. "Where do you really want to go to school?"

"USC . . . but I don't want to spend another year at CCSF," Juice admitted.

"That's a shame. You want to go to school here, but you're willing to settle for less. Don't you know that anything worth having is worth working for?"

In his heart, O.J. knew Goux was right. If he wanted a pro football career, the years spent at USC would give him national media exposure and excellent coaching to prepare him for the NFL. It would prove to be a wise investment that paid back huge dividends. O.J. decided to stay in junior college and pass the geometry classes he needed to get into Southern Cal.

But The Juice still didn't have a clear path to USC. Eye-popping offers continued to roll in from other schools, each more golden than the next. The temptation became too great. Some colleges were bidding more money than the pros, and he reluctantly decided to bolt to greener pastures.

But once again, the hand of fate grabbed O.J. and gave him a not-so-gentle shove in the direction of Southern Cal. Oddly, his ultimate good fortune came disguised as a threatening phone call.

"This is Tom Hamilton," barked a stern voice on the other end of the line, "and I'm the Commissioner of the PAC–8." Hamilton warned O.J. that if he signed with any other school, he would be thoroughly investigated. If there had been any money, or a car, or even the slightest hint of a shady deal involved in switching schools, he would find out. The offending school would be penalized— but far worse—O.J. would be banned from major college football.

He understood the ominous message loud and clear: He would play for Southern Cal . . . or else.

The spring of 1967 found O.J. and Marguerite setting up house in a small second-floor apartment barely a block away from USC's main campus in L.A. For the first time in his life O.J. Simpson's day was structured. He studied in the morning, worked out and went to football practice in the afternoon, then logged a few more study hours each evening at the USC library, where Marguerite had landed a job. Late at night, the young lovers would walk home together, hand-in-hand.

Life was great when it was simple.

Meanwhile, USC football coach John McKay was wringing his hands, eager to shape the raw talent he had recognized in O.J. on the first day of spring practice in April 1967. A quarter-century and an unthinkable turn of events later, that same John McKay would be wringing his hands along with the rest of the country as he went on national television to urge O.J. to end his bizarre odyssey on the L.A. freeways.

But back in their first sessions together, it was still an innocent game. Seven times he had ordered O.J. to run the ball straight up the middle. And seven times The Juice squeezed through the tough and talented Trojan defense. "He busted them backward," beamed an amazed McKay, who had seen enough. Sparing his rising star the chance of getting injured during spring drills, he turned O.J. over to the Trojan track team.

The Juice's blazing speed immediately grabbed the spotlight. He was part of USC's world record-setting 440-yard relay squad and ran the 100-yard dash in 9.3 seconds, finishing second at the NCAA finals, all of which helped Southern Cal win the team championship.

But it was his exploits off the football field that made O.J. a household name. McKay's 1967 Trojans were one of the best college football teams in history. USC capped off a 9–1 season with a Rose Bowl romp over Indiana. Five players were first-round picks in the NFL draft. And the well-oiled football machine ran entirely on Juice.

In Southern Cal's second game, he shredded national powerhouse Texas' defense for 158 yards. O.J. scored his first touchdown and looked up to see Tommy Trojan galloping onto the field. It was impossible to tell who was more thrilled: "The dude on the white horse," the wildly cheering fans, or O.J. Simpson himself.

But it was the spectacle he put on in a nationally televised game against legendary football power Notre Dame that turned The Juice loose all across the country. The undefeated and number one-ranked Irish had built a 7–0 half-time lead, but O.J. scored three touchdowns and gained 150 yards on 38 rushes to lead the Trojans to a stunning 24–7 win.

One sportswriter wrote: "O.J. shouldn't stand for Orange Juice. It should stand for 'Oh, Jesus'— as in, 'Oh, Jesus, there he goes again!' "

In the final game of the season, arch-rival UCLA led the Trojans 20–14 in the waning minutes of the game. It was third-and-eight from the USC 36. In the huddle, O.J. stared at Trojan quarterback Toby Page. "Give me pigskin. I want it!" his eyes demanded. The Juice squirted around the end, cut back, then reversed his field and zipped 64 yards on a spine-tingling touchdown run to lift his team to a 21–20 triumph.

By now, O.J. seriously coveted the prestigious Heisman Trophy. He had wanted it more than anything, ever since he had been mesmerized by the rough-hewn statue of a runner captured for all time in bronze. He first saw it at the home of Heisman-winning USC tailback Mike Garrett. Now, as a USC junior, The Juice was named to every All-American team; he was UPI's Player of the Year, as well as the national rushing champ with 1,543 yards under his belt.

But he didn't get the Heisman.

Instead, UCLA quarterback Gary Beban did, and O.J. finished second. In no time, the Trojans' 14–3 win over Indiana in the 1968 Rose Bowl had become little more than afterthought, because O.J. now had two very important things on his mind—the Heisman Trophy and a baby.

Marguerite was pregnant.

"There are two kinds of great running backs," O.J. once told an interviewer. "The side-steppers and the challengers. I'm a side-stepper. I never let them hit me square, and if I can avoid them altogether, I do.

"Each week, I study the films, and on the field I always look for the baddest dude on the other team. I get it in my mind he's never gong to hit me. My favorite tacklers are the little cornerbacks and the safety. I run at those guys and sidestep the linemen.

"Actually," O.J. confessed, "I run like a coward. I run away. I don't like to get hit." Unfortunately, those innocent words would prove to be chillingly prophetic two short decades later.

Although O.J. still had a year remaining at USC, he was keeping his options open. He had been briefly tempted by a $65,000 three-year deal offered by the Montreal Alouettes of the Canadian football League. After all, a career-ending injury could pop up at any time, and NFL salaries had shrunk considerably since the merger with the American Football League.

The big-bucks bidding wars for college players was over. Yet in the end O.J. again decided to keep his eye on the big prize, on the prestige and the power that comes with being an NFL super-star. You don't get too many big ad deals or movie roles playing in Quebec.

And the football season ahead was filled with question marks. Most of the important senior players from the Rose Bowl championship team had graduated, but a lot of people had faith in the spunky kid from Potrero Hill. "Give me O.J. and ten cheerleaders and we can beat the Green Bay Packers," bragged one fan. Another said he was "Horatio Alger wearing a jock strap."

And The Juice didn't let them down.

Southern Cal was steamrollering its competition and had piled up a perfect 8–0 record by the time they faced cross-town rival UCLA, the final barrier to a PAC–8 championship and another trip to the Rose Bowl. Again, the work load fell squarely on O.J. and dependably, he shouldered it well, ripping through the shell-shocked Bruin defense for 205 yards on 40 carries and scoring three touchdowns in a 28–16 Trojan romp. But the season ended on a sour note. USC tied Notre Dame, 21–21, then lost to national champion Ohio State, 27–16, in the Rose Bowl.

Yet, during O.J.'s time at USC, the Trojans had a sparkling 19–2–1 record, winning two PAC–8 championships and one Rose Bowl. The Juice also set an NCAA record of 1,709 yards during his senior season. He broke or tied 13 school records and walked away with every award in the land. But nothing could top the feeling of pride he had when he finally became a landslide winner of the Heisman Trophy he cherished so much. And, at the award ceremony, USC announced it would retire his number 32.

The requisite big-money ad offers were pouring in, but O.J. was casting a wary eye to the storm clouds looming on the horizon. The NFL draft was coming up, and the Buffalo Bills had the first pick. The news sent a shiver down his spine. Thriving in sunny Southern California, O.J. felt as if he were about to be sent to Siberia.

In early January 1969 he went to Dodger Stadium for a joint announcement with friend Steve Sogge, who had just signed a Dodger contract. O.J. had hired an agent, Chuck Barnes of Sports Headliners. L.A. Dodger manager Tommy Lasorda, then a spirited scout who had signed Sogge, said with his characteristic chutzpah that he had something for The Juice, too.

"We have this unsigned contract waiting for O.J.," Lasorda said. "We figure he might want to switch sports." But years before two-sport superstars Bo Jackson and Deion Sanders came along,

O.J. mulled the tempting offer over for only a moment, before answering, "Nah!"

Bills owner Ralph Wilson had a nightmare task ahead of him. If O.J. was coming to Buffalo, he would have to be dragged kicking and screaming to town. He had never eaten Buffalo wings or wick-on-a-stick and he wasn't anxious to try such delicacies. And then there was the snow.

"I've never been to Buffalo, but my image of the town is cars stalled in blizzards with snow piled to their roofs," O.J. gulped. "Is it really that bad?"

"Well, it's not Honolulu," Wilson admitted.

And the Bills weren't the only bidders. The Orlando Panthers of the Continental League offered O.J. $600,000 a year to play football and hawk orange juice, with part of the dough to be paid by the Florida Citrus Commission. The Indianapolis Capitols offered $400,000, plus a dollar-per-person over the previous year's attendance. The San Antonio Toros offered 80 percent of their attendance revenue. Everyone wanted the kid from California.

In the end, the lure of the NFL won out. On August 10, O.J. reluctantly shuffled off to Buffalo to ink a deal worth $300,000. Nearly three thousand avid fans turned out to greet him at the Greater Buffalo International Airport, but Marguerite stayed home. She wanted as little as possible to do with the grimy, industrial town.

The mayor gave O.J. the keys to the city, and Miss Buffalo, Kathy Karpinski, gave him a peck on the cheek. A local sports columnist wrote that, counting exhibition and play-off games, there were just "21 games until the Super Bowl!"

Team veterans treated the bonus baby like any other player, making him stand on the training camp dining table and sing the USC fight song, standard hazing for rookies. On the first day of practice O.J. couldn't find a helmet that fit him, so he worked out bareheaded.

He was miserable. The Bills were dreadful, winning just eight games during his first three seasons there. Coach John Rauch didn't like his form as he ran the ball and used him mainly as a decoy. "Those were wasted years," O.J. later fumed. "They were restricting my physical ability. They weren't using me right."

But there was light at the end of the tunnel. The Juice convinced the Bills to make his friend Al Cowlings one of their first-round draft picks. And by 1971, Bills owner Wilson had finally had enough. He fired Rauch and hired Lou Saban. The new coach vowed to make O.J. the keystone of his offense.

The Bills hit rock bottom with a 1–13 season, but Saban had already began building a powerful offensive line to blast holes in opposing defenses. He brought in a six-foot-four, 250-pound All-American guard named Reggie McKenzie, whom O.J. would later call "the soul of my pro career" in his "suicide" note.

By 1973, the bulked-up Bills were ready to open the floodgates and drown the rest of the league in Juice. He rushed for more than 200 yards in three games and for more than 100 yards in 11 of Buffalo's 14 games. He scored 12 touchdowns. And he shattered the league rushing record with an incredible 2,003 yards. The Bills finished with a 9–5 record and barely missed the playoffs.

O.J. was the toast of the town, even though he often and openly expressed his hatred for living in Buffalo. He had even casually said of nearby landmark Niagara Falls: "Once you've seen one waterfall, you've seen them all."

The elusive runner captured four NFL rushing titles by 1977. O.J. was ranked the greatest living American hero by boys and girls through high school in a *Ladies Home Journal* poll. But his playing career had crested now, and he suffered a knee injury midway through the 1977 season that required an operation.

Finally, the Bills traded O.J. to San Francisco for five draft choices. He played little for the 49ers during his final two years, but at least he was again playing football where it had all begun, and—surprise—good old A.C. had joined the 49ers, too.

O.J.'s football career in college and the pros had made him a beloved hero, and he set a slew of pro records to go with his college marks. When he retired he ranked second among all NFL rushers with 11,236 yards, averaging 4.7 yards every time he touched the ball. He had scored 61 touchdowns rushing and had run for more than 200 yards in six games.

His only professional regret was that he never got to play in the Super Bowl.

A Stormy
First Marriage

The first true love in O.J. Simpson's life was Marguerite Lorraine Whitley, a busty, statuesque beauty he had met during his days at Galileo High School in San Francisco. But his best friend Al Cowlings, the same man who some 30 years later would drive the white Ford Bronco with a suicidal O.J. huddled in the back and lead police on a 60-mile odyssey that would end in surrender and arrest for both of them, also had his eyes on her.

"When O.J. first met and fell in love with Marguerite, it almost destroyed his relationship with Al," said one long-time friend. "At Galileo High in late 1966, both O.J. and Al—who was a lineman on the team—were football heroes and the best of buddies. They studied together, partied together and knew all the same girls. As it happened, Al started dating Marguerite first. Al liked Marguerite and wanted to impress her, but he felt he needed some help. In those days, Al had a stutter and felt that he couldn't tell Marguerite everything he wanted. So he asked his buddy O.J. to help him out.

"Well, O.J. told her lots of things all right. In fact, he wound up spinning more yarn for himself than he did for Al and ended up winning Marguerite for himself. It didn't set too well with Al. Shortly after O.J. and Marguerite started dating, Al saw them out together and got really mad. He angrily yelled at O.J. and even tried to roll their car over. But a week later, after Al had cooled off and he could see that Marguerite's heart was with O.J., he forgave his old pal and they patched things up."

Ironically, the night A.C. returned O.J. to his Brentwood driveway, it was Marguerite's son who came running up to the Bronco to reach his father, only to pushed away by Cowlings with 95 million television viewers watching. How the years had come 'round.

Once O.J. and Marguerite started dating, they became inseparable, and they were married in June 1967. At the time of the marriage, Marguerite was not quite 19 and O.J. was a handsome, muscular man just twenty years old. The happy newlyweds' first home was a modest, second-story apartment near the University of Southern California's campus, south of Los Angeles. O.J. and Marguerite had moved their meager belongings into the tiny apartment when O.J. selected USC over the more than fifty other colleges which had tried to recruit him.

In the beginning of what was eventually to become a rocky 13-year marriage, O.J. and Marguerite spent some of their happiest days together at the small off-campus apartment. Marguerite clerked in the USC science building library. O.J. was busy with his studies and traveling and playing football, but he and Marguerite were very much in love.

The happy couple spent hours listening to the Supremes, Ray Charles, and the Reflections. Marguerite kept their apartment tidy, cooked up O.J.'s favorite pasta dishes, and helped him every way she could with his studies. Marguerite was on top of the world during those days. She was young and beautiful and everybody envied her because her chiseled, athletic husband was obviously destined for stardom.

Attention throughout the football world was building on O.J. His pictures were in all the papers and on TV. There were calls from reporters and admiring fans. On the USC campus, fellow students and friends started referring to O.J. simply as "he." Such comments as "There he goes," or "Isn't he something!" or "I don't know how anybody can stop him!" were frequently heard when O.J. and Marguerite walked hand in hand across the campus.

An interview with a *Los Angeles Times* reporter on October 6, 1967—only five months after their marriage—reveals just how happy O.J. and Marguerite were together in those days. But, despite their immense love for each other, the interview also offered faint hints of future problems in the marriage. With typical conviction, Marguerite told the reporter that the O.J. Simpson she knew at Galileo High had been a "terrible" person.

O.J. agreed. "I didn't have any goals," he said. "I goofed off a lot. It wasn't my home situation, even though my parents were separated. We still did things as a family. But I was sort of aimless."

Here is how O.J. told the story of beating out his long-time friend Al Cowlings for Marguerite's hand. "Marguerite knew a tackle on my high school team," O.J. said. "He was my best friend and I just sort of happened to be around. I had a good season that last year both on the field and off. I played well and I found a good girl."

Then Marguerite told the interviewer: "After the marriage, I think he found a purpose in his life. With all the public attention he was getting from football, he became more occupied and had somewhere to put his energies. He had something to do with himself."

During the interview O.J. poured out his hopes and dreams. "After graduation from USC," he said, "I'd like to play eight to ten years as a pro. Like Jim Brown," he explained, noting one of his long-time heroes. "I want to get out while I'm still on top, before I get too banged up.

"Then I want to go back to San Francisco and work with kids. When I was coming up, I remember some of the people that worked with me. Lots of guys come out of high school and they're not quite developed. I'd like to try to help kids like that." At that point, Marguerite left the interview and returned to her clerk's job. O.J. talked openly about their marriage.

"You sure have a lot of adjustments to make when you get married," O.J. told the reporter, "but me and Marguerite are making them. We like it here in L.A. I never thought I'd get a chance to go to a school like USC. Now I realize how lucky I have been."

Earlier, O.J. and Marguerite had introduced the reporter to their pet parrot Harvey, who squawked and pranced around the tiny apartment. "We're going to get Harvey a wife," Marguerite said, "and we're going to name her Mildred. Harvey and Mildred. Doesn't that sound like a nice name for a couple?" At that comment, O.J., in a more serious tone, explained: "Only reason we have Harvey is to keep Marguerite company while I'm on the road. Harvey is great for that."

During the years that followed O.J.'s and Marguerite's stay in the tiny apartment, his road trips became more and more frequent. He was sky-rocketing to fame, while Marguerite spent more time alone. This arrangement inevitably caused marital friction.

But during those same years O.J. also brought a huge measure of fame and fortune to both himself and Marguerite—more than either of them had ever imagined. During that same period, O.J.'s acting career had begun to blossom, and he made several movies, including *The Towering Inferno* in 1974, *Killer Force* in 1975, *The Cassandra Crossing* in 1977, and *Capricorn One* in 1978. O.J. had become a superstar in sports, television and film. He was earning millions, but it also meant he was away from home. More and more, Marguerite was destined to spend her time alone, perhaps busying herself as O.J. intimated, by pacing back and forth in their empty apartment, waiting for him to come home and cleaning out the bottom of Harvey's cage.

Then, in December 1968, O.J. and Marguerite bought a beautiful new home at 3005 Elvill Drive in the exclusive Bel Air section of Los Angeles. The two-story, traditional-style mansion, built earlier that year, was a model of California grandeur and provided a sweeping, panoramic view of the Hollywood Hills and downtown Los Angeles further south. Their neighbors included some of the most famous names in show-business, including Zsa Zsa Gabor, Elizabeth Taylor, and Howard Hughes.

The couple needed the sprawling, four-bedroom mansion to house their growing family. On December 4, 1968, Marguerite had delivered a beautiful baby daughter, Arnell. Son Jason, who would become the apple of his father's eye, was born next. During those early years with the kids Marguerite's daily hours were consumed in a typical full-time routine of diapers, baby bottles, and nursery school.

As O.J.'s career continued to soar, he was away from home for longer spells. Cracks began to appear in the marriage. Although O.J. did not file for divorce until March of 1979, there were serious problems as early as 1973. According to divorce records, Marguerite was traveling back and forth between their L.A. home and San Francisco and talking to lawyers about what one attorney called her "present and past marital problems."

From early 1973 until early 1978, the marriage was marked by several separations and reunions. During one of these separations, O.J. met and fell in love with the stunning teenage beauty Nicole Brown. They were already living together before the divorce from Marguerite was final.

According to court records, there were numerous contacts between Marguerite's and O.J.'s lawyers, trying to decide how much O.J. should pay Marguerite in a possible divorce settlement. Their mounting marital problems were complicated further in September of 1977, when a third child, Aaren Leshona was born. A few months after her birth, in late January of 1978, O.J. and Marguerite finally sold their house in Bel Air. They had vacated the house in July of 1977 so they could move into an even bigger place, a fabulous, gray-stone mansion compound at 360 Rockingham Drive in the exclusive Brentwood section of Los Angeles. But the new home was not enough to save the faltering marriage. On September 8, 1978, O.J. and Marguerite agreed to a formal separation, citing irreconcilable differences. O.J. moved out of the Brentwood mansion, leaving it to Marguerite and the three kids.

Then tragedy struck. Twenty-three-month-old Aaren Leshona died of respiratory failure on August 28, 1979, a week after she had somehow fallen into the family swimming pool. A family member had pulled her out, but when paramedics arrived, the child was unconscious and had no vital signs, according to fire department officials.

Using mouth-to-mouth resuscitation, paramedics had revived the child by the time they reached the emergency room, but a hospital spokesman said the girl never regained consciousness.

O.J. learned of the accident just before an NFL home exhibition game. Only minutes after the news was reported to him, he left for Los Angeles to be with his family. As he rushed down the hospital hallway, he was reportedly heard screaming, "She murdered my child, she murdered my child!"

The rift between the estranged Simpsons was never truly healed. In a January 28, 1980 letter Marguerite's attorney charged that:

• O.J. had allowed Jason in his bedroom while his girlfriend Nicole was present.

• Throughout the divorce proceedings, O.J. had tried to make it appear that he looked with equal favor upon both his children—even getting them equal parts in a TreeSweet commercial. But the sad fact was that he showed huge favoritism toward his son, and this alledged behavior had emotionally affected his daughter.

• O.J. had been trying to "win over" Jason by driving a wedge between Jason and Marguerite, and telling the child that he was going to live with O.J. and "Nicole."

• O.J. had been rude and inconsiderate toward Marguerite when he came to visit the children. Often, he appeared at the house without notifying her beforehand.

O.J. and Marguerite finally signed an agreement on March 3, 1980, to dissolve their marriage. The divorce proceedings—which spanned more than five years and included at least six attorney changes by Marguerite—was a heart-wrenching affair, and the worst-case scenario for a couple with children.

In the decree, O.J. and Marguerite agreed that O.J. would buy out her share of the Brentwood home for $600,000 to be paid in cash. Court papers say the house was worth $1.7million at that time. O.J. agreed to allow Marguerite and their two children to remain in the Brentwood home for four more months, until June 30, 1980. After that date, Marguerite would optimistically "be in a position to find another home and be able to occupy it," the papers said.

He agreed to buy out her share in his commercial endorsements, which at that time included Hertz, Acme Boots, TreeSweet, and NBC television, for $500,000, of which $100,000 was to be paid in cash and the remaining $400,000 to be put in a trust account.

Marguerite was granted primary custody of the couple's children, Arnell and Jason. Marguerite was to get $5,300 each month as support for six more years—totaling $371,600—which was to come out of the $1,000,000 that O.J. was owed as deferred compensation in his Buffalo Bills contract.

O.J. agreed to pay $1,500 a month for the children as well as all reasonable medical and dental expenses, their private schooling, summer camp expenses, and up to $400 per month for the children's therapist.

The agreement urged Marguerite to use the $600,000 cash payment she was receiving for her equity in the Brentwood home to buy another home for herself and the children. Marguerite also got a family van and her personal Mercedes-Benz, all furniture and furnishings in the house, as well as all of her personal property, including jewelry.

But it wasn't quite over. According to court papers, when O.J. went to the house to change the locks and take it over on June 30, 1980, he found Marguerite there—refusing to budge. He ordered her out, and she threatened to call police and charge him with physical abuse, libel, and slander. Finally, O.J. left.

On July 6, six days after the deadline had passed for Marguerite to vacate the Brentwood home, her lawyer filed a motion asking that the divorce agreement be overturned. The agreement gave her a total of more than $1.5 million, but Marguerite felt she deserved more for having to put up with O.J. all those years. She complained that she was still in shock over her child's death and was talked into signing the agreement by O.J. and his lawyer.

"The stress came about due to the death of my daughter Aaren Leshona Simpson and pressure by Mr. Simpson to consent to the agreement and settle the issue," she claimed. "At the time, I failed to recognize the significance of my signature on the marital settlement agreement and failed to contest or question any of the declarations which designated Mr. Simpson's separate property."

On the following day, O.J.'s attorney filed a motion asking the court to boot Marguerite and the children out of the Brentwood home. He noted that Marguerite had accepted everything under the judgment, but when she was asked to vacate the house—as agreed to in the settlement—she had not done so.

The judge agreed with O.J., refused to nullify the divorce agreement, and ordered Marguerite and the children out of their home. O.J. moved into the fabulous mansion and was soon joined there by his blonde sweetheart, Nicole. Shortly afterwards, Marguerite bought a house for herself and the two children. Three years later, in late 1983, O.J. sued for custody of then 13-year-old Jason, but the court turned him down.

After the divorce from O.J., Marguerite disappeared from the local social scene. In April 1992, she married furniture salesman Anthony Thomas, a New York native who was nine years her junior, and settled down quietly in Los Angeles. Following the death of Nicole Brown Simpson and Ronald Lyle Goldman on June 12, Marguerite Simpson went into hiding, allegedly with friends in Palm Springs, to avoid the world's press.

Throughout his marriage to Marguerite, the darker side of O.J.'s personality, which cops believe led to the death of Nicole and her friend, remained hidden from public view. But there were clues even then that the home of the all-American Simpsons had concealed terrifying explosions of violence within its walls.

When O.J. and Marguerite finally sold their old house in Bel Air so they could move into the Brentwood mansion, the buyers were Gloria Pall, a 1950s beauty queen and real-estate broker, and her husband at the time. Gloria was shocked and dismayed at what she found when she entered that Bel Air home. Here's her chilling description.

"On January 23, 1978, tears streamed down my cheeks as I stood in the double-garage-sized kitchen overlooking all the broken and cracked appliances. Nothing was in working order and the house couldn't have been more than nine or ten years old.

"Then I stood and viewed all the broken windows. Every door had been kicked in or pushed in with a fist or maybe somebody's head. All of the locks were broken. The master bedroom—also the size of a double garage—had a large cracked mirror, as if something had been thrown against it.

"As a real estate broker on Sunset Strip for many years, I have seen lots of 'fixers' or houses that were advertised in 'as is' condition. But when I saw the 3005 Elvill Drive home, I had never seen a home so rampaged, smashed, and trashed. It looked like somebody had tried to use the house for a punching bag. It looked like someone had taken out all kinds of frustrations and hatreds on the house.

"I looked at all the damage and wondered to myself what had been going on in that house. What kind of person could have so much violence inside?"

The Business of Running

O.J.'s coaches were always saying that you had to have a game plan for after football. O.J. was no fool. He knew his playing days would end someday, and he wasn't going to end up like a punch-drunk fighter or a washed-up football jock hungry for whatever work he could get with the team.

So the cagey San Francisco street kid devised a strategy that not only turned him into a money-making machine and a household name, but eventually transformed him into America's pitch man, one of the greatest commercial spokesmen—white or black—that the country had ever seen.

A major driving force in his push for after-football success was the lesson O.J. learned from the "other" great athlete in the Simpson clan, his older brother Melvin Leon Simpson. O.J. definitely didn't want to end up like him.

Melvin could have been somebody. He was faster than O.J. in high school, winning the 100–yard dash in the city track meet. He could fight better than O.J. too; he won the city Golden Gloves championship.

But when Melvin came back from the jungles of Vietnam, he ran into walls. While O.J. was making millions as a star running back, Melvin was working as a dishwasher, chasing his dream to be a singer. In 1980, as O.J. was hanging up his cleats, Melvin was working as a doorman at the Clift Hotel in San Francisco, tipping a top hat for quarters.

Of course, Melvin was probably the only doorman in town who drove a Mercedes. But the flashy set of wheels came from O.J., not from his tips. The hard life had soured Melvin. He told one interviewer: "O.J. may be number one in everything else, but I'm the number one son." Melvin was bitter. No wonder they called him "L.J." around the Clift Hotel—"L.J." for Lemon Juice.

Melvin and his bitterness taught O.J. one thing: You don't get anywhere with a frown on your face. By the time Melvin had given his interview, O.J. had already parlayed his athletic fame and handsome, smiling face into a fortune. O.J. had begun to put his after-football plan into action while he was still breaking tackles and sprinting for the end zone. He sniffed out commercial endorsements and opportunities to show his friendly smile off the football field—like guest spots on top TV shows.

In 1974, The Juice set the pro football rushing record of 2,003 yards. Besides earning him innumerable awards, it also made him the most recognizable athlete in America. The Hertz Rent-A-Car people wooed the galloping jock and created the famous TV ad showing O.J. as a businessman in a hurry, racing through a crowded airport and hurdling luggage to get to his rented car—where a pretty girl is waiting to hand him the keys.

Even Hertz was stunned by the success of the ads. Their sales skyrocketed, doubling their profits. It was a remarkable breakthrough. Most of

Hertz' customers were well-to-do whites, but that didn't stop them from following in a handsome black man's wake and renting Hertz. Even Hertz' chief rival, Avis, had to acknowledge O.J.'s effectiveness as a pitch man by running an ad with the slogan: "You don't have to run through airports to rent our cars."

Yes, America loved O.J. like no other black athlete before him. Certainly, Jim Brown had been just as famous a football player, but he never captured the white audience the way that O.J. did. Soon other companies, including Chevrolet and RC Cola, wanted O.J. to pitch their stuff.

In 1980, just after his retirement from football, O.J. demolished forever the myth that a retired black athlete couldn't sell products—with a TV commercial for Dingo Boots. There he was, high-stepping for 30 seconds in a pair of $65 cowboy boots. The ads also ran in *Penthouse* and *Playboy*.

The most startling thing about this endorsement was that the Dingo people had picked O.J. to replace Joe Namath, the popular and handsome *white* football star. "We turned to O.J. because he's been so visible, he's universally recognized," they explained.

But O.J.'s plan involved more than leaping over luggage or selling cars, or boots. As his football career was winding down, he launched his own movie production company, Orenthal Productions, with Mr. Orenthal James Simpson, President. Columbia Pictures had given him offices on its lot as part of the corporation's new minorities-in-pictures program. His first film was a made-for-TV trifle called *Goldie and the Boxer.* It not only won its night, it pulled in the highest rating of any NBC Movie of The Week in two-and-a-half years. A sequel was planned to reprise the saga of the little orphan girl who adopted a fighter and became his manager. O.J. would produce and star in that one as well.

Just one year out of the NFL and O.J. was a movie mogul. Everyone wanted his opinion, his endorsement. He came out for Jimmy Carter over Ronald Reagan. He said the Russians "weren't ogres, just people." And he left one interviewer dumbfounded when he told her he wanted more children, but he didn't want to remarry. Now *that* was controversial!

Smiling, dashing O.J. could do no wrong as far his adoring public was concerned. In 1980 he said, "All the older players in the NFL took drugs when I was first coming into the league." When the interviewer had the nerve to ask him if *he* had used drugs to get up for a game, the street-smart charmer flashed his winning boyish grin and replied: "I didn't need them. I'm naturally up."

For the newly retired O.J., 1980 was a vintage year, proving to him that he'd beaten the after-football jinx. He had the hit movie, the new commercials, and he co-hosted the Olympics on TV. A college had offered him a coaching job. There was even an opportunity to buy a piece of an NFL team. When a woman asked him what his fantasies were, he surprised her by ignoring sex and talked about his new business instead. "Winning an Emmy or an Oscar," The Juice replied. "I always put my fantasies in the realm of goals. The Oscar or the Emmy says you've reached a level of competence in this business and I would love to have one."

Of course, all businessman, even the most successful, have their ups and downs. Not every production would turn out to be as successful as *Goldie and The Boxer*. By 1983, things had soured. A final shot for a hit TV series—an all-black soap opera called "Heart and Soul," with O.J. as executive producer—died as a pilot. And O.J. had invested a bundle of his own money just getting it off the ground.

But The Juice remained charming and confident. He was used to battling hard and playing to win. He decided to combine "acting" with his football background and grab a lucrative job as a sportscaster. ABC hired him to work with Howard Cosell, a legend who was soon to retire, on Monday Night Football for a staggering $750,000 over the 1983 season.

O.J. was a hit. *Sports Illustrated* raved: "Simpson comes across as warm, sincere, and enthusiastic. He has an intensity and radiance about him that help compensate for his lack of language skill. For a rookie in the booth, The Juice is unusually perceptive." Monday Night Football's ratings were drooping, and Cosell had just recently made what was viewed as a racist remark. "Look at that little monkey run," he had said of the Washington Redskins black wide receiver Alvin Garrett. The comment caused a furor and helped Cosell out the door. O.J. was now number two to Frank Gifford, and Joe Namath was brought in as the third man.

The Juice knew that primetime exposure on Monday Night Football meant more than 20 million viewers a week and a fat paycheck. It could lead to more movie roles, more speaking engagements at $25,000 a pop, and more invitations to sit on corporate boards. And if he boosted ABC's Monday Night Football's ratings, he could name his price.

But O.J. Simpson, who had never graduated from Southern Cal (his degree would have been in sociology), still had too much ghetto-jive talk in him. *Sports Illustrated*, which had praised him when he began in 1983, began to slam him. The same critic who had seemingly loved him a year before now wrote: "Simpson is repetitive, windy, and obscure in content, if not locution. Worse than that, he contradicts himself."

But critics weren't as important as the ratings, which also continued to tumble. In 1985, a poll by *Sport* magazine signaled his demise. When asked to name their favorite sportscaster, they cited CBS's John Madden first, NBC's Merlin Olsen second, and CBS's Dick Vermeil third. O.J. didn't even get a vote. And when the same magazine asked its readers which football announcer they would fire if given the chance, O.J. got the most votes, followed by Joe Namath and Terry Bradshaw.

O.J. did a great job co-announcing the 1986 Super Bowl, but it wasn't enough to save his job at Monday Night Football. In what was described as "the biggest shake-up of announcers in network TV history," ABC fired both O.J. and Namath two months after the Super Bowl, replacing them both with a single veteran announcer, Al Michaels. O.J. was offered a demotion, covering college football for less than half the money at $300,000 a year.

The Juice had thought 1985 was a great year.

He'd married Nicole Brown and was inducted into pro football's Hall of Fame. But his career was on the skids. He had tried out for a new TV series with Carroll O'Connor, something called "In the Heat of the Night" and was beat out by Howard Rollins, the same actor who'd taken another role, in the hit movie *Ragtime*, away from him.

Even Hertz seemed to be slowly pushing him out of the picture. He'd been doing his spots in tandem with golfer Arnold Palmer since 1982. It hadn't worked and Hertz lost market share each year after that. Then Hertz made actress Jamie Lee Curtis its spokesperson, with O.J. and Arnie relegated to standing behind her, grinning instead of speaking. The final insult came when O.J. was given ad work to do for an obscure Hertz subsidiary. He was now reduced to doing little print ads in trade journals.

But while his ego was bruised, his pocketbook was still healthy. O.J.'s net worth was approaching $10 million by the late Eighties. Orenthal Productions was still producing the occasional TV show, and his other company, O.J. Simpson Enterprises, which was managed by Nicole's dad and owned pieces of hotels and restaurants as well as a Hertz franchise, was thriving. The Juice was also doing color analysis for NFL games on the sports cable channel ESPN. O.J. wasn't going to shrivel up and die just because he had been fired by ABC.

Keeping other options open, he put millions of his own dollars on the line with a group that had the inside track to obtain an NFL expansion franchise in Phoenix. That investment opportunity evaporated when Billy Bidwill's St. Louis Cardinals jumped to the Arizona city in 1988. For a time, O.J. seemed forgotten. But two opportunities soon came along to revive his career.

The first, a film titled *Naked Gun*, had become a surprise megahit that would eventually spawn a series of sequels. Next, NBC tapped him to co-anchor a revamped Sunday pre-game show with Bob Costas. O.J. described his hectic business life as being like one of his old Hertz commercials. "People find it funny to see me in an airport," he said. "I'm always running because I'm always late and they really find that funny."

By late 1993, his total yearly take was back to well over a million dollars and his net worth was $12 million. O.J. was back on top again. He now sat on the board of directors of Infinity Broadcasting, the fast-growing media chain that syndicated Howard Stern, the Greaseman, and the "Don and Mike" show. He took a similar position with the Forschner Group, a knife distributor. And the two

Naked Gun sequels had also become moneymakers, boosting his stock as an actor.

But with the shocking double murders and his arrest, O.J.'s fabulous career as an actor, sportscaster, and product spokesman immediately became a question mark. Hertz has already dropped him from their roster of celebrity endorsers, and the most prominent athlete in America now faces the grim prospect of a life behind bars—or worse.

The Beautiful
Nicole

O.J. Simpson met the beautiful, blonde young woman named Nicole Brown when she was an 18-year-old waitress working at the Daisy Club in Beverly Hills, California. She had been on the job only three days and had barely moved out of the family home into a Los Angeles apartment at the time of that fateful meeting. Her sister Denise, 36, revealed that within days of meeting Nicole, O.J. moved her out of the apartment that she had just started living in and into another one because he didn't like her living with a male roommate.

"O.J. came in and fell in love," said their mutual friend Michael Dubasso. "He quickly moved her in." Another mutual friend revealed: "When he met Nicole, she was 18 years old and he had already come into his celebrity. She was right out of high school, this sweet young thing. She didn't even know who he was. He scooped her up, brought her into Beverly Hills, brought her into his life—and dammit, she was his."

Nicole married O.J. in 1985, shortly before the birth of their first child, a daughter named Sydney, who is now nine. Their second child, a son Justin, is six. They had been living together for about two years while he was in the process of breaking up from Marguerite. And O.J. wanted them to stay together despite the difficulties in their relationship. Even after their divorce in 1992, they tried to keep up the public image of the "perfect couple," often being seen together with their two children or at parties.

However, Nicole wasn't star-struck by the larger-than-life football hero, TV sports analyst, movie star, and Hertz pitchman. Friends said the relationship was deeper.

"She loved the person, not the figure," said Denise, who was working as a model in New York when her sister first met O.J. Simpson. "When she fell in love with him, she fell hard . . . before they got married, it was always O.J. But things got sour. Things go bad."

Denise added, "I was living in New York and modeling when she told me about him. I said, 'Oh, who's that?' She said, 'Oh, he's a football player or a dirt digger.' They were really great for each other."

She may not have been star-struck, but she *was* robbed of her youth. In a 1992 affidavit, Nicole said that she had briefly attended junior college but that she had had to quit because her husband "required" she be with him constantly. Apart from her job as a waitress, she had also started work as a sales clerk in a boutique, but quit after only two weeks out of frustration over not making any sales.

"These two jobs are the sum total of her employment experience," her attorney said. Her sister Denise revealed that Nicole had also briefly tried modeling, but that in fact, she hated it. "It wasn't her deal," Denise said. "She didn't want to be a model. She didn't want to be in the limelight.

She wanted to be a photographer. She loved photography."

The court documents at the time of the divorce offer a window into the relationship between O.J. and Nicole but they also reveal a girl who lost many of her formative years. She said in her filing: "By the time I was 19 years of age, we were living together most of the time. I traveled back and forth between Los Angeles and San Francisco to be with him. I only attended junior college a very short time because he required me to be available to travel with him whenever his career required him to go to a new location, even if it was for a short period of time."

She continued: "I have had no other college education, and I hold no college degrees. I worked as a waitress for two months. Prior to that, I was a sales clerk in a boutique. These two jobs are the sum total of my employment experience. I worked on my own as an interior decorator, mostly for O.J. and his friends. I no longer have that opportunity."

Born in Frankfurt, Germany—her mother's homeland—on May 19, 1959, Nicole grew up in Garden Grove, California's Royal Palm Estates, with her three sisters and brother. She was an active member of the Brownies and Girl Scouts.

"Her mom and dad were so nice," said Rhonda Dzandzara, whose sister was close to Nicole. "They tried really hard to make sure their kids were raised right and cultured. Dance lessons. Singing lessons. Anything those kids wanted or felt they had a talent for, they got."

Nicole graduated from Dana Hills High School in Dana Point, Orange County, in 1978, where she was a homecoming princess. Her parents—mother Judy and father Louis (also known as Lou)—still live in the area in the exclusive gated community of Monarch Bay where they moved in the mid-1970s. It was there, just steps from the beach, that Nicole enjoyed her teenage years. Her father was a small business investor who eventually came to manage part of his son-in-law's business, O.J. Simpson Enterprises, which owned pieces of hotels and restaurants as well as a Hertz franchise. Her mother had dabbled briefly in modeling. The Browns also have another daughter, Dominique, and a son, Ralph Baur.

"All the sisters were very pretty, very popular, very nice," said Valerie Rigg, who graduated between Denise and Nicole. "I remember thinking, 'The Brown sisters are going to go someplace.' It wasn't their beauty alone. It was something about their personalities."

Nicole seemed especially destined for big things. Rigg recounted, "People said somebody wealthy and famous would nab her. She just seemed bound for that. No one was surprised that she was with O.J. Simpson. Nothing was said about their age difference, or race. It was just these two beautiful, famous people."

Simpson, who used to say that back in high school he was "one of the baddest cats around," was, in the 1980s, one of the world's best paid, best-loved, and most recognized former football players. There was nobody who didn't know who O.J. was from his playing days, his commercials, or the *Naked Gun* movies. Now Nicole had become a part of that life. Rigg added: "Nicole was famous to us. She was very famous in our eyes."

Though Nicole was not the oldest of the Brown sisters, she was viewed as the most mature. Bill Prestridge, who recalled her from his journalism class, said, "I remember her presence, her bearing. She didn't have that girlish laughter."

Nicole was a popular student and "campus beauty," according to instructor Harlen Chambers, who said she was a member of the homecoming court in 1976, her senior year. Nicole's ambition when she left school was to become a photographer. In high school everyone called her 'Nick' and they laughed when she kissed a pumpkin at the 1974 homecoming dance when her sister Denise was the homecoming princess.

"We had a good time back then," wept Denise, "and I miss her. I miss her and love her a lot."

As a graduating senior, Nicole left notations beside her 1976 yearbook picture admonishing classmates to "be yourself, don't be a phony; you don't have to do anything." Allyson Becktel Doherty, who rode in the back of a baby-blue convertible with Nicole as one of the 1976 homecoming princesses, recalled: "She came on campus and everybody was wowed. She was good-looking and gregarious."

Nicole's home economist teacher, Jo Hanson, remembered: "Everybody was in awe of her. We get a lot of beautiful students. But she was the ultimate beauty. The girls liked and admired her. The guys were in love with her." But it was Nicole's father who escorted his daughter to the homecoming dance, Hanson said. "I thought she was going to be a model or a movie star," Hanson said. "I used to tease her, saying, 'I should get your autograph now.' "

On the eve of her death Nicole was ebullient about her new life without O.J., her sister Denise admitted. They had tried to reconcile but instead decided a week and a half before her death to go their separate ways. At a dance recital for their daughter, O.J. Simpson sat apart from Nicole but talked with the family. Denise said: "He said, 'I'm on the red-eye tonight.' "

At Mezzaluna restaurant with her children, parents, and sisters, Nicole talked of spending more time with her family, of going to Club Med and camping at Yosemite. She talked of resurrecting her childhood plans of becoming a photographer.

Denise said that Nicole was a kind, generous and loving daughter, sister and friend. "Her sense of caring and her nurturing spirit mad her a most sensitive and adoring mother to her two children." According to friends she was funny, sometimes opinionated, and an aficionado of the good life.

She drove a white Ferrari with the vanity plate L84AD8—which spells out the message "late for a date." Leslie Letellier, who manages a boutique near the Brentwood condo Nicole rented after her divorce form Simpson, said: "We're a little Melrose Place around here and Nicole Simpson was our Heather Locklear. She was beautiful and flirtatious. You'd see her driving down this street looking hot in her white Ferrari."

Nicole spent much of her time working out at Brentwood athletic clubs or jogging on yuppie San Vicente Boulevard, which sweeps its way from the ocean right through the center of the wealthy, up-market Brentwood, the Hollywood entertainment industry's bedroom suburb. She liked to dance at Renaissance, a popular club on nearby Santa Monica's Third Street Promenade. Usually, she danced there on Thursday nights, often until 2 A.M., according to 37-year-old Ray Barron, a bartender at the club who also lived in Brentwood.

He said, "She was very charming, very attractive, fun to be with. There was always a group of guys hitting on her. She was a sexy dresser, a good-looking woman. You could see how somebody could become very attached to her."

The bartender said that she really lit up a room. "Even on nights when five hundred people jammed into the club, Nicole seemed to stand out. Occasionally, she could be seen holding hands or kissing someone, but more often she tended to stay with a female friend and she seemed more interested in dancing than trying to meet men. She was a nice lady—she wasn't sleazy by any means. I always thought she was very classy."

The bartender got to know Nicole because they owned the same type of dog: an Akita, which is a prized Japanese breed known for its fierce protectiveness. Not too long before her death her dog Kato escaped from the yard, as he would again on the night she was murdered, and Barron had returned Kato to her. Nicole was grateful and invited him into the house for coffee.

The bartender revealed that there were pictures of her children in the Brentwood condo but no obvious sign of her marriage to Simpson. To an outsider, it seemed as if he had been erased from her life. "She never, ever mentioned O.J.," Barron said. "She really didn't go too deep into her personal life."

Denise Brown, meanwhile, has set up her own private shrine to her little sister. Her every morning now starts with a flicker of a flame dancing atop a pure white candle on a table. The table is covered with photographs of Nicole. Every morning Denise has her own private conversation with her beloved, lost sister. Denise said, "I tell her how much I miss her and I pray to God that he's looking after her. And I pray that justice will be done."

The Marriage
From Hell

In February 1985, just eight months before their first child Sydney was born and about six years after they first met, O.J. Simpson and Nicole Brown were wed under a billowing white tent at O.J.'s sprawling estate in Brentwood. It was the first marriage for the 25-year-old, brown-eyed blonde beauty, who had been with O.J. since she was a teenager just out of high school.

They had already been living together for years, and it looked like Nicole was on the brink of the type of fairy-tale future that most girls can only dream about—and long for. That summer O.J. was inducted into the Football Hall of Fame in Canton, Ohio. In an emotional acceptance speech, he thanked "my wife, Nicole, who came into my life at what is probably the most difficult time for an athlete—at the end of my career. But she turned those years into some of the best years I have had in my life." His brand new bride, sitting in the bleachers in front of the dais, beamed proudly back at her husband.

It was easy to see why O.J. had fallen in love with Nicole—and why he had to make certain she never wanted for anything. Although she was not a classic beauty, she posessed a remarkable electric quality that drew attention towards her whenever she walked into a room. "She was a dramatic person, a person with physical presence," said one of O.J.'s former broadcasting colleagues. "If you asked me whether she was beautiful, I'd say no, she was not beautiful. If you asked me whether she was elegant, I'd say not necessarily. But she was electric. As for her personality, she had a vivacity, a spirit about her that was just magnetic. If you were in a roomful of people, your eye turned to Nicole. There was something unusual about her. She was a willful, spirited person—a party animal. She loved to say, 'I want to go dance all night.' "

Though she was high-spirited and hot-headed, a woman who had grown up expecting to get her way, Nicole was clearly devoted to her husband. Shortly after their wedding she became a full-time mom and wife. Three years after Sydney was born, Nicole gave birth to their son Justin.

"From the minute she woke up in the morning, she was scrambling around making everything nice for her children, her husband, her home," a friend said. "She would be the one up on the roof, putting up the Christmas lights."

Even Al Cowlings, O.J.'s best friend, was amazed by Nicole's newfound domesticity and said so to her older sister Denise. "Denise, I would not believe a woman could love a man as much as she did, bringing him coffee every morning, in bed," he said. "She was so in love with him."

But becoming Mrs. O.J. Simpson meant much more than love and motherhood. Nicole moved into his $5 million, Tudor-style mansion in one of the most exclusive residential areas of Los Angeles. Her neighbors included the likes of Oscar-winning actress Meryl Streep and the heads of Hollywood's great agencies and studios. It was more than just a community, it was the preserve, the private domain of the most influential and powerful men in Hollywood. These were the industry's royalty, people responsible for the making of $50 million movies and people upon whom President Clinton might call for their opinion or to attend a White House function because he simply needed their clout whenever Asian dignitaries or heads of state came to Washington.

The Simpsons' palatial home was surrounded by extensive grounds and well-tended gardens; it featured a private gym, a swimming pool, lavish dining rooms, a fully staffed kitchen and extravagantly plush bedrooms. When Nicole decided to add her personal touch to the sprawling mansion, she was given an open-ended expense account to remodel from top to bottom. Money was no object. The kitchen and pool were modernized. Other amenities were added. The home was expertly refurbished by professional interior decorators. Nicole even had a mini playground built on the front lawn for the children. Whenever she needed anything, all she had to do was call on her 24-hour-a-day small army of personal servants and housekeepers. Like most "industry" wives, she had become, in her own right, the manager of her own company—the O.J. Simpson household.

Summers were spent at their $1.9 million-dollar Laguna Beach house, situated in an exclusive oceanfront enclave, one of the most beautiful homes in the area. In typical Hollywood fashion, the house was occupied only a few months out of the year, mostly during the blazing days of summer when the L.A. basin bakes in 100-degree heat and the seafront communities are 30-degrees cooler from the ocean breezes. Of course, the house was never rented. Instead, like the country estate of a baron or a duke, it stood empty, waiting for the summertime and the Simpsons to pay a visit.

The couple maintained a bi-coastal lifestyle. O.J. owned a large apartment in New York City, and Nicole traveled east several times a year—for a month at a time—to shop on Park Avenue or to catch Broadway shows. Whenever they went on one of their annual trips to Hawaii, Vail, Aspen, or Mexico, it was first-class all the way—unless, of course, O.J. hired a private jet. Life with him was an all-expenses-paid trip. Nicole didn't have to worry about bills or mortgages or even mundane things like groceries.

On top of all that, she received an allowance of $6,000 a month in "spending money." Whenever she left her sprawling estate to go shopping, to take an exercise class, or to take her children to the park, she could use either a chauffeured limo or drive any one of O.J.'s fabulous luxury cars. These included, in addition to the now-famous white Ford Bronco, a set of twin Ferraris, a Mercedes convertible, and a black Rolls-Royce.

O.J. and Nicole loved to socialize together. They belonged to the best country clubs and navigated within the best social circles. They threw lavish parties for local celebrities at the beach-front home and the Brentwood estate. "They'd make up games for everyone to play," said Pam Schwartz, a close family friend. "Nicole would have a huge crowd and cook for everyone."

A woman who lived next door to the couple at Laguna Beach recalled: "The only thing we heard from O.J. is how much he loved Nicole. Sometimes I'd look at the two of them up on their deck and I'd say to myself, 'Wow, what a lucky couple.' "

But behind the facade of a perfect life lurked a dark saga of beatings and betrayal. Court documents and police logs reveal that there was a sinister, non-public side to the marriage. Nicole called the cops repeatedly and complained about O.J.

beating her up—but most of the calls were hushed up. After all, he was an all-American football hero, a powerful business executive, and a renowned sportscaster with NBC.

For example, just months after their wedding, cops were called to the Brentwood house. When they arrived, Nicole and O.J. were out in front. She was sitting on top of a car, crying her eyes out. He was pacing back and forth. The car had a shattered windshield. When questioned, O.J. admitted that he had smashed the window with a baseball bat. "I broke the windshield," he told the officers. "Don't worry about it; it's mine. There's no trouble here." This was Brentwood. He was Hollywood's O.J. Simpson. His word was good as gold for the police. There was no trouble at all.

They simply left the premises and the incident was forgotten. This is how life is often lived at the most powerful levels of the business where people who make lots of money for the entertainment industry are simply left alone, no matter what happens. Hollywood is a state of mind as well as a place, an attitude which says that as long as what you do generates money and keeps the machine going, you must keep doing it no matter what.

Then in 1989 after a New Year's Eve party, there was a more serious disturbance. A frantic Nicole called the cops again. As officers arrived, police records show that she ran out of the bushes wearing only a bra and sweat pants and yelling: "He's going to kill me! He's going to kill me!"

Nicole later described the terrifying beating to a friend. "She told me that at one point, when she was curled up in a ball and he was beating and kicking her, she thought he was going to kill her," the friend said.

Nicole was taken to St. John's Hospital in nearby Santa Monica and treated for a swollen and blackened left eye and cheek and a cut lip. There was also a hand imprint on her neck.

When officers informed O.J. that this time he was going to be arrested, he began screaming. "You guys have been out here eight times before, and *now* you're going to arrest me? This is a family matter. Why do you want to make a big deal of it? We can handle it." This time, unlike the times before, the Simpsons' domestic dispute had broken the surface tension of Hollywood complacency and bubbled into the judicial system. But here, again, the system put another stopper in the bottle.

Incredibly, it took almost six months before Simpson was formally booked. Under a deal in which he pleaded no contest to spousal battery, Judge Ronald Schoenberg fined him $700, sentenced him to 120 hours of community service, two years probation, and ordered counseling—which O.J. eventually arranged to get over the phone! The appearance of the law was maintained, but would it do any good?

Deputy City Attorney Alana Bowman, who heads the unit that handles domestic violence, was left bitter and disillusioned by the sentence. Perhaps it seemed to her that it was not real punishment and that there would be no real rehabilitation. "The judge didn't feel he should go to jail," she said. "He sentenced him to three months of counseling—by phone—to accommodate the traveling he had to do for work, and it wasn't therapy in domestic violence."

According to Bowman, Nicole told the city attorney's Victims' Advocate that she feared for her life. "She was very frightened," says Bowman. "She said it was only a matter of time before he killed her."

Princeton-based psychologist Dr. James Mastrich, a family therapist who specializes in abuse problems and is the author of the book *Strong Enough for Two* suggests that slaps on the wrists in domestic violence cases may actually worsen the situation. "If an abuser doesn't go to jail when the court intervenes, if charges are dropped, or the system looks the other way, the abuser may feel empowered. He was right. He can get away with anything."

"He was very possessive," said Corey La Russo, a professional golfer who caddied for O.J. at the Riviera Country Club in Brentwood from 1991 to 1993. "He'd say, 'If I ever caught her with another man, I'd kick his ass.' He didn't want to catch anyone with his wife, and he was adamant about it. He put her on a pedestal. He'd say: 'Hey, she's all I need. She's the most beautiful thing in the world.'"

At first, Nicole didn't seem to mind the possessiveness. She may have felt that it was O.J.'s way of saying "I love you." But it soon it became clear that his jealousy fueled violent tirades. And, there were those who believed it was Nicole's personality that triggered his rages.

"She wasn't Little Suzy Homemaker," said an NFL player and friend of O.J.'s. "She had an alcohol problem. She'd get drunk and say and do things you normally wouldn't do. I don't want to tear down her character, but I don't want you to think this is a one-sided thing. The fights were screaming matches. She knew how to set him off." Another acquaintance recalled: "They definitely had a combative relationship. You could see them going at each other. Nicole knew how to press all of O.J.'s buttons."

So much violence. Yet so many people made excuses for it, and others turned a blind eye, not wanting to see it in its full horror for fear their conscience would force them to intervene—to "get involved." Judges, cops, even O.J.'s friends in the sports and entertainment world might have helped. But no one did. That is another part of the Hollywood way. You don't intervene, you don't do anything to upset the apple cart until something forces you to do so. In 1989, if the court didn't send O.J. to jail, then the Hollywood community where O.J. worked was off the hook.

The incident in 1989 "should have been a red flag," sports commentator Dick Schaap said on ABC News. "His friends should've said, 'Hey, O.J., what's wrong? How can we help you? How can you help yourself?' But apparently because he was O.J., because he was everybody's hero, it was sort of allowed to slide. It didn't even get much coverage in the newspapers. An amazing number of people, when they heard about it now, said, 'Oh, I didn't know that.' And it was there. It was in the papers, but it wasn't a big story."

It has been widely reported that there were many calls to 911 that, as one source put it, "were never converted to the police blotter." In fact, many people close to the couple actually believed that the 1989 beating was a one-time occurrence. They say they had no idea that O.J.'s abusive behavior was constant and relentless.

"If their friends had known," said Donna Estes, one of Nicole's confidants, "no one would have allowed it to go on. We would have helped him get help. We wouldn't have ostracized him or covered it up. If he had been forced to face this, maybe Nicole would be alive."

Dr. Mastrich says that if, at times like the 1989 crisis in the Simpsons' marriage, a therapist or counsellor can encourage the battered wife or girlfriend to call the cops, it sometimes can end the behavior right then and there. If the abuser feels his victim will not try to stop him, he becomes even more empowered to keep up the abuse. "When you call the cops," Mastrich says, "and don't press charges or drop the charges later on, it will, in essence, reinforce the person's behavior."

Oftentimes spousal abuse is a pattern of behavior that occurs over and over again. The incident that involves the cops is not the first-time occurrence; it is one of many. And when the woman drops the charges, it ends up enabling the abuser to keep up the pattern of abuse. In Nicole's case, as the evidence now coming to light shows, abuse seemed to be part of a pattern, a pattern that continued long after 1989 and even after the Simpsons divorced years later.

Until Divorce Us Do Part

Fed up with the brutality and the womanizing and perhaps even in fear for her life, Nicole finally left O.J. in February, 1992—four days after their seventh wedding anniversary. Days later, she filed for divorce, citing "irreconcilable differences," just as Marguerite had done twelve years earlier.

Many friends believed that Nicole still loved O.J., but that she just couldn't handle his abusive behavior anymore. "When she did divorce him, (the violence) is what it had to do with," said a close personal friend of Nicole's. "She said she just couldn't take it anymore. She had to put up endlessly with lies and bed-hopping, and then his massive control of her. Any kind of independence she would show, would enrage him. He loved her, but he thought of her as a possession."

During this second set of divorce proceedings, the judge this time determined that O.J.'s estate was now worth $10 million and that his gross income for the previous five years averaged a staggering $1.1 million. Nicole had at first asked for $30,000 a month in alimony and $13,000 a month in child support. But in the end she was awarded a lump sum of about $433,750, the couples' $550,000 San Francisco condominium, $9,000 a month in alimony and $10,000 in monthly child support.

Although Nicole claimed "irreconcilable differences" in her divorce petition, the true reason for the split, she confided to friends, was that the football legend famous for running through airports and jumping over suitcases in Hertz Rent-A-Car TV commercials was in reality running after other women and flitting from bed to bed. "I'd never trust him to keep his pants zipped up," the willowy California blonde told a pal.

O.J. cheated with so many women, Nicole reportedly told a friend, that she was afraid he would get AIDS. Women flung themselves at the handsome Hall of Famer the way they threw themselves at Magic Johnson, who ultimately and tragically, did get infected with the AIDS virus. "When I saw what happened with Magic, I become scared to death that O.J. would become infected with the AIDS virus, as well," Nicole told her pal. Indeed, it was what well might have been another reason to fear for her life.

When she had became pregnant with her daughter, Sydney, O.J. had promised her that his affairs were over. But Nicole later confided to friends that she knew of at least twenty occasions when he had cheated on her. And while the smooth-talking sports superstar crooned to journalists that he was a "one-woman man," his frustrated wife says she repeatedly had to confront the sordid reality of living with a philandering husband, with all the attendant lipstick-smeared shirts, sexy letters, and mash notes.

The last straw came, friends say, when Nicole called her husband at his hotel room while he was on a trip, and a drowsy woman answered the telephone. Steeling her heart against hearing yet another feeble explanation, and finally accepting the fact that he would never change, the pals say, Nicole told her handsome husband that their marriage was finished.

A sheepish O.J. reportedly returned home with a bouquet of roses and promises that he would reform. But this time, his excuses fell on deaf ears. Coolly and calmly, friends say, Nicole faced the man she loved, and told him she was getting a divorce. Thunderstruck, O.J. broke down and began sobbing about how much he loved her and their children, the friends add. But Nicole stuck to her guns. True to her word, she filed for divorce two months later.

Under California's community property divorce law, Nicole Brown Simpson could have gotten 50 percent of all the assets and income acquired during her marriage to O.J. But, the already once-divorced football legend had talked the his then-girlfriend into signing a prenuptial agreement three months before they got married in February, 1985.

Hammered out after seven months of negotiation, the pact limited Nicole's claim on O.J.'s assets to far less than the queen's ransom of nearly $480,000 a year she had requested in her suit to cover such luxuries as $2,500 a month for pet care, hair care, toys and presents, $3,200 a month for designer clothing, and $3,000 for travel and entertainment.

Nicole pleaded with the court to allow her to continue the "exceptionally affluent" lifestyle she had enjoyed with O.J. during their marriage. This included the white Ferrari, the annual vacation in Hawaii, summers at their $2 million home in Laguna Beach and New York apartment, ski trips to Vail, sojourns in the finest hotels, dining at the best restaurants, a personal trainer, and a nutritionist. In court documents Nicole explained that O.J. insisted that they have only the best. "The house was extensively remodeled a few years ago," she noted, "and no expense was spared to update and modernize the kitchen, pool and other amenities."

Meanwhile, O.J. cried poor, claiming that he couldn't afford a bigger settlement since he was also supporting his mother and his two adult children from Marguerite. His NBC salary had been reduced by $100,000 in 1992; two of his fast-food Pioneer chicken franchises had closed down after the L.A. riots, and he lost a wad of money on investments, he stated in court papers. And he complained that Nicole refused to take responsibility for her life and stand on her own two feet.

"Mrs. Simpson has done nothing but play, taking nice vacations, spending time exercising and entertaining and being entertained," he said. According to Lester Wallman, a New York matrimonial attorney and coauthor of *Cupid, Couples & Contracts*, if much of O.J.'s $10 million in net worth was acquired during his marriage, Nicole was foolish not to have tried to overturn the prenuptial pact.

"Courts often throw out unconscionable and overreaching prenuptial agreements, where one spouse tries to hog everything for themselves," he explained.

But Nicole may have been afraid to push O.J. too far with her divorce demands. Dr. Susan Forward, a psychotherapist Nicole was seeing to help her cope with the divorce, recalls how her patient confessed she was afraid O.J. would kill her.

According to Dr. Forward, author of the books *Men Who Hate Women and the Women Who Love Them* and *Obsessive Love: When It Hurts Too Much to Let Go*, Nicole was a "battered wife" and O.J. suffered from a "classic case of obsession."

Crying and desperate, Nicole told her therapist how O.J. had beaten her during the marriage and screamed threats on her life. Then why didn't she leave him? The answer was shockingly simple—because she loved him so much.

In cases where someone is divorced from his partner," Mastrich writes, "what does continuing abuse say? Oftentimes people who are separated but still involved with each other are just as intense as if they were still married because their egos are wrapped up in each other. Separation or divorce doesn't make it automatically go away. In fact, sometimes divorce and separation only make the tension and violence worse because it hits abusive, domineering men squarely in their ego, sense of territory, and challenges their perceptions of dominance. That explains statements that abusers sometimes make to their divorced or separated spouses such as 'If I can't have you no one can.' 'If I can't have you I won't be OK.'"

It all often boils down to a boundary issue, especially among men who were abused as children, boundaries crossed, territory violated, and children left feeling a sense of powerlessness. That doesn't go away, it simply lingers, festering like an infection deep down inside your psyche and waiting to explode when life's stresses become too great. That's when the violence gushes to the surface like an erupting volcano and burns through relationships, scorching anyone in the abuser's path.

The San Francisco Giants' new outfielder, ex-Met, ex-Dodger, Darryl Strawberry has been accused in court of battering women on more than one occasion. In his autobiography *Darryl*, Strawberry writes about the time he was arrested for pulling a gun on his wife in their Encino home. "I don't remember exactly what my wife said before the violence began because I was deaf and blind with fury. Maybe I should have listened more closely. But whatever it was, she said it again, only this time loud enough for half the block to hear. Suddenly I was out of control and I cracked Lisa across the top of her head with a thudding punch that echoed through the whole house . . . her quivering lower lip was puffy where I'd caught her with the heel of my hand as it came down . . . she grabbed a metal rod from somewhere and whipped it with such full force toward my rib cage as if she were swinging a bat . . . then my own temper erupted and before I could stop myself I ran to the closet where I kept my .25-caliber semi-automatic pistol. . . . My brain was on fire with evil voices. What did I say as she stood there ready to whack me again with that rod? 'I'm going to kill you, bitch!' "

But Darryl also writes about the dramatic moment he had to confront his often-absent father who had come home to beat his mother and his brothers who were determined to challenge him. Darryl was an abuser who'd been abused as a child. It's a pattern so typical that many psychologists say that when there is abuse in a family, you will almost always find abuse in the abuser's childhood.

Dr. Mastrich says that in cases where the abuse continues across a divorce or separation, where the physical abuse in the marriage becomes stalking during the separation, more abuse, and even threats to kill the abused spouse, it's because the abuser can't recognize the new boundary that's been created. Look for a pattern of abuse in childhood, Mastrich writes, because it's the childhood abuse that creates the feelings of powerlessness and downright fear.

When you are a kid and you're in a powerless situation where an adult can come and beat you up, you learn tremendous fear, you learn tremendous helplessness—the term is "learned helplessness." If we are subjected to situations which we're powerless to control, like a father beating us, we learn to be externally oriented, to look into the outside world for someone to rescue us and to love us. Whatever we need to get, we have to get from the outside even if it means obliterating the boundaries between people in order to get it.

Now, go thirty years into the future. We're in a relationship. But that doesn't solve any problems because despite whatever we accomplish in our life, we still have this irrational ancient mindset that we're not OK unless we get what we need from the outside. Given the circumstance that can occur—add alcohol or drugs that lower inhibitions and put people in touch with their demons, many people can be capable of violence.

Where we see this in a boy whose father abused him and his mother, the child sees a validation in abusing women. He might even blame his mother for putting up with the abuse or for not protecting him. He may feel it's OK to be an abuser of females. The child has two levels of anger and one level of identification. The kid grows up seeing women abused and knowing that nobody stopped his father. If the kid becomes an abuser when he grows older and doesn't himself get stopped.

He may go through a number of marriages without being stopped. He feels no need to stop. If he hits the brick wall of another marriage where he's being forced to stop, he may be forced out of the marriage but not necessarily out of the abuse unless he's physically put away. If he confronts the law and is not put away, and everyone in his life looks away, then he may feel there is simply no need to stop. He has no "impulse control" unless people physically intervene in his life. The older he gets the longer it goes on until something stops him or he does something he can't simply walk away from. This is a scenario that plays itself out all too often, especially among men living outwardly powerful lives whose demons are nevertheless present and active during moments of challenge, confrontation, and stress.

Late for a Date

After the divorce, O.J. continued to date other women, favoring stunning women like Victoria's Secret model Paula Barbieri, who appeared on his arm at business functions and star-studded galas. While he showered Paula with expensive gifts and clothes, Nicole—single for the first time since she was a teenager and brand new high-school graduate 15 years ago—tried to make a life for herself and her children. A life independent of O.J.

Nicole and the kids moved out of the Brentwood mansion, but they didn't get very far at first. She found herself a roommate and rented a town house about a half-mile away.

Then in January 1994, Nicole bought a $650,000 condominium, also in Brentwood, less than two miles from the house she'd shared with O.J. Nothing, in the Hollywood bedroom communities is geographically very far from anything else. Nestled among palm trees and thick bushes, the two-story Mediterranean-style stucco condo was barely visible behind the gated entry. Aside from its red tiled roof, not much of the house can be seen from the street, and that was how Nicole wanted it. To approach the front door, visitors had to use an intercom entry system located at the top of the small flight of stairs in front of the metal security gate.

Nicole decorated her new home like an experienced interior designer. She hung large, colorful modern art on the cream-colored walls. In the living room were expensive Lalique crystal figures. In a loft overlooking the living room was a StairMaster. There were many pictures of her children, but no obvious signs of her marriage to O.J., except for the white Ferrari. In addition, there was a brand new $30,000 black Jeep Grand Cherokee parked in the driveway.

Despite its lavish, pricey homes, Brentwood maintains a small-town feel. Residents take pride in their neighborly, quiet, and safe community. They go jogging often and at all times of the day and night, and people are commonly seen strolling with their dogs at one in the morning. In Brentwood, people flaunt their sense of security with as much facility and pride as they under flaunt their wealth. Nicole was no exception, often walking her prize-winning Akita down the windy South Bundy sidewalk, greeting her neighbors along the way.

Brentwood Gardens is a shopping area marked by exclusive boutiques and elegant restaurants that cater to locals and the hordes of tourists that descend upon the area every Saturday and Sunday to try to catch a glimpse of one of Hollywood's "beautiful people." Nicole bought her groceries at the Westwood Ho market right on San Vicente, an upscale market where valets park shoppers' fancy cars. "She was quite a shopper," said one source. "She went on spending sprees at some of the most exclusive and expensive stores in Brentwood—like Boulmiche, Rebel and Moda Sport. She was always dressed exquisitely and wore beautiful jewelry."

Nicole maintained her year-round tan by frequenting a neighborhood tanning booth called Le Beach Club. She jogged near her home and was also a member of an exclusive private exercise club called The Gym. "She strove for the perfect body and would work out for hours on end every day," another source revealed. "She was in incredible shape. She worked out very hard and, at 35, had the body of a 20-year-old girl."

Nicole also maintained an extremely active social life and became almost a regular fixture at some of the area's most expensive and trendy bistros and cucinas, like Tuscany and Mezzaluna. Occasionally, she frequented the clubs in Westwood, Beverly Hills, and Santa Monica. On some Thursdays, for fun, she'd put on a skin-tight black outfit and head to her favorite Santa Monica club, the Renaissance.

Despite the hours at the gym and the late nights on the town, few people could ever criticize Nicole's parenting skills. She was a full-time mother, and everyone agreed that she put her two children ahead of everything. "She gave her kids the best," said one source. "She sent them to the best and most expensive private schools, took them on trips and gave them private lessons."

Nicole believed that the children needed a dad and encouraged O.J. to drop by her home to visit them. "She was a terrific mother," said friend Grant Cramer. "She wanted the children to see as much of their father as they could."

But Nicole was only human; she was single, outgoing, beautiful. She enjoyed the attention she received from young men, and her dates were maddening to O.J., reportedly driving him into a fury. One friend said that he was particularly upset by her latest boyfriend, a handsome young man in his twenties. "It really got to O.J. when Nicole began dating him," the friend confided.

Among Nicole's throng of admirers was Ronald Goldman, a 25-year-old waiter and part-time model. He had met Nicole at Starbucks for coffee and at The Gym where she "made herself the center of attention to a lot of young, star-struck guys," according to shop owner Letellier. Like Nicole, Ron was an habitué of the West side restaurant scene, friendly with the packs of waiters and club owners, anxious to learn the hospitality business so that maybe someday he could become a restaurant owner. Nicole, reportedly, was fascinated by the restaurant business also, and the two struck up a casual friendship based on shared interests.

The manager of the Brentwood gym, John De Bello, said, "Ron was a naive and innocent guy, a real puppy dog, someone who wanted to be loved. He and the others sort of idolized her. She was a rich, bigger-than-life blonde, out of place with these young boys. I remember telling them, 'She's gonna break your hearts.' "

In the days and weeks before their gruesome murder, Ron and Nicole were seen frequently together. Neighbors saw Ron at Nicole's house playing with her two children. "I thought they were married," said eyewitness Beverly Newman. "I thought they had adopted a little black boy and I thought how nice that was. Almost every night he would be out playing with the kids."

The couple were often spotted having dinner at the Cheesecake Factory in Brentwood. But people who knew them both well insist that Ron and Nicole were nothing more than very close friends. "We had all seen them together, but always as a part of a group," said Letellier. "If something was happening between them, it was recent and hush-hush. I never heard of Goldman going out with her anywhere. It was just a group of neighborhood people meeting at the gym, jogging, drinking coffee at Starbucks."

Although Nicole tried hard to live her own life, she continued to have contact with her ex-husband.

And O.J. was often seen driving down the street that led to Nicole's home. To the outside world, it seemed like they still enjoyed one another's company, attending celebrity affairs and fund-raisers together, showing up at places with their kids like parents who were still married.

Some insiders, however, claimed that O.J. was still obsessively in love with Nicole and that he was pressuring her to get back together. Others say that Nicole could never really live without him.

"Maybe it was a fantasy of Nicole's to think that she could ever leave O.J.," a friend said. "They were both crazy about each other. It was like they were in each other's blood."

Still others maintain that it was Nicole's financial need that kept the two in constant contact. "When Nicole was married to O.J., she grew accustomed to a very lavish lifestyle," a source close to Nicole explained. "When she got divorced, she wasn't ready to give that lifestyle up." Even though she received nearly a half million dollars in cash and $120,000 per year in child support when she divorced O.J., friends feared that Nicole was still having trouble making ends meet. If spending money on Nicole was one of O.J.'s ways to keep up the appearance of their being still together, it also fits a pattern that powerful men sometimes display. It's the way you can hold onto a possession that you don't want to lose, but it was a game that Nicole might have needed to play as well because she had spent almost every day of her life from the weeks after her high-school graduation relying on O.J. for money. Her only real-life experience as an adult was as O.J.'s companion or wife. The transition would not be as easy as Nicole thought it might be.

"For the average person, that seems like a lot of money," the source said. "But for Nicole, who was used to the good life, that amount was not near enough." So the former Mrs. O.J. Simpson, whose entire work resume consisted of two months and two weeks of low-level employment, looked to O.J. for support.

"Even after the divorce," said the source, "O.J. would pay for things. When she was with him, he would spend money like he did in their married days. He'd take her shopping, buy clothes for the children, toss her a couple thousand here and there." In fact, one high school sweetheart claimed that Nicole saw only dollar signs when she met men. "When Nicole was dating, her first questions were usually, 'How much money do you make?' and 'Are you rich?' " he said.

In the year before she died, things between Nicole and O.J. began heating up. They were doing more and more things together. "They began dating again in March 1993," said a source close to the couple. "That April, they went to Cabo San Lucas with good friends and then to Hawaii in July. They also spent romantic weekends in Newport and Laguna Niguel."

By October, 1993, the two were dating up a storm. O.J. brought Nicole to Dallas for the Cowboys' Thanksgiving Day game against the Miami Dolphins. By December, friends and acquaintances on both coasts started whispering about a possible reconciliation between the two. Insiders said that O.J. was pressuring Nicole to remarry. And O.J. didn't deny the rumors that were spreading.

For example, one time while he waited for a clerk to wrap some gifts at Theodore's, a boutique in Brentwood Gardens, O.J. began talking about his life with Nicole. He told the clerk that he aimed to get back together with her and that whatever had happened between them had been his fault. "He said there really wasn't anyone he wanted to date," Jodi Kahn, the store manager, recalled. "He said, 'I'm really trying reconcile with my wife.' He seemed very happy about it."

O.J. and Nicole were also seen together at Super Bowl '94. "It was really lovely," said a broadcasting colleague who went out with them during game week. "I thought they were getting along well. I didn't get any impression other than that they were still in love, that they wanted to get back together. I got that impression from her as well. They were putting the marriage back together, and the vision in O.J.'s mind was that they were going to remarry. He had even recently stopped seeing other women, which for O.J. was a sign of real commitment."

Sometime soon after the Super Bowl, O.J., Nicole, and their children chartered a yacht in Florida called Miss Turnberry for two days at $10,000 a day. Then, just a few months ago in April, he took Nicole to Mexico where she confided to someone at a grocery store who might have asked that "we're getting back together."

Back home in California, they were seen out together at expensive and party restaurants in the Brentwood area—like Tuscany, the Daily Grill and Louise's Trattoria. "They seemed to get along on a more than cordial basis," said high-profile Century-City attorney and friend Howard Weitzman, Michael Jackson's lawyer, who would later represent O.J. in the hours after police began investigating the murders. "The kids came first with respect to how they related to each other. I know O.J. always referred to Nicole as one of the world's great mothers. He had great respect for the way she took care of and treated the children."

On the surface, it seemed like O.J. and Nicole were heading toward a happy reconciliation. But insiders, police reports, and even Nicole Simpson's own therapist told an entirely different story. "After they separated, O.J. kept pursuing her," said Nicole's therapist Susan Forward, who counseled her throughout the divorce proceedings and in the period afterward.

"She'd be out for a drink at a bar, and suddenly he'd be there, threatening and screaming at her, 'If I can't have you, nobody can!' " It was as if what she had feared most in 1989 after the assault was now fully realized; she was becoming terrorized.

Witnesses said he stalked her, driving by her home at all hours of the day and night just to catch a glimpse of her. Even though they were divorced, he was still terribly jealous and couldn't bear to see her dating other men. "She could see him outside her house," said a source close to Nicole, "and he was constantly showing up at restaurants and bars where she was socializing. She was terribly concerned about his temper, his jealousy and possessiveness."

Neighbor Beverly Newman also heard the sounds of what she described as "big fights" coming from Nicole's condo. "You could hear a woman, then you could hear a man," she said. "All the neighbors heard it, not just me. He was just yelling at her, like 'Get out!' They weren't arguments like would happen normally in your home. They were screaming fights."

One friend reported that O.J. frequently told Nicole and her pals that if he ever caught her with anybody, he would kill her. Worried, the friend warned her that the threats ought to be taken seriously. "But then she would say, 'Oh, he'd never do that. He's just making noise,' " the friend said. "Then in the next breath she'd say, 'I can't make him mad—he'll kill me.' "

Several people recall seeing Nicole with a black eye, and she told others that O.J. had slapped her around on a number of occasions since their split; that he would often show up unannounced and bang on her door until she came out to talk to him.

Susan Forward, determined that Nicole was "a classic battered wife." Forward said that Nicole complained that O.J. was stalking her and appearing in windows and that he had "threatened her life repeatedly. She was in living terror," Forward revealed. "He was always accusing her of seeing other men. If she went to a gas station to get gas for her car, O.J. would demand to know if she was seeing the gas station attendant and there'd be a big fight.

"She told me, 'O.J. is so insanely possessive and jealous that there's no telling what he might do. He gets so angry I know he could kill me someday.' "

After the marriage ended, police were called to Nicole's homes many times and they said that 911 calls from her complaining about O.J. were an "ongoing problem."

Eventually, the Los Angeles Police Department released the tape of one chilling "911" call made by Nicole just eight months before she was killed. In the tape she repeatedly begs the dispatcher to send police to her home. It was on October 25, 1993, that O.J. flew into a rage after seeing a picture of an ex-boyfriend in her photo album. He sped over to Nicole's home in his White Ford Bronco and pounded on the back door. She wouldn't let him in, but finally, he burst through the back door. Not knowing what to do, Nicole ran up to her bedroom. O.J. raced after her, all the while screaming obscenities at her. She tried to calm him down. She told him the children were sleeping, but he didn't care. The rampage continued.

O.J. stormed out of the house, but wouldn't leave. Instead, he stayed in the backyard, yelling obscenities. Terrified, Nicole ran back downstairs to the kitchen and dialed 911.

"Can you send someone to my house?" she asked, obviously distressed.

"What's the emergency?" asked the dispatcher.

"My ex-husband has just broken into my house and he's ranting and raving outside in the front yard," Nicole said as calmly as possible.

The dispatcher asked whether O.J. had been drinking. "No," Nicole replied. "But he's crazy."

After the call, the dispatcher warned police officers in the area to respond to Nicole's town house. Meanwhile, O.J. continued screaming and yelling obscenities and threats at Nicole. In terror, she called the dispatcher again.

"Could you get somebody over here now, to Gretna Green," Nicole said, choking back the tears. "He's back. Please."

The dispatcher asked her for a description of her husband. "He's O.J. Simpson," Nicole said. "I think you know his record. Could you send somebody over here?"

"What is he doing there?" asked the dispatcher.

"He just drove up again," Nicole began sobbing into the phone. "Could you just send somebody over?"

"Wait a minute," said the dispatcher, "we're sending police. What is he doing? Is he threatening you?"

"He's going fucking nuts," sobbed Nicole.

The dispatcher attempted to calm her down and told her to stay on the line.

"I don't want to stay on the line," Nicole said fearfully. "He's going to beat the shit out of me."

"What is he saying?" asked the dispatcher.

"Oh, something about some guy I know and hookers and keys and I started this shit before and—"

The screaming outside grew louder.

"And it's all my fault and now what am I going to do, get the police in this and the whole thing. It's all my fault, I started this before," Nicole continued, somewhat incoherently.

Suddenly, O.J. charged back into the town house, ran up to her bedroom and began pounding on the door.

"Are you in a locked room or something?" asked the dispatcher.

"No," came the terrified response. "He can come right in. I'm not going where the kids are because the kids . . ."

Nicole attempted to maintain the conversation

but O.J.'s ranting distracted her.

"O.J.! O.J.!" Nicole pleaded with her husband. "The kids are sleeping!"

But nothing could calm him.

"Is he upset with something that you did?" asked the dispatcher.

"A long time ago," Nicole was crying. "It always comes back. No one can talk, listen to him."

O.J. stormed back downstairs. Nicole put the phone to her breast and begged him to leave.

"I don't give a shit anymore!" yelled O.J.

"Would you just please, O.J., O.J., O.J., O.J.," Nicole pleaded. "Could you please. Please leave."

But he still wouldn't go.

Tired of waiting for the police to arrive, Nicole told the dispatcher she was leaving to look for them. The cops finally got there and calmed things down. But they took no action because Nicole refused to press charges. And even after that terrifying incident, she continued to see O.J.

"Nicole still had a lot of loving feeling for him," said Forward. "She kept seeking the love of the man who beat her. Nicole would lie curled up on my couch, crying, with no make-up, torn jeans and stringy hair. She looked like a helpless waif. She was trembling in fear when she told me, 'I'm trying to get my life together. But it's on my mind every minute—what is O.J. going to do next?' "

Near the end of Nicole's life, she and O.J. had a loud fight at a picnic over their "reconciliation."

"He wanted to know whether she was going to marry him again or not," a source revealed. "He was really pressuring her." She ran to the bathroom crying. She said she could never remarry O.J.

Visions of past and present abuse haunted Nicole. Despite her love for O.J. and her desire for a family, she couldn't forget the horror of life with her ex-husband. She decided that she would not remarry him ever. About three weeks before her death, Nicole broke the news of her decision to O.J.

"She finally sat down and told him as nicely as she could that she didn't think things would ever work out between them," said a source. "O.J. was floored by the rejection and huffed off."

Nicole's sister Denise later recalled: "She was so happy. She had broken up with O.J. a week and a half before. She was going to start her life over. It was going to be without O.J., with her children. She had just gotten it together, and it was so exciting. I was so happy for her. For the first time in her life, she was able to have her own friends."

But, in the wake of the breakup, Nicole was still terrified.

"She just couldn't shake the fear," the source said. "She told me a few days before she was murdered, 'He's beaten me pretty badly in the past and I'm really afraid that one day he might just go too far and kill me.'"

She was afraid to date other men. She became increasingly worried about O.J.'s behavior. "She'd just given me a book about obsessive love," said Nicole's best friend. "She told me it's hard to deal with a man who is obsessively in love with you. They can't let go."

On Sunday, June 12, the day she died, Nicole canceled a blind date that her friend had arranged. Another source confided: "She said that it was safer for her to keep her distance from dating until the whole thing with O.J. blew over."

KCOP-TV's graphic reconstruction of how the bodies looked when they were discovered at the crime scene by police responding to a neighbor's report.

Juice: A Gallery

Nicole Brown
Simpson

Ronald Lyle Goldman

June 13, 1994. The trail of blood.

The hotel in Chicago where O.J. stayed the morning after the murder and where, he told police, he cut his hand upon hearing the news of his wife's death.

Juice: A Gallery

The home in the Potrero Hill section of San Francisco where O.J. Simpson grew up.

1959. O.J. Simpson (4th from left) and his Potrero Hill Receation Center baseball team.

In 1968, USC senior and Heisman Trophy winner
O.J. Simpson poses with the trophy in New York.

1973. In a driving blizzard, Buffalo Bills running back O.J. Simpson turns the corner and leaves the Jets defenders on the ground as he heads for the end zone.

Juice: A Gallery

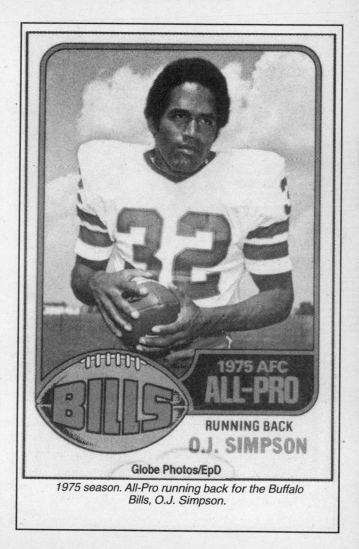

Globe Photos/EpD

1975 season. All-Pro running back for the Buffalo Bills, O.J. Simpson.

O.J. and first wife Marguerite and their children Jason (l.) and Arnelle.

O.J. in an early print ad for Hertz. O.J.'s television and print ads for the rent-a-car company helped create the commercial sports-celebrity industry.

September 18, 1974. O.J. and New York Jets Quarterback Joe Namath at the "O.J. is Alive and Well and Getting Roasted Tonight" TV special.

1984. O.J. poses with his ABC Sports colleagues from "Monday Night Football" (l. to r.) Don Meredith, Jim Lampley, Frank Gifford, and O.J.

Juice: A Gallery

April 3, 1979. Actress Melissa Michaelson cannot resist touching the makeup on O.J. as the two wait between scenes on the set of the Columbia Pictures Television production of "Goldie and the Boxer," O.J.'s first televison movie for his own Orenthal Productions.

"Frogmen,"a pilot for a TV series starring O.J. Simpson.

O.J. and Nicole share a private moment of intimacy.

Juice: A Gallery

October 1981, at St. John's Ball. Beverly Hilton Hotel (l. to r.) Eunice Simpson, O.J., Nicole Brown.

O.J. and his kids out for fun in the park.

O.J. Simpson and Nicole Brown in the early years before their marriage.

At the March 16, 1994, premiere of Naked Gun *33–1/3. O.J. brought along his then ex-wife, Nicole, and children Sydney (center) and Justin (front).*

Juice: A Gallery

September, 12, 1992. O.J. and Paula Barbieri leave the Flushing Meadow Park stands after the U.S. Open Tennis semi-finals in Queens, New York.

A shock to the world. O.J. in handcuffs on the morning after he arrived at the Brentwood house upon his return from Chicago.

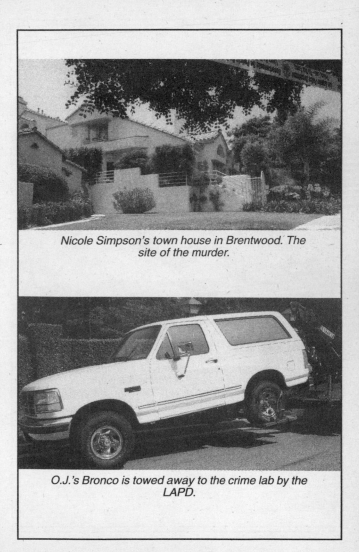

Nicole Simpson's town house in Brentwood. The site of the murder.

O.J.'s Bronco is towed away to the crime lab by the LAPD.

A distraught and exhausted O.J. drives through crowds around his estate during the week after the murders and before he was formally charged with the crimes.

O.J. and his first attorney Howard Weitzman during the anxious moments in the early hours after O.J. returned from Chicago.

O.J. with daughter Sydney, and son Justin at Nicole's funeral service.

Juice: A Gallery

Ron Goldman's family at his funeral. Goldman's father is fourth from the left, holding Ron's sister's hand.

Juice: A Gallery

*What the press referred to as O.J.'s "suicide" note,
written on the morning he disappeared.*

The incredible chase. With A.C. Cowlings at the wheel of the white Bronco and police and CHP units in slow pursuit, O.J. huddles in the rear of the car with his blue revolver at his head.

Juice: A Gallery

A.C. Cowlings, the Bronco driver and O.J.'s best friend during his football days; (top) and after he was booked by the LAPD after the chase.

BK4014054 06 17 94
LOS ANGELES POLICE JAIL DIV

L.A. District Attorney Gil Garcetti talking to reporters.

Juice: A Gallery

For the defense: Two members of O.J.'s powerful defense team. Alan Dershowitz (l.) and F. Lee Baily.

The L.A. prosecution team of David Conn (l.) and Marcia Clark.

At his June 22, 1994 arraignment, O.J. and defense attorney Robert Shapiro confer at the defense table.

LAPD chief Willie Williams tells a reporter that his is "the dumbest question" he ever heard.

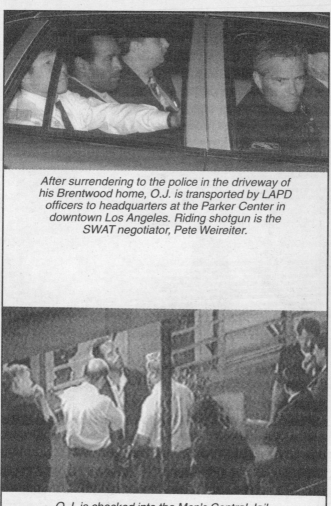

After surrendering to the police in the driveway of his Brentwood home, O.J. is transported by LAPD officers to headquarters at the Parker Center in downtown Los Angeles. Riding shotgun is the SWAT negotiator, Pete Weireiter.

O.J. is checked into the Men's Central Jail.

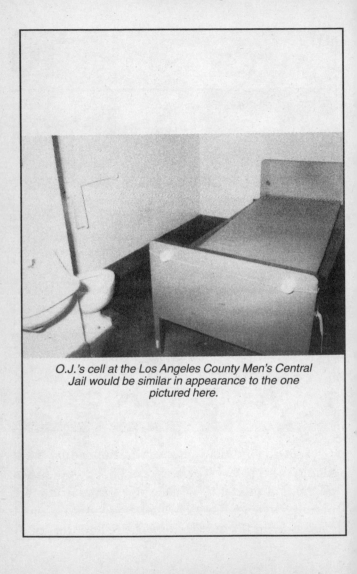

O.J.'s cell at the Los Angeles County Men's Central Jail would be similar in appearance to the one pictured here.

A Boy With A Dream Face

Ronald Lyle Goldman was the handsome other victim. The guy who wanted to have his pictures taken as a model now has, in a tragic irony, his pictures everywhere. He had a face that almost everyone thinks they recognize. He had the good-looking boy-next-door appeal that women remember and men admire. He also seems to have been universally loved and remembered by people who got beyond his handsome exterior.

Just who was he? Was he simply an unlucky guy at the wrong place at the wrong time—a classic Good Samaritan? Somebody who stumbled onto a crime scene just in time not to get away? Could it be that innocuous? Or was Ron Goldman a secret lover of Nicole Brown Simpson?

According to his friends, and they are legion, he was great-looking guy with a big heart who was always there for a friend whenever he was needed. He had the good looks of a model with a body sculpted by daily weight-lifting sessions and tennis, and a magnetic personality that friends said made them want to hang around him, just to see what he would be up to next.

The 25-year-old Goldman was born in Chicago, Illinois and raised in Buffalo Grove, a nice, quiet middle-class suburb just northwest of the city. He attended Adlai Stevenson High School in Lincoln–shire where he was on the swimming and soccer teams and friends say he fit in with all kinds of cliques because he belonged to none of them. According to Brian Swislow, a Chicago pal of his, "Ron was a passionate kind of person who put his heart into the world."

He was a teenager who looked adults in the eye when talking to them. He baby-sat for his Buffalo Grove neighbors and shoveled their snow without being asked. And always, he was protective of his little sister, Kim. His 1986 high school yearbook contains his nickname "Soul Man" and his wish "I want to become a psychologist and live life on the wild side"—something of a prophetic statement.

Goldman moved to California in 1987 with his father, Fred, his step-mother and his sister Kim after attending a year of college at Illinois State University at Normal. Once in California, Goldman blossomed, turning from a skinny teen into a tanned tennis instructor. He even once appeared on the Fox-TV dating show "Studs." And when he was asked by the host how he would rate himself on a scale of one to ten, Goldman held his hand up at eye level and joked "I'm way up here. There really isn't a scale for me."

Although he loved what the club scene in Southern California had to offer, he shunned alcohol and drugs and, like most young Californians seeking careers in the industry, he was fanatical about his diet. He spent hours in the gym buffing his body to perfection. Craig Clark met Goldman five years ago when both were waiters at the Pier View restaurant in Malibu, a casual beach front spot popular with the locals. After work on weekends, the two would hit one club after another, from the Sagebrush Cantina in Calabasas to the more upscale Westside or even Orange County, winding up early Monday morning with breakfast. "Anywhere that was hot," Clark said.

Even so, Goldman did not drink or take drugs and stuck religiously to a low-fat diet, friends said. "Ron never drank or did drugs," confirms Tracy. "When he went to clubs he only drank water. He also watched everything he ate—limiting his fat intake and making sure he was only eating healthy foods. His body was perfection and he was very proud of the way he looked."

Clark said that when Goldman moved to Brentwood 18 months ago he cut back on socializing, but still spent weekend nights on the town, often getting into clubs for free because he often knew the clubs' owners. Goldman recently promoted a nightclub party himself, inviting the guests to a hot Santa Monica club called Renaissance.

"From the minute I moved to California, life with Ron was a big roller coaster ride," said Mike Pincus, a 25-year-old lifelong friend who had known Goldman since they went to kindergarten together in Buffalo Grove and who moved to L.A. a year after his friend did. Pincus and others said Goldman, an aspiring 6-foot-tall model who was registered with Pro Sport, often dated beautiful women who were drawn to his dark good looks.

Goldman moved to Brentwood 18 months ago and set up housekeeping with his then girlfriend on Gorham Avenue, just behind the Brentwood Gardens shopping center. According to Tracy Le Pera, "I never met Ron's ex-girlfriend, but he always used to talk about her. They broke up about six to seven months ago after a two-year relationship and he was real upset. Also, he had trouble making his rent after she moved out and when he got the job at Mezzaluna, it really helped him a lot."

Prior to working at Mezzaluna, Goldman had been working as a waiter at the Cheesecake Factory, a mid-range, casual spot located nearly adjacent to Brentwood Gardens and just 3 blocks away from Mezzaluna.

It was at the Cheesecake Factory that Goldman was sought out to pose for an advertisement, according to Kim Goldman, his 22-year-old sister who's a student at San Francisco State University. That opportunity inspired him to pursue a career in modeling and he put together a portfolio. "Ron was a good-looking guy and people would approach him," said Kim. "He thought he could use some extra money and he figured there was nothing wrong with taking advantage of his looks."

Before becoming a waiter, Goldman and worked as a tennis coach and employment headhunter. When he was younger, he had been a camp counselor and had volunteered to help disabled children. Recently he had become licensed as an emergency medical technician, but he had decided not to pursue that field—he had told friends that he eventually wanted to own a bar or restaurant in the Brentwood area. "He tended to get into something and then say, 'Oh, well, maybe not.' His sister said. "He was in the process of trying to pinpoint where his niche was."

Although "he did a lot of different things . . . the one thing you could say about him is . . . he's really good with people," Kim said. "People are just drawn to him." Friends and family members say that despite his apparent affection for the fast lane there was another, more down-to-earth side to Goldman. They said that his true love was tennis and that his great talent was working with children—teaching them to play the game he loved or helping out at a center for kids with cerebral palsy.

Kim Goldman said that what her brother wanted most was to marry and have a family. "Because we grew up with a lot of upheaval, he wanted more stability," she said. "But he took it one day at a time. He rolled wit the punches and he did the best he could with what he had. He was very loving and he didn't have a mean bone in his body."

Goldman had formed up a small group to hang-out with in Brentwood that consisted of both guys and a few girls. They were so close and did so many things together that they started calling themselves "Brentwood Place" in a take-off on the popular TV show "Melrose Place."

"I first met Ron last January," recalls Tracy Le Pera, one of the members of the "Brentwood Place" gang. "He was living behind Brentwood Gardens and he had become friendly with some of the guys I hung around with. Ron was into his modeling and hoping he was going to hit big in the business, but if it didn't, he was thinking about opening a restaurant or bar in Brentwood. He knew it would be a long time before he had the money to do that, but it was a dream of his."

"On Sundays we would play softball and then have a barbecue together or dinner at one of our apartments. We were all very close—more like brothers and sisters than just friends." The "Brentwood Place" gang loved doing things in groups. Other members of the group included Goldman's good friends Mike, Dave, and Jeff. All of the guys were extremely good-looking and all of them worked out at The Gym on San Vicente Boulevard. "We used to all go to the movies, sit around one of our apartments and watch TV, and hang-out at Starbucks in the morning for coffee. This is where Ron met Nicole."

Nicole, who was newly free of O.J. and out on her own, was also a regular at the Starbucks coffee shop on San Vicente. She met Ron there when one of the guys in the group approached the attractive California blonde and invited her to join their group for coffee. "Ron met Nicole at Starbucks around February," recalls Tracy. But it was only in the last few months that they had become close pals. He loved being seen with her and in her Ferrari. You know, she had a lot of pizzazz—she was O.J.'s ex, she was blonde and sexy and she had this incredible car. What young guy wouldn't like to hang out with her?"

But the other guys in the group were smarter than their pal. Nicole had told all of them that O.J. had beaten her and that he had an incredible temper and because of that, they were cautious about their relationship with her.

"Nicole actually liked Mike and Dave," Says Tracy. "But they were too smart to get involved with her. She had told them about O.J. beating her and they weren't going to put themselves in a position where it could happen to them. I don't know why Ron didn't listen. I guess he thought she needed a friend and he became one. They used to go out dancing together and Nicole often would go to Mezzaluna. I think her neediness appealed to Ron and he was just trying to be a good friend."

Nicole was a real looker and even though she was ten years older than her new friends, the guys in the group liked being around her.

"She always dressed in very sexy short cropped tops and shorts. She had an incredible body and I guess she liked to show it off. She wasn't particularly friendly and she would only speak when someone asked her questions. I always thought she was a bit lost and confused about who she was. I just couldn't understand why a 35-year-old woman wanted to hang out with 25-year-olds. Maybe she just wanted the attention," said Tracy.

"I never met any of her girlfriends because she always came in alone and joined our group or met with Ron or one of the other guys. What's strange now, though, is that I remember driving by the place a few times and seeing O.J.'s car there. Now, after what's happened I shouldn't be surprised. He was always spying on her and I'm sure he must have seen us all at one time or another and been jealous. After all, these guys were really great looking and a lot younger than him," Tracy surmised.

Goldman's death was a great shock to everyone, but his friends are still grieving over their loss.

"Ron was a really nice great-looking guy with a big heart," Tracy remembers sadly. "He would do anything for a friend. One time I was locked out of my apartment and I called him and told him I was at the store. When I got home, there was Ron waiting, ready to help me. He was just like that."

As Goldman's relationship with Nicole became increasingly closer, they were often seen together around Brentwood, and according to Tracy Le Pera, he had even met Simpson a few times, but they were not friends.

All of Goldman's friends contend that he and Nicole were "just friends," nothing more. And in fact, Goldman himself insisted that his relationship with Nicole was just platonic. According to Barry Zeldes, a Brentwood clothier, Goldman had told him that he was meeting more girls just by being seen with Nicole and driving around in her Ferrari than he ever had before he met her.

Zeldes said he asked Goldman point-blank two days before he died whether he was sleeping with Nicole Simpson. As Zeldes recalled it, Goldman laughed and said no.

"If O.J. caught me with her, he'd probably kill me."

And other Goldman friends echo the same.

"He definitely would have told me if he was seeing O.J. Simpson's ex-wife," says Mike Pincus. "That's just the kind of guy Ron was. Whenever he was dating someone, we all knew about it."

"Believe me, if Ron was having an affair with Nicole we would all have known. They were just friends," admits Tracy. "I know nothing sexual was going on between them, because Ron would have told us.

"We all used to play "Truth or Dare" and because we were all such close friends, we always told the truth or accepted the dare. If Ron had been sexual with Nicole, he would have bragged about it to us. We were all like family and share our most private lives with each other. Whenever Ron had sex, he always told us about it. So if he and Nicole had been doing anything, we certainly would have known.

"Ron and I had lunch exactly one week before he died. We had a real heart-to-heart talk and it was then that I knew what a really sweet guy he was. He told me all he wanted was a girlfriend and to settle down. He wasn't into one-night stands or flings. He had really big heart and he would do anything for a friend.

"The night Ron was killed, he went home from Mezzaluna before he went to Nicole's," continues Tracy. "The reason I know is that he called one of our friends and told him he was going over there. It's just too bad that he always had to be such a good guy. If he hadn't volunteered to return those sunglasses, he might still be alive today."

Goldman's funeral was packed with grieving family members and close friends of the good-hearted young man whose life ended far too soon.

"At the funeral, Ron's sister Kim was so shaken that she wanted to throw herself into the casket with him," reveals Tracy. "Ron was very close to Kim and she's an absolute doll. He was also close to his father, who is one of the nicest people I've ever met."

A grief-stricken Fred Goldman had the following to say about his beloved son: "Bottom line, he was a good kid with a good heart who didn't deserve this. I feel ripped open. Given his generous nature, it's not unlikely that Ron would have been the one to offer to return this gal's glasses."

Eight days after the double murders, Brentwood Village is trying to put itself back together. But the word is out: "No one is to discuss Nicole or Ron." From Mezzaluna to The Gym to Moda Sport clothing boutique, the word has come down. It's like the village is in mourning and they want to remember these two young beautiful people as they were and go on with life as usual.

On a very hot Sunday just two short weeks after the murders, Ron Goldman's pals pinned black circles with the letter "R" on the sleeves of their white tee-shirts and, in addition to grieving together, they played softball together, just like before. Only, they know they're not kidding anyone with their bravado. Nothing will ever be just like it was before.

11

The Opposing Team Becomes Women

The time bomb inside O.J. started ticking in March 1992, when Nicole filed for divorce, citing irreconcilable differences. That's a legal term and it can mean a lot of things, but in O.J.'s case it had chilling implications. Nicole could have used words like "wife beater," "jealous and obsessed to the point of rage," or simply "a husband who is a threat to my life."

The tragic truth is that, from the moment Nicole made the decision to divorce O.J., he became a man who apparently couldn't live with her or without her. True, the two did get back together, at least publicly. There were dinners, dances and vacations on sun-kissed beaches. On the surface, it seemed like they were lovebirds once again, somehow able to recapture the passion and romance that once made them the darlings of Hollywood.

No one saw the other side—the violence, the screaming, the shrill, hysterical profanity, glass being smashed, and doors kicked in. But this is what was happening behind the scenes; the man who had become an American treasure was slowly yielding to dark forces.

After a romantic reconciliation trip to Mexico, an ecstatic O.J. asked Nicole to come back to him, but she turned him down. And that sent him hurtling into the depths of despair. The hero who had everything money and success could buy had lost the one thing he wanted more than anything—Nicole.

The rage boiled inside him as he sat in the silence of his home, listening over and over to the Beatles' sad, haunting lyrics in "Yesterday." Aretha

Franklin's and Frank Sinatra's songs of love only made the heartache more unbearable. O.J. tortured himself with the same painful questions. Who was Nicole with tonight? Was she in love with someone else? Were they making love?

The tragic scene was played out day and night, week after week, month after month. The fury inside O.J. was steadily building like a volcano about to erupt. When he was on the road working, he managed to hide his feelings, but those closest to him seemed to know the score.

"It was an ever-changing situation with O.J.," says his friend and fellow broadcaster, Al Michaels. "One day it looked like he would move back to the house and there would be a reconciliation. Other times it looked as though there were still problems to be worked out. Here you had two very strong people, public figures who handled it well. But what went on behind the scenes—all you can do is speculate. Of course, everybody has a dark side. I have seen O.J. get angry. I've seen him lose his temper, but it was no different from anyone else."

No different? Tell that to O.J.'s personal cook, George Mutascu, who watched with growing alarm as an argument between the football star and Nicole escalated into a violent all-out attack. It happened the night before the break-up. O.J. and Nicole were having dinner at Hollywood's famous Spago's restaurant, and a couple of men started openly flirting with Nicole. By the time they got home, O.J. had turned into a vicious, terrifying monster.

Mutascu recalled seeing Nicole with the top of her dress torn off and her hair messed up. "You *fucking* pig!" she screamed at her enraged husband. Then she ran to her bedroom and slammed the door. But doors, like defensive backs, have never been a problem for O.J.

Mutascu, who cooked for Simpson before and after the break-up, picked up the story: "He ordered her to open the door, but Nicole shouted: 'Fuck you, get out of my life. Stay away from me! I'm tired of all the fighting and the jealousy—you need help.' The next thing I heard was the door being kicked in and O.J. shouting: 'Who in the fuck you talking to? You looked like a slut tonight. No woman of mine acts the way you do, you slut.'

"Nicole shouted back: 'Just get away from me, I don't want to fight with you. Just go away, you're making me sick.' "

O.J.'s violent outbursts were nothing new to Mutascu, who spent two years with the living legend. But he had learned to keep his mouth shut.

"The first thing O.J. said to me when I was hired was for me to keep his personal business off the streets. He said he couldn't—and wouldn't—tolerate disloyalty. He was never the mellow kind of guy you see in public and on television.

"He always seemed to be moving, even when he wasn't. He was always searching for something. He never really felt safe or secure. I've traveled the world and I've met a lot of people, and I have learned that the eyes are the windows to your soul. And I saw nothing but pain and frustration in O.J.'s eyes. Even when he was with friends, it was as though he was still alone with his thoughts.

"There were times he would sit in the living room for hours in the dark, deep in thought and listening to some of his favorite singers. He loved listening to Aretha Franklin and Frank Sinatra. But the song he played most was the Beatles 'Yesterday'—he'd play that over and over again.

"O.J. lived in the past after Nicole had gone. He talked about his USC days and his exploits with women, the drinking parties and how he loved the freedom. But to me he was a man living in torment because of the devastating blow of Nicole leaving him. He didn't know how to live his life without her being in the house. It seemed to make him feel less than a man."

O.J.'s violent temper took on many different faces, and even boiled to the surface when Nicole was nowhere in sight. The day after the divorce, he went around the house and smashed everything that reminded him of his ex-wife. He hurled sample bottles of perfume she had left behind against the wall and smashed a coffee table she had bought to pieces with his foot.

In his football days, people used to say O.J. had the grace of a cat, the speed of a jaguar, and the strength of a lion. But now he had turned his lean, athletic body into an instrument of destruction. Said Mutascu: "He is the strongest man I have ever seen. He could easily destroy anything in his path."

And if his closest friends are right, that brute strength grew even greater when he used cocaine. Fellow football legend Jim Brown believes the drug played a big part in Simpson's life—and his fall from grace. "O.J. has been in denial for a long time," Brown told a TV interviewer. "When he started on the stuff, way back in his football days, it got out of control and he lost his first wife. And that wasn't the end of it. When I hear Nicole begging for help on that '911' call, he had to have been on something, and I believe it was cocaine.

"His pattern of spousal abuse, the anger, the violence is all on the record. It was down-played by the press, mainly because of his image. When O.J. was playing ball he was dynamite because he let it all hang out. He used the anger and the violence to a positive end. But when his day on the field ended, the object of his anger took a different direction—the opposing team became women."

After Nicole walked out on him, there were lots of other women in O.J.'s life, and like Nicole, they were always stunning beauties. Hours before the killings of Nicole and Goldman, he phoned to make a date with *Playboy* playmate Traci Adell, a size 36D brunette model. He got her number from a mutual friend and gave her a call after seeing her photo spread in the magazine.

"The call was out of the blue, but he seemed like a very nice man," Adell said. "He didn't seem like he was in a bad mood or anything. But he kept comparing me to Nicole. He said things like: 'You are so different from my wife. She's blonde and you are brunette.' We talked for over an hour."

It wasn't difficult for the handsome hero to have his pick of women. At restaurants and parties they hovered over him like bees around a honey pot. But the relationships never lasted. They met, shared a couple of drinks and then headed for the bedroom. He was always on the lookout for another Nicole, but never seemed to find her.

"That's why he had such a terrible time with permanent relationships," said Brown. "He was obsessed with Nicole, whether he was with her or not. In his mind she was still his woman. He *owned* her. And that's trouble right there—when a man feels he actually owns a woman. It nearly always ends in tragedy.

"Every time I saw O.J., I'd ask about Nicole and he'd say: 'My woman is just fine—why shouldn't she be? She has me and everything else in the world she needs.' It wasn't just what he said but the way he said it. There was that tone in his voice."

Others, like Brown, saw that O.J.'s life was out of control, but he refused to listen to anybody's warnings. "Years ago I talked to O.J. and suggested he should get some counseling, that it might lighten the stress that he always seemed to be going through," said Brown. "His response was: 'Oh, man, I'm getting help, but I don't have time to sit on a couch telling all my personal feelings and business to a shrink, someone I don't know at all. It's just too tough for me.'

"My guess is that there must have been some terrible things that happened to O.J. when he was growing up, because how he sees women and his position as a man in the world is very disturbing. To O.J,. a man needs to be able to control women.

And in today's world, that kind of thinking just won't wash."

When he finally did get some therapy—he was ordered to do so by a judge after his 1989 no-contest plea to wife-abuse charges—he was allowed to have counseling over the phone. But he remained the same hollow, tortured man he was before. It was the beginning of his slide into deep depression—the tragic, downcast man millions saw in court after he was charged with murder.

"When I spoke with O.J. in jail he was a lost soul—depressed, at the bottom," said ex-New York Giant and former actor Rosey Grier, who was one of the few people O.J. agreed to see in the Los Angeles County Jail. Grier is also a minister. "It's very sad to see a guy you've known for years completely on the edge. It's like seeing someone die right before your eyes. This whole thing has upset me deeply, very deeply. I spoke with O.J. about the Bible and advised him to keep the faith."

Grier's relationship with O.J. goes back to their football days, and it's painful for him to watch these grisly chapters of his old friend's life unfold. "The guy I've been hearing about and reading about now is a stranger to me," Grier said. "The O.J. I knew was compassionate, caring, and sensitive. He was a heck of a human being. I don't recognize the angry, violent man that's being viewed by the world. All of us sports guys had our wild moments as young men, and I was no different. But O.J. was always the center of a million women.

"There's no doubt he liked the good life, and a lot of good things happened to him. But having that kind of exposure only made him more complicated. I think he had a need to really have it all—women, money, everything. Owning things became an obsession."

And women were possessions. O.J. prided himself on picking them up for a lunchtime "quickie"—no strings attached. Once, during a lunch interview with a reporter, he asked a beautiful restaurant hostess to feed the parking meter for him. When she came back to the table, she told O.J. what a wonderful Mercedes he had. He offered her a ride and it went on from there. Later, bragging about the conquest, he laughed and said coldly: "At least I got her back to work in time for cocktail hour."

One woman who became an exception to his taste for one night stands was beautiful Paula Barbieri, the focus of O.J.'s "suicide" letter after Nicole was murdered. He wrote: "Paula. What can I say? You are special. I'm sorry we're not going to have our chance."

The 27-year-old *Vogue* magazine cover girl and

Victoria's Secret model was shocked by the mention in O.J.'s note. Even though friends said they were romantically linked, her publicist Tom Hahn insisted the two were only good friends—"like brother and sister." But a friend of the ravishing 5-foot-9 redhead from Panama City, Fla., confided that said O.J. had presented a $15,000 sapphire and diamond bracelet to Paula just weeks before he was charged with murder.

In fact, they began dating in early 1989, shortly after the infamous New Year's Day incident in which Nicole told cops O.J. had hit, kicked, and threatened to kill her. A friend said: "Paula is religious. She wasn't crazy about being the "other woman," but O.J. can be very charming. He showered her with clothes and jewelry. He told her he wanted to marry her and have a family."

But O.J. refused to keep his word. "Paula was devastated," the friend said. "She had been the other woman for three years. She got anxious and finally left O.J." The curvy cover girl dated a string of men, including actor George Hamilton, before she hooked up with director Dean Hamilton.

"Within weeks, Paula married Dean," the friend said. "But the marriage lasted only as long as the courtship. After his marriage ended in 1992, O.J. begged her to come back to him. "Paula really loved O.J. She passed up big modeling jobs in Europe just to be with him. Then out of the blue, just before the murders, he gave her the beautiful bracelet. She was convinced he wanted to get serious." When O.J. was accused of murder, Paula was shattered. "She's known him for years," the friend said. "And he never so much as touched a hair on her head."

Except for Paula, O.J. could never seem to establish a real romantic relationship after Nicole. A longtime friend wondered whether the problem was cocaine. There were plenty of signs. "Whenever I saw him, he always seemed super-hyper," the friend said. "He had this habit of sweating on his upper lip when he talked, and sometimes he would ramble on and on about all the boards he was on—Pioneer Chicken or this or that. He'd talk about how really important he was as a businessman."

Mutascu never saw drugs in O.J.'s life after he left Nicole, but he suspected it with some of the guests. "There was always a lot of drinking going on," Mutascu said. "I personally never saw drugs. But there were many times when I saw people going into the bathrooms or the bedrooms looking perfectly straight, and they'd come out with their eyes ablaze and walking as if they'd been on a trip to Mars.

"There were always women available at these parties of O.J.'s because he loved being around women. They hung on his every word. I saw three women get into a fist fight over him at one party. They were the ones who looked most like Nicole. He might even date them three or four times. After that he wouldn't even be able to remember their names. It was always Nicole. Having lost her was major failure for him, and O.J. couldn't live with failure."

As if to compensate for the personal disasters in his life, O.J. often boasted about his wealth and power to his staff. "He told me one day how money and success had come to him so fast," Mutascu said. "Right from his USC days, he was king of the hill and everything that followed only turned him into a sports god or hero. He said money meant very little to him. He had forgotten what it was not to have money. It seemed to be always there.

"He told me one day: 'You know something George, I could flush a million bucks down the toilet and not feel a thing. But if you don't have the right person in your life, there's an emptiness. Sometimes I wake up in the morning and I ask myself just who the hell I am.' O.J.'s a very serious man. There's very little comedy in his life. He loved to play the social game, but there was no playing around when it came down to himself and those he loved."

Many people have wondered about O.J.'s dark side, but his TV colleagues didn't have a clue. Was it just the TV 'old boys' network sticking together to support one of their own? NBC's Dick Enberg said: "It's tragic, incredible, most difficult to believe. I hope it isn't him, although evidence seems to be mounting." And sportscaster Bob Costas said on CNN's 'Larry King Live,' "O.J. was not the most talented broadcaster I ever worked with, but he was the most good-natured person you could hope to be around. Almost anyone who has spent time around O.J. considers him a friend, because he had that kind of personality."

Was it that difficult to see the dark side of O.J.? Did his TV partners simply look the other way, or did he build a wall around himself to cloak the pain, the bitterness and the rage?

12

COURTESY KCOP

Say It
Ain't So

Sometime after 9:45 P.M. on June 12, 1994, the bronzed and beautiful Nicole Brown Simpson became Los Angeles County Coroner's Department homicide victim No. 94-05136.

The case report makes eerie reading:

Sex: Female; Date of Birth: 5/19/59; Age: 35;

Height: 65in.; Weight: 129lb.; Eyes: Brown; Hair: Blonde; Teeth: Own; Condition: Poor.

"Poor" hardly described the condition of O.J. Simpson's former wife. The report says: "The decedent was lying at the foot of the stairs at the gate. She was in a fetal position, lying on her left side, wearing a black dress, no shoes. Her legs were positioned under the stationary portion of the gate and her arms were bent at the elbow and close to her body.

"Coagulated and dried blood stained the walkway leading to the decedent. Paw prints were present at the sidewalk, consistent with a dog present/leaving the location. . . . Blood stains were present on the decedent's legs, arms and face. Examination revealed a large, sharp force injury at the decedent's neck, with smaller injuries to the left side of the neck."

Nicole's friend, Ronald Goldman, was dead by her side. "Decedent 94-05135 was seated in the dirt, slumped to his right side," the report says. "His back was against a small tree stump and iron fence. He was dressed in blue jeans and a light colored cotton-type sweater. His clothes and face were stained with blood. Numerous sharp force injuries were observed at his neck, back, head and hands. Another wound was present at his left thigh area.

Lying near the decedent's right foot was a business size white envelope containing a pair of eyeglasses."

Ironically, Sunday, June 12, had started out happily for both O.J. and Nicole. He played golf at the Riviera Country Club. In the afternoon he joined Nicole to attend their daughter Sydney's dance recital at Paul Revere Junior High. They sat apart and left separately, but eyewitnesses saw no tension between them. O.J. hugged his little girl and told her he had to leave early to get ready to fly to Chicago.

After the recital, Nicole, along with Sydney and her son Justin, had dinner with her family and several friends at the trendy Mezzaluna restaurant, just 500 yards from her Brentwood home. The party broke up around 8:30 P.M. and Nicole took her children home and put them to bed.

At this point, confusion sets in. Staff at Mezzaluna say that Nicole phoned them shortly after 8:30 P.M. to ask them to look for a pair of glasses that had been left behind. Goldman, who was on duty as a waiter that night, volunteered to run them over to Nicole's house. The case report shows that Nicole's mother called her at 11 P.M. to tell her that she had left her glasses at the restaurant and to make arrangements to retrieve them.

The time difference was crucial to O.J.'s alibi—
that he was on his way to Chicago at the time of
the killings. If Nicole did not call the restaurant
until after 11 P.M., then Ron Goldman would not
have come before O.J. met his limo at the front gate
of his estate and his alibi holds. If she called at 8:30
P.M. and Ron Goldman had come over earlier, it
does not.

Police found Nicole's and O.J.'s children asleep
in the house. After making arrangements for their
care, two officers were dispatched to O.J.'s mansion, just a few blocks away, to tell him the tragic
news. The superstar was not there, but the cops
noticed suspicious brownish-red stains in the
driveway that they thought could be blood.

Dawn was breaking and news of the killings
was already spreading rapidly to news services and
television stations. Local affiliates dispatched correspondents and wired the information to their
network news bureaus. The pack of journalists was
set to descend. Dozens of reporters, along with
camera crews and sound trucks, surrounded
Nicole's house, trying to pry information loose
from tight-lipped investigators who did not want
to be blindsided by correspondents who were
watching their every move. *Globe* reporter Chris
Doherty was among them. He watched as police

removed the bodies and soaked up the ocean of blood with white towels. He pressed close to the gate and saw the grisly paw prints Nicole's dog had left as he tracked through the human carnage.

Meanwhile, in Chicago, O.J.—who flew in on the redeye—checked into his hotel at 6:15 A.M. He made a flurry of phone calls from his room, including at least one to his girlfriend, Paula Barbieri, before the Los Angeles police contacted him, told him the tragic news, and ordered him to return home immediately. The cops issued a terse but ominous statement. "He was in Chicago when we contacted him," said Lt. John Dunkin. "Where he was last night is something we don't know."

O.J. was rushed straight from the Los Angeles International Airport to his mansion while the army of reporters flocked from Nicole's home to his. O.J. was used to this. The media had followed him around for years and he knew how to walk through them without the least bit of discomfort. But this was different. The air was already buzzing with rumors that something shocking was about to happen. As *Globe's* team waited with the others, O.J.'s lawyer Howard Weitzman sped through the gates. There was a hushed conversation with police officials outside the door, too far away for reporters to hear.

Weitzman and the police officers went into the house. And then—the image that shocked the nation was broadcast over the air as a group exited from the house—O.J. Simpson in handcuffs! Another hurried conversation between Weitzman and the cops and the handcuffs came off, but O.J. was hustled into a police cruiser and whisked off just like a common criminal. Before the patrol car sped off, O.J. turned to the reporters and said: "I know nothing." They were the last words he would say in public until he pleaded "Not guilty" to two counts of murder with special circumstances one week later.

O.J. maintained his ignorance of the events that befell his former wife. His denials of any knowledge were so strong that directly against Weitzman's advice, O.J. agreed to be questioned alone by police. For the next three or so hours, he was grilled intensively at LAPD headquarters in downtown Los Angeles while a portable crime lab pulled up to his house and stayed there for the rest of the day. Meanwhile, a crack team of Chicago police investigators swarmed over his vacated hotel room, gathering every little scrap that could be used as evidence.

Yellow police tape was stretched across the driveway of O.J.'s L.A. estate. There were pieces of cardboard marking small reddish-brown stains leading up the driveway toward the garage. Unnamed sources also reported that a blood-stained glove was found inside the house and that it matched another discovered near the butchered bodies. Cops towed away O.J.'s late-model white Ford Bronco XLT.

"We are not going to rule anyone out as a suspect," Commander David Gascon announced. "We will pursue whoever we need to pursue until we bring the party to justice."

But Weitzman was steadfastly denying his client had anything to do with the killings. "He's shocked," the attorney said, adding that the murders were thought to have taken place at 11 P.M. and O.J. was probably on his way to the airport or already there at that time. "His reaction is and has been shock. He is really grieving both for his wife and children. This is a trauma."

Police sources, though, were telling a different story as the first dramatic day drew to a close. "O.J. is the only suspect," said one. And another predicted ominously as The Juice left police headquarters: "Simpson's release is a temporary thing."

On Tuesday, June 14, a numb and drained O.J. Simpson huddled behind the vine-covered walls of his Brentwood mansion with family and close friends. Outside, the media, photographing all those who entered and exited through the gates and curiosity seekers milled around like sharks in a feeding frenzy. Had we seen this all before when Heidi Fleiss was arrested the previous year or, more to the point, when police searched the Century City condo and Santa Barbara estate of Michael Jackson? An already jaded public wanted to take this in stride. But they could not. This was a bigger story, and promised to get bigger with each new day.

The besieged football legend looked emotionally and physically drained by the events of the past 48 hours. For the first time in public, O.J., who had always seemed forever young, was beginning to show his age. He clearly looked tired. If those who believed he was guilty of the double murder were right, then he had been operating at a superhuman pace the entire time: planning and executing the gruesome slaughter of his ex-wife and her friend, rushing at break-neck speed to cover his tracks and make the late-night flight to Chicago, and hiding evidence there before returning to L.A. twelve hours later.

The release of rumors, innuendoes, and the slightest unsubstantiated suspicion was relentless. And all the time, the media blared the details of the horrific crime and the gruesome trail of evidence which appeared to implicate O.J. as the only possible culprit.

In just a few days, the athlete-actor-broadcaster had lost the woman he loved, was being linked to her killing, and had seen the wholesome image he'd built up for over thirty years severely tarnished. It seemed to be more than any one man—even an athlete with O.J's extraordinary powers and stamina—could bear.

"His wife has been murdered and now he has people pointing the finger at him," said attorney Weitzman. "It's awful. O.J. had nothing to do with these tragic circumstances. He is depressed and devastated by Nicole's death."

A stream of friends and kin poured through the gates of the mansion to give their condolences over the loss of his beloved ex-wife and offer their affection and support. *Globe* reporters witnessed O.J.'s sister arrive to hold his hand, along with singer Jermaine Jackson, and close pal Bob Chandler, a former pro football teammate. "Those who care about him are the ones coming here to see him," said singer Dionne Warwick, who also visited.

Meanwhile, Weitzman got busy with damage control, talking with the press about O.J.'s movements during and since the gruesome killings and discussing rumors of damaging evidence that police had allegedly found at the crime scene. Whatever was happening behind the closed doors of the homicide team investigating the murders, Weitzman remained publicly upbeat and aggressive.

Of the bloody gloves, Weitzman snapped: "Pathetically false. I've been told there is no glove with blood at Mr. Simpson's. It's a real tragedy. It makes it look like something exists that doesn't."

Globe learned that police apparently took a pair of white athletic shoes from the Brentwood house. Sources close to the investigation said the rust-colored stains on the driveway at O.J.'s estate had turned out to be blood, and that the football legend had scratches on his body when he was questioned by police on Monday.

Rumors swirled that an arrest of the football star was imminent as mounting evidence appeared to link him to the slayings.

Weitzman noted the strain on his client and said: "Not only is he going through a tremendous grieving period, but all these rumors about his possible involvement are circulating.

"He came back here, cooperated, and has not been officially told he cannot leave or that he is a suspect. But he has to sit here and listen to all these rumors. It's really a horrible time for O.J."

Two thousand miles away in Chicago, cops searched for the murder weapon on the grounds surrounding the hotel near O'Hare Airport where O.J. had stayed. They also found a towel stained with blood and a broken glass in his room.

Weitzman coolly explained this, as well, saying: "I can tell you after O.J. was informed of his wife's death, he was in the bathroom and slammed his hand down on the sink. That's what police found—a broken glass and a towel with blood on it."

Again the lawyer steadfastly denied that O.J. was about to be arrested—or even that he was a suspect. "There has been no indication by law enforcement to me of that fact," he said. "They've been communicative and we are in touch."

But as *Globe* and other newsman pressed Weitzman about the persistent rumors of arrest, he conceded: "I hope that's not true, but as we know, they arrest innocent people on occasion. I am convinced that he is innocent."

Lawmen were keeping mum, at least officially, about the evidence they'd collected and refused to label the football legend as a suspect. "We have made progress in the investigation," Commander

David Gascon, the LAPD's chief spokesman, told the press. "There is no indication at this point that any arrest is imminent."

A spokesman for the coroner refused to divulge details about the slayings and the condition of the bodies, explaining that police asked for a "security hold" on the information. But a police source leaked to Globe that both Nicole and Goldman's throats had been slashed.

And another source close to the investigation said that while the times of death hadn't been fixed, detectives believe there had been plenty of time for the killer to commit the murders and then drive from Brentwood to the airport and catch the 11:45 flight to Chicago.

Then therapist Dr. Susan Forward dropped another bombshell. Claiming she had treated Nicole on two occasions after her 1992 divorce from O.J., Forward said the football star's wife complained that he had threatened her, saying: "If you ever try to leave me—I'll kill you." Forward described Nicole as an abused and battered woman who was stalked by her obsessed husband.

"He would follow her to restaurants and bars and make scenes and threaten to kill her," said the therapist. "It was very extensive—punching, kicking, severely beating her."

It was a devastating description of a relationship, plunging like a flaming meteor into a primordial soup of rumor and suspicion.

O.J. and Weitzman huddled much of the morning in the Brentwood mansion, but as the madness outside with mobs of media and gawkers escalated, they later managed to slip away to a secret location where O.J. could breathe easier and his attorney could think.

It wasn't easy. Crowds of fans and thrill seekers lined the narrow street in front of O.J.'s home, battling with TV and newspaper reporters from across the country and around the world—all of them trying to catch a glimpse of the beleaguered sports hero. Cameramen perched on top of vans while reporters shimmied up walls and peered through gates.

O.J.'s neighbor, actor James Garner, did a slow burn as he tried to snake his car down the street through the sea of spectators.

"I thought they were filming a movie here," said another neighbor, Lindy Kummings. "I went up and asked: 'Is this a movie, or is this for real?'

As nightfall approached, there was another shocking news release, this time from O.J.'s side of the table. His attorney Howard Weitzman suddenly announced to the media that because of

"other professional commitments and my close-
ness to O.J." he was dropping the case. The attorney said he would still be involved as "an advi-
sor." It wasn't until the following day that the
stunned world would learn who O.J.'s new lawyer would be.

The full weight of the double tragedy came
crashing down on friends and family as they
mourned the deaths of Nicole Brown Simpson and
Ronald Lyle Goldman at separate private memorial services on Wednesday, June 15.

Meanwhile, the prosecution was turning up the
heat in their investigation, and a new defense team
was shielding O.J. Simpson. And everywhere, the
press was ready to pounce like a pack of blood-
thirsty piranha. The former NFL star began the
brutal day by hiring one of L.A.'s top criminal defense attorneys Robert Shapiro to defend him. The
high-profile specialist in difficult cases, who has
defended celebrities like Johnny Carson, Marlon
Brando's son Christian, and baseball star Darryl
Strawberry, is legendary for telling jurors that it's
"better to let 1,000 guilty men go free that to allow
one innocent man to be convicted."

It didn't take long for Shapiro to grab headlines. His first maneuver was to present his client's

alibi to the news-hungry media. "At the time this murder took place, O.J. was at home waiting to get into a limousine to take him to the airport. He was going on a trip that had been planned well in advance for a promotional event in Chicago. I have introduced myself to members of the Los Angeles Police Department to offer complete cooperation with them in their investigation to solve this crime."

However, Shapiro's statement conflicted with O.J.'s original story that he had already been en route to Chicago when Nicole and Goldman were slaughtered. Investigators confirmed that the former football star was indeed on the American Airlines flight to Chicago that left LAX at 11:45 P.M., but insisted that he had time to commit the crime, change his clothes, take the 20-minute drive to the airport, and still catch the plane.

Bit by bit, police released information and witnesses came forward that opened up holes in O.J.'s public alibi. The trial in the media had begun.

Now the limo driver claimed that when he arrived at O.J.'s house at 10:45 P.M. Sunday night, his fare was not there. The man reported that about 11 P.M., he saw someone outside the house, and then a sweaty and agitated O.J. climbed into the back of the limo.

The story was further complicated when, Kato Kaelin, a family friend and caretaker living in the guest house at the estate, said that he, not O.J., met the limo that fateful night, and that the star came out of the house a few minutes later.

Kaelin's lawyer, William Genego, said: "My guy saw O.J. coming out of the house to the limo. He does not know where O.J. was when the limo arrived. He could have been in the house, as far as he knows. But at no time did he say that O.J. was not at home."

As the beleaguered Hall of Famer continued to take refuge behind the gates and ivy-covered walls of his estate, his new counsel gave the world a glimpse of the private hell he was enduring.

"He is extremely depressed," Shapiro said. "He is under the care of a physician to help him through this very difficult time of grieving and he is going to remain in seclusion with his family to grieve over the loss of the mother of his children."

One of O.J.'s friends put it more bluntly: "He looks like he's in a state of shock, like someone who doesn't comprehend what happened."

Meanwhile, friends were flocking to boost O.J.'s spirits. One pal, Mark Slotkin, fumed: "They ought to be out there looking for the real person," as he brushed past *Globe's* reporter outside the home.

An anonymous member of the LAPD homicide squad revealed that cops had "definitive" physical evidence linking O.J. to the murders. But police spokesman Lt. John Dunkin said only: "There are fingerprint, footprint, hair, fiber, and blood samples to be analyzed."

Other sources confirmed to *Globe* that Nicole and Goldman's throats had been slashed during the attack, and that Goldman had struggled desperately with the killer.

"It wouldn't surprise me if he put up quite a fight to help Nicole," said Goldman's dad, Fred. "It does not surprise me that Ron was the person who offered to return Nicole's mother's glasses. His manager told Ron he didn't have to, but Ron said: 'I don't mind, she lives close by.'"

The cops also tried to solidify their case by releasing reports prepared by the officers who responded to the 911 call from Nicole Simpson on New Year's Day 1989, during which she claimed her husband had beaten and threatened to kill her. But the day of legal jockeying ended in the tearful privacy of memorial services held for Nicole and Goldman.

A disconsolate Fred Goldman appeared publicly and said of his slain son: "The bottom line is that Ron was a good person from the top of his head to the bottom of his feet, from the inside to the outside. He was a special human being. He didn't deserve what's happened."

Next, if media onlookers expected an explosive situation at memorial services for Nicole Simpson as O.J. met and mourned with members of her family, it failed to materialize. O.J., wearing a dark suit, spent 90 minutes at a visitation service for Nicole at O'Connor Laguna Hills Mortuary in Orange County. O.J., with his children, looked every bit the grieving husband as consoled Nicole's family. He appeared to be simply a husband whose wife had been murdered, not the murder suspect himself.

"It was all friendly," said Nicole's sister Denise Brown. "I went to see my sister. I wanted to tell her I love her and miss her and say good bye for the last time."

While prosecutors and the defense team were taking pot shots at one another on Thursday, June 16, the Los Angeles police dropped a bombshell: They had found the murder weapon—a blood-encrusted military-style entrenching tool with a sharp-edged shovel and a pick ax-like fold-down arm! *Globe's* photo editor, Ron Haines, dispatched one of his assistants to an army surplus store to buy one for picture purposes, but by the time she got back to the office, the cops had backtracked, saying that Nicole and Goldman had been killed with a "substantial knife."

Two things were becoming clear: Police and prosecutors were being stung by leaks inside their own departments, and it was just a matter of time before charges would be brought against O.J. It was clearly the time for public silence, but the sniping continued as new disclosures were made by the police.

LAPD sources confirmed that blood and pieces of flesh found at the scene of the murders matched O.J.'s blood type, but admitted that it would take months to complete the more conclusive DNA tests. And a woman jogger told cops that she had seen a vehicle that matched O.J.'s parked across from Nicole's house the night of the killings.

The incriminating case against the sports hero was also growing, based on investigations taking place halfway across the country. Chicago cops were using metal detectors to search an over-grown mini-jungle behind a gas station located across the street from the O'Hare Plaza Hotel after a witness told them he'd seen someone looking like O.J. in the area early Monday.

The LAPD sent their own investigators to help

out. "We're here to collect evidence the Chicago Police Department has assisted us in acquiring," Detective Bert Luper said. "We are trying to pick up evidence, re-interviewing employees, and doing the legwork that is necessary in any homicide investigation."

One source claimed the cops found a blood-soaked ski mask in O.J.'s mansion, but the defense quickly debunked the story. When they demanded to see evidence, the cops admitted the mask did not exist. Meanwhile, Shapiro hauled out a new pair of hired guns—renowned forensic scientists Dr. Henry Lee of Connecticut and Dr. Michael Baden of New York.

Another witness also spoke out for O.J. Sports photographer Howard Bingham told reporters that he was a passenger on the flight the football star took from L.A. to Chicago. He said he shook hands with O.J. twice and there were no cuts or blood on his hands.

"I am shocked," Bingham said. "He did not seem nervous. He seemed completely normal. He seemed like O.J. He was talking to me about his golf game. He wasn't bleeding. I just hope the right guy is caught. This whole thing is unbelievable."

As the press leaks continued, officials became increasingly frustrated. They admitted that reporters were often calling up to confirm rumors just three minutes after the information had been discussed behind closed doors. "Leaks are not a police issue," said Police Commander David Gascon. "Leaks are a media issue. We just hope the media is responsible and nothing is done to damage the investigation."

L.A. Police Chief Willie Williams, who had just returned from Philadelphia, was feeling the heat, too. The press was grilling him about the slow pace of the investigation and demanding to know if O.J. was still a free man only because of his celebrity stature. "We're trying to do a homicide investigation, with two people dead and the world watching us," he countered. "We want to be careful. This is not taking a long time. We're doing a very expeditious investigation while leaving no stone unturned.

"We are not doing anything special or extra because of Mr. Simpson. Most homicides are not solved in the first 24 hours—but you don't have people watching those cases."

Shapiro, meanwhile, was warding off rumors of his client's impending arrest. "All this is press speculation," he said. "The police have not made any official statement as to who or whom they are looking at." However, he assured the cops that O.J.

"will be available at a moment's notice."

He also said that if the football star was facing arrest, he would be allowed to surrender himself. "As in any case where we are coöperating with authorities—and given my reputation with the court—I would hope we would be extended that courtesy."

Friends and family said their final farewells at funerals for Nicole and Goldman. "I don't know if I ever told you how proud I am of the man you have become," sobbed teary-eyed Kim Goldman at services for her dead brother at Westlake Village." Hundreds of people then walked across the lawn to Goldman's gravesite at Pierce Brothers Valley Oaks Memorial Park.

O.J. attended Nicole's services at St. Martin of Tours Catholic Church in suburban Brentwood with their children, Sydney, nine, and Justin, six. Dressed in a black suit, the former NFL star hugged well-wishers. After embracing the priest, he joined the mile-long procession for the 50-mile journey to Ascension Cemetery in Lake Forest where Nicole was buried.

Shapiro told reporters of the plea Nicole's mother made to him at the service. "Mrs. Brown told me: 'Please take good care of him. The children need their father.' " At the end of the heart-breaking ceremony, O.J. climbed into his limo for the drive home.

First thing the next morning, Shapiro got the news that the defense team had dreaded: The District Attorney's Office called at 8:30 A.M. to tell the lawyer that authorities had filed murder charges, citing special circumstances that could make his client eligible for the death penalty. They told Shapiro to surrender his client by 11 A.M.

Shapiro made a beeline to the San Fernando Valley home of Robert Kardashian where O.J. had been waiting, away from the press of reporters. The Juice was just waking up when his lawyer broke the news that he was being charged with two counts of murder. As the deadline drew near, there were numerous delays in getting O.J. ready to turn himself in.

Two doctors, an internist and a psychiatrist, visited him, and tested him for an enlarged lymph node. O.J. called his children and his mother, then dictated a change in his will to his personal attorney. He then sat down to write three letters.

Shapiro was on the phone every 15 minutes to update authorities about the delays as the 11 A.M. deadline approached. O.J. was in another room while Shapiro spoke to the police. It looked as though O.J.'s week of freedom was coming to an end.

But the drama was about to take another shocking turn.

13

In the
Wind

It had been five days since the slashed and bloody bodies of Nicole Simpson and Ronald Goldman, their wounds still oozing onto the saturated ground and penetrating the concrete, were discovered crumpled at the gate of her $650,000

Brentwood condo and the LAPD was finally set to announce that they were ready to take the great O.J. Simpson into custody.

Without a doubt it was to be their most important arrest since Charlie Manson, certainly of greater notoriety than former L.A. police chief Daryl Gates' on-camera arrest of accused L.A. rioter Damian Williams. The media was alerted and summoned downtown to the Parker Center for a press conference announcing the coup, the result of painstaking investigation and the reward for not jumping the gun with a premature booking.

The circus was in full swing. Video vans hummed outside and photographers jostled for the best vantage points. Inside, newsmen jockeyed for position, too, and furiously scribbled notes for hungry editors. The TV crowd rehearsed their on camera reports.

There was only one thing missing—O.J.

LAPD Commander David J. Gascon had said that the football legend was due to turn himself in at 11 A.M.; an arraignment was scheduled for later that Friday afternoon. But the clock ticked on and the prisoner of the hour was still nowhere to be seen.

At around 2 P.M. L.A.'s finest had to face the bitter fact. They'd lost their man. The most celebrated murder suspect in recent years, the suspect whose surrender they been negotiating with his lawyer, the most recognizable face in the U.S., not to mention Los Angeles, had simply disappeared. They'd promised the press a show, and now the press listened, gasping in disbelief as the LAPD spokesman explained that, no, the police did not have him under surveillance, and that, no, the police hadn't the vaguest idea where he might have gone. First he was there, at his friend's Encino home. Now he wasn't. It was almost as if he'd slipped through a seam in the universe. And there was nothing the police could do about it except put out an all-points and hope that someone—anyone—spotted him.

With his jaw set firmly, fighting back his fury, LAPD Commander Gascon stood before the microphone and announced to an incredulous audience: "Mr. Simpson is a wanted murder suspect— two counts of murder, a terrible crime. We need to find him. We need to bring him to justice.

O.J. was doing what he'd always done best, the one thing he knew he could always rely on—he was running.

Up to that point, there had been a strangely casual, kid-glove treatment of a suspected double murderer whom the police had charged with mercilessly snuffing out two young lives. But then, how could he run? Where would he hide? O.J. Simpson has a face so famous that most people think they know him better than they know their own neighbors. He was being dogged by the media and the cops—the whole world was watching. There was no escape.

But escape he did, pulling off a disappearing act that would have made Houdini proud. Just how did he manage it? It was a classic shell game, launched at his wife's funeral in Brentwood with the help of an off-duty cop and A.C., his best buddy. O.J. had hired Police Sgt. Dennis Sebenick to direct security for the somber occasion. But the 25-year-veteran officer did more than that—he masterminded a plan that allowed the Hall-of-Famer to vanish, not only from the prying eyes of the press, but the police as well.

Here's how it worked. While the press milled outside O.J.'s Brentwood home, a black man in a dark suit, wearing sunglasses—just like O.J.—was hustled into the house by Sebenick. It *had* to be him, thought everyone who saw him, but in truth, it wasn't. O.J. at that moment was miles away, driving to the San Fernando Valley house of his friend Robert Kardashian.

A.C., who was the man masquerading as O.J.,

and lawyer Robert Shapiro knew exactly where he was, but they weren't telling. Nobody was. "I didn't think I was hiding him from the cops," Sebenick said later. "Absolutely not. After he was 'wanted' I would have to tell somebody. Not before."

But the law was closing in on The Juice. The night before, O.J. had been heavily sedated. The next morning Shapiro had arrived up with a doctor and a mental health specialist to give his client the bad news: He had to turn himself in to face charges of double murder. The lawyer had promised the police he'd deliver The Juice at 11 A.M.

O.J. was just waking up, and he appeared to be severely depressed and on the verge of suicide, Shapiro said later. He also wanted his client to undergo a physical examination because a swollen lymph node had been discovered in a routine examination earlier in the week.

After the examination, O.J. wrote three letters—one to his children, one to his mother, and one "To whom it may concern"—and then dictated a change in his will. The 11 A.M. deadline passed but Shapiro assured the authorities that the surrender was nonetheless only 45 minutes away. After all, he was right there at the house, wasn't he?

The deadline passed; again Shapiro called

downtown, and police told him a squad car was on its way to pick up their suspect. The lawyer, the doctors, and several legal aides went upstairs to discuss O.J.'s state of mind and the fragile situation. Kardashian went with them.

Downstairs, Al Cowlings watched over his shattered life-long pal, who was talking about his mother, his dead wife—and also threatening to kill himself. Police were just minutes away when O.J., armed with a pistol, suddenly decided to bolt. Cowlings went with him, explaining later that he feared his friend was going to blow his brains out.

The fugitive jumped into the back seat of A.C.'s white Ford Bronco, trembling, gun in hand. He demanded to be taken to Nicole's grave, saying he wanted to say good bye one last time. They pulled away minutes before three police officers arrived in a black and white squad car to collect their famous suspect.

Shapiro and the others came down to greet the officers. "I was concerned that he was suicidal," Shapiro said. "He was completely despondent. I asked the officers to allow us to go with him, to sit on either side so he wouldn't throw himself out of the car." Kardashian was going to tag along behind.

But it was too late. The psychiatrist went to get

O.J. and discovered that he had fled, along with Cowlings. While O.J. and A.C. slipped through the L.A. streets unnoticed on their way to Nicole's Anaheim grave site, all hell broke lose downtown.

Police brass were fuming that they'd let him get away and that Shapiro hadn't made good on his promise to bring O.J. in to face the music. The normally unflappable lawyer was so embarrassed by the latest turn of events that he held an impromptu press conference to explain the debacle, and then dropped the additional bombshell that he thought his client was going to kill himself.

Next, Robert Kardashian stepped up to the microphone to read a dramatic letter O.J. had left before he skipped. It foreshadowed yet more tragedy:

To whom it may concern:

First, everyone understand I had nothing to do with Nicole's murder. I loved her, always have and always will. If we had a problem, it's because I loved her so much. Recently, we came to the understanding that for now we were not right for each other—at least for now.

Despite our love, we were different, and that's why we agreed to go our separate ways.

It was tough splitting the second time, but we

both knew it was for the best. Besides, I had no doubt that in the future we would be close friends or more.

Unlike what has been written in the press, Nicole and I had a great relationship most of out lives together. Like all long-term relationships, we had a few downs and ups.

I took the heat New Year's 1989 because that's what I was supposed to do. I did not plead 'no contest' for any other reason but to protect our privacy and was advised it would end the press hype.

I don't want to belabor knocking the press, but I can't believe what is being said. Most of it is totally made up. I know you have a job to do, but as a last wish please, please leave my children in peace. Their lives will be tough enough.

I want to send my love and thanks to all my friends. I'm sorry I can't name every one of you, especially A.C.—man, thanks for being in my life.

The support and friendship I received from so many, Wayne Hughes, Louis Marx, Frank Olsen, Mark Packer, Bender, Bobby Kardashian. I wish we had spent more time together in recent years.

My golfing buddies—Alan Austen. Mike, Craig, Bender, Wyler, Sandy, Jay, Donny—thanks for the fun.

All my teammates over the years, Reggie—you

were the soul of my pro career. Ahmad, I never stopped being proud of you. Marcus, you got a great lady in Catherine—don't mess it up. Bobby Chandler, thanks for always being there. Skip and Cathy, I love you guys—without you I never would hare made it through this far.

Marguerite, thanks for the early years. We had some fun. Paula, what can I say? You are special. I'm sorry, I'm not going to have, we're not going to have our chance. God brought you to me, I now see. As I leave, you'll be in my thoughts.

I think of my life and feel I've done most of the right things. So why do I end up like this? I can't go on. No matter what the outcome, people will look and point. I can't take that. I can't subject my children to that, This way, they can move on and go on with their lives.

Please, if I've done anything worthwhile in my life, let my kids live in peace, from you, the press.

I've had a good life. I'm proud of how I lived. My mama taught me to do unto others. I treated people the way I wanted to be treated. I've always tried to be up and helpful, so why is this happening?

I'm sorry for the Goldman family. I know how much it hurts.

Nicole and I had a good life together. All this

press talk about a rocky relationship was no more than what every long-term relationship experiences. All her friends will confirm that I have been totally loving and understanding of what she's been going through.

At times I have felt like a battered husband or boyfriend, but I loved her, make that clear to everyone. And I would take whatever it took to make it work.

Don't feel sorry for me, I've had a great life, great friends. Please think of the real O.J. and not this lost person.

Thanks for making my life special. I hope I helped yours.

Peace and love.

O.J."

He had drawn a smiley face in the letter "O" but they were still chilling, heart-rending words.

It was the second time that day that the specter of suicide had loomed over O.J. Before the rushed press conference had been called, the wires were burning with the shocking news that was quickly disintegrating into false rumors that O.J. had killed himself in his late wife's abandoned Brentwood condo.

Meanwhile, thousands of gawkers had gathered on the quiet street, craning to get a glimpse inside the den of death. Swarms of hungry news choppers circled above hoping for a sneak peak at something, anything. It was a zoo. The pandemonium had been triggered by Nicole's father when he dialed 911 from inside his dead daughter's home and reported that O.J. had called saying he was on the way, and that he was "going to join Nicole." But it was another one of the Juice's jukes; he was actually headed south.

Over at the D.A.'s office, Gil Garcetti was issuing a stern warning. "I want to say to the entire community," he told the gathered press, "Mr. Simpson is a fugitive from justice right now. If you assist in any way, you are committing a felony. You will be prosecuted as a felon. You can tell I'm a little upset and I AM upset." Secretly, he was fearful his suspect had fled the country—no one had thought to confiscate O.J.'s passport.

All over Southern California, eyes were peeled, hoping to be the first to spot Al Cowling's white Bronco and its hunted passenger. An All-Points-Bulletin was put out, but there was no sighting. In police parlance, O.J. was "in the wind." Television stations and radio announcers also joined the chase. Spurred on, perhaps, by the ominous sound of O.J.'s note or by images of the O.J. that everybody loved taking his own life in the final cul-de-sac of his own desolation, announcers described the Bronco and read the license tag number over the air. Helicopters from police and sheriff's departments, law enforcement agencies and news departments, spread out over the LA freeway system, hovering over the ribbon of asphalt, their camera aimed at the cars beneath them, crawling along like an army of ants. But throughout the afternoon there was only silence and everybody was asking, "Where's O.J.?"

Finally, at 6.25 P.M. that Friday afternoon Bingo! A young couple saw the Bronco on the 5 freeway in Orange County and called the California Highway Patrol. Minutes later, Orange County Sheriff's Deputy Larry Pool caught sight of license plate number 3DHY503, and called it in to dispatch. Just as suddenly as O.J. had disappeared, the chase—albeit in a surrealistic slo-mo—was on. Soon, the white Bronco with O.J. inside was being pursued warily by a phalanx of police cars over L.A.'s spaghetti network of freeways.

Now the news choppers homed in, swarms of them, formations of them like a air cav assault team chugging over the Mekong River towards an unsuspecting village. News cameramen swung their legs out over the open space and aimed their lenses at the slow-speed chase playing out on the high-way below. But what was beamed into living rooms everywhere around the world was more than simply a chase. Television viewers had grown tired of such chases, it was a show, a spectacle, an apocalyptic vision of what we had become. Crowds of cheering fans had piled onto overpasses, screaming support for their hero.

"Run, O.J.," they cried, voices harsh and gritty in the afternoon heat, throats choking on smog and car fumes. Guilt or innocence; law and order; these had become empty words. This was show biz. This was drama. This was the Super Bowl for real.

This was no longer about O.J., it was about all of us, millions and millions of fans and rubbernecks suddenly beamed up from the monotony of their everyday lives and now wanting to be part of the greatest chase in the history—the cops caught flat-footed, a private couple spotting the missing car, and now, "live in L.A." the chase of a lifetime. The manhunt the police had promised was reaching its ultimate climax and all of us would be there to see how it ended. We were a part of the great spectacle by proxy, the circus maximus, the Roman forum.

This was history. For sports fans and spectators, this became the ultimate reality show. As the bizarre scene was transmitted by scores of cameras to their respective uplinks and thence from satellite to satellite, bounced 'round the globe, and played out on networks throughout the world to nearly hundreds of millions of viewers riveted to their screens. Here were witnesses not only to O.J.'s agonizingly slow journey to captivity but to the desperate American fascination with its larger-than-life heroes.

"Hello, 911."

"This is A.C. I have O.J. in the car," the scratchy voice crackled over the cell phone to a 911 relay deep in Orange County. It was the voice of Al Cowlings coming seemingly from out of nowhere. Cowlings was driving while his friend sat in the back with a blue steel .38 revolver pointed at his own head:

Officer: "O.K., where are you?"

Cowlings: "I'm coming up the 5 freeway."

Officer: "O.K."

Cowlings: "Right now we're O.K. but you gotta tell police to just back off. He's still alive. He's got a gun to his head."

Officer: "O.K., hold on a minute—"

Cowlings: "He just wants to see his mother. Let me get him to the house."

Police units ahead of the slowly moving Bronco were directed to clear the traffic from the usually jammed San Diego Freeway in advance of A.C.'s reaching the interchange. Now they drove from the 5 to the 405 and turned north towards Sunset Boulevard. Lanes filled with cars parted to let them pass.

People cheered from the freeway shoulder, whooping and barking in the growing dusk as if O.J. actually had a place to run. Past familiar streets they drove, restaurants where he and Nicole might have eaten on Sunday afternoons, along streets where he and his beautiful Nicole had once driven in what was now simply another life. They turned onto the Sunset exit ramp and headed toward Brentwood, crowds following them on foot, hoping to get just a glimpse of the now tragic hero slumped in the back of the Bronco, clutching a picture of his kids, still holding the gun to his head.

News commentators flying low overhead, almost, it seemed from the close-ups they were getting, at tree-top level, were stunned with amazement as the Bronco headed for O.J.'s street.

Everybody wanted a piece of the action now as police had to hold back the fans and spectators, now waving signs and posters cheering on their hero. The Bronco was only a few feet away from

O.J.'s driveway. Would it turn? Would the driver make a desperate attempt to break away having faked the police out? Or, as seemed most likely, was this the final stop? Would the action play out in O.J.'s own driveway in the lengthening shadows of dusk. Would his glory fade away when the spotlights went off, growing dimmer and dimmer in the darkness until it was only a memory?

Finally, fifty minutes after he was first spotted, Detective Tom Lange, of the murder investigation team, got a call through to O.J.'s cellular phone. Lange talked to him off and on, trying to calm him and persuade him not to hurt himself—but all he'd say was that he wanted to see his mother.

The procession had made its way through winding streets to O.J.'s Brentwood mansion past throngs of newsmen and well-wishers. SWAT teams had only made it there just 15 minutes ahead of their quarry, and they thought they'd managed to evacuate everyone except O.J.'s friend Bob Kardashian.

Then the Bronco made the turn, police units rolled into position behind it, and A.C. stopped the car and parked in the driveway with O.J. still inside. For just a moment, everything seemed under control. Then, the football star's eldest son Jason rushed up to the car and lunged for the door handle. A frantic A.C. shoved the young man away.

"He was yelling at us that Simpson had a gun," recalled Sgt. Mike Albanese who oversaw the tense negotiations for O.J.'s surrender. "He was saying 'Don't do anything stupid. Get the police away.' "

But officers weren't about to risk losing their man twice in one day. They stood their ground—there was no way O.J. and Al Cowlings were going to hit the road again. Whatever the outcome, this was going to be the end of the line. For tense minutes, as the shadows grew, the police negotiated with O.J. They first had to deal with a frenzied A.C. who was frantically gesturing to them about the gun. He was in the way. His agitation, justifiable though it might have been, was keeping the police from getting direct access to O.J., the object of the entire chase. But the police were cool. They waited A.C. out, showed him there was no way to go, told him that he was the problem as long as he kept them from talking O.J. into putting down the gun. They finally managed to coax A.C. into the house and calm him down.

Now it was time to deal with O.J. himself. With helicopters still buzzing overhead, more heard than seen because of the increasing darkness, negotiator Pete Weireter strained to hear O.J.'s weak, exhausted voice over his cellular phone. Outside searchlights from helicopters sent shafts of bright white beams into the mobs gathering in the darkness. The crowd around the house was growing, pushing and shoving to get a better view of the goings on in the driveway. Police tried to control them, tried to keep open an avenue of escape for the moment they had to escort O.J. downtown. They knew that moment would soon come. It was only a matter of time.

There inside the van, O.J. held out for his final few minutes of freedom. Anxious to use the bathroom, thirsty for a drink of water or, better still, orange juice, still desperate to talk to his mother, O.J. negotiated with members of the SWAT team who were inside his house. As O.J. talked to Weireiter he hugged family photos to his chest, and to all observers, he looked like a shattered shell of a man. At last he agreed to come out of the car, unarmed, setting three conditions—that he could use the bathroom, have a drink, and phone his mother in San Francisco. Then, he walked from the car to his house and collapsed into a waiting officer's arms.

"I'm sorry for putting you guys out," O.J. told them. "I'm sorry for making you do this."

14

4 0 1 3 9 7 0   06 1 7 9

Prisoner Number 4013970

I'll do anything to stay out of that cell. I'll sit here and read."

They were pitiful words, caught by a live microphone, and they betrayed the helpless desperation of a tightly coiled athlete who'd just been sprung from his tiny cage.

But the grim, dazed mask he wore during his first court appearance was gone. O.J. was alert and responsive this time, determined not to spend a single unnecessary second in the claustrophobic holding cell marked with a special red stripe. He'd felt like a sideshow freak and he'd learned something. Space was precious. He had room to breathe.

But the eyes and ears of the world were riveted on him again, as they had been throughout his last few hours of freedom. Almost a hundred million people had watched in fascination and disbelief his bizarre flight on the freeways with a gun to his head and his final surrender that seemed to take forever. The ratings had outscored the Super Bowl and the Persian Gulf War.

Strange. One minute the entire world is watching you. The next minute, you are prisoner number 4013970 in solitary confinement under a 24-hour suicide watch.

No more mansions, servants or fancy meals for The Juice. His new home was a 7-by-9-foot cell on the second floor of the Men's Central Jail in L.A., down the hall from the prison's psychiatric section. Among the previous celebrity inmates of the so-called "high power unit" were actor Todd Bridges, who was eventually acquitted of murdering his housemate; Evel Knievel, who was convicted of assaulting his former P.R. rep; and The Night Stalker, serial killer Richard Ramirez, convicted of killing 13 people.

O.J.'s cell was stripped down to bare essentials—a sink, a toilet, a bunk. And so were his clothes. No belt, no shoelaces—just a blue jumpsuit with "L.A. County Jail" emblazoned on the back. The only special privilege he was eventually granted was a medically prescribed cervical pillow for his neck. On the first weekend of his incarceration, the only eyes on Number 4013970 belonged to the sheriff's deputies who peeked in on him every 15 minutes round the clock to make sure he hadn't found some way to end his misery, permanently. His meals were served in his cell, and he ate them alone. He was allowed to spend a half-hour a day in the exercise room, but one of the greatest athletes in the world is only allowed to walk and stretch. There is no gym equipment. "Weight plates and bars could be used as weapons," Deputy Sheriff Larry Mead explained.

Even while he was doing calisthenics, O.J. was monitored constantly by deputies. Showers are not exactly a luxury, but he is only allowed one every other day under the watchful eye of his jailers. Never alone.

The megamillionaire was permitted just $40 in

cash, which he could use to buy magazines and newspapers. Books from the prison library are free, and he could have a TV rolled into his cell for a couple of hours each day. Visitors are permitted from 10:00 A.M. to 3:00 P.M. and 5:00 P.M. to 7:00 P.M., but he can only see them through a glass partition down the corridor from his cell.

O.J.'s first visitor was his attorney, Robert Shapiro; his second, and last, on that freshman jail weekend was a psychiatrist who spent four hours with him.

Shapiro said that O.J. was depressed but composed—for the most part. "He wished me a happy Father's Day and asked me to spend the day with my two boys," the attorney revealed. And then he started to cry and said, 'I wish I could spend the day with my children.' "

That, of course, wasn't possible. O.J. wasn't eligible to be released on bail. There is no bail when the charge is double homicide. Besides, 8-year-old Sydney and 6-year-old Justin hadn't even been told yet that their father was in jail, or that he was due to be arraigned on charges of killing their mother and Ronald Lyle Goldman. Since the funeral, they had been staying with their maternal aunt, 36-year-old Denise Brown—who, save for her dark hair, looks eerily like Nicole.

Neither Shapiro nor the sheriff's office would say whether O.J. had been given the mild tranquilizer Meprobamate, which is commonly prescribed in California prisons. Of his psychological state, Shapiro would say only that there was "concern . . . for his mental and emotional welfare."

By Monday, before he was arraigned, O.J. was still numb, though veteran suicide counselor Thomas Caffrey believes that he had probably "already partially worked through the major issues" that were plaguing him when he threatened to take his life on Friday. "He's . . . in that unthinkable place [prison] and survived it hour by hour," Caffrey said. "The longer he tolerates that experience, the more realistic he will become and the stronger he will be."

Yet strength was not on display later that morning when O.J. was brought before Judge Patti Jo McKay on the ninth floor of the Los Angeles Municipal Court building. Robert Shapiro was at O.J.'s side. Across the aisle were District Attorney Gil Garcetti's impressive prosecution team of Marcia Clark and David Conn, both members of the D.A.'s Special Trials Unit, which specializes in tricky, high-profile, highly publicized celebrity cases. The two prosecutors and their boss were hungry: Garcetti had so far failed to move ahead against Michael

Jackson in the child molestation investigation, he'd taken a real beating in the first Menendez trial where both defendants had *admitted* killing their parents, and now the press had accused the D.A.'s office and the police of giving special treatment to O.J. Simpson. After all, hadn't he been allowed to disappear just days earlier? It was embarrassing. Now prosecutors came into court publically stating their intentions to go to the mat with O.J.

Dressed in a dark pin-striped suit and white shirt buttoned to the top, O.J. stood with his hands at his side, eyelids heavy, sighing deeply and frequently during the 9-minute hearing. Among the people lending their support in the courtroom was his good friend Robert Kardashian, who had read reporters O.J.'s desperate "suicide" note on Friday. O.J. was aware that his beloved mother could not be there, that she'd been admitted to California Pacific Medical Center for a heart problem exacerbated by what had befallen her son.

That, too, was weighing heavily on him.

The Hall of Famer softly answered "Yes" three times when asked to confirm his name, whether he understood the charges being brought against him, and whether he had discussed those charges with his attorney. When the court clerk read those charges aloud, and mentioned his ex-wife's name,

O.J. winced. Seeing this, Shapiro placed a comforting hand on his client's shoulder.

O.J. then entered a plea of not guilty.

After the hearing, hard-as-nails prosecutor Marcia Clark, who joined the district attorney's office in 1981, met with reporters and tried to undermine the sympathy that, inadvertently or not, O.J. appeared to be attracting.

"He is the sole murderer," she said in a firm, tight voice. "We had two young people with their lives stretched out before them . . . murdered in a brutal and horrible way."

It had became abundantly clear during the initial hearings that the legal fight would be an unparalleled match-up of legal talent.

Howard Weitzman, O.J.'s first lawyer, seemed the ideal man for O.J. to have in his corner, having worked what U.S. District Judge J. Lawrence Irving said was "the legal miracle of the century" when he got automaker John DeLorean off the hook after a videotaped cocaine deal.

Weitzman had also represented Mike Tyson when former wife Robin Givens sued him for libel, and Michael Jackson in his recent legal showdown with a 13-year-old boy who accused the singer of molesting him. He's also represented Kim Basinger, Elizabeth Taylor, Marlon Brando, heavy metal singer Ozzy Osbourne—and Mary Brunner, the only member of Charles Manson's gang who was charged with murder but not convicted.

Colleague Mona Soo Hoo says that Weitzman not only has a great legal mind, but he's "charming and jurors tend to like him and follow him." But Weitzman didn't get to call O.J.'s legal plays for very long. On Wednesday, June 15, just three days after the slayings, he resigned, giving the explanation that he was too dear a friend of O.J.'s to be as objective as he needed to be. Weitzman also claimed that he was "too busy" to give the case the time it needed.

However, attorney-client friendships are not uncommon, and this particular challenge was right up Weitzman's alley. It would seem that whatever else he was doing certainly could have been turned over to an associate at his firm.

What, then, happened between Weitzman and O.J.?

Sources close to the case say that O.J. called Weitzman's office from Chicago to say that he was in trouble, and asked the attorney to meet him at the airport. But Weitzman didn't get there in time, and O.J. either felt deserted, scared, hurt, or all of the above. By the time the two got together, the media had been all over O.J.—and, more importantly, he apparently felt that their relationship had been strained. Yet Weitzman is still very much involved in the case as consultant to the defense team, which now includes the legendary F. Lee Bailey and Harvard law professor Alan Dershowitz, who successfully appealed Claus Von Bulow's conviction for the murder of his socialite wife, Sunny. Attorney Thomas Puccio later defended Von Bulow in a second trial and won. Dershowitz also appealed the convictions of Leona Helmsley and Mike Tyson.

Defense lead counsel Robert Shapiro is one of the most tenacious defense attorneys in the nation. Unlike D.A. Garcetti, who made the rounds on the talk show circuit from the very beginning, Shapiro has confined himself to press conferences, insisting: "At no time do I plan on doing any interviews or any shows with anyone."

The 51-year-old, New Jersey-born lawyer is Weitzman's equal and takes a common-sense approach to the trial process. "I like to slowly take control of the courtroom," he once said, "and make the court a friendly place to find my client not guilty."

He also works hard with his clients before the trial, preparing them for their testimony and the grilling they'll receive. He videotapes them to show them how they'll look to a jury—playing the part of a ruthless district attorney himself. Among his many celebrity clients are Johnny Carson, whom he rescued from a drunk-driving charge, and Marlon Brando's son Christian, for whom he plea-bargained in the murder of his half-sister's brother.

If Weitzman and Shapiro have anything in common besides their high rate of success in the courtroom, it's the curious habit they have of mis-placing clients or key witnesses. To be fair, of course, attorneys can only do so much to guaran-tee that third parties will show up at a trial or be on hand when police show up to arrest them.

Prior to O.J.'s sneaking out the door when the police were en route to take him into custody, Shapiro also had the misfortune of watching Chey-enne Brando skip town and head for Tahiti. Weitzman is Michael Jackson's attorney. When the child molestation investigation reached the criti-cal stage, they met in Mexico. Jackson then abruptly canceled his concert tour and fled to a hideout in England while lawyers wrangled over his fate.

The prosecution's Marcia Clark, meanwhile, is as successful in obtaining convictions as Shapiro is in getting his clients off. Her triumphs include the conviction of Robert John Bardo for the brutal murder of actress Rebecca Schaeffer. She was also successful in convincing a court to hand down the death penalty to Albert Lewis and Anthony Oliver, who killed a pair of churchgoers in 1989.

O.J.'s defense will be complex and multifaceted. A mountain of evidence will have to be dealt with, and Shapiro will have to create reasonable doubt in the jury's mind regarding each blood stain or article of clothing. New York defense attorney Marvyn Kornberg, experienced in cases like this one, points out: "When they say his blood was found at the scene, they're saying his blood *type* was found there. He's simply one of (many) people in this world with that type." While DNA testing was also ordered, the science is so new and complicated that it is not considered conclusive in many cases. A skilled forensic scientist can certainly cast reasonable doubts on the process, if not the results.

Perhaps for that reason, O.J. hired Dr. Henry Lee, head of the State of Connecticut's forensic lab and a veteran of five thousand homicide investigations, and Dr. Michael Baden, of New York's state forensic lab and former chief pathologist for New York City, to help with his defense. Lee is particularly skilled at reconstructing crimes, and he has a way of captivating juries with his knowledge and winning manner as he throws black ink on white paper to show how splattered blood flows, or explains the most complex chemical processes in the simplest of lay terms.

Lee and Baden will also explain how things like the cuts on O.J.'s hand may not have been caused by a fight with Nicole, but by punching a glass in his Chicago hotel room when he learned of her death. Chicago police who examined the scene and removed a bloodied towel from the room say that O.J. told them he cut himself that way.

The forensic defense can be successful, but UCLA criminal law professor Peter Arenella predicts that if the forensic evidence looks like it isn't going to favor O.J., that wouldn't necessarily be the end of him. Not by a long shot.

In that case, Arenella says, his "likely defense will be to focus on his confused mental state at the time of the killing." Kornberg, however, believes that would be a dangerous tack: "It would be suicidal to have an insanity defense," he says. "If Simpson took gloves to the scene, he certainly understood his actions." Also, other legal experts have said, insanity defenses tend not to work in California.

Whatever the outcome of the trial, it is unlikely that O.J. will be able to simply pick up where he left off and return to his previous endeavors. Topping the list of post-trial woes, experts predict that his advertising career is finished.

What began nineteen years ago as endorsements for Hertz at $300,00 a year grew to include a roster of clients including Dingo Boots, TreeSweet Orange Juice, Wilson Sporting Goods, Shindana Toys (which once made an O.J. Simpson doll, now a superhot collector's item), Hyde Spot–Bilt Athletic Shoes, and more. Even mother Eunice got into the act, shooting a commercial for MCI last year.

Marty Blackman of Blackman and Raybar—a consultant who works with advertising agencies looking to hire athletes—says that because of the arrest, "Not a company in this country" would hire O.J. Jeff Jenson, a sports marketing reporter for the magazine *Advertising Age*, agrees. "If there's one thing advertisers don't like," he says, "it's scandal. They don't want to risk having a blemish on his character that could rub off on them."

Advertisers aren't the only one who don't like it: Time Life Custom Publishing dropped the idea of putting O.J.'s picture on the cover of their upcoming coffee table book celebrating the sixtieth anniversary of the Heisman Trophy.

Even if he beats the murder rap, O.J.'s finished, says Jensen. After listening to the police tapes of the star abusing his wife, the public will be saying,

" 'Look at what he's done in the past.' His advertising career is over."

O.J. also serves on the board of directors of three large and powerful companies: Infinity Broadcasting Co., one of the nation's largest radio station company; the Forschner Group, which markets Swiss Army knives and Victorinox cutlery; and the Kushner Locke Co., which makes TV programs and motion pictures. Ironically, O.J. was reelected to the board of Infinity Broadcasting—which pays him $15,000 a year—on June 13, the day after the murders. None of the boards planned special meetings on the matter.

As for continuing to work as a sports commentator on NFL Live, NBC, his employer since 1989, says it is in "no rush to make a decision," according to network spokesperson Ed Markey. Chances are very good, however, that his voice will become so familiar at his trial, and that viewers will be so accustomed to hearing him and seeing him in that context, that he may be unable to resume his on-camera duties.

His career in Hollywood is quite possibly finished for the same reason. It's one thing to be typecast as a character. To be typecast as a defendant in a double homicide is considerably more difficult to overcome. "On the other hand" said one agent, "that could help him escape the good-guy parts he's been forced to play. After the trail, people could picture O.J. in a J.R. Ewing kind of part." The agent also points out that the CBS TV movie he made with Elizabeth Montgomery, *A Killing Affair*, will probably get a lot of airings in the near future. However, neither Warner Brothers nor its producers have decided what to do about the hour-long TV pilot "Frogmen," which O.J. recently finished. Obviously, he won't be available for a series in the near future, and although airing the one show would definitely earn its producers and advertisers ratings in the stratosphere—especially if the weapon turns out to have been a knife from the show, as some investigators think—it isn't likely to happen.

O.J.'s films on videotape are renting briskly, and his education training film For *Goodness Sake*— a comedy in which he talks about the importance of being a good and moral person—is selling like mad. Copies of the 24-minute film are being offered by the maker, Mentor Media, in both O.J. and now non-O.J. versions.

To continue to support the lifestyle to which he'd become accustomed, O.J. will have two immediate avenues open to him following an acquittal. One is to write his memoirs, which would earn him an advance in the neighborhood of $2 million dollars and royalties that could net him five times that amount. (True-crime author Joe McGinniss was offered a reported $1 million dollars just to write his own book about the case.) Another option would be to consult on or even star in a film based on his experiences. That would be brutal for him and especially for his children, but he may be in no position to turn it down.

In 1977, O.J. told *People* magazine, "I often wondered why so many rich people commit suicide. Money sure isn't a cure-all. That's why I throw on my jeans and try to stay loose." It's advice he'll need to follow himself over the months to come and, if he's found guilty, through the years of appeals. He could spend many anguished, tormented years in that prison he so quickly grew to hate.

Only time will tell which way it goes. But one thing is certain: neither O.J. or his stunned fans, nor the system that brought them together, will ever be the same again.

Photo Credits

The editors of Globe *and Princeton Publishing West would like to thank the following for the use of photographic material:*

AP/Wide World
Celebrity Photo Agency
Globe Photos, Inc.
KCOP-TV
OnLine USA
Ron Galella Ltd.
UPI-Bettman